UNDERTOW

Beverley Shaw

Undertow

First Galleon Edition, September 2025

ISBN 978-1-998122-25-7

Published by Galleon Books
Moncton, New Brunswick, Canada
www.galleonbooks.ca

Cover photographs © Collette Robertson, Saltbox Media.
Used with permission.

This is a work of fiction, one whose story will pull you in, or under, and have you believing that these characters are real, that you know them. They may stay with you for some time. That is the sign of excellent fiction, dear reader, but they still are figments of the author's imagination, and now yours. Enjoy.

The author acknowledges the financial support of Arts Nova Scotia.

Library and Archives Canada Cataloguing in Publication
Title: Undertow / Beverley Shaw.
Names: Shaw, Beverley (Violin teacher), author.
Identifiers: Canadiana 20250280892 | ISBN 9781998122257
(softcover)
Subjects: LCGFT: Novels.
Classification: LCC PS8637.H3825 U53 2025 | DDC C813/.6—dc23

UNDERTOW

Beverley Shaw

GALLEON

This book is dedicated to my mother, Olive Shaw.

Nova Scotia
August, 2016

Sнᴇ ᴡᴀʟᴋs ᴛнᴇ ʙᴇᴀᴄн, ᴡᴇᴀʀɪɴɢ нᴇʀ ʙᴀᴛнɪɴɢ sᴜɪᴛ under a summer frock, trying to decide if she will go for a swim, or take a moment to relax at the base of the red earth cliffs she sees ahead. She tries to match the rhythm of her breathing to her strides—in two, out three, in three, out four. When she sees sandpipers or sea gulls running ahead of her, the image of their small bodies against the sunlit water imprints itself on the surface of her eyes.

If this were one of Bill's films, she would meet someone on the beach and start an off-beat relationship with them, or she would remember something from her childhood which would start a small avalanche of revelations. But at this time of the morning, the beach is mostly empty, and her memories are not of childhood these days. The recent past keeps crowding her mind: words with Bill about his screenplay, words with Tim before she left New York, and one solitary wordless moment since her arrival here that she is still processing, or avoiding.

She isn't sleeping well in this place: last night, she dreamt that dark hair was sprouting up all over her body. It covered her arms and chest, her face, began to grow inside her mouth, poking through her tongue like tiny wires: filling the cavity of her jaw until she could no longer speak.

Usually, she is a reluctant sea bather, but today she is drawn to the water, wanting to feel weightless, taken over by the shock of the icy Atlantic. The air isn't as hot as it was yesterday; the wind makes the surface choppy, punctuated by white caps. Leaving her towel and sandals in the sand, she finds it's easier to get in than she anticipated. Giving herself to the push of the waves and the suck of water under her feet, what she notices most is sound. The roaring of the sea, rather than the cold, takes over her senses. When she surfaces, she turns to see the shoreline. The small hump of her dress and sandals is no longer directly in front of her, but further to the right. The pull of the waves must have disoriented her, causing her to move diagonally.

Swimming parallel to shore, she continues to move away from the spot where her clothes lie, but the bottom isn't flat—it keeps scraping her shins and ankles. She swims a bit further out, not quite over her head, but deep enough to find the freedom to kick, to extend her legs without touching bottom, to move and be moved freely. She's just beginning to find the form and power she learned in swimming lessons as a girl, when a large wave lifts her up.

For one second, she feels herself rise, as if about to shoot into the sky like a flying fish. There is a blue-green roaring all around. Then the wave breaks. It has the weight of a sandbag on her back. She feels herself fall—the queasy stomach thrill of a roller coaster plummet. Then she is bouncing along like a toy on the seabed, her legs scraping gravel.

She surfaces long enough to inhale a lungful of sweet air and to see blue sky, then is sucked under.

She opens her eyes and the blue around her is dark, almost black. She sees her hands flailing in front of her, foreign objects, white amoeba-like creatures. Her legs, useless appendages hanging from her hips, are like empty stockings, pulled along by the current.

She is pushed to the surface, takes a ragged gulp of air, is sucked down again.

On her third time up, she senses that the shore is nearer, but the undertow pulls her out into the choking darkness once more. She hears the words *'rip tide'* and *'undertow'* in her head—warning words that were posted in the parking lot. She surfaces, and is pulled under. She sees the words spelled out in front of her now, as if on an imaginary computer screen: *Under*, and then *Tow, Rip*, and then *tide, under*, and then *tide, rip*, and then *toe*, no; *tow*. She is being forced to the surface again. She sees herself as if viewed from below, a body pushed towards the incandescent, sunlit surface of the waves, to be submerged after one gasp.

She thinks, no one knows I'm here. What a ridiculous way to die.

Anyone caught in a rip tide should swim parallel to the shore until free of the current. These words appear on the screen in her mind as she breaks the surface again. An invisible force like a hand swivels her body around, and she begins to move her arms and legs in a semblance of the front crawl, side stroke and breaststroke all in one. It is a wild movement, not the purposeful, forward-moving strokes of an athlete, more like a spasmodic dance. The word *free* dances in her head. *Swim parallel to the shore until free.* Each time she is allowed to the surface for a gasp of air, she feels an intense pain in her chest. She wonders if she has done something to her ribs, or lungs. Eventually, a wave envelops her, lifts her, and spits her closer to the shore. She feels her feet touch bottom before the wave can suck her out again, and she lunges forward, staggering, pushing her arms, shoulders and chest through the sea barrier until the sound of her own breathing starts to take over from the pursuing crash of the waves.

| 1 |

FRED HAS NOTICED HER EVERY MORNING, eating breakfast on the balcony, looking out over the sea. She sits with her back to the view, sunhat shading her face and an iPad or paperback by her coffee cup. He thinks she has a Catherine Deneuve look, but the younger staff at the resort don't get that reference. She always has a croissant and coffee and goes down to the beach afterwards.

There is speculation about which of her two companions the woman is with. She seems too young for the older one, the fiftyish guy who is footing the bill. The younger guy, skinny with glasses, doesn't seem right either. Which doesn't stop rumors of a threesome. They are all staying in one suite.

If the men make it down to breakfast at all, they do the full buffet deal—bacon, eggs, sausages, fruit—and linger to read on their phones, or argue about baseball and movies, the younger guy leaning against the railing to smoke. The older guy wrote his home address down in the registry as simply 'New York'. They have booked in for two weeks—a rarity, even in summer. This little resort is usually a stop on the way to somewhere else.

On the drive to and from work, Fred savors the sea air moving through his nostrils and chest. He lives in Halifax, in a neat bachelor apartment, and every time he returns home—tips and/or paycheque in hand—he appreciates the simplicity of his life: no more joint business ventures, no more art gallery, just the clean exchange of services for rent and food money, his car payment, the occasional evening out or bottle of wine that he drinks while watching Netflix. His list is all foreign TV shows and independent films. He likes to search stuff on IMDB, and read the names of the directors and writers.

Last night, scrolling through trailers, his hand froze on the mousepad when he saw the profile of the young woman from the resort moving through the frame.

It must be a passing resemblance, he thought, but then she turned to the camera. Her nose and mouth, that slightly quirky look despite the classic cheekbones and blue eyes. He checked the credits and saw her name—Sophie Langstrof. Under 'Producer,' he saw Nathan Ackerman, the older of the three guests. 'Bill Reese, writer/director' must be the pale, thirtyish guy who smokes on the balcony.

Fred decided to check out the film, and to say nothing to the rest of the staff about this discovery. He would hold this secret close, its power to set him apart. It would give him a special relationship with the three guests, although he would not tell them, either. They were involved in some creative endeavor which, contrary to the speculation of the resort's horny little waiters and gossipy chamber maids, transcended sex.

Having extracted himself from his relationship with Jamie, Fred likes the idea of transcending sex.

The film wasn't bad; a romantic comedy with references to art, a token gay couple thrown into the mix. The couple were incidental to the plot, but at least they were fairly normal people; neither party animals, nor gurus to the straight. Sophie, the main character, was cute, confused, coming out of a relationship which had stifled her. The film was released two years ago, but Fred had never heard of it.

Fred prides himself on his ability to sleep well and soundly, much better than in the old days. But occasionally he has disturbing, anxiety-filled dreams about animals. The animals change from dream to dream—a snake one day, a bear the next, a cat the next. Last night, after watching Sophie's film, Fred dreamt that he was in an outdoor museum or a zoo. There were all kinds of birds behind glass—stuffed maybe, but Fred knew otherwise. He slid the glass open and felt a surge of satisfaction as the birds burst out in a beating of wings up into the sky. But then they all started to fall apart, like rusty airplanes. A blue jay's tail lay spread like a peacock fan in the grass, a grosbeak's wing nearby. Worst of all, a small sparrow, who seemed to catch a current of wind for a few feeble yards, tumbled to the ground as if dead, then moved in a spasmodic, maimed way. When Fred came closer, he saw a prickly pine-needle growth slowly covering it, obliterating feather, beak, and eye.

He woke sweaty and sick to his stomach, with a weight of anxiety that pulled him back to his time with Jamie: holding his head over a toilet, flushing multiple substances down the drain, listening in silence to tears, threats, and occasional apologies. Yet he couldn't remember feeling anxious at that time. When he thinks of those days, Fred can't remember feeling anything at all.

This morning, his shift is later than usual. When he arrives, Sophie and the two men are nowhere in sight. The dining room is being cleared of breakfast dishes. A German couple argue quietly over a map and coffee. A family from Maine are at the desk getting directions to the nearest theme park.

Nathan and Bill come out onto the balcony when Fred is setting the tables for lunch. Bill is squinting slightly. Nathan looks comfortable in the sun, in a blue cotton shirt and linen trousers, sunglasses momentarily perched on his forehead as he approaches Fred, smiling.

"Have you seen our friend, Sophie?" he asks.

"No sir," says Fred in his best head-waiter voice. "I'm afraid I only just arrived. Perhaps the staff at the front desk?"

"Yeah, we asked them," says Bill. "She went out for her walk about two hours ago."

Fred keeps his face expressionless. "She may have lost track of time. If I see her, I'll let her know you're looking for her."

When Sophie still hasn't turned up by lunch, he feels the first queasy beginnings of alarm. At the same time, he can't repress a voyeuristic surge of excitement. Has there been some kind of dispute between the three?

Fred debates asking Bill and Nathan if she took her bathing suit with her on the walk. He looks out at the whitecaps, notices how deserted the beach still is, sees the sand cliffs in the distance. His excitement immediately dies. The sweaty, claustrophobic feeling from his nightmare returns. Maybe he should alert the rest of the resort staff, but he can't figure out how to word it.

Or should he make that final leap towards a 911 phone call?

If they took him seriously and sent out search parties, only to have her turn up safe and sound, how would that look?

Slowly, over lunch hour, a schism develops between Fred's outer world of calm place settings, offers of wine and coffee, and an inner world of catastrophic images. The absent-mindedness with which he does his job is not pleasant. The smooth rhythm of his day has been lost. He notices that Bill and Nathan do not come to lunch, and feels a growing irritation towards the three travelers, and towards himself for becoming so interested in them. He feels unreasonable shame about the fascination Sophie's disappearance holds for him.

On his after-lunch break, he finds himself walking the beach alone, in completely inappropriate polished work shoes, looking for her. Chances are, he will meet her on her way back and exchange a word or two. He tells himself this is what he hopes for, what he wants.

As he walks, he thinks of seeing the three travelers leaving for dinner in town yesterday. Sophie was between the two men, not holding anyone's hand. There was an easy intimacy in the way they bent their heads towards each other in murmured conversation. They returned just before Fred's shift ended, and Sophie dropped her silk scarf as she went by the desk. Fred moved in quickly to retrieve it. She took it from him, smiling, and said to her companions, "Think I'll take a walk before turning in. See you in fifteen minutes or so." Her eyes were fixed on Fred as she spoke, but she wasn't really looking at him.

"Watch yourself Sophie, wouldn't want to get lost in those dangerous Nova Scotia streets," said Bill.

"No, wouldn't want to do that."

As she headed towards the door, Fred saw the younger man shrug.

There is something up ahead, a lump in the sand which Fred doesn't think is seaweed. He approaches with caution. It's a neat pile of clothes, a sundress and beach towel with sandals on top to keep them from blowing away. He stops, experiences a moment of infinite stillness, the blood audibly pumping in his head. He has felt this only once before in his life. This impulse to turn and run, to seek out others, to do anything to escape this moment, to escape the potential knowledge he does not wish to have.

Then he looks up and sees someone moving towards him from further down the shoreline—a stick figure that morphs into a thin blond woman in a black one-piece bathing suit. When she gets close enough for him to make out her features, relief explodes in his chest. He feels like crying. If he could, he would embrace her as a long-lost sister, soul mate. But something is wrong. She's moving erratically, stumbling slightly, as though drunk.

He hurries forward, his service industry persona taking over.

"Are you alright?" he asks.

She starts, looks up at him as if she had no idea he was there.

"I think so," she says. "I went swimming and got pulled out by the undertow. I think I might have hurt myself, broken a rib, maybe."

"You're not far from the hotel, Miss Langstrof," he says. "Can you walk the rest of the way?"

"Do we know each other?" she asks, looking up again.

For one moment, he imagines telling her he has seen her movie and read her bio on IMDB. He even indulges in a brief and strangely adolescent fantasy about having a conversation with her about films, watching her face register surprise at his intelligence and good taste.

"I'm on staff at the hotel," he says. "My name is Fred? I usually serve you coffee in the morning."

"Right, of course. Sorry, I'm not thinking very clearly right now."

"That's understandable."

He gathers her clothes and towel in one hand, putting his other hand under her elbow. It seems like the right thing to do. Not surprisingly, given how shaken she is, the patina of glamour and sophistication he noticed when she first arrived has gone. Instead, she has a gawky, brainy quality, reminding him of one of his best friends in high school, a girl who was never at home in any social situation, but who played the piano like a pro. He lost touch with that girl, with a lot of people, after he got together with Jamie.

"Your friends have been looking for you," he says.

She doesn't answer. Then, after about ten meters of slow walking, she says, "I could have come back sooner. The whole thing was probably over in a few minutes. But I sat for a while getting my breath back. I just didn't want to move."

"Again, understandable," he says.

"I guess so."

After a few paces, she stops.

"This is not how I want it to be," she says.

Her voice sounds as if it's on automatic pilot, as if she is speaking within a dream. She's staring down at the sand, as if trying to spot something she has lost.

"Sorry?" he says, his anxiety returning. Is she having some kind of emotional breakdown? He hopes she's okay to walk the rest of the way.

She starts to walk again. "When we get back, I'd like to book a single room for the rest of my stay please," she says, her voice both formal and childlike.

"Of course." Again, he allows his professional persona to take over. "That shouldn't be a problem. But perhaps the first thing to do is to get you checked out by a doctor? There's a small clinic not far from here, although if you think you've broken something, you might need an x-ray, which would mean going into the city."

"I need to put my dress on," she says, stopping again.

He hands her the dress, a loose canary yellow cotton shift which she pulls on from the bottom up, avoiding lifting her arms. She winces as she puts her right arm through the hole.

"Maybe you could take me to the clinic?" she says.

He is silent for a moment.

"I'd have to let them know at the hotel. I'm supposed to be working the evening shift."

"Right, of course. I understand." She starts walking again. He notices how thin she is—her skinny, sand-encrusted legs. "Are there cabs out here I could take?"

The possibility of leaving work in the middle of the day gives Fred a giddy sense of freedom.

"Tell you what," he says, "my car's in the lower parking lot. We'll go there so you won't have to climb the steps. Then we'll drive to the front entrance and let them know. The dining room's slow today. They can spare me. But you'll need to get some ID from your hotel room."

She thanks him, and when they arrive at the car, Fred opens the passenger door for her before settling behind the wheel. The sun-warmed upholstery feels hot through his black trousers. Once at the entrance, they get out together. He leans on the car for a moment and mentally rehearses his explanation to the front desk, but Sophie heads straight to the doors. Following, he sees her turn down the corridor towards her suite, and wonders what she will say to the two men she shares it with.

On the way to the clinic, Sophie lightly touches the wooden cross hanging from his windshield.

"This is beautiful," she says. "Did someone give it to you?"

"My mother. When I moved a couple of years ago, I found it in a box of stuff I hadn't opened since I left for college. Reminds me of my childhood I guess."

She lets go of the cross.

"Are you Catholic?"

"No, far from it. I grew up in the United Church."

She probably has no idea what he's talking about. There is no United Church in the States.

"They performed gay marriages before any other church did," he explains. "They see Jesus as a radical social reformer. Emphasize the 'Judge not and thou shalt not be judged' part."

"Lucky you," she says.

Fred's church background is something Jamie always scoffed at, having grown up small-town, fundamentalist Baptist. Unable to envision any other kind of Christianity, he used to call Fred's hometown congregation a bunch of politically correct "wolves in sheep's clothing," not noticing the irony in his choice of a biblical metaphor. There are some things you can't escape, Fred thinks, no matter how hard you try.

As they drive through the village, Sophie looks out the window at the well-maintained houses, summer homes mostly, owned by a mix of Americans, Germans and wealthy Nova Scotians. Fred notices the tidy gardens, the summer foliage of green and gold. He feels like a kid playing hooky, or a tourist.

When was the last time he was a tourist—worry free? He can't count the trip to Bermuda with Jamie. There were too many times when he found himself second guessing Jamie's motives, too many times when he awoke to Jamie's body slipping between the covers at unpredictable hours of the night. Nor can he count the ski trip they took a few months after they first started dating. Jamie hurt his back, and Fred had done the same thing then that he's doing for this woman now. He drove Jamie to the hospital, sat patiently in the waiting room, filled out his prescription. He has often wondered if the painkillers were what set Jamie off again. He said he was clean when they met. Who knows for sure.

At the clinic, Fred is content to drink a juice from the vending machine and stare out the window at the green summer day. Time seems suspended, until Sophie comes out and tells Fred that the doctor doesn't think she needs an X-ray, unless the pain gets worse, or she has shortness of breath. The doctor has also recommended Tylenol. Not, Fred notices, the heavy-duty prescription painkillers given to Jamie that time.

She seems to have recovered her sophistication and poise. And there is something different about her—a slow, thoughtful quality. He supposes a near-drowning must be a sobering event. As they stand at the counter of the pharmacy next door while she buys her Tylenol, she flashes him a slightly crooked smile. The last vestiges of the Catherine Deneuve resemblance vanish with that smile, but Fred still thinks she is lovely. It's a smile that, for the first time, is uncomplicated, friendly, without the shadow of any thoughts getting in the way.

Pulling out of the parking lot with Sophie by his side, he has the strange sensation, briefly, that he is an actor in one of her movies and they are improvising a scene together. He feels at ease, as though they are colleagues or creative allies, not too close, but comfortable with each other. He wonders why she has booked a separate room at the hotel, but only briefly, idly. He will probably never know her more than he knows her now. There will be no complications, no repercussions from this act of kindness.

Already he is retreating into his own life. An ocean current is pulling him farther from the shore, just as she seems to have found her footing on dry land.

| 2 |

Hᴏw ʟᴏɴɢ ʜᴀᴅ ꜱʜᴇ ʟᴀɪɴ ᴛʜᴇʀᴇ, in the shelter of the dune? As they drive back from the clinic, Sophie turns this thought over and examines it like a sun-bleached shell. She remembers the overhang of eel grass, the hot sand, the quiet wind. She almost wishes she were back there.

She had huddled into the dune, the sand beneath her cheek pulsing like a heartbeat that seemed to come from deep below, under the earth, from a place she could sense but never see. The stretch fabric of her wet bathing suit clung to her as the salt dried on her skin, her flesh pulled tight over the awkward angles of her bones. Her shallow breaths had threatened to split open the pain in her side. She tried to slow down and match the deep, sonorous inhalations of the sea. The waves, pulling back from the shore, seemed magnetic, as if they could draw her to them again, just as they had when she had first walked in. She had curled in a fetal position, hanging onto a tuft of eel grass, terrified that she might find herself running down to the water's edge, to be tossed around in that clothes-washer churning again.

No, she doesn't wish she was back there. Instead, if she could, she would keep driving with this stranger by her side, away from the beach, the hotel lobby, from other voices and faces. He's a nice person, this man. On the beach, he had gallantly held out her dress to put on over her bathing suit. He spoke in a calm voice. She judges him to be in his late thirties or early forties— short, curly dark hair, neat, clean-shaven, with small, wire-framed glasses. She wonders what his life is like, where he lives, if he's married, single, straight, or gay.

"Thanks for helping me out, Fred," she says when they get to the hotel parking lot.

Walking away from him into the hotel lobby, she feels weightless, a shining vessel. At her core, there is another heartbeat, as unknown as the one she felt when she lay curled on the sand. It's official now, a fact. Still inaudible to the outside world, but there, all the same. The test she had taken soon after she arrived here, the one inescapable discovery she had been trying to avoid, has been confirmed. She took a second test in the bathroom at the clinic, and had an impartial witness to the double lines on the pee stick.

"Chances are, this experience will not have affected the baby," the doctor said.

The baby. Behind the doctor's back, multi-coloured containers were stacked like toy bins in a kindergarten, filled with bandages and needles instead of toys.

"Although on TV, women miscarry every time they fall off a horse or slip on a bar of soap, our bodies are actually more efficient than that." The middle-aged doctor, with her Scottish accent, had a Mary Poppins quality about her. "How far along do you think you are?" she said.

Turning down the corridor to the hotel suite, Sophie has an image of her last time with Tim. The feel of his weight, his skin, and the red curtain in the window that seemed to pulsate with her body just before he came. That was about a week before things turned sour, a week before she told him she had made up her mind to join Bill and Nathan instead of going on tour with him. Had they been careless, or was it intentional?

"This is a planned pregnancy, a positive thing, yes?" the doctor asked, shooting her another look from under her bangs. "Or do you have any concerns you'd like to discuss?"

"No," Sophie said. "No concerns. I just want to check that everything's okay."

"Everything's okay," she tells Bill and Nathan. "The rib could be broken, or it might just be bruised."

She comes further into the room, fingers the key in her pocket, the credit card with which she had reserved a single room for tonight. "But there's something else I need to tell you. I'm pregnant. I already guessed, but the doctor confirmed it."

There is a look of astonishment on Nathan's face. On Bill's side of the room there is silence. She can see Nathan trying for congratulatory heartiness. He walks forward, taking both her hands in his, while the lines on his forehead deepen, betraying mental calculations she can guess at—*Can we do the main bulk of the shooting before she starts to show? Is she together enough to keep working?*

She would like to recapture the calm she felt coming out of the doctor's office. She imagines making her way to the single room she has booked, closing the curtains and lying on the bed's clean sheets, attempting to listen to that unknown heartbeat within her, in silence.

Nathan is still holding both her hands in his, just as he did when she came in earlier to tell them she had hurt her rib and was going to the clinic. He had wanted to come with her then, had grabbed his keys, with that purposeful look on his face, the one he often had on set. She had to argue, pretend to be less hurt than she actually was. All the while, she was aware, as she is now, of Bill standing in the background. Aware that Bill probably thought her extended absence that morning had been some reaction or statement on her part about the film. It was laughable, almost, but at the time she felt too fragile to laugh.

"I haven't decided what to do yet," she says. "Except that I am planning to have the baby. I'm only about a month along so I don't feel different. I'm not nauseated or anything."

Nathan lets go of her hands, makes a move as if he wants to hug her, then changes his mind. He backs up, gestures to the sofa, and when she sits, he comes and sits beside her. Bill remains standing by the window.

"Sophie," Nathan says. "Lots of actresses have gone through this. We can make it work, do most of the shooting before you show. We'll just have to wrap up the pre-production stuff now and get started back in New York in a week or so."

In the past, Sophie has been grateful for the way he likes to gather all the messiness of life and turn it into something flowing, something functional.

"We're only halfway through the screenplay development," says Bill. Sophie can hear invisible quotation marks around the words 'screenplay development', the official title Nathan used to define this trip with his backers.

"I need to think things through," she says. Recognizing that her voice sounds tight and high, she modulates her breathing and pitch. "It's a lot to process. I haven't even told Tim."

"Of course," Nathan says. "I didn't mean to pressure you. Take the time you need. Talk to Tim. We can work to your time schedule. Maybe, if necessary, do some shooting from the chest up."

"Like hell we can," says Bill, still standing by the window. "This is my film, not some crappy situation comedy with head shots of people sitting around on sofas."

"It's not like I planned this," she says. "It's just one of those things."

Bill raises an eyebrow, a look he has usually reserves for other actors, not her.

"Well, your contract is also just 'one of those things', Sophie," he says.

She avoids looking at Nathan. Like her, he is probably thinking about the unsigned document in her inbox. She had let it slide, knowing Nathan wouldn't hassle her, because they had already made two films together, because he trusted her to get it to him eventually, because they were friends.

She tells them about her single room, saying she needs space to think, and retreats to the en-suite bedroom. There is a loaded silence while she packs, broken only by the sound of the coffee maker and Bill opening the sliding doors to the balcony. When she comes back into the living room, Bill is still out there, smoking. Okay then, she thinks. Lately, when Bill is around, another Sophie clings to her like a shadow, a person only Bill can see and about which she knows nothing. She's tired of feeling like someone else in his presence.

Unable to decline Nathan's offer of help, she walks beside him as he wheels her suitcase down the hall.

"Get a good night's sleep," he says. "Don't try to make any split-second decisions when you've just come through a stressful event."

Sometimes split-second decisions are the right ones, she thinks, at least when she's acting. Then again, this isn't acting.

The colours of her new room are different from the suite, a darker bedspread and curtains, and there is only one window, facing the lawn rather than the sea. The curtains shut out the late afternoon sun.

Sitting on the bed, she feels a twinge of nausea. Her body playing tricks on her? Or maybe the result of the pain in her side. She decides to take one of the Tylenols the doctor recommended, to help her relax. Tomorrow, she will see about booking an earlier flight home. Then she will do other, practical things. Make a doctor's appointment. Call Tim.

She picks up her phone to make a list, but instead starts scrolling through YouTube. George Clooney, with Amal on his arm. An HIIT fitness video, introduced by a fresh-faced Scandinavian woman. Try yoga instead, her mother would advise. Her mother will want to see her as soon as she learns this news. Sophie imagines her barging into their Brooklyn apartment, while her father follows, picking up scattered belongings—a silk scarf, a dropped earring, a handkerchief, a vial of homeopathic remedies. What remedy would you take for shortness of breath, a sore rib, anxiety induced by an unplanned pregnancy, Sophie wonders.

Scrolling some more, she encounters Beyoncé swimming and swirling in an underwater hotel room, bubbles magically reversing themselves back up her nostrils. Inhaling sharply, she coughs, eyes watering at the pain in her ribs. She lies down and closes her eyes. Beneath her eyelids, there is the sea, the hospital, Nathan's smile topped by worried eyes, and Bill's face, guarded and speculative. No longer a face she knows.

Even before that first test result, days after arriving at the hotel, she had been feeling her commitment to this project wavering, her belief in it balanced like an insect on a blade of grass. It could go one way or another, depending on the direction of the wind. When Nathan had suggested including her in these collaborative weeks with Bill, she had been excited, had felt like she had just gotten an A plus in a high school English essay.

It was the collaborative part that was turning out to be a problem, though. Yesterday, the three of them re-watched the final cut of the last film. As they watched, Nathan was like a proud dad at a little league game. She, herself, felt no affinity with the girl on the screen, her fiddly mannerisms, her hair twirling. Later, when they were reading through a scene in the new film where her character meets an ex-boyfriend at a party, she had questioned the girl's awkwardness. "Maybe some water has gone under the bridge since then," she said. "Maybe she's moved on."

Bill's stare. "Maybe she hasn't, Sophie, even if you have." A remark that nailed her to the wall like a butterfly on a pin.

Nathan was the teamwork guy, always wanting to create a safe and respectful environment for actors. But Bill, why had he gone along with this idea? Nathan told her Bill had wanted her there when he had pitched this idea to him. But why? She would like to recall the good parts of their working relationship. All the times she made him smile, all the times his tense and scrawny shoulders relaxed, just because she delivered a line the way he wanted. The times he said, "Oh *yeah*," in a jubilant voice, at her delivery of some smart and sassy bit of dialogue.

But instead, she remembers an incident, during the second film, when she had gotten carried away in her feedback, when she felt like she was on to something, some motivation that even Bill wasn't aware of. She doesn't remember what it was now, only that sense of being interested, being alive to her work, being at home in her opinions. Her confidence was a little over-the-top, maybe. At some point, she noticed Bill was no longer dialoguing with her, but moving his head in little minute shakes, staring into her eyes, silently commanding her to shut up. Then saying sotto voce: *You don't get to do that. Don't fucking tell me how my character's supposed to react.*

It was only one incident. He didn't do it again.

Maybe this attempt at collaboration isn't worth it, she thinks, shifting her head on the pillow and adjusting her torso to avoid complaints from her injured side. A part of her has been envisioning an opportunity to go beyond speaking the words of others, to be part of creating something new. But she also wants the old Bill back, the one whose appreciation of her acting constantly boosted her ego. The pain in her side sharpens as she thinks, maybe it isn't possible to have both.

Outside her window, the ocean's roar is faint but continuous. Listening, she briefly loses awareness of her surroundings—this sturdy mattress, these heavy white bedsheets. Instead, she feels the pull of the undertow once more. The separate life that is within her body seems less real than her sense of still being battered by waves—as if she is no longer solid muscle and bone. As if she is nothing at all.

| 3 |

At Fred's building, Joan and Krystle are sitting out back on the bit of concrete all four apartments share as a patio. They are well underway, he can see. Krystle—twenty-four years old with pale skin, black hair, and a taste for sketchy boyfriends—has three empty Keith's bottles on the picnic table in front of her. Joan, who is forty years Krystle's senior, lounges on a deck chair smoking, a box of wine by her side.

"Looks like you've had some sun, Joan?" Fred says, eyeing her puffy eyes and lobster-red skin.

In response, Joan lifts her bathing suit strap gingerly off her shoulder to reveal a strip of skin so white that it almost sparkles against the burnt red on either side.

"We went to the beach," says Krystle. "She's paying for it now."

Joan nods, eyes closed.

"Joan," says Fred, who has never burnt in his life, thanks to a small parcel of African heritage from his biracial mother, "sunscreen?"

Krystle guffaws. "Where's the fun in that?"

Once inside his apartment, Fred limits himself to two glasses of his own wine, which is better than Joan's, but only slightly. Sitting in front of his laptop, he considers rewatching Sophie's movie, but opts for YouTube instead. There are raised voices upstairs, a door slams. He turns up the volume on Graham Norton.

The next day, returning home from a short morning jog, he sees two cop cars parked in front of the building. Slowing his pace to a shuffle, he feels a faint echo of what he felt yesterday when he saw Sophie's clothes in the sand. Two male cops and one woman are trying to wrestle Krystle's latest boyfriend to the ground. Fred has the familiar urge to turn around and keep running, but is unable to look away. The guy is so skinny he could be a kid throwing a tantrum, but it takes all three of them to get him to a place where they can cuff him.

"He fucking trashed my car!" Krystle is yelling at a fourth cop, another woman. "How am I supposed to get to work? You asshole, Cory!"

After Cory has been driven away, Fred only half listens while Joan details the timeline of events—Cory threatening suicide, Cory stealing Krystle's car, Joan calling the cops. In his other ear, he hears the cop ask Krystle what Cory is on. "Cocaine," she begins, "speed, oxycontin, benzos." The officer makes no sound, just writes.

"Didn't sign up for this," says Joan. "This used to be a quiet neighborhood. And you know? He used to be a nice boy. I know his mother. He lived with her until he started trashing her apartment and stealing from her purse. He keeps running out of money for all that stuff he's on. The last time she kicked him out, he told her she was abandoning him. Jesus."

"Yeah well, if he's taking benzos," says Fred. Or not taking them due to a lack of funds, he thinks, remembering Jamie throwing dishes on the floor, a cutting board across the room. Fred told a mutual friend at the time that none of Jamie's tantrums scared him, which was true. He remembers saying, 'When he's in that state I just think, 'Dude, grow up.' It all seemed, at a very deep level, like some kind of act, like Jamie was winding himself up, intoxicated by his own rage, then wallowing in remorse afterwards like a comfortable warm bath. Then again, maybe not, Fred thinks, given all the chemicals running interference in the guy's brain.

He comes out of his memories to see Joan's eyes on him, sharp and sober.

He wishes today wasn't a day off. He would rather witness the drama at the resort with the actress Sophie and her film buddies than the drama in this four-unit building. He should do his laundry, but does not relish the trek to that basement room with the dirty and peeling vinyl floor and the overflowing plastic bin full of dryer lint. He decides to take some of his tips from last night to a nearby café for brunch.

When he returns, feeling slightly more grounded after eggs benedict and sparkling orange juice, Joan is sitting on the front step. She tells him the cops took Corey to the hospital, but after keeping him waiting for two hours, they sent him away again.

"I guess you have to kill someone to get noticed," she says. "Or yourself."

Hyperbole, Fred tells himself, a figure of speech, the words, 'kill yourself'. Still, when he goes inside, he finds himself automatically calling his mother. Since moving to her apartment in Clayton Park, she has lost touch with many of her Dartmouth friends and, like him, no longer goes to church. He gets it. Events in their shared life have raised questions that the gentle Christianity of his childhood just can't seem to address. And his mother was always an outsider in that crowd—her African hair mostly straightened into a submissive ponytail. Skin the color of honey, not chocolate, leading people to speculate about her origins—Mi'kmaw? Italian? Mexican?

One positive in her recent life is that her job at the hospital brings in enough for vacations— Newfoundland, Quebec, even as far away as Scotland once. Hard-won luxuries. She studied for her GED, and later did her book-keeping course, all while raising him. He remembers that basement office she shared with his father, how his father's desk got emptier and emptier, while the box with files neatly labeled 'Credit card,' 'House Insurance,' 'Car Insur-ance,' 'Power bills' migrated to her corner of the room, next to her calculator.

When his mother answers, he does not tell her about the drama in his building, or even the drama at the resort. Instead, when she asks how things are going, he says that he has been enjoying watching films lately. "I'm thinking of getting tickets to the Doc fest," he says, recalling a poster he saw at the café.

"I love documentaries," she says. "Saw a great one on the History channel last night, all about Bonnie Prince Charlie."

Bizarrely, she has developed a fascination with all things Celtic since she went to Scotland, especially the music, which she finds sublime—even hokey renditions by North American YouTubers. Did she choose this topic because of his history degree? As a typical BA who now waits on tables, he can dredge up enough of his history-loving past to recall Bonnie Prince Charlie, but can't understand his mother's dead-white-guy romanticism.

When he sees an opening to do so, he brings the conversation closer to home.

"How's Aunt Flo?" he asks.

"Crazy as ever," she says. "She published her book. Gave me a copy."

"No way!" he says. "Have you read it?"

"All that talking to spirits stuff? I haven't got the time."

"But aren't you curious?" he asks. Aunt Flo's book intrigues him. It's a memoir of ghost encounters, some of which involve ancestral family members. Ghosts or not, it might be cool to explore history that is rooted in his own genes.

There is a brief silence on his mother's end, and he wonders if he has touched a nerve. Maybe talking to the dead is the last thing she wants to do.

"You can borrow it if you like," she says.

"Or buy it," he says. "You know, support the cause."

"I guess," she says.

Fred remembers talking to Aunt Flo about the book. He'd been helping her wash dishes in her house in Shelburne, last Christmas.

"I've seen some things, I can tell you," Flo said. "Went into an old house once. A girlfriend of mine moved in there after she got married. I smelled smoke and saw this woman in an old black dress on the upstairs landing, pointing at the ceiling. Later, when they checked out the attic, there were signs of a fire."

He felt both envious and spooked by this story. While quietly wiping wine glasses and stowing them in her cupboard, he started to suspect that Flo was subtly suggesting he should try talking to spirits too.

"After my dad died, I met him in a dream," she said. "Had a long conversation. Forgave him some stuff."

That would be Fred's white grandfather, dead long before Fred was born, who abandoned his family when Fred's mother was ten. She has never talked about him much, but things may have been different for Flo, who was the oldest. Fred can't recall anything he would like to say to his own father, although he remembers trying to voice such things to his university mental health counsellor years ago.

"Good for you," he said to Flo. Now, he wonders what he meant by those words.

After hanging up from his mother, he goes round back to the fence where he has secured his bike, planning to go for a ride. But he finds only his flimsy chain lock, cut and lying on the ground. For a moment he stands perfectly still, staring at the useless metal links in his hand, trying to decide how he feels about losing a crappy $150 Canadian Tire bike whose gears never worked properly anyway. Then he imagines Cory trying to sell it for drug money and starts to laugh. One step forward, he thinks. He would never have laughed three years ago, when Jamie pulled shit like this.

He hears footsteps in the gravel behind him and turns to see Krystal standing there surveying the cut lock.

"Fucking Jesus! I'll kill him!"

"We don't know for sure it was Cory," he says without conviction.

"Yeah, right."

He feels his phone vibrate in his pocket, reaches in and opens it.

There's a new text. Reading it, Fred is suddenly alone in a place he doesn't recognize. He is no more aware of Krystal's presence beside him than he would be of a speck of dust on the wind.

The text says, *Baby, I want you back.*

Fred's first thought is 'This can't be real. It must be a scam. Jamie disappeared off the planet with his blond, hard-faced girlfriend, two years ago.'

His second thought is, 'Why didn't I block his number?' He prepares to delete the text, but his finger hovers over the screen, without complying. The words pulsate, evoking Jamie's face, the last time Fred saw him. That meeting was on a street downtown, with the girlfriend, who laughed a lot at inappropriate moments, prompting Fred to assume she enabled Jamie in ways he never had. He had tried to catch Jamie's eye, but Jamie's gaze was constantly on the move.

The words on the screen throb along with his accelerated heartbeat, filling his head with a whoosh that blocks out Krystle's meaningless, high-pitched words in the background.

His third thought is that this is as close to seeing a ghost as he has ever come.

| 4 |

During her ride home from the airport, heat bounces off the urban surfaces of metal and pavement, even though the sun is low in the sky. It envelops Sophie as she trudges up the stairs of her and Tim's Brooklyn brownstone. The apartment, which she moved into with Tim two years ago, has been a major source of gratitude in her life. Tim had stayed here with his great uncle when he was an NYU student. The uncle was a cellist, and Tim inherited the rent-controlled lease after the uncle died. Sophie never met him, but she noted the reverence Tim held for him, much more reverence than when he spoke of his orthodontist and pediatrician parents in California. Sometimes the music thing skips a generation, Tim said.

When she met Tim, Sophie was slightly intimidated by how grounded he seemed. He had a stable place to live, teaching assistant hours at NYU, a regular gig with his band, and frequent work as a session musician—the height of competence, compared to her. Despite her early success in *Liza*, the teen tv show that had been her first break, she was couch surfing, auditioning for commercials and off-Broadway shows, making cheery phone calls to her mother, lying about how great everything was. But Tim didn't see any of that. He just kept telling her she was lovely.

When she enters the apartment, she notices a drooping ivy plant on the end table by the sofa, its leaves dry and browning along the edges. She leaves her suitcase at the door, takes her overnight bag further into the room and sits down. This is the sofa where she told Tim about her plan to go to Nova Scotia with Bill and Nathan. Tim was standing in front of the bookcase, in front of the photo of her parents on the Brooklyn Bridge and the one of his parents by a giant tree at Redwood State Park. Sophie almost got a crick in her neck looking up at him.

"Nova *Scotia*," he had said. "What are you talking about?"

"It's partly a location scout for Nathan, partly a chance to work on screenplay development with Bill. Nathan says it's beautiful up there, just the spot to get creative juices flowing."

"You have to go to Nova *Scotia* to enable the creative juices to flow?"

Looking back now, she sees his point. Compares their claustrophobic, three-person unit, all alone by the seashore, to the summer camp vibe of a regular shoot. Tons of people. Everyone working long hours together. Everyone oversharing, and emotional.

"It's nuts," said Tim. "There's nothing in your contract to say you need to give over two weeks of your personal life to get 'creative juices flowing'."

"I don't *have* to," she had said. "No one's saying I *have* to. It's an opportunity to be more involved in this film. It feels kind of exciting. Empowering."

"Jesus. You sound like you're on the festival circuit."

"I'm just trying to explain!"

Her voice wobbled like a teenager's. She thought, *I hate this*, staring at a patch of carpet, Tim's eyes on her.

"So that's it then," he said. "Instead of coming on tour like we planned, and even though shooting doesn't start until September, you're gonna drop everything and run off with those guys so they can *empower* you?"

The flat blankness of the tv screen is a focal point for the emptiness of the apartment, sucking her attention like a black hole. In the past, on evenings like this when Tim was on the road, she would have called him, cozying up to the phone as to a warm flame.

Maybe she could text. *You forgot to water the plants…Had a near death experience in Nova Scotia…Am pregnant.*

She goes to the kitchen and puts the kettle on. As she waits, she fills a measuring cup with water for the neglected plant. The water slowly fills the cup and overflows. She feels again the ocean dragging her body like a prop dummy along the sea bottom. Carefully drying the outer surface of the cup, she remembers her arm reaching towards the place where the sun hit the ocean's glassy surface, where there was air she could see, but not breathe.

The kettle boils, making a high-pitched squawk. She turns it off, goes back into the living room and waters the plant, her hand shaking slightly. The dull thrum of pain in her side makes her wonder what exercises are safe for her rib, which might or might not be broken. She doesn't know what is safe, because she is pregnant. She's afraid to drink a glass of wine. She is pregnant. She sits on the sofa, adjusts a cushion at her side, pulls her laptop out of her overnight bag at her feet, then lets it sit idle beside her as she looks towards the large, south-facing window and the Brooklyn skyline. This city, her chosen home, shimmers, mirage-like, in the heat. She feels a retroactive pull back to the person she used to be—an awkward, upstate kid with hippy parents.

Tim's tour schedule is on the laptop. Today is Sunday, so no show tonight. He might be out for a meal with the band, or sitting alone in his hotel room.

Her phone is also in the overnight bag, in an outside pocket.

Panic rises within her, barely containable, as though she is back in the sea.

She pulls the phone out and puts it on the coffee table, then picks it up, and finds Tim's number. It rings. Three times.

"Hey?" he answers, in a slightly surprised tone.

"Hey," she says. The casual-sounding syllable is laughable. Except that she's crying. She hasn't said a fucking thing yet and she's crying.

"I'm pregnant," she chokes out. "I found out in Nova Scotia. It must have been that afternoon, you know."

There is a silence on the other end. It surrounds her tentatively, creeping fingers of darkness in the stillness of the room. Then his voice, barely audible.

"Sophie."

"I'm going to keep the baby," she blurts out. "I don't know what I'm going to do about anything else but I'm going to keep the baby."

"Well of course you're going to…Sophie."

The silence again, tasting her tears and sweat, filling her ears with the roaring insistence of sound.

"Look, I'm almost done here. One more week, but the big gigs are over, just some small ones in bars along the coast. I could cancel one or two if necessary. The guys will understand. Do you want me to get an early flight home?"

All day she's prepared herself for this conversation. Has imagined, at best, a continuance of chilliness and distance between them; at worst, a full-out argument, ending in solitude.

She sits on the carpet, leans back against the sofa.

"You want to be with me?" That high pitched, kiddie voice again. "I thought…"

"You thought what? Sophie, what do you take me for? What did you think I was going to say?"

Every time he says her name, Sophie, she feels the distance between them being erased, bit by bit. Every time he says it, she feels herself becoming a real person; someone named Sophie, a grown woman with a body, a heart, and mind. Not this jagged mass of nerves, these disconnected parts and flashing mental images. Not these hands moving through water, these dummy legs dragged along the ocean floor.

"But," she says, "before I left, things weren't very good between us."

"Yeah, well, I was pissed off about you not coming on the tour. Obviously, I don't give a shit about all that now. We need to get together and talk. Do you want me to come home early?"

"No," she says, her voice steady, her body sinking into the carpet and the floor beneath it. "It's okay. Finish the gigs. We'll talk when you get home…

"Thank you," she adds.

"For what?"

"For offering to come home. I'm gonna go now."

"I love you, Sophie."

"I love you too," she says. Ordinary words, so simple, like a hand reaching out in the darkness. They have always come so much easier to him than to her. Why, she doesn't know.

| 5 |

Anne is buying Rudy new shoes. She hands him the first of three pairs she has pulled off the metal shelves. Rudy has the shakes as he ties the black laces. Anxiety or a side effect to his medication, she can't tell which. She has chosen this decent, small-sized store, knowing Rudy can't handle the noise, crowds, and fluorescent lights of the mall. She spent time in the mall this morning though, looking in the windows of the stores aimed at high school and college kids, to see what was in style. She also sat in the food court and stared at other people's feet, the over-large boy/man feet of high school sophomores and college freshmen shopping for the fall term. She tried hard to avoid letting her eyes wander up their shapely blue-jean clad legs to their fresh or acne sprinkled faces. She tried not to notice their laughter, their casual shoves and punches at one another, some holding hands with their girlfriends, the occasional one holding hands with a boyfriend. She tried not to take too much to heart the grace and ease of their youth.

"You should walk in them," she tells Rudy, "to make sure they're a good fit."

His feet look enormous to her. They are identical to Nathan's feet, she notices. And when he stands up to walk, he towers over her. She tries, and fails, to connect this gangly body to the tiny white and pink being that emerged between her thighs twenty years ago, eyes closed, not bothering to cry until the attending physician, a girl who looked younger than some of Nathan's nieces, rushed in to suction the afterbirth off his face. "Leave him the fuck alone," Anne had wanted to say, but didn't.

Rudy walks towards her in black running shoes, carefully, as if following a prescribed path, or on a tight rope. "Hmm," he says, "Hmm," which is his default noise when he can't decide what to say, what to feel.

"Do you like them?" she asks.

"Oh," he says. "Like them. Do I like them."

She glances at his face, sees his nervous smile, more of a brief spasm really, nothing that touches his eyes. Other people might think he's being sarcastic, but she knows better, knows the focus it requires for him to connect his words to the shoes, or to speak at all.

"Walk to the end of the aisle and back," she says. "Make sure the toes aren't pinching or the heels rubbing. Check them out in that mirror down there."

Luckily, it's only a foot mirror, coming up to his knees. Full length mirrors can be precarious territory for Rudy. As he walks down the aisle in that careful, slightly teetering way, Anne has the fantasy that there is an invisible cord connecting him to her, that she's holding one end and the other is attached to his back, just between his shoulder blades.

"They seem to fit," says Rudy.

She sees in his face that he is listening to his own voice, as if it's coming from far away. He is slightly surprised by his own words, uttered in that flat monotone. His voice is like his walk, which cannot stray from the tightrope, the middle line. She would like to feel that these attempts at normalcy were some kind of achievement, as the doctors do. She would like to envelop Rudy in that loving support that the nurses at his hospital day program offer, as if he were a child learning basic skills; walking, talking, going to the shoe store, a blank slate to be written upon, a tiny emergent being, becoming, becoming.

Except that he is not. He is not. The "not" of his not-becoming looms in her mind, three letters denoting the fading away of everything he used to be, the boy she used to know replaced by this hidden, distant young man, dissociated from the sound of his own voice, from the feel of his feet on the carpet, his big man's feet in these fashionably neutral black running shoes.

When she thinks of the days before she and Nathan had Rudy, she remembers how the endless possibilities of her future life seemed to branch out in front of her like a tropical sea fan. She remembers talking late into the night with Nathan, fantasizing, considering how many children to have, whether she might take up a teaching career or get a PhD. Whether she and future children might travel to some exotic film location with Nathan. The theme that ran through these fantasies was always the warming glow of family: Nathan by her side, that sense of belonging to something, a social unit she had helped to create. Nathan and Anne, Anne and Nathan. Those words propelling her into a glittering, widening future. But Nathan's film locations did not turn out to be exotic, she had a miscarriage after Rudy and didn't try for more, the PhD never beckoned strongly enough. And then Rudy got sick, driving all such considerations from her mind.

"I think I'll do some cleaning when we get home," she says, easing the car out of the shoe store lot. "Dad's home tomorrow," she adds, by way of explanation. Rudy makes his noncommittal 'Hmm' as he looks out the window.

When they get home, he follows her in silence to the front door, carrying the shoebox gingerly, as if it might explode.

"I'm going to vacuum downstairs," she says over her shoulder to him as they walk in. "Maybe tidy your room and the bathroom, and then come down while I do up there."

Rudy has a pair of noise canceling headphones in his room, which he puts on when she vacuums or uses the food processor. She always warns him before she does anything noisy. She's doubtful he will get his room in a decent enough state for her to clean it properly but he may at least clear a pathway for her. They might be able to avoid negotiations about what to throw out.

She starts in the living room, the tidiest room in the house, and then makes her way into Nathan's office. Devoid of Nathan's presence, it has a still, expectant quality. Books on the movie business line the shelves, there is a calendar with black and white movie stills on the wall, framed family photos on the small, makeshift shelf he has put over the desk. This is her husband's domain, with its own separate character. In the past she has found it warm and comforting, like Nathan.

On the desk is a snapshot of Nathan, Bill, and Sophie, taken on the set of their last film—an outdoor shot, with blurry figures in the background, suggesting a moment of stillness amidst frantic activity. Who was taking the photo? Bill stares at the camera, an unreadable expression on his face. Sophie, in the center of the frame, smiles vividly. She looks young and relaxed. Nathan's head is turned in profile, watching Sophie, watching Bill.

Just as Anne is about to start the vacuum cleaner, she hears a sound coming from Rudy's bedroom. It is unidentifiable, a low humming, or moan, that she can't connect to any familiar image in her mind. Not music. Not his air purifier. She walks upstairs, feeling that she should be going quicker, but all her pre-cleaning energy has evaporated, leaving her legs heavy and stiff.

When she opens the door to his room, she can't find him at first. Then she sees him—crouched in the corner, between the bed and the wall. His hands are clasped on the crown of his head. He reminds Anne of pictures she has seen of people held at gunpoint: criminals at bay or soldiers captured in the street by an occupying force.

"No…" he's saying, his voice rising in increments. "No, no, no, no…"

Anne rushes to his side and crouches, putting her hand on his arm.

"Get away from me!" he shouts, "Who the fuck *are* you?"

The back of his hand, which has suddenly become an unknown, heavy object, catches her face, right on the bridge of her nose. The thwack of contact is vaguely surprising, bringing everything into hyper-focus. Her hand flies to the place where the pain is. It throbs like a migraine, but there is no blood.

"Jesus," she says, behind her hand.

She should have known better than to take him by surprise with touch. She had learned that at one of the support group meetings.

Even as this thought crosses her mind, she is aware of anger coursing through her. It's a relief, this anger; cool, white, and cleansing; replacing the heaviness of anxiety and the thick cotton-wool fog of grief which has been clogging her thoughts forever, it seems. There is absolute silence in the room, until it is broken by a long, shuddering intake of breath. Rudy's breath.

"It's me," she says, her voice muffled and nasal sounding behind her cupped hand. "It's Mom." Because he might be mistaking her for anyone. If this is a full psychotic break, she might have to phone 911. She imagines the explanations; the danger Rudy might be put in by under-trained EMT's. But what other choice will she have, with Nathan away?

Rudy looks at her.

"I know who you are," he says. "I'm sorry. I didn't mean..."

She takes her hand away from her nose, which is still throbbing. She wonders what she will look like in the morning.

"I can't, I can't..." Rudy is saying.

"Can't what?" she says. "Tell me what you can't do."

He is crying. Briefly, she recognizes him, the same boy whom she comforted in the past over bike accidents or skinned knees. As quickly as it has come, her anger evaporates, but it leaves something in its wake that Anne can't quite identify. Something white and cool, despite his wet eyes, despite his resemblance to the boy she used to know. When he says: "They haven't gone away, you know," his words enter her body at chest level and sink like a stone in her belly.

"They haven't gone away?" she says.

"The demons. They're still there. The pills, all the shit I'm taking doesn't make them go away."

She breathes, swallows. Wonders if she's up for this conversation. Manages to drag slow words out in response. "They're still telling you..." to cut people, was what he has told her in the past, demons hovering in the background, or crawling out of the computer screen and clawing at his feet as he lay in bed. "They're driving me crazy," he had yelled, unaware of any irony in this statement.

"The pills don't help at all?" she says finally.

He shakes his head. "Just makes it so I don't do what they say."

"Right," she says, grasping for something to move forward with. "Right, well, that's better, isn't it? If you don't have to do what they say?"

He's still looking at her. At least he is aware of something, someone, outside of his head, outside of that locked, dark world encompassed by the shell of his tightly curled body. Arms wrapped around his knees, he is rocking slightly.

"Until the next time," he says. Once more, his voice has something in it, something that she recognizes, that cuts through the medication and the demons and all the things about him she will never understand.

"I can't go back there," he says. "Don't make me. I know I hit you, but it wasn't what I meant to do. I can't go back to the hospital and get pumped through with so much Risperdal that I'm a fucking zombie."

"Rudy," she says. "I don't know if you remember what you were like that time, but we had no choice but to take you in."

He had thrown a lamp, his eyes huge, pupils dilated like those of a wild animal at night. She remembers him trying to get out of the car on the highway, yelling, "They're shooting from the helicopter!" She remembers climbing over the gear shift to get in the back seat with him, Nathan locking all the doors from the driver's side, somehow managing to keep driving. Nathan's eyes in the rear-view mirror, watching them both.

"As soon as they could, the doctors lowered your dose," she says.

"And is that it? Up the pills, down the pills, round and round and round the pills! In the ward, out of the ward, back again in the fucking ward!"

An angry red is moving up his neck to his face. Anne notices his enlarged pores, the stubble on his chin, the slight sheen of sweat on his forehead.

But she's not afraid. She finds his repetition of the word "fucking" reassuring. He is using it the way other kids his age use it, for emphasis, for effect. He's using it the way she once used it, before she adopted her careful, polite, mother's persona.

"Is that it?" Rudy says again, more quietly this time.

"No," she says, remembering her tears in the psychiatrist's office: her unanswered pleas. "That isn't it," she says. "There has to be a better way."

Her words come out slowly, because she is still carrying in her belly the stone weight of Rudy's voice, talking about the demons. "There has to be more we can offer you than this," she says. But something moves her to add: "Whatever it is, whatever we try, you are going to have to work hard at it. We can't do this for you."

She would like to see beyond his red-rimmed, wet eyes into some kind of neutral territory where his thoughts exist. Beyond terror, beyond childhood, beyond his constant, debilitating need. He is quiet now, still in the corner, his arms and shoulders slightly more relaxed, his hands on his knees a little less white with tension. The colour in his face is slowly subsiding. She can hear him breathing. She sits with it, tries to breathe along.

…

The next morning, Nathan calls to say that he plans to break up the drive home from Nova Scotia by visiting his friends Keith and Linda in Maine.

"I may be late," he says. "Don't wait up for me."

She's mostly relieved. In the mirror this morning, she noticed a slight swelling where Rudy hit her. If she ices it, by tonight even that should be gone. When Nathan asks after Rudy, she tells him Rudy made it to the day program four times this week.

"Great, great," Nathan says.

After she hangs up, it occurs to her that, last night, she made a promise to Rudy. It was implicit in the words, "There has to be more we can offer you than this." She wonders if the doctors would approve. Probably not. But that's what parents do. Make promises all the time, even if they don't say them aloud. I will look after you. I will stand by you.

When Nathan gets home, she will tell him they need to do more research, look up every possibility, even if it seems like snake oil. She will reach out her hands to him and say, "Enough, enough. I am done with this." But what is she done with? Watching Rudy take his meds? Taking him to the day program? Trying to explain? She says inwardly: "What are my options?" and then thinks, "What options?"

There is no sound from upstairs, where she hopes Rudy is still asleep. Through the kitchen window she sees the sweep of their lawn and driveway, which is lined with the jack pines she and Nathan planted when they first moved here. Now they stand over ten feet tall. Beyond their ranks, the driveway ends, and the road begins.

$$| \, 6 \, |$$

SHE WATCHES RUDY TAKE HIS PILL. It is in one of those compartmentalized pill boxes, which Dr. Green has said are helpful, but are not, he specifies, a replacement for watching Rudy take his medication. Only 51% of patients are 'compliant', he said, a word she hates, but recognizes as accurate in this situation. Relapses into psychosis can, according to Dr. Green, permanently harm the brain, make Rudy lose ground. 'Lose ground towards what?' she's wanted to ask. 'Where is he going?'

Rudy puts the pill in his mouth, rolls it around before swallowing his water, a slight smile on his face, half ironic, half something else. This pill watching is a daily occurrence. The only alternative, according to the doctors, is long-acting injections every month, a treatment reserved for acute cases. Anne tries to imagine what kind of substance would stay in the bloodstream and change the chemistry of someone's brain over that long a period. She envisions a black dye pumping its way through Rudy's body, sending out tendrils towards his thoughts. But where do those thoughts, those voices and fears live? In Rudy's brain, his belly, his heart?

Last night, when she told Nathan she thought they needed to do something different, try something new, she saw a familiar, wary look come into his eyes.

"Anne," he said. "I think we're, you're, doing a pretty good job as it is."

"I'm not talking about how good a *job* anyone's doing," she said.

"Maybe," he said, "we can find some time tomorrow to talk properly when he's at the day program."

Understandable, she thinks now. It was bad timing. He had just arrived home, had just told her the news about Sophie. So she had put the Rudy talk on hold and made him a cup of lemon ginger tea.

"Bill is seriously pissed off," Nathan said, sitting across the table from her. "We'd have an outside window of three months to shoot before Sophie starts to show, and we'd have to start right away. Meanwhile she's waffling—I'm not sure what her status is with the boyfriend. That might be the problem."

Anne had looked Sophie up when Nathan had first hired her. She was dismayed by how lovely she was, and meeting her at film-openings and parties hadn't reassured her. She's slightly ashamed of this reaction. Mostly, Nathan takes a chummy and avuncular line with young actresses. Still, they are a strange breed, actors. All that faking of pain and sex and tears. Can't be good for the character. She wonders how Sophie will deal with impending motherhood. No matter how inept a person is at parenting, it can't be faked.

In a way, it was a relief, last night, to listen to the story of Sophie going missing, then running off to the hospital. The plot was like one of the mystery novels Anne liked to read before bed. She could feel Nathan warming to her, his voice relaxing as he spoke. When they reached a natural stopping place, like a lull in a piece of music, she said, "You probably need an early night after all that driving."

"Actually, I think I'll go for a walk to stretch my legs," he said. "Join me if you like."

She should have said yes, she thinks now. She should have walked with him in the twilight, even though she felt bone weary. But she didn't. She followed him to the door, looked out through the porch window to the driveway.

"You go ahead," she said.

When Nathan kissed her good night, she was careful to avoid bumping her still tender nose against his stubbly cheek.

After Rudy has had breakfast, Anne drops him at his day program and continues along Route 9, towards her mother's retirement home. A few maple trees have already started to turn, even though it's only early September. Global warming, probably, a weakening in the fabric of things. She pulls into the parking lot of her mother's home and notices signs on the lawn. Keep off the grass. They have obviously applied weed killer, adding carcinogens to the myriad ways these frail elderly residents could pop off at any time. She resolves to take her mother for a walk in the nearby state park, with the view of the river, away from here.

The receptionist in the lobby buzzes Anne in before she has to ring her mother's apartment number. The wide and carpeted halls to her mother's door always fill her with relief, despite the weed killer outside. No stairs, handrails everywhere. A certain staid uniformity to the décor, but lots of natural light in the lobby and other common areas. Clean. Much better than some places they could have chosen.

The door to the studio apartment is unlocked, and when Anne enters, she sees her mother rise slowly from an armchair on the other side of the room. Backlit by the window behind her, her face is in shadow.

Anne embraces her mother gently, noticing how she has to stoop to do so, remembering that she and her mother used to be the same height. Her mother is wearing russet-coloured slacks and a turtleneck sweater and silk scarf that remind Anne of English Department soirées her parents attended when she was little, and later, the public lecture series established in her father's honour after he died. In years past, she had occasionally taken her mother to these lectures. Her mother would enter the room with an air of regality; there was no other word for it—standing to survey the audience with a slow sweep of her head before sitting down. She invariably caught the eye of some old friend or other, but as the years went by, there were fewer people to come up and kiss her on the cheek. Lately, she has lost interest in those talks, preferring to go to concerts instead, and Anne has found it less and less possible to get away from Rudy to join her.

When Anne suggests they drive to the river for a walk, her mother wrinkles her nose, "It's too much trouble," she says. "Getting in and out of your car is a bother for me these days."

Anne thinks of all the times her mother had insisted she pull herself away from a book or the tv to get some healthy fresh air.

"Well at least let's enjoy the sunshine in the courtyard," she says.

She hands her mother her walking shoes and a footstool, and searches for something to say during her mother's laborious process of putting the shoes on and tying them. Her mother's book club seems like a safe topic. But when her mother tells her they are reading Harper Lee's *The Watchman* this month, her heart sinks. She hated that book, but for different reasons than her mother, who has embarked on a slow, halting, literary critique. Anne had been horrified by the adult Scout's capitulation to the men in her family, whose creepy paternalism towards Black people turned the heroics of *To Kill a Mockingbird* into a sham. She felt as if one of her favourite childhood reads had been forever tarnished.

"Some people think Lee was pressured into publishing it," she says, getting her mother's cane now and handing it to her so she can hoist herself upright.

"Possible, I suppose. She may have been losing her mind at the time, like a lot of people here."

Anne does not point out that her mother is almost the exact age of Harper Lee at the time of her death. They walk in silence through the lobby to the front entrance, her mother hesitating at the front door, trying to decide if she needs her fall jacket.

"I have my key," says Anne, "I'll get it."

She goes back to retrieve the jacket, a utilitarian Helly Hansen number, and ends up carrying the unneeded item of clothing for the duration of their slow amble around the parking lot. The late summer sun warms their shoulders. In the back courtyard, there is a trellis on the walkway, adorned with white roses that are browning at the tips, and a pond with a bench facing it. Anne stops and waits for her mother to lower herself down on the bench. In the pond, koi and giant goldfish swim around each other in slow, hypnotic circles.

"Will Rudy be starting back in school soon?" asks her mother, staring at the fish.

"Mom," says Anne, "that will not be happening this year. Rudy is doing really well, though."

These days, she tones down any mention of Rudy's illness to the point of making it sound like an adolescent rough patch. She had tried to explain more fully, when Rudy was hospitalized last year, but her mother's obvious confusion, her questions about whether Rudy had a drug habit, and the conclusions Anne felt she might be drawing about her own and Nathan's parenting, had discouraged her from going into much detail.

They sit silently for a while, Anne trying to internally bolster her comment about how well Rudy is doing, despite his inability to return to school. She is considering taking Rudy to a naturopath, which would be another taboo topic, here. When her mother was hospitalized after the first in a series of falls that made it impracticable for her to continue living alone, Anne had been astonished by her uncharacteristic meekness around the doctors and nurses. And since then, her mother has rebuffed suggestions of massage therapy or acupuncture for her aching back, calling anything other than surgery or physiotherapy 'pseudo-science'.

"Is Nathan back from…where was it again?" asks her mother.

"Nova Scotia."

"Ah yes, Nova Scotia…your father and I had a lovely holiday there once."

"Really?" says Anne. "When was that?"

"Oh, years before you were born. Before we were married, in fact."

"No way!"

She has half a mind to tease her mother about what would have been a pretty illicit jaunt back then. The late fifties maybe? Surprisingly, this topic has never come up, even when she and Nathan bought their cottage.

"It was our real honeymoon," says her mother, with a slight formality to her tone, layers of meaning there that Anne can only guess at. "After our wedding, he had so much preparation to do for the fall term at the university. That year was his first full-time teaching job, you see."

"So where did you stay in Nova Scotia?" Anne says.

She wants to add, 'Did you have to wear a fake wedding ring, like in the old movies?' but her mother's demeanor, her precariously upright posture, deter her.

"We went to Cape Breton. Beautiful scenery. But the ocean was far too cold to swim. The nicest spot was on a big lake. We stayed in a cottage. Absolutely deserted. So different from Cape Cod or Nantucket…We could swim there, with no one around to see us."

"Ah…" says Anne, again afraid to tease, afraid to lose this glimpse into an intimate reminiscence.

"Was Nathan's trip successful?" says her mother.

Anne takes a breath.

"Not very. It turns out his lead actress is pregnant, so the film's on hold for the time being."

"The blond one, with the crooked smile?"

"Sophie. Yes."

"Well, how very careless. I would have thought in this day and age…"

"It can happen to anyone," says Anne, surprised to feel offended on Sophie's behalf. She thinks, but does not say, that after confessing to a romantic adventure in her own youth, her mother could be a bit less judgmental.

"There were far fewer options in my day, but I managed not to have it happen to me," says her mother.

Anne recalls a version of this conversation when she was in her teens. How the early birth control pill was horrendous, how it made her mother nauseated all the time, how she "managed" despite being unable to take it, in ways that Anne was too squeamish to ask about.

"Well," she says, slightly ashamed to feel a trace of her fifteen-year-old squeamishness once more, "Good for you."

On her way home, Anne stops to walk on her own at the Franny Reese State Park, choosing the shortest trail, having told Nathan she would be back in time to pick Rudy up.

The pressed earth of the gravel path feels soft after the tarmac of the parking lot. There is a steep hill on her right, strewn with dead leaves, some of which have tumbled down to the path to make a satisfying crunch when she walks. On the incline, young trees hold onto the earth, their roots exposed, occasionally making long and tortuous forays down the hillside to gain purchase, but still managing to stand upright. Neat, waist-high rock walls, evidence of human attempts to slow erosion, line the trail in places. When she looks beyond the rock wall to her left, she notices the perpendicular uniformity of the trees, the way the sun shines through them.

The trail leads past the ruins of the Cedar Glen Estate. As a teenager, Anne would have been fascinated by its roofless, crumbling stone walls. If this place had been open to the public then, she would have probably climbed that stairway leading nowhere. She would have plotted imaginary Gothic novels, with herself as protagonist, dressed in a flowing white Victorian nightgown.

She can see the Hudson through the woods on her left now. Its blue grey is intersected by the evenly spaced silhouettes of the trees. When she climbs the steps to the Mid-Hudson Bridge and looks down at the water, the illusion of a uniform body of water vanishes. The river is actually a multiplicity of movements, dark ripples shot with glints of sunlight. Giant swaths of surface water rolling along, like the surface of the blue parachute her gym class used to play with in grade school. But the river's movement is continuous, oblivious, in no way dependent on excited children's hands.

On her way back to the parking lot, she passes the ruins again, and their decaying architecture makes her think about the toppling of symmetry, the crumbling of stone into stone. Earth to earth. There is something comforting about the ephemera of human history. She wonders if the human lives which evolved here and have now vanished, really matter after all.

| 7 |

SHE SEES TIM THROUGH GLASS DOORS. He's on an escalator coming towards her. He could be anyone, but his height distinguishes him from the other disembarking passengers. The carefully erect way he holds his head, the set of his shoulders, the slight stubble on his chin. When he hugs her, she's overcome with shyness, enveloped in familiar textures and smells—the suede jacket, the arms around her back, the stubbly cheek resting on the crown of her head. For a moment, they are enclosed in a bubble of silence, as hordes of people move around them. She wants this stillness more than anything. She wishes they could stay like this, wishes there were no need to talk.

Thankfully, he either senses or shares her mood, and the cab ride home goes by in almost trance-like quiet. When they are stuck in traffic, she takes his hand for a while, and he raises it to his lips, completely unaware of the sweetness of this gesture. She turns to see his face. He's looking out the window, his eyes thoughtful behind his glasses, his lips warm and dry on her fingers.

When they speak, it is in slow, unhurried sentences, completing each other's thoughts, as though they are composing a song together.

"You okay?"

"Yes."

"Feel any different?"

"Yes, but not in the way you mean."

"Oh?"

"Something happened before I knew for sure."

"Something good?"

"Something scary. I almost drowned. Got pulled out by the undertow when I was swimming and tossed around by the waves. Might have broken a rib, but I don't think so."

"Sophie."

"It's okay, the doctor said it's okay. Shouldn't affect the baby."

When she says the word 'baby', there is a brief moment of something in his eyes. Awe maybe, or the cautious beginnings of joy.

"You are so beautiful," he says as they pull up to the curb. Inside, when she offers him a cold beer from the fridge, he says, "Come sit with me."

The naive and direct way he takes her hand and leads her to the sofa. So sexy. She looks at his face—his half-smile, his eyes drinking her in—and thinks, I've missed this. I need this. She wonders why she agreed to go off with Nathan and Bill when Tim didn't want her to. She contrasts her trance-like state, meeting Tim at the airport today, with how she felt meeting Nathan and Bill to board the plane for Nova Scotia together. Nathan had hugged her, then gone to check his bags. It was then that Bill kissed her. A quick, firm kiss on the lips that could have been familial, but there was something proprietary about it. She pulled away quickly, wondering if she was being paranoid. She would have preferred a hug, like Nathan's, and noted that Bill had waited until Nathan's back was turned.

She had put this out of her mind when they arrived in Nova Scotia, and Nathan had chatted, the entire journey, about the film and their plans for the week. Collaborating on screenplay development, location scouting. Carried away by Nathan's enthusiasm, she neglected to notice how little Bill joined in the conversation. She felt excited in a reckless sort of way, refusing to dwell on her argument with Tim, or even on her late period, which she put down to a change in routine. She had been so convinced that she knew what was best for herself and her career, before she took that test in the hotel bathroom, before her encounter with the sea.

All of that so different from how she feels now as she sits next to Tim and tells him about the shock of the double line on her pregnancy test, about her appointment with the doctor in Nova Scotia. For some reason, she does not talk about the ocean, the terror of being buffeted by the waves. They do not mention the film either. Future decisions hang in the air, an unspoken presence.

"Have you seen a doctor since you got back?" he asks.

"I have an appointment on Wednesday."

"And the timing for all this is?"

"I'll find out for sure after I see the doctor, but I'm thinking April or May."

Again, there is silence. Tentatively, he puts a hand on her belly.

"It's amazing," he says.

She tells him how she spent her last night in Nova Scotia barely sleeping, trying to get to know the new heartbeat inside her body. She recalls how that imagined heartbeat steadied her, allowed her to feel still, despite hallucinogenic memories of her time in the sea.

They talk until long after shadows have replaced the sunlight creeping across the living room floor. She asks him about the tour, and he describes the times his playing surpassed what he thought he could do, and the other, frustrating moments when his intuition deserted him and he slogged his way through solos as though wading through sludge, hearing his sound, correct and stodgy, just trying to find a safe foothold in the harmony.

"Only happened a couple of times, though," he says. "It gets better the more we play."

She asks him if he's hungry and they cobble together a meal with all the produce she bought at the organic food mart and deli down the street. Afterwards, she is overcome with exhaustion—a heavy, voluptuous languor that she rarely experiences, or rarely allows herself to experience, she's not sure which. They cuddle on the bed, deep slow kisses and Tim's hand exploring her body with a new gentleness, but they do not fully make love. She wonders if he's worried about hurting something—her rib, or the baby—but she's too sleepy to tell him it's okay, she's okay, better than she's been for a long time.

But in the early morning, when she wakes beside him, her stomach is roiling. She stumbles to the bathroom while he sleeps. She does not vomit, but kneels beside the toilet wishing she could, regretting the rice and stir-fry of the night before. She takes deep breaths, lying on the floor, the cool tiles comforting against her clammy cheek. Gradually, the nausea passes, but it has taken with it her joy, and definitely her plan to wake Tim up with playful morning sex. Her side is hurting, and she's afraid to swallow a painkiller. Even the thought of water is taboo, nausea hovering in the background, waiting to strike.

She makes her way to the living room and pulls her phone out of her purse, hoping to find some online remedy for morning sickness, but sees instead a text from Nathan: How are you? Three simple words containing all the questions she has avoided asking herself or discussing with Tim.

I can't, she thinks. I can't work right now.

Suddenly, this baby no longer feels like a gift. Even the sweetness of her time with Tim last night is out of reach.

She goes quietly back to the bedroom to get her hairbrush, her underwear, and clothes. Tim does not stir. His inert form is a foreign lump on the bed. She thinks: He is the parent of my child. The words 'parent' and 'child' are no more real to her than memorized dialogue. What business have they trying to do this, make a life together, raise a child? The nausea swells again like a huge wave inside her, and she barely makes it to the toilet this time before vomiting up what feels like the entire contents of her stomach.

The last time she was sick like this was when she was eighteen. The morning after she lost her virginity. That LA cast party from *Liza*, all those teen actors crammed into one apartment, all those drinks poured, stiffer and stiffer each time, she is sure, although she tasted the alcohol less and less. All the sex. A threesome down the hall between her best friend Amy, Ryan, the costar of the show, and some girl whose name she couldn't remember. When Chad, whom Sophie considered vaguely to be a nice guy, pulled her onto the couch beside him and later led her to a bedroom, she thought, "Why not? Now is as good a time as any." At the same time, once he was actually standing over her, skinny white legs and erect dick jutting out from under his Karl Lagerfeld shirt, her teenage drink-befuddled brain had registered him as both ridiculous and terrifying. Now, still kneeling helplessly by the toilet, she wonders why her memory chose to toss up that particular image, the last thing she needs.

Tim is awake. She hears his low murmur of concern and knows he's standing in the doorway, bleary-eyed, staring at her hunched back in its light cotton night shirt, which is now drenched in sweat. She's not sure if she wants him here, but is grateful for his hand under her elbow as she stands to wash her face at the sink. She avoids looking in the mirror, unsure whether it is his face or her own that she does not wish to see.

That afternoon, her mother calls to say that Jack, her younger brother, will soon be coming home from China, where he has been teaching English as a second language.

"He's taking some time to travel. Wants to go to Vietnam, Laos, and Thailand," she says. "He thinks he'll be home in time for Thanksgiving, but you can never get a firm date out of him."

There is excitement in her mother's voice, but also a familiar combination of affection and pique at her unpredictable, globetrotting son.

After her early morning vomiting spell, Sophie has a hard time focusing. She knows she will need to tell her mother about the baby, but the words *not yet* pass through her mind. She has assumed her mother will be joyful with grandmotherly expectations at the news, but now, she wonders what tone will be used to tell others about this unplanned event. Will her parents decide she has carelessly fucked up her current career prospects? Once, when she was fourteen, she considered not enrolling in summer theatre camp again that year. When she had idly tossed the idea out over the supper table, her mother had put down her fork and stared at her as if at a stranger. Nothing was said, but Sophie had imagined a speech bubble emanating from her mother's mouth, containing the words *lazy, time wasting, after all we've sacrificed to pay for those camps.* She changed tack mid-sentence and never entertained the idea of an idle, theatre-free summer again.

"I think it's great Jack is doing all this travelling," her mother says, "though he doesn't seem to have any plan for when he comes home. He wants to stay with his friend Noah for a while, that's about all I can get out of him. I just hope he knows what he's doing. He needs to find something he can sink his teeth into, develop his will."

The last three words penetrate Sophie's blurred consciousness.

"What does that mean, 'develop his will'?"

"When was the last time he finished anything he started, Sophie?" says her mother. "He's always been so aimless. So unfocused. Not like…"

Sophie feels heat rising to her face, a prickling of anger sending goose-bumps along her arms and hands, along with an odd sense of claustrophobic panic that arouses her nausea once more.

"He's twenty-four years old, Mum. How focused were you at that age?"

She winces, realizing that her mother was only two years older than Jack, two years younger than Sophie is now, when she gave birth to her first child. She had been focused enough, then, to choose a midwife and water birth for Sophie's arrival, although some people would not call that focused, just arbitrary and weird.

She clears her throat and searches for another topic to cover the awkward pause, and settles on the only one that comes to mind—a surefire way to keep her mother busy and distracted.

"So what's the latest on the Trump man and the election?" she says. "I lost touch when I was away."

Her mother sighs. "Don't get me started," she says. "Have you heard he hired that insane Steve Bannon as CEO of his campaign a couple of weeks ago?"

For the next ten minutes they enter the territory of electoral politics, which feels inexplicably safer than talk of her brother—or her. At the same time, her mother's rant about the appalling state of journalism in this country, and how the education system has a lot to answer for if people think a shoddy crook like Trump is going to save them, sets Sophie's teeth on edge. It's not like she doesn't share her mother's anguish. Each crazy bit of news makes the country she grew up in seem less and less recognizable. But her mother's intensity irritates her all the same.

As she draws the conversation to a close, Tim comes into the room to get dressed.

"My mother is the queen of drama," Sophie says, putting her phone on the night table.

"Ah…that's where you get it from," he says, fluttering his fingers over the ticklish spot near her ribs.

"Fuck off," she says, laughing. Secretly, she fears he's right. There are some things you can never get away from, no matter how hard you try.

| 8 |

Fred watches an art film at the Oxford theatre, part of the doc fest he told his mother about. The film is a career retrospective of a Nova Scotian painter, with musicians' interpretations of his works. On the screen before him, musicians talk about the paintings they have chosen to interpret and why, the stories they see glimmering beneath the surface of the still-life canvasses. Fred likes these conversations, which have nothing to do with the daily grind of hand-to-mouth living, or gender, or sex, or race. He likes the way the people in the film spend their time—looking at art, speaking, singing, listening, all for the sake of something undefinable but real. He likes their faces, their heads bent over guitars or pianos, their eyes watching something Fred cannot see. He also enjoys watching stills of the paintings—women and men turned in profile, agricultural or coastal landscapes, technically precise, representative images, the kind of art Jamie always scoffed at.

There is another unanswered text on his phone, burning a hole in his pocket like a still-smoldering cigarette. *I hate the way things ended between us.* No kidding, thinks Fred, as if he's the one responsible for that shit-show. In the months following their split, he had sent mutual friends to check on Jamie when his texts turned suicidal. And then they had dried up, presumably because of Liz, or Linda, or whatever her name was. Fred is hoping the same will happen now, without him having to take further action. But he can't help wondering where Jamie is—Montreal? Halifax? The last possibility makes him jumpier than he cares to admit, even though he never shared his new address with any of their mutual friends.

To his mild dismay, one of those mutual friends appears in the lobby after the film—Jeff Logan, an artist who used to occasionally exhibit in the gallery. Jeff's white head, with its Santa Claus beard, asserts itself in the crowd. He catches Fred's eye, beams and surges forward, grabbing one of Fred's hands in both of his, pumping it up and down as if he and Fred are long lost buddies.

They stand together, two lone men in a sea of social groups.

"Pretty good film, eh?" Jeff says. "Always wanted to play an instrument. Am reduced to being a patron though."

"Well, a patron is good," says Fred uncertainly, imagining Jeff in an embroidered eighteenth-century jacket and powdered wig, like the emperor in the movie *Amadeus*.

"Yeah… I host these open-mic nights at my café. Amazing, the talent in this town. We're having one tomorrow night. Would love to see you there."

Fred thinks an open mic night at Jeff's café might be stretching his recent resolution to get out more. "I'm working at that time," he says reluctantly, knowing where this might lead.

"And where is work these days?" says Jeff, inevitably.

"I've picked up some shifts at the Peninsula Inn and Resort."

"Really," says Jeff.

"Just helping out in the dining room," he adds, as if it's a hobby. "There's less work now that the tourist season is ending." An organic transition, he would like to imply, instead of what it actually is, the beginnings of a financial crisis that will send him into a tailspin, scanning job ads at night, acutely conscious that he's pushing forty and still trying to get by on seasonal work.

"Well now, that's a coincidence," says Jeff, a tentative expression on his face that is at odds with his confident, gregarious vibe. "Just had a staff member leave to have a baby, and we're pretty busy right now, at least over lunch hour. With our location, the seasons don't affect us much. Don't suppose you'd be interested? The tips won't be as good as at the resort, but I'd be happy to work around your schedule."

Is it just laziness at the thought of firing off another volley of resumés that leads him to accept? The café is on Agricola, within easy walking distance of his apartment. He agrees to help with the Wednesday and Thursday lunch shift, this coming week.

"See how you find it," says Jeff. "It'll just be me and you there on those days. We are pretty low key. A few regulars who work in the area come for lunch on weekdays. Most of the high traffic is on the weekends. I hang work on the walls," he adds. "Mostly my own, but I like to take other people's stuff too, if you know of anyone interested."

Is he talking about Jamie? Fred wonders.

"People miss the gallery," Jeff continues. "All the events you used to hold there. It was a happening spot."

"Until it wasn't," says Fred. To his own surprise, he decides to take the bull by its horns, address the elephant in the room—all the clichés he can think of to describe the air Jamie takes up in a space, even when he no longer inhabits it.

"Jamie was in pretty rough shape for a lot of that," he says. "It's tough trying to run a business with a partner who's an addict."

Jeff nods his head sagely, as if they are commenting on the weather. "Got it," he says and, after a slight pause, "Do you know what he's doing now, where he is?"

"Montreal, as far as I know," says Fred.

"Ah," says Jeff, turning his eyes away to scan the crowd.

The next day, on a phone call with his mother, Fred tells her he has landed "a few shifts at Jeff Logan's café," once more trying to make it sound as if his serving career is a hobby. She isn't fooled.

"Not making enough at that fancy resort?" she says. "They're lucky to have you, you know that?"

"Thanks, Mom."

"Just the truth. Bet you could run that place better than the clueless owners."

"Ah, but would I want to?" says Fred, thinking about the hopes she probably had for him when he went to university, the hopes she still had for him when he was running the gallery, until he couldn't hide the mess any longer. He has disappointed her, wasted his opportunities, while she had to fight so hard to get ahead, after the dearth of education available to her in Shelburne County. "Fifteen black kids in a class, three white," she would say, "We thought we were the lucky ones when they worked with those three instead of us. There were teachers smoking dope and playing guitar. Dating kids in Grade Eleven. I could tell you some stories."

When Fred had gotten his scholarship to McGill, his mother had looked him in the eye and said, "Go, you have to go." He remembers his gratitude, and at the same time, something he couldn't quite pinpoint—the inkling of which still makes him ashamed. Annoyance—at her, not his father—the woman who had done everything for him up to that point. He felt so tired by the fucking weight of his homelife, pity for her situation warring with an urge to shout: *You*. It's you who have to go.

"You met Jeff once, at the gallery," he tells his mother. "White hair and beard? He paints landscapes."

"Okay," she says.

"How's Aunt Flo?"

"I'll give you her book next time you come to visit," she says. "She's giving a reading at the library next Friday."

"Are you going?"

"Haven't decided yet," she says. "What about you?"

"Have a shift at the resort that night."

"Hmm."

Will she go without him? She's independent in almost all things, except when it comes to encounters with her family, when she seems to need him on her arm, proof, maybe, that he is okay, she is okay. That they are survivors.

"Did I tell you about the drama that happened at the resort a couple of weeks ago?" Fred says. "A woman went missing, and I found her on the beach. She got caught in the undertow and nearly drowned."

For the rest of their conversation, he makes a meal of that story, the coincidence of finding Sophie's film on Netflix. The trip to the clinic. He doesn't mention the memories that trip evoked, memories he has been trying to forget, a task that is becoming more and more difficult, with Jamie's second text still in his pocket.

"That's the thing about the ocean," his mother says. "You have to respect it. People from elsewhere just don't get that. Like those fools that go stand on the slipperiest rocks at Peggy's Cove and think the waves only exist in their selfie videos."

"I don't think she was that foolish, just unlucky," he says. "She seemed like a nice person, but mixed up. Distracted, sort of. Like she was working something out. Definitely intelligent."

"Yeah, well, there's intelligent and there's intelligent. Some fellas with a string of letters as long as your arm after their name couldn't boil an egg to save their life."

"Maybe there are more things than boiling an egg," he says.

His Aunt Flo would say his encounter with Sophie was fate. Fate that his routine was interrupted by a glimpse into a life that wasn't his own, that revolved around something more than putting meals on the table. Fate that memories had been stirred up. Fate that he had run into Jeff at the doc fest and landed a new job.

He knows his mother fears such talk, scorns deviating into the flights of fancy required to make art, or to believe in spirits and destiny. Listening to her calm, alto voice, a trace of her rural roots in the way she says, 'those fools' and 'some fellas,' he remembers the only time he witnessed her lose that calm. A sudden, unbidden image of her running out of the house after she found his father, doubled over as if someone had sucker-punched her in the belly, saying 'Don't go in there. Don't go in there.' When the cops, in tandem with the laughably useless ambulance, showed up, Fred, just home for study leave, had to do all the talking. He remembers how she stayed absolutely silent until the EMT's emerged, carrying the covered stretcher. It was only then that she started to scream.

He and his mother talk more about little nothings, the traffic jams— how the city always waits until September to start construction, just in time for everyone going back to work at the universities—how she can't find the right shoes for her walks with her hiking club, how the leaves outside her window are starting to turn. At the end of their call, he says, "Take care, Mom," noticing, as if listening to himself from a distance, that there is a new tenderness in his voice.

"You too," she says.

Fred wonders why Sophie should come up in his conversations, take up residence in his psyche the way she has. One thing he knows about himself is his absolute lack of interest in women. He tried sex with a girl once when he was in college. It had been a surreal and alienating experience, like learning a technically complex dance to ambient music with no back beat. But there is something about the memory of Sophie that he can't shake. The way she came to the table alone every morning, the way her fingers handled her coffee cup and smoothed the pages of her magazine with care, the way she turned her face to the sun.

Maybe, he thinks, if he were the artist in that documentary he watched, he could have painted her. She could have become a profile against a landscape of sand dunes and mud cliffs. Maybe the painting could have become a song, and the song could have become a story. Maybe all of the random encounters in his life could have populated paintings, or songs, or stories, if there were time for such things. His mother's story could have become a song or a painting too, her childhood and adult struggles noted and displayed with pride, instead of being swept up in the current, lost amid the flotsam and jetsam of constant change and the need to get by.

| 9 |

THERE IS NO WAY FOR SOPHIE TO MAKE PEACE with her newly unpredictable body. Even dry toast tastes like vomit. Her once-loved mint tea has an unpleasant, faintly metallic tang. Ginger tea burns like fire when she brings it up again. She pictures herself of two months ago—all the jogging, the core training, the stretching. Now, even going for walks is risky. She is overcome by the city smells, combatting the urge to puke before she can make it home. The only improvement in her circumstances is the rib, which is aching less. Probably only bruised, her New York doctor has said.

Scrolling through Nathan's unanswered texts, she tells herself decisions have to be made, even though her brain feels like cotton wool. Guilt fills her chest and constricts her throat when Nathan's voice answers after two rings—warm, solicitous, asking her how she's doing.

"I just can't shake the nausea," she says. "And I'm tired all the time." Into the silence at the other end of the line she adds. "I've been thinking about the film. You just wouldn't be getting the real thing. My heart wouldn't be in it."

Her heart. What has her heart got to do with it? And who is this person trying to wrangle her way out of a job? No one she knows. After all she has done to get her career off the ground.

"If you and Bill need to go with someone else, I'll understand," she adds.

"Sophie," Nathan says eventually. "You know that's not an option. The distributors, all of our backers, are counting on the combination of you and Bill. If I'm being totally honest, more you than Bill. Your performance is what made the last two films popular. It's what got us the international distributors this time round."

Even now, a familiar hunger for flattery and validation wars with her nausea.

"I'm sorry. I'm sorry… is there any way you can delay things until at least my next trimester, or until after the baby is born?"

What the fuck is she saying? Does she see herself as one of those superwomen showing up for work, baby and breast pump in hand, to put in a full day and then breastfeed all night?

Her mother's horror stories about her own infancy. Not one poo or breast infection left out, as if to underline the sacrifices made. When Sophie was a teenager, those stories nearly turned her off the idea of motherhood entirely. Scared the crap out of her in fact.

"I'll do what I can, Sophie," says Nathan. "But most of the funding is time sensitive. I'm sorry you're feeling unwell. But I'm also sorry that the film may not happen. There's not much I can do about it. There is no legal document between us. But I went ahead assuming that contract would be signed, because it was you, and because of the last two films."

And there it is. He has said the words neither of them had yet spoken. *The film may not happen… no legal document.* In a way, she's grateful. But she cringes at the new businesslike coldness in his voice.

"I'm sorry" she says again. "I love working with you, Nathan."

Which is true. She would be lost without him on the set. Always there in the background, giving her confidence, making it all seem less overwhelming, making it all seem possible.

"Take care of yourself, Sophie," Nathan says, in a slightly gentler tone of voice.

After she hangs up, tears in her eyes, she recalls getting the call from her agent, Patty, when she was seventeen, about her first big break, the role in *Liza.*

The show was canceled after two seasons, but it was perfect at the time: not big enough to make her famous, but enough to make truly decent money. She remembers a champagne dinner with her parents, who never drank anything other than gifted bottles of wine. She remembers her father telling her to manage her money, to draw a small monthly income and leave the rest invested. She wishes now that she had gone for more TV roles, the solid income. The films with Bill and Nathan added only a small chunk to her savings.

In the kitchen she pours herself some bubbly spring water, which, oddly, helps settle her belly. Tim is at the table, scrolling through his phone. She says nothing about Nathan.

"Still okay to go see your parents tomorrow?" he asks. "We can put it off. Say you're not feeling well."

We're really excited and we hope you are too, she imagines saying, calmly sitting on the threadbare sofa across from them, holding onto Tim's hand as she speaks, his presence blocking a barrage of boundary-invading questions from her mother. During the *Liza* years, her mother ended phone conversations to LA by asking if there was "anyone special" in her life. Sophie said "No" curtly, during her first few months of wallflower solitude, and had continued to do so after her encounter with nice guy Chad, who turned out not to be so nice after all.

Her father won't ask invasive questions, but he will think them. She's certain he sees her wound up in various incomprehensible hormonal emotions, as colourful and haphazard as her mother's silk scarfs.

The next day she sits, as predicted, on her parents' sofa, but she isn't holding Tim's hand. Her mother is between them with an old photo album from Sophie's summer theatre-school days. Sophie glances out the window at the sun-dappled maple trees as Tim leafs through the photos—Sophie as a nineteenth century governess, a fairy princess, a little girl from Kansas with ribbons in her hair.

"Isn't this a riot?" her mother says. "We were so lucky to have that school in this little town. Don't you think?"

"Absolutely," says Sophie.

Her mother wafts a plate of homemade macaroons from the coffee table in her direction. Sophie resists the urge to push it away.

"We had a pretty big lunch before coming here," she lies.

Tim raises his eyebrows but says nothing.

"That's Pam," says her mother to Tim, pointing at one of the photos. "She was a great teacher. There for the whole five years."

"Actually," Sophie says, "there was someone else the first year."

"Oh right, I forgot about him," says her mother. "What was his name again?"

"Russel." Sophie takes a macaroon, nibbles at the edges, then surreptitiously hands it to Tim to finish. "He was a creep, Mom. Don't you remember Jeannie's mother complaining about him?"

"Something about inappropriate theatre games? But then, Jeannie's mother tended to be over-protective."

"Well in this case she was right, take my word for it."

Sophie was only twelve that year. She remembers the bearded and scruffy Russel's voice, feels a resurgent twinge of nausea.

"This will improve your spatial awareness as well as your connection to each other," Russel had said. Everyone was supposed to move blindfolded in a circle, half the class going in one direction, the other half moving the other way, without touching, until a prayer bowl sounded. Then they had to stop and explore with their fingertips the face of whoever was closest, like blind people. All the girls were trying to maneuver themselves in front of James, a British boy with shoulder length hair.

"Remember all the theatre games Pam did?" says her mother. "Murder and Graveyard?"

"Interesting how adolescents always love games that refer to death," says her father.

Sophie remembers seeing shapes and layers of light and dark through her blindfold. When the prayer bowl sounded, she found herself touching and being touched by a short wiry presence with a beard. Russel's fingertips scrolled through her hair and face. Made their way to her neck and her chest towards her tiny, budding breasts. Even at that age she knew enough to wonder what her parents would think, but she didn't tell, because the whole thing felt too weird. Exciting and embarrassing at the same time.

"Pam also got us reading stuff." she says.

"*Alice in Wonderland, The Wizard of Oz,*" says her mother, pointing to the photos again.

"Miller's *The Crucible* and some Shakespeare when we were in high school. And whenever the energy level seemed low, she would put on music—James Brown, usually—and tell us to dance for five minutes exactly, and then get back to work."

"Sounds like a born teacher," says Tim.

"Yeah, looking back, I think I was sort of in love with her."

No wonder. Pam's curly black hair was always falling loose from clips or hair bands when she went up to any kid who mumbled their lines on automatic pilot, getting right in their faces and saying, 'Come *on.*' Sophie was never on automatic pilot. She thrived in the limelight, aware of the other kids watching her.

She stands up, suddenly restless, and says, "I quit the film."

Which is precisely not how she intended to tell them. There is silence, then a concerned noise, halfway between a sigh and a squeak, from her mother. Sophie shakes herself awake, and gets back to the script in her head.

"Tim and I are expecting a baby sometime in April," she says. "I was going to keep working but I'm not feeling so great. I don't think I can manage the film right now. But we're really excited and hope you are too."

After a full five seconds, her mother explodes into hugs and congratulations. And five minutes later, she's handing Sophie worn paperbacks and hardcovers of out-of-date pregnancy and birth guides, unearthed from the same basement that produced the photo album.

"One of the most wonderful experiences you'll ever have," she says.

"Sure Mom, I'll just forget all the poo and vomit stories then?" She meets her father's blue eyes, which are appraising, curious.

It seems it's going to be alright. They are not plying her with questions. They will not make her feel like a kid who has just come home from a bender.

Tim, at her side, and the little fucker inside her, making her feel so miserable all the time, are keeping all of that at bay. Her parents see her as a person in her own right. Relief wells up inside her, less intense but similar to what she felt when she told Tim over the phone, and he kept saying her name.

She scrolls through her phone for part of the car ride home, then pretends to be asleep. She wants to bask in gratitude towards her parents, transcend the usual feelings that crop up during family visits, mostly guilty irritation at her mother. Tim occasionally reminds her that her mother's heart is in the right place—he would take her mother's bossy effusiveness over his family's uptight silences any day. He is right, she knows, but ever since she was eighteen and living in LA, Sophie's had sensed a wistfulness, even desperation, under the surface of all her mother's offers of help, and has been unable to shake a feeling of claustrophobia in her company.

Once back in the apartment, she drinks more soda water and lies on the sofa with her phone, but the screentime does not take her mind off her belly. She decides, again, to give yoga a try, dredging her memory for a class she took before the pregnancy. Downward dog is out, but eventually she manages a shaky tree pose, while staring at an art poster on the bedroom wall.

The poster is a print of Monet's *Garden at Vétheuil*. There is a child on the garden path, wearing white. Monet's son, she has been told. But he looks like a girl, in his white, loose-fitting clothing and hat. On either side of the path, sunflowers tower above him. In the foreground are China pots filled with spikes of ornamental grass. Vaguely sketched-in figures of a woman and another child hover in the background. Behind them, there is the low roof of a farmhouse, deep blue sky above.

The whole painting suggests late summer languor. Deepening shadows along the path. Lush vegetation. The still, inquiring tilt of the child's head in its white bonnet. Sophie wonders why he is so far ahead of the others, if the shadows are long because it is evening, if the people in the background are also family. If the woman in white is his nurse. She wonders if it is August or September in the painting.

The late summer days of her own early childhood stretch behind her, tug at her back body. Long before theatre school, before the need for speech or interaction. Long before Tim, Nathan, and Bill. A world without boredom, a continuous sequence of revelations. Her paths were wilder than the path in this painting. Trails through the woods to a backyard fort under a spreading pine tree and the local swimming hole.

Sophie's belly is mercifully still for the moment, and the room is quiet, or as quiet as it gets, with the traffic outside. Tim noodles on his guitar in the living room, his restless fingers running up and down the instrument's neck like scurrying mice. It's a sound she has found annoying in the past, but today the music blends seamlessly with the traffic sounds. There is no sense of time passing, of the pressing weight of obligation, the need to make plans for this approaching life. Time is suspended, balanced, just as she is, on one leg, the sole of her foot grounded on the floor, her torso, arms and fingertips reaching towards the sky.

| **10** |

Nathan has offered to talk to Bill on her behalf, but Sophie feels she owes Bill an explanation. She wants to make him understand that her abandonment of his project is nothing personal. They are friends. During those shoots, he always claimed never to stroke egos, but he stroked hers all the time. It was the way he looked at her, the way he drew her in. And bar that time when she had talked too much about her character, she had always known what to say to lighten his mood. Once, when he was horrified by imperfections in a rough cut and buried his face in his hands, she made him laugh when she said, "If we fucked up that badly, maybe it'll be a cult classic."

Their shared history has got to count for something. But each time she pulls out her phone to dial his number, she is bothered by two memories: that swift kiss on the lips at the airport, and Bill's face when he found out she was pregnant. It was slightly revolted, as if she'd vomited at a party or something, as if he was looking at some other person, someone he had never seen. Sometimes she doubts she has ever looked into someone else's eyes and actually seen herself reflected there, or at least the person she thinks herself to be.

Tim is at band practice, and she is again lounging in bed after another early-morning vomiting spell. There is a plate of rice crackers by her side. Taking cues from her mother's various dietary experiments, she's testing to see if gluten might be aggravating the problem. Her hand hovers for a moment over the green call icon below Bill's name. Then she thinks, fuck it. What will be will be.

When he answers, she adopts her cheeriest, lightest voice, the one that has made him laugh in the past.

"Sorry I've gone silent for the past few weeks," she says. "I thought I'd, you know, touch base to see how you're doing." To her own ears, this sounds neither professional nor particularly warm. Apparently, he agrees. His silence is a classic Bill silence. It says, I am thinking, I am taking my time to respond, and I am choosing words fit to use in this situation.

"Well, this is a surprise," he says eventually. "I'm fine, thank you."

"Good." She clears her throat, tasting the remnants of morning vomit, flat ginger ale and rice crackers. "I don't know if you've had contact with Nathan over the past couple of days. I've let him know I need to leave the film. I just wanted to say that it's nothing personal, or anything to do with your screenplay, which is great."

"Really," he says again.

Has he got a lie detector shoved somewhere?

"Really," she says. Her words tumble out, some planned, some forming in her mouth before her brain has time to register. "To be honest, I'm puking my guts out several times a day. My head doesn't feel screwed on right."

"Don't worry about it," he says quickly. Too quickly. Has she given too many details? He's notoriously squeamish, once turned pale and nearly passed out when he cut his finger on set.

"I wish I knew a little bit more about how I'll feel later on, or after the baby is born, but it isn't fair to keep you and Nathan on the hook. That's why I suggested you might want to go with someone else."

Again, there is a Bill silence. Sophie looks around the room, focuses her eyes on the Monet painting, wishing she could join that kid on the garden path. She thought this phone call was the right thing to do, both for the sake of their friendship and for her career, but now she isn't so sure.

"Look Sophie," he says. "I think we can both agree—that film is dead in the water without you in it. You're in every frame. Anyway, it doesn't matter that much. I've started working on something new."

She exhales, turning her face away from the phone so he can't tell she has been holding her breath. "I'm sorry to hear that," she says. "I mean, not about the new project, that's great…but I'm sorry you've lost interest in our film."

"*Our* film?" he says.

Shit, shit, shit.

"You know what I mean," she says.

"Didn't you say at one point that you were tired of that character?"

"Not exactly. I…"

"Didn't you say you were getting too old for her?"

"Well, yes, but I was joking…"

"Didn't you spend half your time on our little script consultation retreat going for long dreamy walks on the beach?"

"While you guys were asleep!" she said, stung. "I was always on time for meetings! Except for that one time."

"Admit it to yourself. You were on automatic pilot in Nova Scotia."

He has a point there, she acknowledges, through her anger and incipient tears. But still. Fuck him.

"You try being one hundred percent focused on a project when you've just found out you've got a kid in your belly!" she almost shouts.

"Obviously, I wouldn't know about that," he says, and again, she can sense his squeamishness.

"Look, Bill," she says, adjusting her voice back to where she wants it to be. "I really enjoy working with you, and I hope we'll get the chance to do more in the future." There is a note of pleading in her voice, which she hates.

"Do what you need to do," he says. "I'll admit I was tired of that character, if you will."

She's at a loss for a reply. Does he think this is all about his film?

"Did you know that it wasn't your character that inspired the first screenplay?" he says.

"No?"

"It was the homeless guy," Bill says. "The one in front of the movie theatre. Based on a real person. The day I saw him; I swear to God I went home thinking I was going to write a social commentary piece. I even considered interviewing him. But when I went to find him the second time, he was passed out cold and I figured the poor bastard needed his rest. Then, when I started to write, what came out was that rom-com. Homeless guy no longer a hopeless case, just someone down on his luck. Homeless guy no longer living in complete isolation. Enter cute little waitress friend who takes life as it comes."

"It was more than a rom-com," says Sophie, surprised to feel defensive on his behalf. "It was funny, sure, but also intelligent, and touching. It really worked, for me and for a lot of people."

"Maybe you and a lot of people aren't my target audience, especially if you're becoming a Brooklyn matriarch."

Did he really just say that? She thinks. Who is this person?

"Take care of yourself, Sophie," he says. "This is a big moment in your personal life, I guess. I don't expect you to give a shit about anything as trivial as my little film."

His words are a weird echo of Nathan's, except the tone is so different.

"Okay," she says, feeling an icy calm wash over her, replacing all her anxiety and guilt. "This conversation is getting us nowhere. I'll talk to you some other time, Bill."

"You do that," he says.

She hangs up. Continues to stare at her phone without seeing it, starts to scroll through emails without reading them.

Once, during the first film, when she and Bill were sitting side-by-side at lunch, trading stories, he told her what had kick-started his career. It was a former girlfriend, who got him in touch with Nathan. Apparently, the girlfriend's brother-in-law was in the film business. Before that, there were years of poverty, crappy TA jobs, countless drafts of his first screenplay. All kinds of social media bullshit and groveling, he said, in an effort to cultivate a presence in the film world.

"Thank heaven for former girlfriends," Sophie had said, meaning it as a compliment, wanting him to know how glad she was that he was making this film.

"Would have got there on my own eventually," he said.

"Sure… She sounds like a good person, though. You said she was an artist? Talented?"

"I used to think so."

"Used to?"

He started to sing, drumming his fingers on the tabletop: "Now she's just somebody that I used to know…" A bullseye imitation of James, one of her co-stars, who perpetually looped that tune on his phone, ear buds wiggling as he nodded along to the bass.

The artist-girlfriend who had put Bill in touch with Nathan was called Angela Menotti. Why does she remember this? Sophie looks at her phone again and, almost without thinking, googles the artist's website. It's a riot of colour—lusciously vaginal looking flowers, nighttime landscapes with naked women's bodies nestled at the heart of tree roots, black branches looming against a moonlit sky. Birds taking flight. Sophie has a hard time picturing the creator of these paintings in a relationship with Bill. He wouldn't go for the mother-goddess imagery. The lack of biological realism in the soaring birds would bug him. Then she wonders what she's doing, creeping this woman. Her nausea flaring, she puts her phone down and imagines being tossed onto a huge junk heap of the people that Bill used to know.

| **11** |

Anne can't remember when she last made a spontaneous lunch date. Now, here she is, about to have lunch with a young woman she barely knows, but who has been on her mind lately. It was a shock seeing Sophie come out of the Brontë exhibit, as if materializing straight from her thoughts.

She sees Sophie sitting in a booth near the window. The sunlight turns her into a silhouette. Girl with a coffee. Girl at rest.

Anne moves forward, unwinds the scarf around her neck. "Such a surprise seeing you today," she says, "on the one day I'm in town."

Sophie half rises but sits down again, managing to make this uncertain movement look graceful. "I know what you mean," she says. "When I saw you, I thought, what are the odds, in a city of five million people?"

Anne undoes the buttons of her soft blue jacket, fingers fumbling a little. She drapes it over the back of the chair.

"I'm starving," she says.

The café has polished wooden tables, a blackboard with vegan specials. Its affluent vibe is soothing after the exhibit at the Morgan Museum—all those plaques about the abject poverty and rigid upbringing of the Brontë sisters. The waiter who brings them the menus is tall, Hispanic-looking, well groomed, impossibly young. Hardly needs to shave, by the looks of it.

Sophie opens her menu, glances at it with a sort of businesslike determination, then shuts it again.

"What did you think of the exhibit?" Anne asks.

"I loved all the little manuscripts from when they were teenagers."

"Did you see the one listing all the books Charlotte wrote before she was fourteen?"

"Yeah. When I saw that I thought, okay, that's how a genius copes with adolescence. I was mostly hanging around church basements in play rehearsals, wearing thrift store costumes."

Anne laughs. "As good a way of getting through those years as any." She thinks of Rudy when he was fourteen; were there clues there that she missed?

This daylight Sophie is different from the glamorous one of premieres and parties. Her fingers on the closed menu have unpolished, short nails, as opposed to the long and perfectly manicured ones. She also seems slightly ill at ease. Maybe she's only comfortable in a crowded room. Anne is the opposite, can barely make it through parties. She knows Nathan is never quite ready to leave when she gives him the signal, but he smoothly wraps up his conversation while wrapping a shawl or coat around her shoulders, doing his best to make their departure seem like a mutual choice.

"I hear congratulations are in order," she says, and notes, instead of a smile, a naked, troubled look on Sophie's face.

"I guess I've kind of messed things up for Bill and Nathan," Sophie says.

Compassion stirs within Anne, as well as some other undefined emotion that is rough around the edges. "Oh well, Bill and Nathan will survive," she says. "It's important to keep things in perspective: A film is a film, and a baby is, well, a baby."

For lunch, there is grilled tofu for Anne and mixed greens with avocado for Sophie, who eats the some of the greens, but only toys with the avocado.

"How are you feeling?" Anne asks.

"Crappy, for the most part. 'Morning sickness' is a misnomer. It should be called 'every-day, all-day' sickness. The doctor tells me it will ease up soon, but no sign of that yet."

"It was like that for me with my son. It did eventually ease up." She takes a slightly guilty bite out of her tofu, which has been marinated in something sweet and is spiced with curry. When she finishes chewing, she says, "My doctor, who was a very sensible woman, told me to eat little bits of things throughout the day, soda crackers, almonds, that kind of thing. It helps."

"Yeah, I've heard that." Sophie twirls a bit of shaved carrot around her fork like spaghetti, putting it into her mouth carefully.

Anne watches Sophie's downturned face. Is she getting enough protein and fat for her condition?

"Nathan said you had an upsetting experience in Nova Scotia," she says. "Got pulled out to sea, actually broke a rib?"

"Rib turned out to be only bruised, but, yes, it was pretty surreal." Sophie toys again with her salad, stabs a piece of avocado, places it into her mouth without letting it touch her lips. "I really liked that place though," she says, after swallowing. "Not the resort so much, but the ocean and the landscape. I've been thinking about it a lot."

"It's beautiful up there," Anne says. "It was our vacation spot every August."

Rudy's chubby sand-encrusted legs, she remembers. Rudy collecting shells in a bucket, turning each one over, deciding which ones to keep, which ones to throw away.

"I grew up near lakes," says Sophie. "Didn't experience the ocean until I was a teenager. It blew me away."

"And you're not turned off it, after your mishap?"

"My mishap," says Sophie. "I guess that's one word for it."

The handsome young waiter comes back, hovers, asks if everything is alright.

"Fine," says Sophie.

"Lovely," says Anne.

When he's gone, Sophie says, "Actually, I think I'm even more fascinated by the sea since all that. I'd like to go back to the exact spot."

Anne raises an eyebrow. "Maybe more happened out there than a bruised rib."

"Maybe," says Sophie.

They share a pot of mint tea after they have eaten, and Sophie says, "I was interested in the Brontë exhibit because I played Jane Eyre on stage when I was seventeen."

Anne watches her cradle the cup of tea with both hands and take a tentative sip.

"That must have been remarkable," she says.

"I often think I would do it better now. I've learned a lot since then. But maybe not, maybe it was good to be close to Jane's age, to come at the material fresh."

Anne is surprised at the thoughtfulness of this remark, then wonders why. The assumptions we make about people, she thinks.

"I wrote about the Brontës in my Masters' thesis," she says.

Now there is surprise in Sophie's eyes. Understandable. She herself wonders how she ever had the focus to write those lengthy pages on Gothic literature, years ago, a lifetime ago. Her mind skitters away from the other writing she did at that period—unfinished poems and journals, all locked away in a storage bin in the attic somewhere. How had she found the time? These days, she can barely manage to send chatty emails to friends.

Looking across the table at Sophie, she's hit by all she does not know about this young woman, and all Sophie does not know about her. Until now, she has been nothing to Sophie, other than Nathan's wife. Briefly, she has an image of the central artifact of the Brontë exhibit: a preserved dress on a headless dressmaker's dummy that had once belonged to Charlotte Brontë, its high-collared bodice with sleeves stuffed with rods, curved to resemble Brontë's slim arms. In front of the stiffly hanging skirt were two small ankle boots, the right one turned out at a jaunty angle, as if about to dance a minuet.

"So sad the way Charlotte died," she says almost to herself. "Just when she was at the height of her powers. They say it was brought on by pregnancy."

"Mmm," says Sophie.

Anne's hand freezes as she reaches for her teacup. *God,* she thinks. What did I just say?

Their eyes meet briefly. To Anne's relief, Sophie is laughing.

"Oh well, I got through it," Anne says. "Presumably, you will too."

"Sometimes I wonder."

"Let's take your mind off it. Tell me more about yourself. How did you get into acting anyway? Sounds like you have a theatre background?"

"Yeah, in my hometown. Started summer theatre when I was twelve. I was tall for my age. Really awkward."

"Hard to picture," says Anne.

"Believe me, I was a mess. Always knocking things over and breaking them. Anyway, something about saying another person's words, doing another person's moves, calmed me down. I started to notice the way this silence would gather around me. Even the kids who teased me would shut up, when I was pretending to be someone else. Kind of pathetic, now that I think about it." Sophie shrugs, half-smiling.

"Not pathetic," Anne says.

"After I grew into my knees and elbows, I started to get leads, and yeah, Jane Eyre was my last role with that school, and my favourite. *If God had gifted me with some beauty and much wealth, I should have made it as hard for you to leave me now as it is for me to leave you...*"

Anne hears both a Yorkshire-accented nineteenth century governess and a teenage Sophie's voice uttering these lines. A role within a role. How do actors do that stuff?

"Now that I look back on it," Sophie is saying, "it's hilarious how I threw myself into that part, staring into my co-star's eyes, who was actually a jerk with zero social skills."

"So was Mr. Rochester."

Sophie laughs.

"And what about film acting?" Anne asks

"Ah," says Sophie. "I have my mother to thank for that. When I told her I thought acting was what I wanted to do, she took me to Manhattan to find an agent. It was pretty intimidating; I can tell you. All I had in my portfolio were video clips of Jane Eyre, and a letter of recommendation from my theatre-school teacher. Every place we went was all huge offices with sterile glass tabletops. My awkwardness came back big time. And then we met Patty."

"Patty?"

"Coolest agent on the planet, in my opinion," says Sophie. "Her office was small. She was just starting out, and as soon as you met her you knew she was in it for the right reasons. Really loved film. Really interested in people. She had all these movie posters on the walls, mostly Hitchcock. I was in a major Hitchcock phase at the time, so that impressed me right away. She eventually got me this role in a teen series, *Liza*, and that led to other stuff, and eventually to Nathan and Bill."

The waiter brings them their cheque, and Anne admires, once again, Sophie's grace as she reaches for it. They split the bill equitably, without fuss.

Sophie reaches for her coat. "This has been lovely," she says.

"I'm so glad we ran into each other," says Anne, aware of the middle-aged formality in her voice.

Stepping out on the sidewalk, they pause, Anne trying to judge which direction Sophie is heading so they can part naturally, Sophie probably doing the same.

"You know," Anne says, "if you really want to go back to Nova Scotia, you're welcome to stay at our cottage. It would be a nice summer vacation for you and Tim and the baby."

Once more, she meets Sophie's eyes. Once more she sees surprise there.

"Well, that's a sweet offer," Sophie says casually. "I might take you up on that someday."

After they have gone their separate ways, Anne walks towards Central Park, unsure of how to spend the rest of her afternoon. She wishes she were young again, like Sophie. Then again, she doubts she ever had Sophie's grace and spontaneity. Too nerdy, too bookish, she still had dreams of being a writer, back then, but Rudy's arrival had superseded all of that. She had thrown herself into motherhood as if it were the only thing she had ever wanted to do. Had thought: There will be time for that, when he's older, when things are easier.

Earlier today, after visiting the Brontë exhibit and before having lunch with Sophie, she had gone to the Morgan Library. Thirty-foot-high walnut bookcases, florets of bronze above their uppermost shelves. Countless books with leather binding and gilded letters. Words, words, and more words. A few tourists milling around, their voices hushed, as if praying to all those words. Anne had lingered on a blue, plush-covered bench, her eyes roaming over the vertiginous ceiling, portraits of Dante, Botticelli, Michelangelo circling above her head like indifferent angels. On the way out she bought a journal in the gift shop, because she liked its old-fashioned leather cover, its faux-antique yellowed pages.

Now, she passes Trump Tower and averts her eyes. If she could, she would bury herself in places like the Morgan these days, and completely avoid screens. She has enough on her plate without contemplating mass insanity taking over the country. Surely, cooler heads will prevail. Just beyond the South entrance to the park, two street performers are gathering a crowd. They start recruiting audience members, mostly young and pretty women. They do aerial somersaults over the women's bowed heads. Anne is afraid to stay and watch, afraid to look away.

Deeper into the park, she finds a bench, and texts Nathan, *Everything okay?* She's not sure she can trust his answer. Nathan had not picked up on the obvious signs when things had first started to go wrong. Rudy was a normal, affable kid until early high school, maybe slightly prone to intellectual flights of fancy, but that was it. But one day— a turning point. Rudy coming home from school with words tripping off his tongue, his hand moving constantly to the back of his neck as if to swat away a fly. Rudy obsessing over the number four. *If all four clocks stopped at exactly four o'clock what does that say about sixteen— an obviously lucky or unlucky number?* A wad of crumpled paper on Rudy's bedroom floor covered with numbers, eventually all turning into 4,4,4,4.

What am I supposed to do with this? Anne remembers saying, her hand shaking as she held the paper out to Nathan. Nothing, Nathan said. He's working something out. He's got some kind of theory he needs to see through. He's a creative kid. Anne had made an appointment with their doctor to get a psychiatric referral. But everything went to hell before that appointment had a chance to take place.

The sunshine is warm enough to make her feel sleepy. She would like to linger here on this bench, until it's time for her train to leave, just as she lingered on the blue, plush-covered bench at the Morgan Library. She feels like she is inhaling, in stasis. She does not know what to do with her hands, which are open in her lap, as if waiting to receive a gift. The journal that she bought at the Morgan beckons her, so she takes it out of her purse, just to look at it, because she didn't bring a pen and she has nothing to say anyway. She does not know where to focus her gaze, where to find a sign, from something or someone, that her life might contain the possibility of change.

| **12** |

JEFF WAS RIGHT ABOUT THE TIPS AT THE CAFÉ. They aren't as good as at the resort, but Fred can walk to work, which is a bonus. He has so far attended two open mic nights, wincing at some painful performances by angsty teenagers. But there was the odd unpolished gem: a high school student singing Townes Van Zandt with a voice like sunlit water, and a poet reading ten lines about visiting his father in prison, his voice neutral and clear in the still air of the suddenly quiet room. Fred can't imagine what it would be like to put yourself out there like that.

Today when he arrives for his morning shift, Jeff is sitting at an empty table, sketching. After refilling all the salt cellars and wiping down the counters and tabletops, Fred can't resist peeking over Jeff's shoulder. He used to love watching Jamie work, when Jamie was still making art.

This work bears no resemblance, however, to Jamie's abstract colour washes. Jeff is mapping out the room with his pen and pencil, reproducing the tables and chairs, the salt and pepper shakers, even the beam of sunlight that slants from the window, with astonishing accuracy.

"Jesus, how do you do that?" Fred says.

"Practice, and lots of it," says Jeff. "But there are tricks of the trade. I could show you some."

"Get out," says Fred. Like Jeff with his open mics, Fred sees himself as a patron, not a creator. When he was with Jamie, he felt like a kid watching a grown-up do magic. It fed Jamie's ego, all that admiration. Fred can see that now. He realizes he may have enabled some stuff, always doing the grunt work, always letting Jamie do his thing.

He watches Jeff some more, sees his pencil jump from spot to spot on the page—lines and vanishing points morphing into chairs and tables and sunlight, until the first customer shows up. While he watches, he hears a whole dissertation from Jeff about perspective, shading, the golden mean. Jeff suggests he come in before opening tomorrow so they can have a lesson, tells him not to worry about proper art pencils and paper. "Just bring what you have, man. We'll make a party of it."

So, the next morning Fred sits, pencil in hand, across from a bowl of apples (he doesn't need to ask himself what Jamie would think of that subject matter). He stares at the fruit more intently than he has ever looked at anything in his life. He tries painstakingly to convince his fingers, which feel stiff, to coax onto the page the semblance of spherical objects, tries to take in Jeff's advice about shading. When he has finished, Jeff is impressed with one of the apples.

"Now that is one round and shiny conveyor of gastronomic delight," he says.

That night, Fred finds himself working late in his apartment to finish one of the exercises Jeff has given him. He doesn't once turn on Netflix or watch the news. After setting aside his pencil and sketchbook, he drifts off to sleep on the couch, then moves to bed when the sun starts to glimmer through the crack between the grey curtains.

In the morning, driving to the resort for a rare off-season shift, he notices with new clarity the silhouettes of the maple trees that line the sidewalks of the old highway. Although he loves this view, he can't quite recapture the feeling he had when he first started driving out here, and is starting to wonder if the tips justify the gas money. He pictures a life in which trips to the South Shore are a luxury, not a necessity, in which, instead of pouring water and taking orders, he is sitting at one of the tables on the sunny balcony with other like-minded people, discussing art. He doesn't take these thoughts very seriously, putting them in the same category as his fantasies about running into Sophie again. He has learned to be distrustful of any dreams of the future.

When he was in university, he thought he might go to grad school, but after what happened with his father, he had returned to Montreal for the final semester of his BA, scooped out and hollow as a dead tree. A combination of Ativan and his previous work ethic got him through his final exams. And then it was his job at the steak house that kept him going. Quick and efficient at serving, he was good at striking up a banter with the customers, in either English or French. Their faces were never concerned or pitying like those of his friends. He broke up with his royally shut-down college boyfriend. The end had been inevitable anyway. Although technically out, the guy was more closeted than Fred had ever been. He couldn't even hold hands in public, and at a time when *Brokeback Mountain* was playing in every theatre in town.

A year later, there was Jamie, love-bombing him all over the place. Sending him flowers, emailing him song lyrics, reigniting his dreams of a future that involved more than just staying sane and checking in on his mother. The idea of the gallery glowed like a beacon in their shared life. It was heaven, until it wasn't.

Pulling into the resort's parking lot, Fred notices the new bite of cold under the surface of this sunny weather. He reaches for his phone to confirm there are no more texts from Jamie. For which, he tells himself, he is deeply thankful. If things were to spin out of control, the way they did before, and tearful phone calls became more than daily occurrences, who would he talk to about it? Barring Jeff, he has lost touch with anyone who has an inkling of what Jamie was like to live with. He spared his mother the details, only told her that he and Jamie had drifted apart. More like collided and smashed each other to smithereens, he thinks.

Sylvia at the front desk has a fresh manicure—blue nails, to match her jacket. What would she say if he started confessing his not-so-romantic past? He's not even fully out to the staff here, although they have probably guessed. They are all younger, and he knows precious little about them. Most see their jobs here as steppingstones. Some are in college; some are considering moving out of province this winter to look for work.

In the hall on the way to the dining room, he glances at a full-length mirror, and wonders, not for the first time, why they decided to put it there. For staff to check their neatness before a shift, or for guests? Catching his reflection, he has a sudden, vivid memory of rifling through the bathroom vanity one day three years ago, when Jamie was out. He was looking for syringes and God knows what else. Closing the vanity door, he caught sight of his face in the mirror, and was sure he saw someone else's profile behind him. The profile disappeared out of the frame, heading around the corner into the hallway.

Heart pounding, he had walked from bathroom to living room and come face-to-face with…himself. A solid figure, not dreamlike, just…there. Same height, same clothes, same hair and glasses, standing in the middle of the room, smiling. Fred could see lines and wrinkles he didn't think his own face had yet, could see something like understanding in the brown eyes behind the glasses. And then the doppelganger, or whatever it was, disappeared.

In his Aunt Flo's book, which Fred started reading last night, every supernatural encounter means something, prefaces an epiphany or monumental change. People reframe memories, Fred thinks. Hindsight is always 20/20. All his doppelganger experience did was reawaken fears for his own sanity. He remembers collapsing on the floor and lying in a fetal position, rocking back and forth, saying something like 'No more,' over and over again. But it was another year before he finally ended things with Jamie.

Today at lunch, Fred serves an affable, if over-sharing, guest from Texas. He can't quite pin down why the guy is here—middle-aged, travelling solo. It doesn't look like business, judging from the jeans and plaid shirt, and mid-October seems like an unusual time for a tourist jaunt. The Texan praises the quiche, and while Fred pours his coffee, says, "Don't tell my wife but this recipe nearly beats hers." Kind of wholesome, all-in-all. He reminds Fred of the next-door neighbour who came and cheerfully helped him shovel his mother out after White Juan. The Texas guy leaves Fred a tip that is just shy of the entire cost of his meal.

"Dude from Texas," Fred says later to Sylvia. "Super generous tipper. Nearly ninety percent."

"Mmm," she says, her eyes on her computer screen. "When you get the chance, check out his car in the parking lot."

"Why? Which one is it?"

"It's just out front, a few rows in. You'll know it when you see it."

For the rest of his shift, he wonders about this exchange. Maybe, with the Texas guy, he has hit on a Bill Gates-type billionaire, all humble-pie and jeans, who drives the latest model of Porsche 911 or something.

At the end of the day, he does, in fact, find the car immediately. Not because it is the luxury vehicle he was anticipating. It's a Ford Focus, whose red exterior is almost completely covered by a slew of bumper stickers. *Trump 2016 (Make America Great Again); If you like your gun you can keep it; The only thing that stops a Bad Guy with a gun is a Good Guy with a Gun; Hillary sucks but not like Monica; Hillary for Prison;* and, in pride of place at least a dozen times over, the confederate flag.

Fred stops two feet away, as if approaching a bear in the woods. A familiar sensation creeps up on him, of not wanting to see, but being unable to look away.

| **13** |

On the way home from a doctor's appointment, Sophie navigates the sidewalk past three eateries in a row, one of them advertising a blue-cheese-melt burger. She feels only slightly queasy, no bile rising to her throat. The word gratitude pops into her mind. *Give your body some gratitude*, her thin and limber instructor used to say in her HIIT fitness classes. She remembers how strong and free those classes made her feel. Now, as her body slows and thickens, gratitude is less about strength and freedom, more about getting through the day without needing to puke.

Her nausea comes back, briefly, when she passes a novelty shop with Donald Trump and Hilary Clinton masks in its window. Why would anyone choose those for Halloween? Tim has taken to watching every news bite about the Trump Campaign lately, barking with angry laughter at each fresh verbal outrage. She dislikes how the news cycle is swallowing his time and attention. He has landed some sessional teaching this term at NYU, replacing a friend who is taking paternity leave—another source of gratitude. The prep and teaching time distract him from the news, but by the time she gets home, he will be done for the day and have plugged into election coverage again.

Crossing the street into her neighborhood, she passes a tall black woman pushing a toddler in a stroller. The child is moaning indignantly, while the woman, who is wearing sweatpants and sunglasses, says vaguely, 'S'okay, baby'.

Sophie wonders what her doctor, a thirtyish woman with sleek blond hair and impeccable mascara, would say if, in response to generic questions about her wellbeing, she had confessed her fear of becoming harried and tired like this woman behind the stroller. But she also looks forward to her approaching roundness, to inhabiting a pregnant body with a Mona Lisa smile and a hand on her burgeoning belly. How shallow is that, she thinks, treating pregnancy as if it's just another role?

When she gets home, Tim is sitting on the sofa with his back to her, his laptop perched on a pile of books on the coffee table. The orange face of the king of sleaze fills the screen.

"The doctor booked an ultrasound," she says, coming alongside him.

He turns to look at her. "Everything okay?"

"Better than okay. I've been having these bubbly sensations. I think it might be the baby moving, but the doctor thinks it's a bit early for that. She wants to check that we have our dates right."

With satisfaction bordering on smugness, Sophie sees a reawakening in Tim's eyes of the joy she witnessed at the airport six weeks ago. She has a sense of the radiant power within her womb, undimmed by political angst and anger. She also glimpses something else which, after a moment, she identifies as fear. Understandable. This is a huge transition for him. It probably still seems unreal; the way it felt to her when she first found out—before her body began to change and validate the unlikely story they have both been swept up in.

They make a meal of spaghetti topped by a jar of her mother's pesto—home-grown basil and garlic with some unusual ingredients, like sunflower seeds instead of pine nuts, and kefir instead of cheese. Tim loves the stuff. Sophie is also fond of it, but she remembers hiding these kinds of additions to her lunch box when she was in grade school. Too healthy. Too messy.

After supper, they curl up on the sofa and watch on old Sinatra film—*The Man with the Golden Arm.*

"Sinatra researched this by looking through a keyhole at an institutionalized drug addict," she tells Tim, reading off her phone.

"That's morally reprehensible."

He's right, she supposes, but watching with renewed interest the claustrophobic withdrawal scenes, the hunched shoulders, the shakes, the fist in the mouth, she thinks, not bad. She has always thought of Sinatra as a singer, not an actor.

"Samara's Halloween party is tomorrow night," Tim reminds her after the film's over.

"Who's going again?"

"Just the rest the band, I think. Maybe Farid."

The thought of Farid, Samara's brother, fills her with warmth. She has acted with him, known him for years. He will save her from the rabbit hole of incomprehensible music talk with the guys in the band. Samara, with her beautiful voice and her big heart, doesn't share their nerdy vibe, but still. Sophie feels a little intimidated by the way Samara pins people down into serious one-on-one conversations.

"She's also planning an election night get-together," Tim says.

"I think I'll pass on that one," she says. She will vote, then avoid screens for the rest of the day. She's got excuses—the baby, her need for sleep.

"What do you want to wear tomorrow?" she asks.

"You could just make up our faces the way you did last year."

They google Halloween makeup ideas on Pinterest. Joker grins, spiderweb eye contours, sexy vampire blood-dripping mouths. Sophie drapes one leg over Tim's lap, planning to celebrate how well she's feeling today. It has been a long time, and she doesn't want him to be too ginger and careful. She wants her body to remember its old joyful patterns.

On the night of the party, she makes up her own face with more care than Tim's, trying for vamp, sexy, not too goth to be pretty. When they get there, she hugs Samara, who is dressed as Tinker Bell. The apartment is filled with beautiful art by exiled Iranians.

Sophie scans the room.

"Where's that adorable brother of yours?" she asks.

And then she sees him, navigating towards her, past Mike and Jason from the band. He's such a beautiful guy, she thinks —those big brown eyes, the grace in his arms and hands. She's flooded with affectionate memories. They are eighteen, partying in LA with other *Liza* cast members. They are twenty-one, back in New York, practicing lines for an off-Broadway production of *The Glass Menagerie*. He is her brother, in all ways but blood.

They hug and he says, "Samara told me. Congrats."

"Thanks! And what's new in your life?"

"Remember Benny, the guy I've been seeing?"

"Sure."

"I just got back from DC, met his parents for the first time."

"Wow!" She can't think what else to say.

Mike, the bassist, comes over to put his arm around her shoulders. He's wearing a long-haired wig and headband, obviously trying for a hippie vibe. "Sophie! With a bun in the oven!" he says.

Jason, the percussionist, trails Mike in a baby outfit, complete with an enormous diaper, a bottle that he has filled with rum and coke, and a bonnet. Is this in her honour? Jason has always reminded her of the acne-pocked kids who hung around in male-only groups on the south wall of her high school. He punches Tim on the arm. "A fucking *father*, man! Who'd a thought? Get ready for those diapers. And… lullabies. You realize the kid's gonna be subjected to the collected works of Radiohead filtered through this bastard's reedy voice from day one? How will that warp him?"

"Who says it's a him?" says Sophie.

The talk turns to tv, fashion trends, celebrity gossip. She's grateful that Samara doesn't bring up election night. Drinks start to flow, and joints get passed around. Although she can't join in the drinking and smoking, Sophie acts inebriated anyway, consciously blurring the logical edges of her thoughts, letting herself float free, enjoying the way the guys in the band treat her like a best bud, at the same time making her feel pampered and sweet. But she also wants to chat alone with Farid. When there is a lull in the conversation and Tim has been inevitably drawn into shop talk with Jason and Mike, she sits beside Farid on Samara's teal-coloured sofa.

"So, what's next for you, Sophie?" he asks. "I mean after…" He looks at her belly. "Last I heard, you were making another movie with Bill Reese and Nathan Ackerman."

"Yeah well, that's pretty much on the rocks. My fault." She gestures to her belly. "I didn't plan on this," she says, "and I've been feeling too sick to keep working. Things are a bit better now, but…"

"You were great in that role, Sophie."

Roles, she thinks. There were two movies, two roles. But she doesn't bother to correct him. Same character, slightly different plots, said a review of the second film. The review had called Bill's screenplay 'intrusively self-conscious'. But Sophie had kept it on her laptop, because it said nice things about her.

"I see other things in your future," Farid continues. "Some tragic part, maybe, or one of those HBO shows that leaves you thinking so much your head explodes."

"Thanks… I think."

"Did you hear about Hugh Wilkinson?" says Farid.

"No, what?"

"Quietly blacklisted from every series he's been hired to direct. His taste for pubescent girls finally caught up with him."

A pit opens up inside Sophie, deep and black enough for her to fear what might come out of it. Wilkinson, a frequent director on *Liza*, was known for his bullying on set. But how did she miss this? Maybe her mother's embarrassingly frequent visits, that first year, had done her a favour.

"I always wondered how you negotiated all that," Farid continues. "I assumed he would have gone for you. You never had problems?"

Not with Hugh, she almost says aloud, thinking of Chad, standing over her at that party, and the painful and unpleasant acts that followed, acts in which her body took part while her brain hovered somewhere above, surveying it all with a cold and fishy eye. She has never fully succeeded in unravelling the messy trails of emotion that particular memory leaves in its wake, has always shied away from labelling it, from using the word that would turn it into something loaded with the weight of misery and trauma. No way is she going there. In any case, there is no correlation between Chad and Hugh

Wilkinson. That night was a one-off, when they were both pissed out of their minds. Chad was only a year and a half older than her—a fellow actor, not her director.

Farid's voice penetrates her thoughts. "You were a class act back then, Sophie. The way you negotiated all that, stayed clear of Hugh and disappeared on holidays to your fancy New England family."

"Fancy New England family?"

"That's what we all thought, anyway."

"My mother was teaching art part-time, and my dad was a janitor!"

"It was the way you carried yourself," he went on, unperturbed. "A little Gwyneth Paltrow, a little Claire Danes."

"You're full of shit, you know that?" she laughs, but her unease deepens. Is that how the other girls saw her? She tries to recall their faces. She rarely hung out with them long enough to hear their stories. She was too fixated on the next day's shoot. Had she known about Wilkinson on some level?

For one perilous moment, acting, which she has often thought of as her life's purpose, seems like an ego-fueled game, one that may have blinded her to the suffering of others. All those teenagers trying so earnestly to please the adults in the room. She and Farid skyping in the evenings to help each other learn their lines, without once acknowledging how fake their characters sounded, all the first world problems the plots were based around. They were trying to act like pros, she supposes. Those attempts suddenly seem meaningless to her, as futile as children trying to make waves by throwing pebbles into the sea.

She sleeps until noon the next day and, just before waking, has a dream that takes place in the bedroom of her suite at the resort in Nova Scotia. Only somehow, the geography has changed. She is on the second floor, and her window looks directly down onto the beach, which is now a narrow strip of sand, like the small, supervised lake beach her family used to go to when they were kids. The sand is littered with brightly coloured toys, parasols, and towels. There is a white lifeguard tower, upon which sits Hugh Wilkinson. She thinks: I didn't know Hugh was a lifeguard, isn't he too old for this gig? Still from her vantage point at the window, she recognizes a small pile of her mother's belongings on the sand—a silk scarf, a novel, reading glasses. She wakes up consumed by the urge to go down the wooden balcony steps to the beach to retrieve her mother's stuff.

But then she realizes she's in her own bed, traces of mascara on her pillowcase. Tim, beside her and still in his makeup, has a debauched David Bowie look. She goes into the bathroom to wash properly. Looking at herself in the mirror, she thinks of her last profile shot, the one on her CV, IMDB, LinkedIn, Facebook, all those pages she has been ignoring for the past three months. Nothing much to add—Quit my latest film. No fucking clue where my career is headed. Whether I even want my career. No fucking clue how I am going to tackle being a mother.

She has been meaning to call Patty, her agent, since praising her so highly to Anne. She thinks of Patty's voice, its purposeful warmth. In the bedroom, Tim is still out cold. Sophie quietly grabs her phone, her jeans and a loose blouse, and dresses in the bathroom. After a careful breakfast of dry toast and jam, she puts on a suede jacket and walks in the crisp morning air and sunshine to Fulton Park. Sitting on one of the metal benches along the park's tree-lined pathway, she watches orange oak leaves swirling through the air to land at her feet.

Patty's receptionist puts her through, as soon as she dials.

"Well, hello, *Lovely*," says Patty. "How the hell are you?"

Sophie, haltingly at first, tells her about the baby and quitting the film. Patty listens as though she has all the time in the world, and it all comes out—how everything went down, how guilty she feels about Nathan, how sad she feels about Bill's coldness.

"It's all fine," says Patty, in response. "This too, shall pass."

"I'm going to be a *mother*," Sophie croaks, slightly surprised at the panic in her voice. "I've just come through three months of hardly being able to eat a cracker without puking. I can't picture what I will do next week, let alone after the kid's born, and sometimes I wonder if anyone other than those two guys will even be interested in my work. Seriously. I don't know what the fuck I'm doing."

Talk about high maintenance. She has taken honesty way too far, has become one of *those* clients.

"Skip the part about no one being interested," says Patty. "You're good at your craft. You have skills, a decent CV. There are no guarantees, but I'd say that when you're ready, we'll find you something."

Sophie takes a deep breath, tries to mirror Patty's calm.

"I was thinking," she says more quietly, "about voice-acting, maybe just to tide me over."

She's not sure where this idea has come from. Maybe it's the intense phone conversations she has been having lately, with Tim, with Nathan, with Bill, with her mother. She feels newly aware of the healing and unsettling power of the disembodied spoken word.

"Yup, that is definitely a possibility," says Patty. "Slightly fewer jobs than there used to be because of voice cloning—they say that might become a bigger deal in the future—but for now, there are still a lot of opportunities—commercials, video games, audiobooks, corporate training."

The conversation turns to making a demo reel using Tim's recording software, and Sophie feels a sweet calm wash over her. She starts to envision a step-by-step way forward, work she can possibly do at her own pace.

When she hangs up, she realizes she feels closer to the person she used to be before the baby, but also different somehow, less restless, less caught up in the web of emotions that usually arise whenever she thinks about acting, the future, and all the choices life compels her to make. Despite all her confusion, something within her has decided, as if for the first time, that she will have a say in how this all goes down. She feels sure that there is a route for her to follow, if she can just set a course and take her time to see her way through.

| **14** |

Anne drains the pecans, thinking they look like tiny, shriveled brains. The recipe, from a grain-free cookbook, involves soaking them overnight and making them into a pie sweetened with honey. Honey is better than sugar. Fermented, natural, in a state the body is better able to absorb.

Behind her, Nathan sits at the kitchen table, responding to emails from his siblings in Montreal. That familiar click, click, click on his laptop. Last night was election night. She guesses what his family is saying: *Come home for Chanukah; Come home for good.* Nathan's elderly mother, who lost European family to the Nazis, is distraught about swastikas painted on public buildings, and rumors of skinheads celebrating the Trump election with the Nazi salute.

The shriveled brains are being smeared with honey now. Anne's hands, as she pours the honey, are small and white, their veins and wrinkles more noticeable than a year ago. Her wedding ring needs to be cleaned, but she dislikes taking it off for fear of dropping it down the drain. She washes the stickiness off her fingers, rubs the soap and water under and around the ring.

It's four o'clock, the light outside waning. Anne's restless sleep patterns appear in her mind's eye—a series of wavy lines, like the ones she once used to indicate her periods in her daybook, when people still used daybooks, when she still had periods.

When Rudy comes downstairs, she is relieved. Who knows what he might be accessing on his computer up there. His shoulders are hunched, hands in pockets, but she tells herself his movements seem freer, less robotic, since his latest round of meds reduction. He says he's going for a walk, and she's torn between celebration and terror at the thought of him wandering off. She remembers a conversation she once had with a mother of a formerly suicidal son, in a support group she went to after Rudy's diagnosis.

"I can't always be watching him," the other mother had said. "I can't always be expecting the worst. These things can be self-fulfilling prophecies."

Only after Rudy leaves does she remember that last year, some woman, walking north on the road towards the church and the empty apple orchards, went missing. Abducted, it was rumored. So many rumors. Which direction is he going? He's already out of sight when she crosses the kitchen to look out the window, where approaching twilight is starting to make the trees into darker silhouettes against the paler glow of the sky.

She would like to go for a walk too, once the pie is in the oven, but she doesn't want Rudy to think she's following him. Besides—where to go? If she heads into nearby Red Hook, she risks seeing celebratory signs on lawns of the few open Trump supporters in her neighbourhood, and she couldn't bear that. If she heads away from town, she will feel uneasy, remembering the woman who went missing.

Amongst all of the things she's afraid of, she realizes she no longer fears the labels that have been put on her son—the strange looks from the ignorant and small-minded. She no longer cares if Rudy acts or looks "normal." She thinks of the "normal" people she saw in the voting booth yesterday, half of whom, presumably, didn't notice or care about their chosen candidate's sociopathy, didn't care that they were sharing their vote with people who drew swastikas on buildings and gave the Nazi salute.

Maybe I should make this pie as a Thanksgiving dessert, she thinks, drying her hands on a tea towel. Holding the bowl of nuts to the light, she wills some imaginary god of plenty to bless them with miraculous feeding and healing power.

"At least the guy can't do anything until January," Nathan says.

No need to ask who he's talking about. Nathan uses the same tone of voice as last night, when he said: "It's still possible, she could still win." It's the same tone of voice he used about Rudy, two years ago, when he said, "He's a creative kid. He's just working something out."

She'd like to think all this political turmoil is just poison coming to the surface, like a wound being drained of its pus. Or like homeopathy, something she has been reading about lately. In order for healing to take place, the layers of illness have to come to the surface. It has to get worse before it gets better. Thinking of Rudy, she wonders what further poison would need to come to his surface, beyond the imaginary demons clawing at his feet, the helicopters shooting from the sky. Thinking of her country, she wonders how many people will have to die or have their lives ruined before its chronic sickness gets better.

She says to Nathan: "Maybe your dual citizenship is a good thing. Maybe we should consider what your sister has been saying."

Nathan looks up from the computer for the first time. "You're not serious," he says. "Anne, we're both disturbed by this, understandably, and so is my family, but what are we supposed to do, put the house up for sale, go bury ourselves in the backwoods of Nova Scotia, uproot Rudy from his support network?"

The last bit about Rudy's support network stings. As if she isn't the one who has set all that up. As if she isn't the one who is constantly thinking about how even their smallest actions affect Rudy. And who is to say that Rudy would suffer from the move or miss his 'support network'? Nathan isn't truly worried about Rudy. It's his career. Even though they own property there, he's always said he would never go back to Canada, the place where, in his youth, obscurity was equated with artistic integrity, success rewarded with skepticism and suspicion, and where the English language film industry was dead in the water.

"Things have changed since you left Montreal," she says. "It's a more international world. You can work from anywhere. You have to travel to film shoots anyway."

"Look, even if I thought it was that easy," he says, "it wouldn't be the way to deal with this. We'd be like rats abandoning a sinking ship. And if Trump manages to stay in power for a full term, which I doubt, the effect of his administration isn't going to stop at the border."

This she can't argue with. But what can they do to rescue this particular sinking ship? She observes, as if from a distant remove, Nathan's calm voice, the way he says *Look*, gesturing with his hands. The way he says *rats*. She feels a second rush of anger at the word *abandoning*.

The oven preheat light goes off. She opens the door and inserts the pie. The door closes with a discreet click. She has a mental image of Rudy, sitting in the passenger seat of her car on the way to his day program, lately without biting his nails or grinding his teeth. She pictures her mother in her retirement home, rising stubbornly out of her chair to greet her. She knows the idea of leaving the country is a fantasy. For the past two years, she hasn't even seen her way to leaving the state for vacations.

She wonders what place elderly women like her mother, and kids like Rudy, have in the minds of those seemingly normal people in the voting booth, in the collective mind of the relentless machinery of change.

Anne notices the pouches under Nathan's eyes, the lines around his mouth. Her annoyance at him vanishes. His life is disrupted too. He, too, is finding it difficult to cope. She has heard snatches of his phone calls, seen sadness in his eyes after a conversation with Sophie, flustered annoyance after one with Bill.

"Maybe we should get away for Thanksgiving," she says. "Go somewhere new for a change, somewhere we can hike and get outdoors, instead of the same old same old."

Right away, she sees the lines deepen on his face—the opposite effect to what she intended.

"Sure, babe, we could do that," he says half-heartedly.

Money, she thinks, feeling like an idiot. And where the hell is there to go nearby that will offer pleasant hiking in November?

"Or we could just do a small turkey supper," she says. "I could go get my mum and bring her out for the day."

"Whatever you think."

A gust of cold wind blows in as Rudy opens the screen door beside the kitchen. He enters, tousled and red faced, like his child-self from a few years ago, but also, too thin—cheek bones too prominent, dark eyes hidden in the shadow of the porch doorway. Anne bites back her questions about where he went, if he met anyone. She says, "We were just talking about Thanksgiving."

"Oh?" says Rudy, eyes still in shadow, his voice flat.

You're right, she thinks. It is a boring topic. I'm bored with it. When I was your age, I probably would have said I didn't give a flying fuck about Thanksgiving. But in my head. Only ever in my head. And now I'm this person who makes polite conversation around everyone's feelings. I am the person who keeps the holidays going, who normalizes life when there is nothing normal about it.

"Probably best to just have a quiet family meal," she says. "I'll bring Grandma out for the day."

She begins to clean her baking dishes and turns on the oven light to peek at the pie. Rudy, she notices, has not disappeared to his bedroom just yet. He is standing by the patio doors on the other side of the living room, looking towards the woods bordering their back lawn.

"Were you on the phone, like, really early this morning?" he says.

Her back gives a twinge as she straightens and closes the oven door. "What time?" she says.

"Like, maybe 5 AM."

"No, definitely not. I was still in bed." She's aware of Nathan sitting at the table, listening.

"Why, Rudy?" Nathan says.

"Oh, I just thought I heard Mom, ordering a prescription or something. Thought I heard your voice too." Rudy's body is half turned towards Nathan, but his eyes are not looking that way. If she were to judge the direction of their gaze, she would guess they were fixed on a point in the far corner of the living room, about halfway up the wall.

"Rudy," says Nathan. "Why would your mum be ordering a prescription at five in the morning? The drugstore is closed at that hour. We were both in bed. I definitely wasn't talking to anyone. What were you doing awake so early, anyway?"

"Maybe you weren't awake," says Anne. "Maybe you were dreaming." She sends these words out to him like tendrils of hope, and statements of fact. *Dreams, sleep,* the difference between what is and isn't really there.

"Right, dreaming," says Rudy, as if exploring the word with his tongue. "You were saying the number 666 out loud, which is weird."

"Definitely weird," she says, looking him in the eye, now that he's no longer staring at the corner of the room. "The pharmacist's number starts with 845."

"I didn't sleep that well last night."

"None of us did. All this election stuff is stressful."

"Maybe I'll take a nap before supper," he says.

"Sounds like a plan. I'll let you know when it's ready."

She feels the tug of the imaginary umbilical cord pulling taut as she watches Rudy go up the stairs. She feels Nathan's eyes on her back. He's uneasy about the meds-reduction. Already he's asked her if she's sure they're doing the right thing.

Once more, she examines the options. Upping the anti-psychotic until Rudy gets the shakes, filling another prescription to deal with the shakes. Medicating him at night so he will sleep better, but then dealing with his lethargy in the morning. Despite her sinking stomach when he was speaking just now, she treasured the clarity of his words, the way he met her eyes with a clear gaze, eventually. And wasn't it a good sign that he asked about what he heard? That he tried to confirm the reality or unreality of it?

No. She won't up the meds unless Rudy asks her to. She will not panic every time he says something that she might not think twice about if he didn't have this diagnosis. He would never admit anything to her again. He is seventeen, soon to be beyond her reach, soon to make his own decisions about how to live with this illness.

The heat from the oven is claustrophobic. She asks Nathan to take the pie out when the timer goes off, so she can go for a walk—towards the apple orchards, not into town. She will walk until her legs feel tired and taut and strong, until her mind feels as clear and free as her body, moving for the sake of moving, for the sake of being alive.

| **15** |

Sᴏᴘʜɪᴇ ᴡɪꜱʜᴇꜱ ꜱʜᴇ ʜᴀᴅɴ'ᴛ ᴋɴᴏᴡɴ which way the tide was turning last night. She wishes she could have gone to bed without awareness of Tim sitting at the kitchen table, frozen to his screen where electoral maps kept popping up, each one grimmer than the next. He had decided not to go to Samara's party after all. Presumably to keep her company, which she should have been grateful for. Instead, she felt both irritated by the invasion, via his laptop, of the chaotic outside world, and guilty at her inability to sit still beside him and submit to the weight of history.

Since then, Tim hasn't touched his guitar—a first since she has known him. From his vigil behind his laptop he says he plans to go to a protest outside Trump Tower.

"You stay here," he says. "It might be a shit-show."

She has been wanting to talk about finances, plans for the baby, her voice-acting idea and getting his help recording a demo reel, but now her timing seems stratospherically off.

After he has gone, her mother phones. "I am so worried for the future of your generation," she says, tearful. Her father's voice on the line is calm and unchanged, but kind of numb. Sophie can relate. Her numbness is punctuated at intervals by the same sort of fear she felt after telling Nathan she was quitting the film, a feeling that something in their collective lives has been changed forever.

She tries watching kids' movies to distract herself, then checks her Facebook page. Patty, posting about Mike Pence. *Has anyone checked out this guy's background?* Sophie has not. *If possible, he's even more toxic to women than Trump! Wants to turn America into an evangelical theocracy! Thinks abortion is a crime!* She has a vivid recollection of her confusion in the first few weeks of pregnancy, when she knew, but didn't want to know. Although she has no regrets about the choice she subsequently made, she can't imagine having no choice to make. She leaves Patty's page and checks the news instead.

Arrests in front of Trump Tower, and Tim isn't answering her texts.

When he finally gets home, close to midnight, there's a manic and panicked energy about him.

"Word is, sixty-five people were hauled off," he says. "They're crazy if they think that's a deterrent."

Is this how it's going to be? she wonders. Her city turned into a battle ground like hot spots in far flung corners of the world? Tim caught in the middle of it? Her feeling scared shitless and weak and unable to feed on his righteous energy? She imagines walking the streets for the next four years, paranoid about the faces she sees, trying to decide who is on the right side.

The next day, her mother calls again. "I thought that 'grab 'em by the pussy' quote would totally scuttle Trump's chances," she says.

Sophie had thought the same, but some impulse she doesn't understand makes her say, "Come on, Mom, you know that wasn't going to happen."

The pussy quote always reminds her of a day in seventh grade, when two thirteen-year-old boys followed her to school, yelling: "What's that under your shirt? Shriveled grapes? What's that under your pants? A hamburger?" Creative wording, actually. Sophie has always laughed at that story, recalling her prepubescent mortification, how she hid her budding nipples behind an over-sized school binder. Now, she contemplates the possibility of middle-school assholes being in public office.

Tim, scrolling through his phone, tells her there is a No-Fly Zone around Trump Tower. For a moment, as she looks at the photos, her anxiety is replaced with a touch of ghoulish excitement—armed guards everywhere, cement barricades and sand-filled garbage-trucks parked along Fifth Street.

"Maybe we should get away, head upstate or something," she says. But, she thinks, where would we go? The whole world is shrinking, like a badly fitting dress. That orange, oversized face on TV screens everywhere.

That night, as they witness the bizarre spectacle of the first family-in-waiting interviewed on *Sixty Minutes* while seated on throne-like gold furniture in their Manhattan penthouse, Tim says, "It will be interesting to see how much of this crap he can actually pass."

"I'm not interested," says Sophie, walking into the kitchen to get a glass of water. "I don't want to see."

Against what she suspects is her better judgement, she decides to text Bill. In contrast to Tim's earnestness, Bill has always been able to make her laugh at the world's absurdities. Besides, surely all of this craziness will have superseded Bill's pique about her leaving the film. There are more important things in life than movies, after all. Even as she thinks this, she is overwhelmed by nostalgia for a time when nothing seemed more important than movies. She wants to rekindle the 'us against the world' vibe she had whenever Bill spent time with her on set, going over notes, or just shooting the shit.

"Hey," she writes. "Shit's gotten a little weird in the world since we last talked."

He responds in twenty minutes.

"Ah," he says. "You would be referring to the Orange One."

"Yeah him," she answers.

There is another pause, during which she goes into the bedroom and puts on her pyjamas. Tim is still parked in front of his screen.

When Bill's next text comes through it reads like rehearsed political commentary.

"It was naive to think a logic-spouting brown man could hold the greasy reins of power in this country. And even more naive to think we could elect someone up to her neck in the establishment, who reminds people of their least favorite schoolteacher."

His thumbs must have gotten a good workout on that one. She doesn't quite get the schoolteacher comparison, but supposes he has a point about the establishment.

She thinks of all the resistance sites Tim has subscribed to, the news already circulating about planned marches, even one that is being organized by high school students, which is kind of touching.

"You planning to go to any demos?" she texts.

His response is quicker this time.

"I have no plans to descend on Washington," he says, "with a mass-generated slogan on a placard, along with the left half of American idiocy."

The left half of American idiocy. Of which she is a part, presumably. Okay then.

She puts her phone aside and crawls into bed. The *Sixty Minutes* interview is over, but now the pundits are having their say, their voices like mosquito sounds from the living room. Her nostalgia returns, but not for acting anymore. She is going back farther, to her childhood, to her fort in the woods, when she knew nothing about politics, or the many ways people are terrible to each other, or all the responsibilities she might have in a new, potentially dystopian, future.

Sleep evades her. She realizes Bill's dismissive and cynical texts make her sick. Tossing off the covers, she swings her bare feet onto the floor and walks into the living room, where Tim is starting to nod off, his laptop still squawking excitedly. She puts her arms around his shoulders and whispers in his ear, "Come sleep. Let's forget about it for a while."

He wakes up enough to switch his laptop off, so she comes around the sofa and reaches for him, wills him to stand up and put his arms around her. And he does.

"I want to cuddle," she says.

"Mmm…me too."

She steps back and puts her hands on either side of his face—framing those thin high cheekbones, the craggy nose, and the blue eyes that, despite all the confidence he exudes, always look uncertain when she stares directly into them.

"Love you," she says, watching the uncertainty in his eyes fade, willing it to be replaced by tenderness and peace.

| **16** |

F RED DECIDES HE WILL SKIP THIS FRIDAY'S open mic at Jeff's Café. It will probably be loaded with political angst after the election down south. Everyone scared a new brand of fascism will creep over the border, all the teenagers outraged, as if it's the first time this kind of thing has appeared in the world.

Fred has noticed, today and yesterday, that the patrons of the café are unusually muted, and that a feeling of gloom hangs over the town, even in the grocery stores. Overkill, surely? Atlantic Canada is miles away, physically, culturally, and politically, from Trump land. Then again, maybe not. Aside from the fact that it's easy for folks like the MAGA-bumper-sticker guy to cross the border, you never know what you're going to find if you scratch the surface of some of the polite white faces in this town. Fred is privy to more racist talk than most people of his heritage, because at first sight, people don't clue into the Black ancestry. Even those who know make assumptions about who he will or won't feel compelled to defend.

Last week, after everyone in his building got notified of a rent increase, Joan started dissing the Syrian refugees across the road. "You know the government's paying Toronto rents for these folks," she said between drags on her cigarette. "Landlords are gonna start expecting that. Before you know it, Abdul and Fatima over there'll have their whole family plus a goat living with them, and everybody else'll be on the street."

Grossed out as he is by these comments, he feels a similar annoyance at the po-faced, Blundtstone-wearing customers who came sadly into the café on the day after the election. Worse still are Jeff and his aging white hippy friends. Fred had to exercise extreme self-control in order to stay silent while a group of those grey heads sat at a table after closing and reminisced about the seventies and the good fight.

On his walk home he hears a text beep from his pocket and notices, almost clinically, how his heart rate increases. He stops under a streetlight, takes a breath, and opens his phone.

Why are you ignoring me?

Jesus, he thinks, as another text comes through.

Are you fucking someone else?

Okay, that's it, he thinks, searching for the block caller option.

I am right here in town. Could look you up sometime and find out for myself.

The level of anxiety that rushes over Fred is beyond reason. As he blocks Jamie's number, he thinks, A) Jamie's always been about words, never action. B) No one from that time knows where I live. C) His mind defaults back to B) and wonders… Jeff. Did he give Jeff his address? He remembers that night at the theatre a couple of months ago, Jeff looking away from him when he said he thought Jamie was still in Montreal. Does Jeff know something he doesn't?

A whoosh of renewed anxiety fills his gut. He considers turning around to go back to the café and confront Jeff, but if the other grey heads are still there, he won't be able to say anything, and then he'll have to explain why he returned. Chances are they've all left, and Jeff has closed shop for the night. For the rest of his walk home, Fred feels exposed every time he crosses a street, every time he's out of reach of a streetlamp, every time a bundled up stranger walks towards him. When he isn't hearing imagined footsteps behind him, he replays the worst of his memories of Jamie.

They lived mostly as roommates towards the end, because Fred knew Jamie was doing it with others, probably in exchange for his stuff. Mostly Jamie kept it quiet, but the last straw was when he brought one of them home. A pale, beefy guy who wore a jean jacket and work boots, whose lips were constantly turned up in a slight smile, as if the joke was on everyone else but him. The two of them came into Fred's bedroom that night—Jamie, to Fred's disbelief, looking at him lovingly, while the pale guy leered.

"What the fuck?" said Fred, jumping out of bed and throwing a robe over his bare chest and boxers.

"What's the problem?" said Jamie, in the kind of voice he hadn't used with Fred in months. "You've got two people who are horny for you. Lighten up and enjoy it."

What really pushed Fred to leave was his own reaction. After the aching loneliness he had been carrying around for months, and in response to the tenderness he thought he saw in Jamie's eyes, there had been a split second of indecision. But sanity prevailed. Looking back, he thinks he can detect his mother's voice speaking calmly and firmly into his ear as he said: "Get the fuck out of my bedroom. And you," pointing to the beefy guy. "Get out of my apartment or I call the cops."

As he packed up his stuff and, once dawn had fully arrived, called his mother to say he would be coming to stay for a while, he had moved around Jamie as if he was a piece of furniture. He can't even remember, now, where Jamie was in the apartment—sitting on the sofa or standing in the kitchen, or both. At that point, his former lover seemed like nothing but a black absence, a silhouette, containing anti-matter. There was nothing left of the troubled addict for whom he once felt so much compassion, whom he once thought he could help—the guy whose face had sometimes looked so raw and exposed that Fred can still weep about it to this day.

"Baby…" he used to say, when Jamie had that look on his face. "Babe, you're worth it. You're worth the work." But after that last night, the memory of those pleading words makes Fred feel like he was the baby. Like he was talking to himself.

The next day, Fred goes in early to his shift at the café, hoping to speak to Jeff alone. He has to wait on the sidewalk until Jeff rolls up on his bike just fifteen minutes prior to opening. Fred cuts to the chase.

"I need to ask you something," he says, as Jeff surveys him over his glasses and takes an unnecessarily long time to unlock the door.

"Sure shoot," Jeff says.

Fred follows him into the café and stands by the counter as Jeff starts to scoop beans into the coffee grinder.

"Have you been in touch with Jamie?"

"Your Jamie?"

"Not my Jamie!" Fred shouts over the noise of the coffee grinder. Checking over his shoulder to make sure no customers are waiting outside the door, he decides to expedite this process even more.

"I've received some harassing texts from him, and I need to know if you know where he is."

The grinding stops, thank God. But this whole conversation feels sordid and embarrassing. Fred has always prided himself on keeping his work and personal life separate. He wonders if it was a mistake to take this job, to work with someone who knew him, before.

"Hey man, sorry to hear that," says Jeff, adopting his most hearty bro-voice.

"Do you know where he is?" repeats Fred, feeling his shoulders rise to his ears, aware that he should be helping brew the coffee and unbox the pastries. But he is stuck to his spot on the floor, as if in some weird game of freeze tag.

Jeff is avoiding his eye, the same way he did when they last spoke about Jamie.

"I had contact with him a few months ago. He said he was thinking of coming back to the Maritimes. Sounded kind of hard up. Looking for a place to live."

"What did you say to him?"

"Hey man, you know I always want to help a fellow artist. It's tough out there. Gave him some leads on apartments. Put him in touch with a couple of mutual friends."

"But you didn't say anything about me? Where I live, for example?"

Jeff stops moving and surveys Fred, a nervous half-smile on his face.

"I was, and am, not privy to that information," he said.

Fred's shoulders start to release their tension, ever so slightly.

"We okay?" says Jeff.

"Sure, yeah. No problem. Just checking," he says, vowing to never again revisit this subject, and to put his most professional day in so far at this hippy dive. His feet become unglued from the floor. He walks around the counter and starts refilling the creamers, checking the levels of the coffee beans and sugar. He pays special attention to laying out each item in the bakery display case as neatly as possible, making sure the counters are swept free of sugar afterwards, and polishing the teaspoons that he puts in the metal container next to the napkins and the tip jar, until they shine.

| 17 |

It's inevitable, Sophie supposes, that this Thanksgiving meal which she has decided to host is not going to feel like an ordinary family celebration. She hears snatches of conversation while she focuses on the cooking.

"Now Trump's saying he's above investigation for his conflicts of interest because he's president. Thinks we live in a banana republic and he's the chief," says her father.

Her mother mentions a bunch of Trump history everyone already knows—the defaulted loans, the scamming of businesses that built his hotels, his history as a racist landlord.

Jack is the last to arrive. Sophie hasn't seen him since he left to teach English in China two years ago. She hugs him, feeling shy. His dark hair and eyes are familiar, but there is a new grownup solidity about him that doesn't match the brother she remembers.

"Hey kid," she says.

"Hey Soph." He hugs her in an exuberant, slightly restless way, pulling back before she does, laughing softly at something. As he ambles around the small apartment, he says, "Sweet!" and "Swanky spot, Soph."

Her mother sets the table, and asks if she can help with anything else. Bending over a pot of potatoes, Sophie realizes that the steamer of turnips, under which she has turned the burner flame on high, is sitting in a dry pot. There is the sickly-sweet smell of burnt turnip flesh—and smoke rising. She grabs an oven mitt before reaching for the pot handle to toss the whole mess into the sink, but the damage is done. The smoke alarm shrieks. Tim cranks open the window while she fans underneath it with a tea towel.

"Whoooooah!" yells her brother in exultation, his bloodshot eyes suddenly taking on a new meaning. She remembers running interference for him when he was fifteen, so that he could make it to his room without their parents noticing he was stoned. But he's twenty-five now, their parents are in the room with them, and this is her first time hosting Thanksgiving dinner. What the fuck is he thinking?

"Sorry, guess turnip's off the menu," she calls out, feeling tears prick behind her eyes. She has been picturing this day, has imagined smiling and placing a perfect turkey dinner on the table. She would like to show her family that she's at home in her life, confident in her budding motherhood. The apartment has been cleaned from top to bottom, Tim hauling the furniture around to attack unseen dust with the vacuum cleaner while she worked on the clutter of musical instruments in the corner and the haphazard CDs on the shelf. Together, they placed the extra leaf in the dining table and softened the edges of the room with candlelight.

She dumps the turnip mess into the compost bin and runs water in the blackened pot, creating another burst of steam and a hiss like a dragon's roar.

"You go girl," says Jack.

She avoids his gaze. "Tim has a new guitar, you should take a look."

Her mother seems to have sensed her need for space, and stays in the living room while she does the rest of the vegetables. But Sophie has to call on Tim's help to get the turkey out of the roasting pan and onto the platter to cool. They stand on either side of it, like stretcher bearers on a battlefield, easing it out with two spatulas, a salad server, and a wooden spoon. Not the kind of maneuver you'd see in YouTube cooking videos.

"Amazing meal," says her mother once they are at the table. "The turkey is perfect, so moist."

"Yeah, well done," says her father, "no pun intended."

Tim and Jack nod with their mouths full, but Sophie is so overloaded with the smells and stress of cooking that she can hardly taste the meat, and only half believes them.

Jack has started to come down, now that he's eating. She takes a sidelong look at him, notices, as if he were a stranger, the long-lashed eyes she would have killed for when she was sixteen, his Adam's apple, the stubble on his chin. During the time she has been with Tim, Jack has had a string of girlfriends. Some of them she met, some not. She wonders how he finds these girls, if he loves and leaves them, or if it's the other way round. She wonders about his life in China for the past two years.

After the pumpkin pie that her mom insisted on bringing, everyone volunteers to do the dishes, so Sophie sits down on the sofa alone. The little bubbly movements in her belly are back. She wonders if the baby has been holding itself in suspension, alert to her every move, every anxiety over gravy or burnt turnips. She would like to picture it protected from stress, cocooned and oblivious. She would like to picture it enjoying the ride, like Blackie, her childhood cat, who would eye her sleepily as she wheeled him around the yard in her doll carriage—never complaining.

Jack comes into the living room and starts leafing through a book of Richard Avedon photos she bought at a flea market last year.

The Trump conversation continues in the kitchen.

"His Cabinet picks?" she hears her father say. "Laughable. And Steve Bannon's not a white supremacist, just a 'decent guy', Jesus."

"Weird time to come back to the country, I imagine," she says to Jack.

He shrugs. "Weird time, weird country, but then, China's no picnic either."

She tries to catch his eye again, but there is no focus there, no desire to do anything but roam around. He was like that when he was a kid—rarely engaged with others, always absorbed in his surroundings.

"Do you remember Anthony at school?" she says. "The way he tried to make you prove your manliness by jumping off the top monkey bars?"

"I have no immediate recollection of that incident," says Jack with a half-smile.

"I told him I'd flush his Pokémon cards down the toilet if he didn't leave you alone, and he ran off crying like I'd beaten him black and blue."

"Well, I do vaguely remember you saying something like that, now that you mention it. But the monkey bars were no biggie. He saved his worst behaviour for that hippie camp mom sent me to while you were in theater school. That place was a clusterfuck—counselors stoned half the time, or absent."

Nonplused, she tries to meet his eye again.

"Did you tell Mom and Dad?"

"Naw, would have been even more of a drag to be stuck at home all day, or worse, tag along with you and the thespians. Those kids came from another planet."

She laughs, noting her slight hurt. "Yeah, well I admit we were kind of nerdy."

"*Kind of?*" he says, and for a moment the brother she has always known appears, despite the red eyes and new muscle mass. But when everyone else joins them in the living room, the Trump conversation resumes, and he goes back to looking at books.

At the end of the evening, Sophie's mother puts her hand on her belly.

"Good luck on the ultrasound," she says, a far-away look in her eyes.

This baby will be the family's first grandchild. Sophie feels a surge of warmth towards them all. She wants to get closer to Jack, now that he's home. She would like to transcend her impatience with her mother, even though her wistfulness makes Sophie feel claustrophobic. She wishes she could laugh about her family with friends, and stay affectionate, the way other people do.

Later, lying in bed, she puts her arm across Tim's waist. With her face buried in his white T-shirt, she says: "Only twelve hours until the ultrasound."

"Mmm…" He is already drifting off.

How strange, she thinks, that their first sight of the inhabitant of her womb will be on a screen. Instead of enlarged angry faces and talking heads, they will see a black and white image of a new life, slowly and inexorably coming into being. For a moment, all the weight she's felt since the election lifts and she's flooded with uncomplicated, anticipatory joy. Her whole body flushes with it.

This is how it's supposed to be. This is what it is to be happy.

The next day, Sophie lies on a table while the technician squeezes blue gel on her belly. The drip of gel tickles slightly, chilly on her bare skin. Tim stands near her left shoulder, facing the screen. When the technician places the ultrasound wand on her, Tim grips her hand. There is warmth and a slight tremor in his fingers. She is certain right now that there is no distraction in his mind, political or otherwise, that he is wholly with her and the baby. As a silvery-grey shadow appears on the screen, Sophie stares hard at it, trying to see the outline of something recognizably human. It is like looking through a kaleidoscope, or at one of those optical illusion drawings created to be seen in multiple ways—a bunny or a duck, an old crone or a chic young woman, depending on how you focus. There is silence in the room except for the sound of Tim's breathing close to her ear. Then suddenly, it emerges—head, shoulders, tiny wriggling limbs. Definitely recognizable. Definitely a baby.

"Holy crap!" says Tim, making both Sophie and the technician laugh.

The technician points to the screen: "Here are the feet. Look, they're crossed. Look, the baby's wiggling them now." Sophie turns her head to look at Tim's face and sees tears start in his eyes.

"It's incredible," he says.

Now the technician is telling them the baby is about the size of a lime—a weird analogy. Still, it helps her visualize this turning and swimming being that could easily fit inside her palm, surrounded by the vast ocean of protection that is her womb. What would it be like to float in there in comfort, without fear, enveloped by liquid and not suffocated by it? What must it be like to be safe and at home, without any awareness that you will soon be spit out into the world—a world of hard and soft surfaces, cold and heat on the skin, darkness and light assaulting newly opening eyes? Just then, the baby turns and faces the ultrasound wand, and Sophie sees its features—the strange ET-like spacing of the eyes, the emerging bone structure. It's at once alien to her, and familiar—like some long-buried memory.

"Hello," says Tim.

The creature on the screen, which is also in her belly, turns and moves its limbs again.

After the technician has stepped out and Sophie is getting dressed, Tim says: "It makes me realize even more than ever that there's something worth fighting for."

No doubt he is referring to politics. She has seen words very similar to these many times since the election, posted on Twitter and Facebook. She has told herself they are right, these warriors for the future, for the kids. But ironically, given her impending motherhood, she cannot focus on anything to do with the future, even for her own baby's sake. All her feelings, all her visualizations, are centered on this moment, this one undeniable fact, the stirring life in her womb. There is a point, directly below her navel, that sucks her attention and energy like a vortex—drawing all the flotsam and jetsam, all the spinning and destruction, into stillness. As the November day turns cloudy with impending rain, she and Tim walk wordlessly to the car, hand in hand, speech suspended like their floating child.

Back home, she puts some salad on a plate with avocados. It took her ages to find ones that were edible at this time of year. Only a month ago, she remembers, avocadoes made her feel sick.

"Remember I told you last month that I ran into Anne, Nathan's wife, that day I took the train downtown?" she says to Tim. "I've been thinking about how sweet she was. Asking how I was doing, not mentioning the film, even offering her cottage up in Nova Scotia as a vacation spot. She really seemed to understand me backing out of the film, or didn't care much."

She stops talking as she rinses the lettuce, enjoys the spray of water, the way it runs off the crisp green leaves. "I guess I don't regret quitting the film. I feel bad about leaving Nathan in the lurch, though," she says.

"What about Bill?" says Tim.

"What about him?" she says, pausing in the midst of spinning the lettuce. She has not told Tim about her two encounters with Bill. He would ask too many questions. He might misinterpret her decisions to call and text Bill on her own, instead of talking to him with Nathan present. She remembers the edge of jealousy in his voice when he said, "You're gonna drop everything and run off with those guys so they can *empower* you?"

Then she remembers Bill's kiss at the airport, and wonders if it would have happened in Tim's presence. At the same time, she feels a weird sort of protectiveness towards Bill. An emotion that might be shame—of what, she's not sure. She recalls all the compliments he gave her on the film festival circuit, all the compliments she gave him in return. He always claimed never to stroke egos, but he stroked hers all the time by not stroking it. It was the way he looked at her, the way he drew her in. Different, she realizes, from the way he worked with the other actors. And for once that thought does not make her feel proud or flattered.

Tim is slicing another avocado, making a lattice work of cuttings in its exterior, removing the skin and laying the neat pieces side by side on a plate. "Have you heard from him at all?" he says.

"Not lately," she says carefully. "Why?"

He cuts the slices in half again and dumps them in the salad. "It's just I've heard some shit."

"Oh?" She turns to him.

"I shouldn't say anything," he says.

"Go on, say it. What shit have you heard about Bill?"

"Just social media shit. Facebook. Twitter. I don't know. Someone told Farid, who told Samara, that Bill has been posting negative stuff about you."

Her face must have changed, because he adds quickly: "He doesn't mention you by name, but people like Farid, who know what happened, are reading between the lines."

"What kinds of things?"

"Oh, bullshit about 'unreliable actors,' and also dissing the whole rom-com genre. Saying he's lost interest in it, wants to move on to other things."

"Those films weren't rom coms," she says automatically.

"Not technically..." Tim says. "Look, it may not have been about you at all. People always blow stuff out of proportion. The guy was probably just letting off steam. Why people choose to do that on Twitter is beyond me. Emulating the commander-in-chief, I guess."

"Don't call him that," says Sophie.

After supper, she sits on the sofa and checks her Facebook post with the ultrasound snapshot of her little alien. Sliding down to the floor with her laptop on her knees, she basks in the hearts and astonished-face emojis from friends. Nothing from Bill. She avoids the temptation to check his page. She feels fogginess in the head, and a sudden stillness, as if she has just woken up from a nap. From her vantage point on the floor, she surveys the room. In about ten months' time, they will have to do some childproofing. Plug up electrical sockets that are in reach, remove the low-lying clutter of magazines on end tables. Maybe they will get a rug that will cushion the baby's hands and knees.

In the peace and warmth of this snug living room, with the comforting presence of her lover only a few paces away, Sophie wishes she could give everyone in the world the sweetness of this anticipatory joy. She wishes this even for Bill, despite having had moments when she has relegated him to the asshole category of her acquaintances. Even though she's starting to draw a line between herself and him in her psyche, she includes him in her well wishes, momentarily convinced that what she is currently experiencing has the power to transform all the pain and chaos of this crazy, fucked-up world, and turn it into hope.

| **18** |

ANNE PLANS A LATE THANKSGIVING LUNCH, instead of dinner, because she knows her mother will fold after eight p.m. Nathan has offered to make both trips to the retirement home, for which she's grateful. She does not try to involve Rudy in the meal preparation, other than handing him the cutlery and glasses to set on the table, which is covered with an ironed linen cloth that her parents gave her as a wedding gift. It has miraculously survived all these years unscathed and stain free, probably because it only comes out for holidays. As Anne fills her mother's plate, her mother asks Rudy if will be going back to school soon. Anne sees Rudy struggling to swallow a piece of turkey, and jumps in to answer. She knows she shouldn't do this. He needs autonomy, needs to develop his own social skills in small, easy steps.

"We'll cross that bridge when we come to it," she starts, but Nathan changes the subject.

"How's the new retirement home, Judith? They treating you well?"

"Oh of course," her mother says, sighing and lowering her shoulders, while Rudy continues to sit in silence. "I was fortunate enough to go to a very lovely concert last weekend. String quartets made up from students at Bard. Mozart and Beethoven mostly." She enunciates her words carefully, as if it's an effort to move her mouth.

Nathan's hand touches Rudy's as the wooden salt cellar is being transferred. For a moment, Rudy seems transfixed, staring at Nathan's knuckles, at the small dark hairs on each jointed bone segment.

Later, Anne clears away the dishes and the remnants of food while Nathan takes her mother home. She sneaks another bite of the pecan pie. Rudy, at least, seemed to enjoy it. Nathan only had one piece, and her mother barely touched hers. When Nathan comes back, Anne offers him a glass of wine.

"I've been thinking," he says, "about Keith and Linda's place in Maine. How great it is."

She wonders why he's talking about this now. It has been nearly three months since he stopped for a visit in Maine, on his way back from Nova Scotia.

"That post-and-beam house. The meditation space, spare bedroom."

"I remember," she says, thinking of another visit there, before Rudy was born, remembering the aura of contentment and peace around the place. Easy to maintain, maybe, when there are no kids, in particular, no troubled kids, to care for.

"Keith and I went for a walk on the trail across from their house. It was so quiet, except for the odd deer. The trail leads through the woods to an old apple orchard."

"Like the one on the way to the Dutch reform church up the road?"

"Older, though. Abandoned. The apples aren't good for eating anymore, but they collect the ones that aren't wormy and make them into cider. Said they would be ready for Thanksgiving. Guess that's why I thought of it."

Anne can hear a longing for a simpler life in his voice, and recognizes that same longing in herself.

"You never talked about that when you got home from that trip."

"No," he says.

She recalls how all conversation on that evening had been consumed by talk of Sophie and her pregnancy. "Did I tell you I ran into Sophie in the city about a month ago?" she says casually.

She knows they have not had any such conversation. And she knows why. It's the guarded look he gets on his face whenever Sophie or Bill's name comes up, now that the film is on hold. The look he has on his face right now.

"How did she seem?" he says.

"Still feeling a lot of nausea, apparently, but she looked healthy, on the whole. We met at the Brontë exhibit at the Morgan museum. Did you know that one of Sophie's favorite stage roles was Jane Eyre?"

He frowns. "Must have been a long time ago. I don't remember seeing that on her CV."

"She was only seventeen. I think it was a high school production or something, but it had a big impression on her. She can still quote whole passages from the proposal scene."

"Yes, well, actors are good at that."

She ignores the slight edge in his voice.

"I think that whole experience in Nova Scotia, her adventure in the sea, had a big effect on her," she says cautiously. "She says she'd like to go back to that particular beach someday."

"Sounds like you had quite the conversation."

"Oh well, you know… stuff comes up."

"It's crap that she never signed her contract, because then her responsibility to come back to the film would be obvious. I wouldn't have to pull out the big guns on a friend. I don't want to be that guy."

"So don't be," says Anne.

"Easy to say, Anne, but if this thing folds completely, we're in serious trouble. I can't keep the backers at bay for long, and recasting isn't really an option. Decisions have to be made."

There is a pause before he turns to meet her eyes. "I've actually been thinking about our place in Nova Scotia," he says. "We hardly ever use it, and it would make more than a pittance if we sold it, being close to the water and all."

She feels a rush of adrenaline, and is not sure if it's fear, or anger.

"Surely it doesn't have to come to that!" she says. "There are other things we could do. There's my dad's trust fund."

She immediately regrets these last words. Her father, with not very well-hidden skepticism about Nathan's career, had wanted the trust fund to be Anne's old age security, and she knows that Nathan, for more than just that reason, hates the thought of using it. She has always felt that, without actually voicing it, he's insecure about her family background. The wealth of her railway magnate grandfather, the intellectual heft of her parents, her dad, a tenured professor for so many years that when he spoke, he always seemed glued to a lectern. The overwhelming Wasp Americana of it, something she would be happy to escape. But Nathan, with his humble beginnings and hard-working Polish immigrant parents, probably envied all that, at first.

"Can we just keep the option of selling that place open?" says Nathan, "This whole thing with the film might not be easy. Aside from being out of work. I'll have to pay back a shit load of money from the pre-production budget."

It's a pity, thinks Anne, that this is coming down just as she has started to get to know and like Sophie. In fact, the reason she's starting to like Sophie is at the heart of Nathan's current dilemma. Her pregnancy has started to make her seem like a person, rather than an actor.

She does not tell Nathan about offering their cottage to Sophie. She probably should have consulted him first. What had made her do it? The only answer she can come up with has something to do with the way Sophie had looked—a still, mindful expression on her face when she spoke of her feelings for the sea.

In the days that follow, Anne takes to walking, as she did on the night of the election, towards the apple orchards, away from town. She has invited Nathan to join her on several occasions, hoping that, together, they might recapture some of the peace he experienced in Maine. She times the walks for after supper, convincing herself that Rudy will be okay. At her request, Nathan has bought software that is supposed to block harmful internet content.

But Nathan rarely joins her, and when he does, never wants to go as far as she would like. He always seems drawn back to the house and to his email and social media sites. Maybe there needs to be a content blocker for anxious and work-addicted husbands, she thinks.

Tonight, there is a light snowfall, the first of the season. She passes the old Dutch reform church and keeps trudging uphill until the wind freezes her cheeks and ears. She sees a flock of wild geese flying overhead in a V formation, heading south. She envies the geese, their wings beating steadily, following signals received by the collective mind of their species, searching from high above the earth for a livable landscape, never staying anywhere long.

After the geese have passed, the silence is broken only by the wind, its iciness nipping at the spot on her face where Rudy's flailing hand had landed, that day back in August. Anne stops walking, realizing that she has gone past the town limits and stepped into the unlit section of the road where that woman was supposedly abducted last year. She turns around and makes her way back downhill, thinking she will ask Rudy how far he goes at night, discuss what might be safe, what might not be.

Coming level with the church again, she stands for a moment at the end of its driveway and surveys the building—the clean lines of its white clapboard, its row of gothic windows and its black steeple, stark against the evening sky. Clouds alternate in mauve and pink cumulus layers above a strip of bright orange on the horizon. Turning to look across the road, she sees other layers, snow-dusted fields beneath rows of naked apple trees. The intersecting geometry of telephone poles and wires. In the distance, purple hills are layered on top of the glow from the setting sun.

I can't do this, she remembers Rudy saying. *Up the pills, down the pills, round and round and round the pills! In the ward, out of the ward, back again in the fucking ward*

I can't go back there, she hears him say. *Don't make me.*

Earlier today, she went into his room to drop off his laundry, and saw a picture of a dead hand on his computer screen.

He was at his day program, and she hated herself for invading his personal space. But she touched the mouse and reactivated the screen as if her hand was moving of its own accord. She felt as if Rudy's mind was stored in that screen, all the broken bits she couldn't understand. What popped up was an article called "The Ice Man," about an intact five-thousand-year-old body found buried in the snow in the Italian alps. There was a picture of the ice man's corpse lying, like meat, in the freezer of an Italian archaeological museum.

It was the colour of burnt umber, dark skin pulled tight across the skull, eyes which seemed to be staring out and down, one arm reaching across its chest as if to brush aside a cobweb or a curtain. A closeup of the hand, for some reason.

Immediately her mind flew to Rudy's face, staring at Nathan's hand at Thanksgiving. Was he thinking of this image? She will never know. And maybe she doesn't want to. How thin can the boundaries be, between her thoughts and what she imagines are his thoughts, before she gets as delusional as him? She wants to say, like Rudy, *I can't do this. Don't make me.* But no one is making her. There is no one here. She is by herself on this frozen hillside.

The next day, prompted by the weather, she goes into Red Hook to purchase a Christmas tree. Last year, she insisted on making this a family ritual, but she can't be bothered this time. Simpler to do it by herself after dropping Rudy at the day program. And this is not Nathan's holiday, although he has always entered into the spirit of it without protest. This year, Christmas Eve coincides with the first day of Hannukah, so she will unearth the Menorah and follow that ritual as well. In years past, when she asked Nathan what Hannukah was like in his household and if there were any special things they should do as a family, he just shrugged and said, "Do what you feel, Anne. It wasn't that big a deal in my house. People think it's like Christmas, but it's not."

Fair enough. Still, she wishes he would see her interest as a compliment, an invitation of sorts, not an intrusion.

After Nathan picks up Rudy in the afternoon, he helps her set the tree in its stand, while Rudy stands by and watches. When Anne fills the stand with water, Rudy says, "I guess the water will keep it looking alive, even though it's actually dead."

She pauses a moment, thinking of the ice man, then says, "Yup. Reanimating corpses is a talent I have. Just call me Frankenstein."

She thinks she sees the edges of his mouth briefly turn up, but she may be imagining that.

Several of the Christmas light bulbs have burnt out. She leaves two boxes of ornaments sitting on the floor beside the tree while she goes to the pharmacy to see if they have any replacements. When she returns, the ornaments are still there, Nathan is on the sofa with his laptop. The tree is unadorned, and Rudy is gone.

"Is he up there on his computer again?" she says.

Nathan looks up. "I guess so."

"You know, it would be great to distract him from that sometimes, get him doing stuff around the house."

"He's fine," says Nathan, eyes returning to his screen.

Anne sits down on the sofa, across from Nathan's armchair, and observes the tree. The black night outside is like a wall, pressing inward, making the room smaller and smaller.

"Last night I dreamed," she says, "that Rudy was this man-sized helium balloon, and that I was holding the string, but he kept flying higher and higher away, and the wind was blowing him, and I couldn't hold on much longer."

"Anne," says Nathan, pushing aside his laptop without closing it. He has that look. The one he gets when she's emotional in their parent meetings with Dr. Green.

"There has to be something better than this," she says, in spite of herself, in spite of all her resolve not to do this, to make this a simple, peaceful day.

"So, what more do you suggest?" says Nathan. "He's going to the day program. He's taking his meds, which I think we can both agree, after the way he was talking about imaginary phone calls on the night of the election, he still needs."

"That was a one off," she says. "Probably caused by stress."

"Yeah, well, life is stressful."

"I don't see any need to change the meds reduction schedule the doctor's laid out for us. We're doing it safely and gradually." She can hear a slight shake in her voice, especially when she says the word 'We.'

Nathan continues. "And you've taken him to a naturopath. And you've changed his diet."

Something in his tone makes her look at him sharply. "You have a problem with that?" she says.

"Of course not. Your meals are delicious. It's great. Really healthy stuff. It's just…"

"It's just?"

"It's just I'm not sure how seriously he's taking all these warnings about the evils of sugar and processed food."

"He's eating what I put in front of him, for the most part," she says.

"Yeah," says Nathan, "but I've occasionally found candy wrappers and chip bags in his garbage can."

"Occasionally? How often? Why didn't you say?"

"So you can make a big deal over him enjoying some ordinary pleasures in life?"

She feels anger brew in her belly.

"So that's what I'm doing when I pay attention to his nutrition and sleep habits and computer use, keeping him from enjoying the ordinary pleasures in life?"

"I'm not saying that. It's just that you're always looking for something more. You're so desperate to help him, you're losing perspective."

She breathes slowly, stares at the undecorated tree.

"What perspective is that?" she says.

"Anne, you're his mother and you're doing a great job. But you can't *make* him better. You're not a priest or a miracle worker. And no one else is either."

"I'm not trying to be a priest or miracle worker!"

"No? You think I haven't noticed some of the sites you've been searching? Energy work? Crystals? Even "past life therapy"? Jesus, I thought that one went out with the eighties."

Humiliation, an explosive catalyst, mingles with her anger. Has he been deliberately checking her search history? She has only glanced at the sites he's talking about, most of the time sticking to nutrition and herbs, but sometimes the more far-out therapies pop up, and she's drawn to them, in spite of herself.

"Okay, you try it for once." She nearly shouts. It is impossible to keep her voice at his near-whisper level. "You try being his full-time caregiver. I'm at the point where I can't even imagine anything beyond this, ever, and I'm not the one who's seeing things and hearing things. Imagine how trapped *he* feels. You, me, the nurses, the doctors, the social workers, can be as calm and rational as we like. We can describe it, analyze it, see it as a set of symptoms, or a spiritual state, or a set of chemical imbalances. We can talk to him, give him pills, give him coping techniques. None of it takes away the suffering. It's like this fucking black cloud, hanging over everything in the house."

She stops, and when Nathan speaks again in a low voice, horror floods through her at the thought of what Rudy might have heard.

"Look, Anne, I think I can imagine how you feel," Nathan says. "But let's just accept that we're doing the best we can."

He stops, closes his laptop. "And you're right. I should be more involved in his care. You can get away more often now that I'm home."

This is not what she expected. She mulls it over, tries to imagine where she might get away to, comes up blank. Her limbs feel heavy and the room swims before her as she slowly makes her way to the Christmas tree and starts opening up the boxes of ornaments. In one box, there is a painted wooden angel, delicate glass balls, silver stars and tinfoil icicles.

She replaces the burnt-out bulbs and then starts to drape the string of coloured lights on the tree. Nathan comes behind her and silently helps untangle them, reaching one end up to the uppermost bough. Once they are all in place and clipped onto their individual branches, he sits down and opens his laptop again.

Her fingers keep working on the tree, while multi-coloured lights cast rainbow shadows on the ceiling. She believes that if her life were a series of simple tasks like this, she could find a place of calm, of rest. Inhaling the sweet smell of the fir boughs, she's reminded of her own childhood Christmases, the hushed awe of expectancy and hope.

She turns to reach down for another ornament and sees that Rudy has come downstairs. He moves towards her, crouches to lift a star out of the box. She holds her breath, holds her tongue, watching his averted profile.

He silently places his offering on the tree's green and passive branches. Together, they hang tiny stars, glass balls and paper snowflakes on the tree. She sees the lights shine through the skin of their hands as they anoint this dead thing they have brought into their house, to remind them of new life.

| **19** |

Fᴿᴱᴰ ꜰᴏʟʟᴏᴡs ʜɪs ᴍᴏᴛʜᴇʀ ᴛʜʀᴏᴜɢʜ the parking lot of a Bayers Road gas station, making non-committal noises as she assesses each Christmas tree for freshness, and determines whether it's the right size for her living room. She has even brought along a saw—an ancient one that used to live in the shed back in their Dartmouth home—so they can trim excess branches and level the bottom right here in the parking lot. After choosing a six-foot high fir for herself, she spots a diminutive sapling over in the corner.

"You take that one," she says. "All you need is a flowerpot and some rocks, and away you go."

He agrees, more to please her than anything else. He does not associate his own apartment with Christmas trees, or family tradition. Just a place to sleep and watch tv. Maybe, occasionally, to practice the drawing exercises Jeff has given him.

He will be picking his mother up on Christmas morning, and then they will drive to Shelburne to spend the rest of the day in his Aunt Flo's noisy and, no doubt, yuletide-stuffed house. There will be extended family, turkey, music. Grandchildren. All the things he is unable to provide.

They stuff the trees in the trunk of his car, which he ties down with rope, and drive slowly to her building in Clayton Park, only a couple of blocks away. He carries her tree upstairs to her apartment and she lifts the vacuum cleaner and extension cord that are waiting and retraces their steps downstairs, sucking up all the fir needles. Like the saw they used to level the trunk, the Christmas tree stand in the corner of her living room is ancient. He remembers it from childhood.

When he was really young his parents would set the tree up together—his mother focused and particular about where she wanted it, how much sugar water to put in the base of the stand, his father mutely but amicably following instructions. Later, when his father was away on sales trips, or in the hospital, Fred remembers taking on the assistant's role, as he is doing now. That was a time when his father had seemed to be nothing more than a slightly embarrassing, unknown presence in the house, a tame animal who hung out in silence most of the time, hurting no one. But then the tame animal went off his meds, settling into a pattern of slow-building mania, crash and burn. Despair. Repeat.

After the tree is up, they spread her string of lights out on the carpet, checking to see which bulbs are good.

"I have something for you," his mother says, opening up a package of fresh bulbs.

"What?"

"Hang on."

She goes into her bedroom and returns with an antique looking photograph in a cast iron frame. The photo is of three young black women. It is blurry and faded—more grey and brown than black and white, although judging from the clothes the women are wearing, it probably dates back only to the fifties. Two of the young women look to be in their teens, their heads tilted towards the center woman as they smile shyly at the camera. They are wearing pale, wispy summer frocks, and their hair is kept off of their faces with bobby pins and hair bands. The woman in the centre is different. Stylish, in a blazer with a tapered waist and cat's eye sunglasses. She looks directly at the camera, her head held high. There is elegance and grace about her, but she does not smile.

Mystified, Fred looks at his mother. She points at the shy smiling girl on the left. "My mom," she says, and pointing to the one on the right, "my Aunt Violet. And this one," she says, pointing to the elegant middle figure, "is my Aunt Lucy."

"The one who saw visions?"

His mother's hand freezes in mid-point. "How do you know about that?" she says.

"Flo talks about her in her book."

"Flo remembers her; I don't. She went down to the States, only came up here to visit a couple of times. I just remember one time when I was four or five, and she was tall and kinda scary. But Flo liked her."

"Well, this is cool," he says, turning the photo over in his hands.

His mother starts to drape the lights around the tree, walking around it, surveying its symmetry.

"Flo calls Aunt Lucy a medium in her book," Fred says. "She thinks that's where she got her own gift from."

"Who knows." His mother bends over a box of ornaments she has placed near the tree. "Thought you might be interested in that photo. Family history and stuff." She unearths a paper bag from the depths of the ornament box and hands it to him. "Take these," she says.

The bag is filled with the smallest of the glass balls that survived his childhood, along with a couple of homemade felt stars and angels that he doesn't remember seeing before.

"Picked those ones up at the craft show," she says, when he asks. "They sell mini lights at the Canadian Tire down the road. Pop them and a couple of those ornaments on that little tree and you're done and dusted." There's an unspoken imperative in her eyes. It's time, she is saying, for him to get his shit together and make the best of his life, despite what has come before. Just like she did.

Christmas day at Aunt Flo's is as noisy as he predicted. Like last year, the house is stiflingly warm by the time everyone has had their turkey. The grandkids all retire to the TV room, staring at their individual devices instead of watching TV. Fred supposes he should get to know them more, but feels intimidated by their air of self-sufficiency, the way they ignore the adults and seem to communicate with each other only through looks and nods. Despite their taciturnity, they share a sense of ease that suggests deep roots in this place. They know where they come from.

He, on the other hand, had no idea where he came from, when he was their age. A skinny white kid with glasses, only faint vestiges of his mother's heritage in his wiry black hair and brown eyes, he had no clue where he belonged. Not with his uptight, cardigan-wearing Nana who visited from England once when he was seven. Not with his Black extended family, who would descend on the house several times a year—the women taking over the kitchen and cranking up the radio, shouting at their own kids when they got too close to the food before it was ready, but only smiling at him. The men heading out to the driveway to smoke and politely talk about cars with his father, who was usually numbed out on anti-anxiety meds.

But here he stands once more at Christmas, beside Flo with his hands deep in dishwater. In advance of this visit, he made a point of finishing her book, *Encounters on the Other Side,* which, all things considered, was a pretty snappy read.

"Glad you liked it," she says easily, when he tries awkwardly to compliment her, without going too deeply into its subject matter, torn as he is between attraction and skepticism. If he could just put aside the snooty little academic in his psyche, he could admit that some of her stories, if true, defy conventional scientific explanation.

"You talked about Aunt Lucy," he says. "Mom gave me a picture of her."

Flo reaches up to a top shelf to stack some plates. "She was the real thing, I figure, Auntie Luce, which is why everyone called her crazy…. But she wasn't crazy. She just saw stuff others couldn't." The plates are stacked, so she moves over to the wine glass cupboard. She's a big woman, broad shouldered and heavy-set, but she carries herself lightly, as if her bones and extra padding are weightless, merely serving to protect her and keep her warm.

"The way I see it," she says, "when people can't find the bridge between us and the spirit world, that's when they start to go crazy. Sometimes they just get stuck and kind of lost, sometimes they're sensitive enough to feel the spirits knocking, but have no means to communicate. Or they're scared, or they only tap into darkness, because of stuff that happened to them in their own past. That's when they start seeing and hearing bad things—maybe like your dad." She looks him straight in the eyes.

That's one theory, he thinks. He doesn't know whether he believes it or not, but there is something in Flo's eyes that he trusts. "What if you don't want to talk to them?" he says, surprised to hear these words coming from his own mouth, his mind suddenly going back to Jamie, to the memory of his fingers pressing the Block Caller option on his phone.

"Then you don't have to," she answers right away, as if she has been expecting this. "They won't make you."

After an uneasy night on Flo's sofa, he arrives home the next day to find that he is unable to unlock the inside door to his ground floor apartment. This has happened before in cold weather, despite slathering the lock with WD-40. The lock is on the landlord's list of stuff to attend to, next time he shows up, whenever that is. His back door always works, but that means trudging through foot-high snowbanks.

Fred can hear Joan's TV through the door across the hall and sighs before knocking on it. When she opens, he says. "Sorry about this, Joan. It's my lock issue again. Do you mind if I take my boots off and cut through to my back door?"

"Of course, sweetheart. I told you before. Don't be trudging through the snow and dog poop." Shiloh, the chihuahua author of the dog poop, sits shivering in her dog bed, next to the TV. She's so elderly, Fred keeps expecting her to keel over when Joan takes her out to do her business. Joan has turned the sound down on the TV, but Fred, glancing at it, can tell it's a true crime doc.

"Sorry," he says once more. "Thought the WD-40 would do the trick. Guess I'll have to call Rick again."

"More like scream. Good luck."

"True crime again?" he says, nodding towards the TV as he unlaces his boots. "Learning some tips? Making a list of your enemies?"

"You said it, right? This one's about a woman who stole a baby, though. Won't be taking notes on that...two of those are enough in one lifetime."

He makes it to the back door, boots under his arm, without getting too drawn into a conversation about her daughter and son-in-law and grand kids in Cape Breton.

Once inside his own apartment, he cobbles together a quick meal with the leftovers Aunt Flo insisted he take, and then finds himself falling into another uneasy sleep, on his own sofa this time.

He sees Aunt Flo in his dream, her face sympathetic, saying "Babies aren't always stolen." Then there is Jamie, saying "Baby, I want you back." Behind him stands the smirking guy he brought home that time. And then, clearer than any of these people, Fred sees a middle-aged woman whom he has never met, thinner than Flo, with a body type more like his mother's. She has Flo's eyes, and he knows she is trying to tell him something.

He jerks awake to the sound of sirens coming through the wall from Joan's TV, and lies still on the sofa for a long time, barely aware of the fatigue in his body, feeling instead as if he's floating, unmoored from physical and emotional pain, unmoored from a long-standing weight he's hardly been aware of carrying.

| 20 |

There is an expression of grim forbearance on the face of the battered angel topping Sophie's parents' Christmas tree. It underscores her mother's dire comments about global warming after Sophie and Tim drove through torrential rain to get here yesterday. But Christmas day has dawned cool and clear. No snow, but not freakishly warm either.

Tim comes downstairs and kisses her mother's cheek. "We are so lucky to be in your lovely home, Molly," he says. It's the kind of thing he comes out with, sincerely and spontaneously, the kind of thing that would sound pompous from anyone else.

Sophie's mother has placed ornaments Sophie remembers from childhood on fir bows around the living room. She has managed to do this in a quirky and creative, rather than cluttered way. Her artistry is permanently imprinted on this house. Her own paintings on the walls. Beautifully dyed and hand-made wax paper stars placed in the windows. While Sophie loves the memories these evoke, she would like to tell her mother that she's not obligated to keep every ornament from years past, or the other memorabilia from her and Jack's childhood, carefully stored in the basement -- especially the clippings from Sophie's early career, which are just plain embarrassing.

When they arrived last night, she led Sophie and Tim to the guest room they had created in Sophie's old bedroom. The bed had a brand-new duvet.

Sophie wondered if similar attention had been given to Jack's sleeping arrangements.

"Where will Jack sleep?"

"In his old room. He's not coming until tomorrow," her mother said. "First thing, he's promised, so we can open presents before breakfast like we always do."

"Sure, whatever works," said Sophie restlessly, hearing these words as a mandate. "Whenever he gets here is fine… it's a holiday, right?"

This morning, as they wait for Jack, her father shows Sophie and Tim his revamped workspace in the garage. A recent sale brought in enough to help him buy a new power jointer and thickness planer. He shows them a photo album of his work, and his Facebook page. Sophie, remembering his school janitor years, feels a glow of pride. Her father is making fine furniture these days, instead of the wooden sculptures she admired so much when she was little. Those never earned him a living wage. But she does not worry about his happiness. She doesn't notice lines of trouble or disappointment like the ones around her mother's mouth and eyes.

When they return to the house, her mother is roaming the kitchen, eyes darting to the window, looking for the beat-up Toyota Yaris that Jack shares with his roommate. Sophie considers asking about her teaching job to distract her, but the last time she did, it led to a tirade about the school administration and how devalued art is in the curriculum these days. Nausea is starting to send subtle feelers into Sophie's gut, as if to remind her she's not out of the woods yet. She goes to the kitchen to look for soda crackers.

"Breakfast time, I think," says her father.

"I was hoping to wait for Jack," says her mother.

There are organic eggs and sausages in the fridge, and Florida oranges on the counter.

"Crackers will do me for now," she says.

"The boy can make his own breakfast when he gets here," says her father. "He's an adult."

In the end, they open one present each to pass the time. Sophie chooses one of two presents from Tim. It's an album by Joshua, a singer-songwriter friend of Tim's who lives in Maine.

"Who would have thought vinyl records would become popular again?" says her mother. "Look, he's even got an insert with lyrics. Now that brings back memories."

Sophie's eyes are drawn to the picture on the album sleeve: a boy lying on his belly on the floor reading a book, another boy on a bottom bunk, lying face up.

This photo, its fuzzy quality, the room, the coloured toys, the dark, rough looking wood of the floor, and the relaxed abandon of the children's bodies, causes an explosion of longing and nostalgia within her. She's slightly mortified, but not surprised, to find her eyes filling with tears.

In the early days of her childhood, she and Jack shared a room, until it became hers alone. At age ten, she pleaded for privacy, and her parents created a small bedroom downstairs for Jack. She remembers luxuriating in her newfound space, no longer embarrassed, when friends visited, by a jumble of Beyblades, Pokémon cards, dirty socks and underwear on his side of the room. Now, she wonders if his bedroom, smaller than hers, was a source of freedom or resentment for him. She can't recall his reaction at the time.

When Jack arrives, it is nearly eleven. They don't notice him come in, because he enters by the patio doors in back and they are in the kitchen, washing up after a feast of sausages and eggs. He carries a knapsack and a bottle of wine, and, to Sophie's relief, his eyes look normal. She is the first one to glance up and notice him standing there, watching them. She hugs him, which still feels a bit weird, because they never did this when they were kids, but it's a routine she wants to establish now that they are adults.

"Ho, ho, ho and all that," he says, taking some newspaper-wrapped presents out of the knapsack.

"Santa slept in, by the looks of it," says Sophie's father.

Her mother jumps up to put together a plate of leftover sausages in the microwave.

"How are the new digs?" says Sophie.

"Oh, you know, digging," he says.

"Bring your breakfast in the living room," says their father, his voice neutral. "Tim, why don't you be Santa?" He gestures to the armchair nearest the tree which is partially hidden now by a mountain of presents.

Really? Sophie thinks. Someone has to be Santa?

Jack says: "Maybe we could have a scrum at the foot of the tree, each man for himself."

"Or we could tear all the labels off, open them randomly and then see if we can guess who they're for," says Tim.

"Forget Father Christmas," says Sophie. "I want to be Mother Christmas. Out of the way, Tim."

"Okay," he says, "make way for the pregnant belly. We do what she says."

Sticking with the drawing room comedy vibe, Sophie starts picking out the least breakable looking presents under the tree and tossing them to people. There is a sense of relief when they start to open things, a quiet lull in conversation, except for exclamations of gratitude or wonder. When Sophie gets to her pile of gifts, she's touched to find a beautiful lacy white nightgown from Tim, loose and comfortable looking but not devoid of sexiness. Her father has given her Zadie Smith's most recent novel, and Jack has given her and Tim the latest Silk Road Ensemble album.

Sophie's gift from her mother is carefully wrapped in old National Geographic maps and decorated with fabric ribbons. It turns out, not surprisingly, to be baby themed… photos of Sophie's birth, in fact, and her first few days. Although she has seen them before, these grainy faded images, like the photo on Tim's friend's album cover, are striking. Molly has compiled and set them elegantly against dark mat paper in a reproduction of an antique photo album. Sophie is unsure what to make of the images of her mother—round, with somewhat indistinct features, surrounded by her midwife and birth attendant, their bent heads unconsciously shielding her pendulous breasts and straining belly from the camera, as she steps into a jacuzzi-style tub built by Sophie's father especially for the event. Her parents believed water births were the gentlest way of bringing babies into the world.

There was a more upscale jacuzzi in the Brooklyn Birthing Center Sophie visited with Tim last week. It had multiple jets of different-coloured water, and reminded her of a scene in one of the Harry Potter books that she had giggled over endlessly when she was ten: Harry talking with a female ghost while trying to hide himself in the multicolored bubble bath in the prefect's bathroom. The room with the jacuzzi also had softly draped curtains, a cushy sofa and a king-sized bed. Definitely not in their price range. The next room they visited had purple walls and a smaller iron-framed bed with a floral bedspread. In the corner, a rocking chair with a rag doll on the seat.

Although she can't relate to her mother's water birth photos, Sophie can almost imagine herself sitting in the rocking chair in the birthing center, before and after the big event, cradling, first, an enormous heaving belly, and later, a blanket-wrapped baby. What happens between those two moments is beyond her imagining, despite the first-hand descriptions she has read, and the video she has watched of a heroic woman squatting on the floor, while something that looks like a blood-covered doll emerges agonizingly slowly from between her legs. She and Tim have signed up for the childbirth classes at the birthing center, but she doubts that many of the strategies offered will make this process easier.

"This is amazing," she says to her mother as everyone gathers round the album, "but don't you want these photos for yourself?"

"I made copies of them all."

She wants to feel uncomplicated gratitude for the time spent sorting and organizing these pictures, but there is that familiar sensation of being hedged in, aware that her mother expects something from her that she doesn't know how to give.

Now her mother is laughing about her eighties haircut in the post-birth pictures, her father is describing what went into the building of the tub, and Tim is asking intelligent questions about the home birth experience. Despite the fact that she is at the centre of all this talk, she feels weirdly invisible.

"You've got one more thing to open, Soph," says Jack, holding out an envelope. Sophie recognizes it as coming from the bag of stuff she and Tim grabbed from the mail delivery back in the city yesterday morning. It's a card from Nathan and Anne—a beautiful abstract watercolour which is seasonally bright—filled with yellows, reds, and greens—but with no text or reference to any specific holiday.

We wish you both well at this exciting time of your lives, Anne has written on the inside of the card. Her handwriting is slanted and precise, with a firm look to her periods and commas. *If you are out this way over the holidays, stop by for a visit.* Underneath this, a simple sentence from Nathan. *Be well, Sophie.*

A detached, observant part of Sophie's mind notices the tightening Nathan's name has caused in her body—a jolt of anxiety that she associates with her shitty phone call and texts with Bill. At the same time, the three words *Be well, Sophie,* cause tears to fill her eyes again. By the time her pregnancy hormones have reached their peak, she will probably be a puddle on the floor. She hands the card to Tim.

"They're not far from here, are they?" he says.

"No, but," says Sophie. "It'll feel awkward if we visit. I've really fucked things up for Nathan. He's probably trying to scramble to pay back the investors as we speak. I hadn't signed the contract yet, because I wanted Patty to look it over, but he'd be within his rights to litigate to get some of the pre-production costs back."

"You're not serious," says Tim.

"I am serious."

"They're such nice people," says Molly, who has only met Nathan and Anne once or twice. "I'm sure he understands the position you're in."

"You'd be surprised how business gets in the way of nice, Mom."

"Have you ever heard of an actor being litigated against in that way, Sophie?" says her father, his voice even, his eyes on the wool scarf he has just removed from the box from Tim and Sophie.

"Well… no," she says. She feels a sudden blip, like a hiccup, in her belly—the baby squirming, turning? She starts to gather the Christmas wrap strewn around the room and fold what's reusable, putting the rest in a recycle bag. She stacks the gifts under the tree.

"Whoa, look at the swag," says Jack. "Guess we must love each other."

That afternoon, she goes for a walk with Jack along the deserted but sunny streets.

"Does it feel weird being back here after all this time?" she says.

"No weirder than anything else… Not much has changed as far as they're concerned," he says, jerking his head towards the house. "Still living in their own little world."

"Not much changed?" says Sophie. "Seriously? The new post-election political landscape? Better not let Tim hear you say that."

"Ah yes, Mr. Trump."

"Yeah, him."

"From what I gather, Clinton was no prize either," says Jack.

There is a beat during which Sophie takes a moment to collect her thoughts, her heart thumping curiously.

"Well but… I mean… She's not perfect, but there's no comparison, surely?" She adds, with a half laugh, "Unless you're going to fall for Breitbart stories about pedophile rings or something."

They pass the candy store they used to walk to after school when they were kids. It's now a cash store. There is a picture in the window of a young couple holding fanned out wads of bills in their hands, slightly manic smiles on their faces.

"Look Soph," says Jack, "nothing is simple, and I've learned over the past couple of years that sometimes the weirdest shit turns out to be real shit."

"But not that shit," says Sophie, heart still thumping. "That's the shit that makes wackos shoot up diners looking for non-existent children trapped in non-existent basements."

"Okay, so maybe not that shit… But how do you know you're not in just as much of a bubble as everyone else? You can't tell me that Bruce and Molly back there are the most politically savvy pair, with their art students and hand-made furniture."

She's stung by the tone of his voice, his use of their parents' first names. Looking at his profile, she wonders what has happened to him over the years. She wonders how much she knows him, despite having grown up with him.

She does not intend to say it, but it comes out.

"God. Tell me you didn't vote for this bunch."

"Vote? Shit no, I didn't vote."

"You didn't vote?"

"Nah, got back a month before it, wasn't registered. And my goal in coming home had nothing to do with all that bullshit."

Within Sophie, moral indignation vies with sibling attachment. She imagines Tim's voice saying: *You didn't vote? It's idiots like you who got him elected.* She hears her own voice say:

"So, what was it like in China, anyway? Did it live up to your expectations?"

"Well since my expectations were mainly to get away and earn enough money to survive, I guess so," he says.

"And you got to travel, Vietnam, Laos, Thailand. Amazing."

"Yeah, it was."

"And the teaching job, what was that like?"

"Crap administration, weird organizational glitches everywhere. But some of the other teachers and most of the students were cool. We were all given these bullshit prefab lesson plans that we deviated from when we could. Not sure I was what the students expected in an American."

"No?" she says, intrigued. "In what way?"

"Oh well, I wanted to know about Lao Tzu, they wanted to know about Facebook and Twitter. They were fine though. By the end, I just got tired of the company and crazy work schedule. Not many people renew their contracts after two years in that job."

"And now you're back," she says.

"And now I'm back."

There is another silence while they cross the street and turn towards home. The pharmacy is the same as when they were kids, a flag blowing in the wind above the door, the RX sign, cards and Christmas bags in the window. Molly has said it's in trouble though. The town has refused the family that owns it a grant for renovations, and sales are down. Most people drive to Walmart these days.

"What are your plans, Jack, now that you're home? Are you going to look for a job, or go back to school?"

Too many questions, she thinks.

"Earned enough to get by and travel a bit over there, not enough to set up a college fund," he says.

"You could look into bursaries or something."

"Yeah?" he says. "I'm not you, Sophie. My high school marks were shit. And what bursaries should I apply for? The 'white male privilege' category?"

This whole conversation is making her body feel heavy with much more than the weight of the baby.

"But do you know what you'd like to do, all things being equal?" she asks.

"All things being equal," he says, "eat turkey right now. I'm starving."

| 21 |

The day after Christmas is a nothing day, a day of over-stuffed bellies and leftovers, of dust starting to collect on the carpet among the needles from the fir boughs, a day of gifts and clothing disappearing into respective bedrooms and of books starting to be read and commented on. Already the political talk has resumed. Syria, this time. Tim and Sophie's father are in the kitchen cleaning up from another overly lavish breakfast prepared by her mother.

"Jesus, Aleppo," says Tim. "Those people are seriously doomed. It was bad enough before. But now with this guy? Who cozies up to Putin?" Molly weaves around the periphery of the conversation, commenting at intervals as she takes dishes out of Tim's hands and puts them in the cupboard.

Sophie thinks back a few years to the desperate-eyed Syrians standing on street corners in her neighbourhood, handing out pamphlets about al-Assad's regime. She had known nothing then, had not yet been witness to one horrendous image after another, courtesy of Facebook or CNN. The flattened buildings, the dark-eyed children covered in dust. The bodies washed up on Turkish beaches haunted her long before she had her encounter with the sea, long before the word "child" carried the weight for her that it carries now.

There is a place within her that feels shaken up, not in her womb exactly, but somewhere deeper. Maybe it's the proximity of her family members, or being back in her childhood home—the same but changed. Or her flutterings of anxiety over the possibility of a visit with Anne and Nathan, and this non-acting life she is leading. She feels she has been thrown into a new existence, partly through circumstance, partly through the perversity of her own nature. And the small, insistent movements she feels in her belly these days remind her there is no going back. She's torn between a desire to reach out to the people around her, and a need to escape. She wants something beyond these kitchen walls, beyond all this talk of suffering.

Jack is in the living room drinking coffee, wandering from bookshelf to mantelpiece, looking at nothing.

"Come for another walk?" she says. She goes to the hall closet without waiting for an answer. "I'll pick up some milk at the corner store," she says to her mother.

When she feels Jack coming up behind her and putting on his coat, she is relieved. And when they start walking into the winter wind, she tells him about being in the waves in Nova Scotia, about the moment when she thought she was going to die, about her time afterwards in the sand.

"The thing is," she says, "I already knew I was pregnant then. I hadn't told anyone, not even Tim. I still hadn't taken it in, couldn't believe that something as small as a blue line on a pee stick could mean that much, couldn't believe that my body, that sorry little flat-chested runt of a body, was capable of doing that."

"Not so flat-chested anymore," he says.

Sophie laughs.

"I'm still trying to get around this myself," Jack says. "You're gonna make me an *uncle*. Fuck. *Uncle Jack*. Sounds like some pervert in an X-rated cartoon."

"Another addition to the *Pirates of the Caribbean* franchise," says Sophie. "Johnny Depp, allowed to be the middle-aged slob that he now is, smoking a pipe in a rocking chair and making eyes at his hot young niece."

"Okay, that's even more twisted than my cartoon."

"You'll be a wonderful uncle," she says. "Seriously. If I can do the mom thing, you can do that."

Yesterday's sun has already retreated into clouds and the temperature has dropped. Her breath comes out visible, lingers in front of her.

"This is going to sound kind of weird, but I didn't realize how much I missed you while you were over there, until you got back." She recognizes this thought as a new one, right now, as the words spill out of her.

Jack looks slightly uncomfortable, which she expected, but doesn't mind.

"Well, thank you," he says. Not *I missed you too*, she notes, but again, this does not bother her. She feels a need to keep talking, or more specifically, to keep talking until Jack starts talking. She can't put her finger on what she feels they are on the verge of, but there is something.

"It's been a weird few years," she says. "The films, the steady work after those two dry years when *Liza* got canceled. Deservedly so, though. It was crap. Especially by the last season. They changed writers about every hour. None of us knew where our characters were coming from. I just assumed mine had borderline personality disorder." She thinks back to the final show, to that creep Hugh Wilkinson, with his barked orders to any actors who had the nerve to ask questions. *Keep it moving, keep it moving… we're on the clock … You're an actor not a fucking auteur, okay?*

"You were right to only watch a couple of episodes," she says, "even if I was pissed off at the time."

"Yeah well, it was bizarre, watching your sister prance around spouting valley talk with a bunch of kids neither of us would have been caught dead with in real life."

"Oh well, that was only the beginning. You missed my love triangle with Blake and Shelley… you might be able to catch the reruns somewhere online if you search hard enough."

"Think I'll pass."

"Fair enough," she says.

"You never came out to the set, that time Mom and Dad visited," she adds, remembering that one occasion both her parents came to LA.

"Got an invite to stay with Noah," says Jack. "At the time it seemed preferable to traveling anywhere with the parents."

The parents. At least it's not "Bruce and Molly" today. Hopefully, she will be a parent who inspires affection in her adult children, not derision, but who knows.

"You weren't doing the wilderness camp anymore that summer," she says.

"God no."

"So, what was that like, really? You said the counsellors were stoned all the time."

"What do you think? A bunch of thirteen to seventeen-year-old kids alone in a cabin in the woods together with no supervision and not enough to do. *Lord of the Flies.*"

"That bad?"

"First year wasn't that bad. I was in the younger group, only six of us in the cabin, and Noah was there. I just had to put up with Anthony—you know, Pokémon Anthony of the monkey bars. Adolescence had not improved him. But the second year was truly bizarre. I got put in a cabin with one of the older groups. There were some kids—the sixteen and seventeen-year-olds— who were really fucked up. Their folks must have sent them thinking they could clean up their act—out of sight, out of mind. And most of the halfway decent counsellors from the year before had left, so the useless stoners were in charge."

"I wonder what happened?" Sophie says. "To make the good staff leave, I mean. Parents would have asked questions if they had known."

"Yeah well, ask no questions, we'll tell you no lies."

Sophie turns to look at his profile.

"We were dumb-ass, pimply kids," he says. "Our parents couldn't wait to get rid of us."

She wants to protest, come to her parents' defense. But he did have an awkward presence at that age. She remembers, with a pang, how scrawny he was. Too old to run around the yard with Noah playing superhero games, too young to date anyone, and he had never been into sports. The good parts of puberty were delayed for him until ninth grade. She thinks back to what she was doing at the time. That must have been the year they did *Wizard of Oz* at theatre school, also the year her mother signed her up with an agency for the first time.

"So…" she hears herself say. "Did you have any run-ins with them—the fucked up seventeen-year-olds I mean?"

They are just outside the entrance of the corner store now, and she stops walking and turns again to look at his face—the stubble on his jaw, the cheekbones the girls like, the dark lashes she would love to have, rather than the blond ones she inherited from their father.

He gives an impatient shrug. "Soph, you don't want to hear about that," he says.

The wind is cold on the street corner now. There is a tightening in her chest that tells her he may be right—she might not want to hear. She puts her hand on his arm and waits for him to turn and look at her.

"No," she says. "I do. I do want to hear, Jack."

Jack nods to the store. "Does she want a pint or a quart?"

"A quart. I'll get it."

Inside the store, she watches her hand take the milk carton out of the fridge and put it on the counter, then count out change from her wallet. The whiteness of her fingers reminds her of how her hands had looked underwater in Nova Scotia, when she was struggling to the surface, just before she managed to break free from the current.

She tries to match the rhythm of Jack's steps on the way home. The crunch of dead leaves and frost on the sidewalk is unnaturally loud, as if she's hearing it through high quality earphones with the volume turned up.

"There was this one kid in our cabin," he says eventually. "He really had a hate on for me. Don't know why he singled me out. I mean he was shit to everyone, but I just bugged the crap out of him, apparently. I think it started when we had this campfire thing on the first night and had to pass a stick around and talk about what our favourite hobbies were. When it got to me all I could think of to say was listening to Radiohead. I guess that marked me out to him as a 'fucking faggot,' his generic insult. You know what it was like back then."

"Yeah," said Sophie. "The lexicon was limited. They had nothing different to throw at the kids who actually were gay. Remember Markie? Always saying 'thank you' and blowing kisses at them when they yelled that stuff?" She gives a laugh that sounds fake to her own ears.

"Well, this was not someone you would want to try blowing kisses at. Whenever the counsellors weren't looking, which was most of the time, he did something—tipped me out of the canoe. Stuck his foot out when we were hiking, 'accidentally' stepped on my leg when I fell. Elbowed me in the gut hard enough to double me over when we played soccer in the field. But the worst was back in the cabin. There was something different waiting for me every night—earwigs in my bed, spit in my water glass, he fucking pissed on my towel once. He used to laugh maniacally when he did shit like that."

"Jesus. He sounds demented," she says.

"He was also twice everyone's size. Built like a linebacker. Did weights back home. Everyone was fucking terrified of him. But the night before we left, I'd had enough, figured if I stood up to him, how bad could it be? If he beat the crap out of me, he and the useless stoners who were supposed to be looking after us would have to answer for the bruises. There were six of us in that cabin, and in front of everyone else I told him he was a useless motherfucker with sawdust for brains."

He stops and lets out an almost silent snort of laughter. "I must have been thinking of your *Wizard of Oz* show, there. Anyway, the brilliance of my repartee was kind of marred by the fact that I was bawling at the time."

They have stopped moving, and instinctively she puts both hands on his arm, as if to keep him from starting to walk again, and then laces her arm through his. There is a gas station up ahead. The sound of hammering, metal on metal, comes from the garage. In the distance, Sophie can see the grey outline of the Catskill foothills.

"But instead of hitting me, all he did was knock me down, flip me over and press his knee into my back. Hurt like hell, I thought it was going to break a rib or something, and I'm screaming, but he's got me face down with my mouth full of this moldy carpet thing they had in front of the bathroom door.

"Next thing I know the pain lets up, cause he's just standing with one foot on my back, but kind of teetering, as if he's distracted, reaching for something. I found out afterwards it was a shampoo bottle on the side of the sink. And then he's pulling my pants down, saying, 'You're a fucking homo, you know that? You'll probably enjoy this, you little faggot,' and he's trying to shove the shampoo bottle up my ass, pulling me backwards, ass to the sky, ramming it in, and all that time there's not a sound in the room, they're all fucking watching it, I guess. Little Anthony with his Pokémon cards? He was there. He saw. He did fuck all."

"Jack..." Sophie says.

"Don't know how long it is until I hear the door bang open and Noah's voice yelling 'Get off him you freak!' I guess he'd gone to get the least stoned of the counsellors, who's yelling some shit like 'Break it up, break it up… fucking kids.' Like it was a normal fight. Don't know if he really didn't see what was happening because the other kids were blocking his view, or if he just pretended not to see. Meanwhile Jackson, that's his name, fucking Jackson, is standing up, having tossed the shampoo bottle through the doorway to the bathroom and is turning his attention to the counsellor, calling him a 'fucking retard' and the other counsellors are running in to protect their own. I'm on the floor pulling up my pants and having difficulty cause it's fucking agony to sit down and no one is looking at me except Noah, and all I can think of to say is: 'Don't tell anyone.' I didn't even thank him. My very first thought was 'This never happened. No one needs to know.'"

He starts walking so quickly that she has to trot to catch up. "And you know what, Soph?" he says. "I still feel that way. I still don't want anyone to know. I've read all the stuff about bullying and male sexual abuse and what have you. Doesn't mean shit to me. I don't want people to define me by that crap moment in my life, to think of me as that guy."

These last words resonate deep inside Sophie. She imagines the fear in that room, the bizarre spectacle of casual bullying taken to that height, while the unreality of the scene froze all those shit-scared little boys in their tracks. She feels her heartbeat, full to the breaking point with the enormity of this secret.

"But you told me," she says breathlessly, struggling to keep up.

"I told you. So, you and Noah know. As well as those other little shits from school that I never see anymore."

A new thought intrudes on the grotesque image that this story has seared into her brain. "Jack," she says. "Is that camp still in existence?"

"Naw, it folded the next summer."

"Do you think someone told? One of the counsellors? Or the boys? Noah maybe?"

"Not Noah, he promised and kept it. If anyone told, nothing happened that I know of."

"But that means that creep is still out there?"

"Him and a thousand others like him." He starts to walk even faster. "And before you say anything about my social obligations, Sophie, I don't even know the guy's last name. He's just a blip on the horizon that I would rather forget."

She is willing herself not to cry. She will gladly accept all the hormonal tears she has recently shed over burnt turnips and Christmas gifts, if she can avoid crying right now, if she can find a way to make him meet her eyes.

"Can you just stop for a minute, please?" she says. "You're walking too fast for me."

He slows to a halt and stares up the street. His breath comes out in a cloud of steam. She knows she can't make this go away. There is no big-sister remedy, all the times she thought she had his back when he was little are reduced to zero.

"I wasn't going to say anything about social obligations. The only person you have an obligation to is yourself."

This sounds straight out of a self-help manual. There is no way she can get this right, but she keeps trying.

"You never told us," she says. "You never told Mom and Dad. If they had known…"

"What?" he says, turning to her with a stiff movement of his neck. "What do you think they would have done to make it better? Sued the camp? Shoved me in therapy they couldn't afford? Treated me like a fucking wounded puppy? You think I felt like talking to them? Breaking their little bubble? Mum had just got through that teaching degree and still couldn't get work. The only thing she seemed to live for was taking you to all those auditions and stuff. Dad was coming home every night from that janitor's job and lighting into me for fucking everything—my mess, my shit grades, my laziness."

Those years rush by Sophie's brain in a confused blur. She feels rootless and lost, trying to make out her memory's sign posts with nearsighted eyes. Okay, she sort of recalls arguments about the state of his room, tension between her father and Jack, tension between her father and mother, for that matter, but all that seemed to occur off stage from where the real action was. It was always something she could get away from. The novels she buried herself in, the play practices. *All those auditions and stuff.*

Her voice, when it speaks, sounds as foreign to her as if she's in one of those auditions.

"Jack, I'm sorry this happened to you," she says.

"Yeah well, shit happens. For every sob story out there, there are a thousand others that are ten times as bad. And it could be worse. It was only once. I didn't get dismembered by a serial killer. I'm not living in a war zone somewhere, getting the shit bombed out of my neighbourhood."

So he had also been listening to the Syria talk, maybe shared her need to seek refuge from that unsavoury, voyeuristic feel to the conversation. She believes she understands why he has chosen to keep this secret.

"But this shit happened to my brother," she says. "And I'm sorry."

There is a silence, broken by two crows calling to each other, as if they are sounding an alarm, a private warning relayed from treetop to treetop.

"Thanks," he says finally, without turning to meet her gaze, and starts walking again, more slowly this time.

| 22 |

RUDY STRIDES TO THE END OF THE DRIVEWAY. Watching him through the kitchen window, Anne remembers his careful, robotic shuffle of just a month ago. Now, he appears to be pushing something huge aside with his forward pacing body, oblivious to the cold, the sun, the scenery. His face shows no enjoyment, but neither does it show any negative emotion, just deep concentration. He is merely involved in the walking process.

She fills the kettle for tea with filtered water, acknowledging what is 'not quite right' with him, the tension in his neck and shoulders, his slight tendency to mouth words to himself as he goes along. But once again, she rejects all her preconceived notions of 'normal.' All of this effort and focus is evidence that her son is alive, human. Occasionally she dares to think that he may, someday, be alive and human to her. She places her China teapot and cups on a colorful papier mâché tray, along with some of her mother's Christmas cookies. As she pours the hot water, she pictures meeting Rudy's eyes on some kind of equal footing—a Rudy who has managed to integrate the quirky, easy-going kid from before his illness with the brain-scrambled, fear-driven teenager. In these imaginings he has become someone new, someone strong and able to acknowledge both.

She tries to put these thoughts aside, as much as she puts aside the catastrophic thoughts that haunt her when he's gone too long. Hope, as much as fear, always carries within it the seeds of betrayal.

Tim and Sophie arrived a few minutes ago, and Rudy seemed unfazed. Anne kept her voice neutral as she introduced her son. He said "Hello" quite passably, before going out. Now, she takes the tea into the living room and joins the conversation, as if this is all normal stuff in her everyday life. Friends stopping by for tea, a Christmas tree by the window, an outwardly healthy son ambulating his body through the room and out of the house of his own accord.

Sitting on the love seat, she looks across at Sophie cozying up to Tim on the sofa, her hair pulled back and no makeup. The wan, pale version Anne had lunch with in Manhattan retained a slight aura of glamour, but today, Sophie merely has that healthy glow some women get in their second trimester. There is a visible bump under her oversized sweater.

Anne assumed Nathan might come join her on the love seat, but he's perched on one of the antique chairs they inherited from her aunt in Pennsylvania. It's an item of furniture that rarely gets used. From the late William and Mary period, it is gorgeously upholstered and reasonably comfortable, but Nathan sits on it gingerly. Anne knows how ambivalent he is about this visit, how much effort it is for him to make small talk and listen to Sophie's non-film-related preoccupations.

Over the past few weeks, she has heard snatches of phone conversations through the door of his office. Positive, upbeat briefings to investors. Keeping all his balls in the air, as he would say. *In a way, it's not a bad thing this particular project's been delayed. Remember the other writer I told you about? Working on the second draft of... I've found a story editor to work with him and have had some new brain waves about casting... I can guarantee that when both these projects hit the theatres, the rewards will be substantial.*

She feels a rush of empathy for him, for the determined optimism in his voice during those pitches, which contrasts with the pouches under his eyes. At the same time, she does not regret her impulse to invite Sophie and Tim. Normalcy, and friendship, are needed now, the only solution to the unspoken words hanging in the air. Everyone is an adult in this room, she thinks, and soon they will all be parents as well.

Sophie tells them about her ultrasound, how clear it was, how weird it was to see the shape floating on the screen and to connect it to what is growing inside her own body.

"Obviously, the technology has improved since our day," says Nathan.

Anne remembers that appointment years ago—trying to peer at the ultrasound monitor to get a sense of a human outline, managing once for about two seconds, then losing it in a snowy globular mass that reminded her of her parents' old black-and-white TV when it malfunctioned.

"Could you tell if it was a boy or a girl?" she asks.

"The technician might have been able to," says Tim, "but we decided we'd rather not know. No need to heap gender expectations on the kid in utero."

Anne thinks, this guy has obviously imbibed feminism from babyhood. There is no trace of the confusion, disempowerment, or anger that still linger for Nathan's generation. Tim is tall and lanky and has expressive hands. Twenty years ago, she would have been simultaneously turned on and tongue-tied in his presence. One benefit of aging is being able to enjoy beauty and youth without all that yearning. As a young woman, she was usually overwhelmed by the creative guys—the musicians, actors, writers. Scared of them, in fact. It had taken the pragmatic, down-to-earth style of Nathan to put her at ease. Not that Nathan wasn't, isn't, creative. She recognizes the talent it takes to do what he does. She recognizes what it costs him.

"Your families must be excited," she says, passing around her mother's Christmas cookies. She hopes to get rid of them quickly, so she can get Rudy back to his sugar and wheat-free diet.

Sophie nibbles on the corner of a star-shaped cookie. "My mother calls the baby her 'one little bubble of hope' ever since Trump got elected," she says, with a crooked smile that reminds Anne of her character in the films. "I think maybe the two things are sort of balancing her out—political angst on the one hand, grandmotherly joy on the other. She can't decide whether to give me advice on prenatal care, or info about the Women's March in January."

"Two totally interrelated subjects, I would think," says Tim.

"Oh definitely," says Sophie, finishing her cookie.

"I can't face the crowds for the march in Manhattan," says Anne. "But I plan to go to a little one in Poughkeepsie."

"That's the one my mom is going to," says Sophie. "Maybe you two can meet up."

"And we'll be at the Manhattan one," says Tim, "for as long as Sophie feels up to it."

Again, his earnestness touches Anne, but also makes her feel old. Secretly, she has been dreading the rally in Poughkeepsie, worried it will be full of smug, self-congratulatory bonhomie, unlikely to solve anything. She can't believe she needs to march for rights she thought were finally givens—equal pay, bodily autonomy, the right not to be leered at, glowered over, or grabbed. As if echoing her thoughts, Sophie says:

"I can't believe we are in this position. I still can't believe he's in. And I don't know how to choose what to start protesting. When I think of all the misery in the world that's going to get worse—the refugees, the poverty, whole ecosystems collapsing… and here we are having to shout and chant what shouldn't even need to be said anymore."

"I can remember feeling this way when Reagan was elected," says Anne. "Now, God help us, they're starting to hold Reagan up as some kind of moderate."

"That's what my mom says," says Sophie.

Okay, now she really feels old. She remembers her parents' horror at the fact that Reagan was an actor, that he came from a world they despised and mistrusted—the world that is such a big part of Nathan's life now.

"My parents used to say it was pathetic that the public could be duped by a Hollywood cliché, and what was the world coming to," she says, smiling again.

"When Arnold Schwarzenegger got in as governor," says Tim, "my dad said, 'They elected the *Terminator*?'"

Anne remembers her father's xenophobic reaction. *The guy can barely string a grammatical sentence together, for God's sake.* He had lived long enough to watch the Obama inauguration on TV. She remembers him saying, "He's got his work cut out for him." It's a good thing he checked out when he did. He must be rolling in his grave today, given the state of Trump's sentences.

"So tell us more about this baby," she says. "Do you have plans for the birth?"

Sophie looks at Tim, which seems odd. Then she says: "My mom wants me to go home and have a home birth with a midwife she knows, but I can't picture it."

"Can't picture a home birth, you mean?"

"No, it's not that. I'm fine with a home birth. Actually, I was born at home."

"Really?" says Anne. "That was unusual back then."

"True. My parents were ahead of the trends."

"Whereas my parents…" says Tim. "I think we'll compromise and have a midwife-delivered baby at a birth centre. We toured one last month. Felt like a friendly spot."

"Mmm," says Sophie.

Again, there is a short pause. Anne says, "I think you're right to examine your options. Looking back, a more natural situation than the hospital would have been better for Rudy and me."

Nathan shifts suddenly in his chair as he reaches for his coffee. "It all worked out though," he says. "Healthy baby, healthy mum."

"Mum too stoned on Demerol to fully experience what was happening after an endless labour in a grim little grey room," says Anne.

Nathan's coffee cup stops midway between the table and his lips. Guilt floods her. She doesn't want to be negative about the arrival of Rudy into their lives, that pivotal moment of bonding, when they became a family. She remembers the minutes after the birth, Rudy wrapped in blankets in Nathan's arms, Nathan saying over and over again "Hey there little guy. Hi… hi." a slightly drunken smile on his face. In that memory, the room was no longer grey, the midday sun shining through the hospital window.

"But you're right," she says, glancing over at him, "it did all work out." Turning back to Sophie, she says, "The main thing is finding what you yourself feel comfortable with, so you can relax and do what's needed when the time comes." She deliberately says "yourself" not "yourselves." Much as she appreciates the sweet and purposeful Tim, there is a limit to male feminist empathy. She can't stand it when she hears fathers-to-be saying things like 'We're pregnant!'

"Yeah, right," says Sophie, a little nervously, it seems to Anne.

"A hospital birth with a labor attendant from our childbirth class was what felt right to us when Rudy was born," she says. "But we have friends in Nova Scotia who had three home births with a midwife. She sounded amazing. They were singing her praises, and the mum seemed to recover from the births really quickly."

"Well, Mary Ellen's that type," says Nathan. "She could run a marathon and bake a four-course meal afterwards. Not everyone is wired that way."

Anne feels a flicker of annoyance. What he means is that she's not wired that way. But how does he know that? How much of her own postpartum funk and nursing difficulties might have been alleviated if she had been surrounded by friends and a midwife for Rudy's arrival, if she had been able to sleep in her own bed, smell household smells and sounds instead of being imprisoned by a bleeping monitor, antiseptic odours and those blank hospital surfaces. How different would it have been if she had known how to choose what happened, rather than submit?

After Tim and Sophie have gone, she and Nathan move around the kitchen, putting away the cookies and washing the teacups. Anne puts her hand on Nathan's arm. "I didn't mean that Rudy's birth was awful, just that we'll never know if the alternative might have been better."

"Things could *always* be better, Anne."

A depressingly familiar comment. She wonders if she will always feel pushy or unrealistic in his presence, just because she wants know all her options, explore the truth. She places a bone-china cup carefully on its saucer on the shelf of the glass-windowed kitchen cupboard.

"The nurse we had, the one with the red hair," she says. "She was great."

"And remember the obstetrician they called in after it was over?" Nathan's voice is warmer now. "The Sikh one with the turban? What was it he said to you when he came in? You were just sitting there naked, refusing to be covered by blankets."

Anne makes a stab at the doctor's Punjabi accent. "It is a hard workout, this giving birth business. One needs a cool down afterwards."

They meet each other's eyes and smile. A narrow escape. But she feels that she has just dipped into a well of sadness, a well that has deepened over the years, overflowing with things they can no longer say.

| 23|

Sophie is cleaning, dusting high surfaces first, then pulling out the vacuum to do the floor.

"I'll do that," says Tim, from the sofa, where he's checking his emails.

"I'm okay," she says. "I'm gonna crash later."

She enjoys actively sucking up dust-bunnies after being constantly served over the holidays—served food and drink by her mother and Anne, political conversation from Tim, disturbing words and images from her brother.

When she and Jack had returned from that Boxing Day walk, Jack had edged past her while her mother had offered her a kitchen chair and a glass of water, saying, "This is such an exciting time. I'm going to love being a grandma." Her mother's face, the way she leaned forward to talk, like a Victorian lady about to smell a bouquet of roses, rattled Sophie. The normally comforting home smells—morning pancakes and fir boughs—made her stomach churn. Everything seemed foreign to her, even the house. Later, lying down for another afternoon nap in her childhood bedroom, she was acutely aware of her family downstairs: her father in his workroom, face impassive and focused, Tim in the living room reading, her mother in the kitchen dealing with the turkey leftovers, and Jack, doing what exactly? Pacing? Flipping through books he was not reading? She wanted to believe he felt better for telling her that horrific memory, but she wondered if he regretted it instead.

Tim looks slightly guilty, watching her vacuum. "I'll do supper," he says.

She should probably eat some green vegetables. Also yogurt. There is a slight stirring in her womb, as if the baby agrees with her.

Tim decamps to the kitchen and opens the fridge door. "Should I do an omelet with the rest of these eggs?" he asks.

"You can't make an omelet without breaking eggs," Sophie says.

Where did that come from? Mrs. Milstein, one of her Junior High English teachers. A dynamic woman with flaming red hair, also pregnant. *You can't make an omelet without breaking eggs*, she said once. *Common idioms are called clichés.* Mrs. Milstein's protruding baby-bump was oddly shaped and seemed to change daily, a fact the fourteen-year-old Sophie queasily noticed, because Mrs. Milstein wore T-shirts and tight dresses.

Tim is looking at her oddly.

"Don't bother with the eggs," she says. "Just lots of green stuff—maybe a broccoli stir fry."

Those junior high memories predate what happened to Jack. Sophie wonders if she will always divide her childhood memories into 'before and after.' She thinks about all the times she disappeared upstairs to her bedroom and Jack disappeared into the basement. Her mother would knock on her door, computer or newspaper in hand, saying "Have you seen this?" An article about acting, or an interview with a fantasy author Sophie was reading. Did her mother ever knock on Jack's door, perch companionably on Jack's bed? Sophie cannot recall the arguments she vaguely overheard through her earbuds between Jack and her father.

She tries to picture Jack's face when he came home from summer camp that year, but nothing comes to mind other than her recent, Boxing Day memories of his face turned towards her, jaw clenching and unclenching, eyes resting briefly on her before turning to look away. *You think I felt like talking to them? Breaking their little bubble?*

Tonight, Sophie has two dreams in which the baby is a presence, with a face and body she can see and touch. In the first dream, the baby, a girl, slips out of her hands in an above-ground pool—like the jacuzzi in her mother's water-birth photos. Sophie is startled by the ease with which the baby slips away. A simple letting go, a lack of tension in the arm, the viscosity of skin on skin. The baby becomes an aquatic creature, diving down, down. The baby is nowhere. Then, as if Sophie's waking self takes charge of the dream, she goes under-water to find the baby, brings it to the surface and starts giving it mouth-to-mouth, the way she once learned in swimming lessons.

She wakes, sweaty and panting, and grasps onto Tim's arm. His immobile, sleep-sodden body helps her to slow her breathing. He mutters, shifts, puts his arm a bit too heavily across her belly, so she turns with her back to his torso, allows his warmth to envelop her while her breathing gradually calms and her heart returns to normal. But it takes her a while to go back to sleep. Faces crowd her mind: Bill, when she told him and Nathan about the baby. Tim, when the election results came in. Jack's face. Online faces—refugees, trau-matized soldiers returning from war. Smiling, deer-in-the-headlights faces of fashion models and actresses at red carpet events. Smug faces of political pundits and the alpha males of the current Washington shit-show. What goes on beneath the surface of that weird display of human behaviour,? If she has been so blind to the suffering of her own brother, what else has she missed?

Then, for some reason, she remembers the face of that nice waiter, Fred, who helped her after she nearly drowned, and of the doctor she later saw, whose calm, appraising gaze was not unlike the face of Anne, when they talked about the baby in Anne and Nathan's living room yesterday. In the early hours of the morning, she slips into a second dream, which fills her mind with sunshine. She has just given birth in the sand dunes, on the beach in Nova Scotia. In the dream, she squats to give birth, like the woman in the home video, pulling the baby out from between her thighs with her own hands. It's a painless experience. The baby comes out looking perfect and at home, its face the delicate creamy colour of brown eggshell, its eyes closed, its breath peaceful. She decides to cover the baby up to its neck with sand to keep it warm—the way children on the beach bury each other for fun.

When she wakes from this dream, she can't remember if the baby was a boy or a girl. What stays with her is the serenity of its face, her own calm deliberate movements of scooping the sand over its naked body, the warm wind and the sound of the sea.

Alone in the apartment while Tim rehearses with the band for a New Year's Eve gig, Sophie pulls up Nathan's number on her phone. His landline, not his cell. She is hoping to reach Anne, not him.

She closes her eyes briefly when she hears Anne's voice.

"Sophie… How nice to hear from you! That was a lovely visit the other day. Did you need to speak to Nathan? He's just in his office."

"No, I…" she says quickly. "Actually, it's you I want to talk to, Anne. I wonder if you have a minute?"

"Sure?"

Sophie hears a slight wariness in Anne's voice.

"I kind of want to brainstorm about something," she says.

Brainstorm, she thinks. An apt word for what she has been feeling, but probably the opposite of what she's looking for in this conversation.

"I loved our visit, too," she says. "Especially all the talk about birth and babies…"

Anne laughs. "Well, that's not surprising. Babies must be uppermost in your mind right now."

"I know this sounds weird, but when we were talking about plans for the birth, I realized that I can't picture it here in New York." She closes her eyes again and sees the birthing center. Nothing wrong with it, really—the baby photos on the wall, the white-sneakered, heavy-set nurse who gave them the tour. "I'm seriously considering going elsewhere," she says.

"Home to your parents' place, you mean?" says Anne.

God no, she thinks.

"Further afield than that," she says. "I'd like to examine all of my options. I wonder if your friend who had a home birth in Nova Scotia would be interested in chatting with me."

Okay. She has said it. Maybe a bit too quickly. But at least Anne knows she's not asking for any Nathan or career-related favors.

She hears Anne exhale.

"I can get you two in touch," she says, her voice its usual level calm. "I bet Mary Ellen would love to correspond with you. Mothers always enjoy sharing their experiences. Of course, the way things are up there might be different from down here. You should probably also talk to some American midwives."

How can she make this sound rational, not crazy?

"Tim and I talked to some midwives at the birthing center," she says. "I'm just not sure…I think a home birth might be what I'm looking for."

"And how does Tim feel about that?"

Sophie remembers Tim's intelligent and conscientious questions at the birthing center tour. Afterwards, the act of filling out the paperwork made him seem more confident, reassured in some way, while she felt more nervous and at sea.

"I'm still just trying to formulate all of this to myself, to be honest," she says. "I haven't even talked to my doctor about it. I may change my mind but, as you can imagine, it's feeling urgent to come to a decision. And sometimes when I'm in that place, I just have to follow my intuition."

"Okay, that makes sense," says Anne, caution audibly returning to her voice.

"You may think I'm crazy, Anne," Sophie says, "but Nova Scotia is still on my mind, and the experience I had up there. I keep thinking about that beach."

Anne's voice, when she answers, is quieter, as if she's in the room with Sophie, sitting beside her, maybe even holding her hand.

"Thinking about it in what way?" she asks.

"I had a dream the other night that I gave birth on the beach," says Sophie. "Obviously," she tries for a laugh, "that option's out, unless I move to Hawaii or some place. But it just seems like my subconscious is telling me something, and the experience I had in Nova Scotia plays into it."

Again, there is a pause. But when Anne answers, her voice has not lost its intimacy or warmth. She's speaking more slowly though, as if carefully choosing her words.

"Wow," she says. "Obviously, this is important to you in a way that only you can understand. When are you due, Sophie?"

"The end of April."

"So exciting," says Anne. "Only four months away."

"When we had lunch in October in the city…" says Sophie.

"Yes?"

"You made a generous offer to me, you said that Tim and I could use your cottage sometime for a vacation."

"Yes," Anne says again. "But Sophie, I was thinking about the summertime, when it's beautiful there. I've never spent a winter in Nova Scotia. Mary Ellen says the weather's like Massachusetts or Maine, only damper and messier. I'm not sure what you're planning but…"

"I'm not planning anything. Just thinking about my options. I'd like to talk to Mary Ellen's midwife."

"And to Tim, of course."

She may have a gentle touch, Sophie thinks, but she sure knows how to hit the nail on the head. A list of obstacles to this idea unrolls in her mind. Everything Tim will bring up when she suggests it.

"I just don't want to say anything until I know my own mind," she says. "Once I know what I want to do, I can figure out the reasons that will make sense to him."

She hears surprised laughter, and realizes how manipulative this must sound. She suddenly feels very young.

"That's one way to look at it," says Anne.

The next day she sits curled on the sofa, once more with her phone cradled in her palm, against her ear. What she notices most about the voice at the other end of the line is its slow, even tone, a slight drawl to her speech that sounds almost Southern, but without the Southern vowels. Claudine, the Nova Scotian midwife whose contact info Anne's friend Mary Ellen had emailed to Sophie last night, sounds like she's waiting for her words to come out. As if the words are already there and she's just choosing which ones to allow to swim through the distance between them. Words about working as a nurse in the north, about 'catching babies' as she puts it. About getting midwifery training and moving to Nova Scotia with her husband. She says she has attended both hospital and home births.

"I was a home birth," says Sophie. "Back in eighty-eight. My mom had me in a big tub on the back deck of our house."

"Well, she sounds remarkable," says Claudine. "Nice for you to have that in your background."

Sophie agrees.

"When I first started," Claudine continues, "a lot of my clients were having huge fights with their families. Most families were scared something would go badly wrong. People are more open to it these days, but still, it isn't for everyone. Your baby is fine and you're healthy?"

"Yes," says Sophie.

"And you're moving up here in the middle of all this?"

All of this? Sophie thinks, for one bizarre moment, that this woman has divined the craziness of the past few months in her life, the film, the election, the heartbreaking conversation with her brother at Christmas. But then she realizes Claudine just means the pregnancy.

"Sort of," she says. "I mean, it might not be a permanent move." God, she sounds like a flake. What kind of parent does this sensible woman think she will become?

"Well as a non-Canadian, there will be a fee you will have to pay, but there would be, anyway, for a home birth. I can email you information on that, as well as a medical history form."

"Yes, please do that, and I will talk some more with my partner."

Partner, a useless word. But she has to call him something. "Husband" is definitely out. "Boyfriend" sounds like they're in high school. She has to imply she has been discussing this with Tim, or this woman might think she's running away from a bad marriage. Sophie is pretty sure Anne's careful questions about Tim yesterday hid a barrel of speculation. She shifts restlessly, switching the phone to her other hand.

"Do you have any other questions about home birth?" asks Claudine's slow, even voice.

Sophie scrolls through a long list in her mind, and decides to go with the one that jumps to the top.

"This is going to sound clueless, but you don't give medication for pain, do you?"

"That doesn't sound clueless. If you are at home, we can't administer narcotics, but there are some things we can do to make you more comfortable. Obviously, having a baby is not a painless procedure."

"Right, of course."

She does feel clueless, though, and young, and cowardly and… not quite there, not quite in the moment. She is haunted by the notion that she's a shallow person, able to mimic the big moments of life, but unable to live them. How the hell is this acting body of hers supposed to split open and push an authentic, squalling, baby into the world?

On one level, the thought of picking up and leaving for Nova Scotia feels almost as blissful as when her feet finally touched bottom that day in the sea. But another part wonders what people will think. Her whole life seems to be about abandonment these days. She abandoned Tim to go to Nova Scotia. She abandoned Nathan and Bill's film. Now, she is thinking of abandoning the country and her family.

But she will not abandon Jack, a voice inside her protests. She cherishes a sudden fantasy of inviting her brother to come stay with her—maybe in Nova Scotia, maybe somewhere else, wherever life takes her and Tim and the baby. She imagines providing a real refuge and family warmth for him, because he might need it. Because she will do anything she can to make up for the blindness of her teen years. Although what Tim would say to all of that, she has no idea.

| 24 |

Snowflakes slowly feather down, occasionally landing at the base of Anne's kitchen window. On the fridge door, there is a reusable whiteboard calendar for the month of January. There's not much on it at the moment, no deadlines, since Nathan isn't working, and no appointments, since Rudy's caregivers are all on holiday. Anne thinks of the deadline imposed on Sophie by the baby—four months away. In Anne's life, four months can go by imperceptibly in a blur of sameness: household chores, appointments with Rudy, visits to her mother. But for Sophie, that time period will transform winter into spring, a fetus into an infant, a young woman into a mother.

Anne makes a stir fry for supper, the first meal of the week that does not involve Christmas leftovers. She considers telling Nathan about Sophie's request for the cottage when they sit down to eat, but instead they talk about when to take down the tree. January 6, says Anne. New Year's Day, says Nathan. They try to involve Rudy, who stares at his plate, chewing. Anne sympathizes. He should be hanging out with friends, making New Year's Eve plans, not being subjected to this middle-aged chit-chat.

Both Nathan and Rudy disappear to their respective rooms after supper. Anne resolves to broach the subject of Sophie's request at bedtime. But when she arrives at the bedroom door, she finds Nathan already under the blankets, asleep with the lights on, a discarded *New Yorker* magazine by his side, his arm flung over his eyes. She goes quietly into the adjoining bathroom to wash and undress, then slides in beside him. She reads briefly before finally closing her eyes.

The next morning, she waits until after breakfast, then, hovering on the threshold of his office door, she asks if he has a minute to talk. He swivels his chair away from the laptop to face her—the light from the computer screen a magnet which they both know is tugging at his peripheral vision.

In years past, she used to come and visit Nathan here, after Rudy was asleep. They would share whispered jokes or look at articles or posts from friends on Facebook, Anne sitting on Nathan's lap in the swivel chair. She even remembers having sex in here once—starting jammed up against the wall between two bookcases and finishing on the carpet.

Now, as she gives Nathan the bare bones of her phone conversation with Sophie, she watches his mouth tighten into thin line—ungenerous, even querulous, an old man's face. She tells him Sophie is interested in spending time at their cottage in Nova Scotia, and that she herself suggested this as a possibility back in the fall. She does not mention Sophie's dreams of Nova Scotia and babies in the sand.

"You didn't think this was something you should discuss with me, first?" Nathan says.

"That's exactly what I'm doing, now. I haven't given her a definitive answer."

"But you're saying you offered the place to her, back in the fall, without telling me?"

"That was ages ago, and it was just because she seemed so moved by the landscape. I didn't think she'd take me up on it. Also, I had no idea, at the time, that you were thinking of selling. Which," she adds, drawing a breath, "there is no point in doing until the spring anyway. Any realtor will tell you that." Before the topic of the house sale can lead the conversation astray, she says, "I think she's considering having the baby up there with Mary Ellen's midwife."

"What?"

"I know. It sounds kind of impulsive…"

Nathan's hand reaches over to close his laptop.

"Kind of? Why the heck can't she do this home birth thing here in New York?" he says. "What can she possibly want to go all the way up there for?"

Anne has been asking herself the same question. It seemed to her, when they talked, that Sophie was searching for motivation the way she would when playing a character. *Once I know my own mind, I can figure out the reasons that would make sense to Tim.* Anne knows that in the past, when unsure if a suggestion she's making is reasonable or wise, she has played similar games with Nathan. Choosing her moments to talk to him, choosing what to say, what not to say. Never giving the whole story, only those bits she thinks will be palatable. Being married does that to a person.

She moves into the room, pulls up a spare chair and sits on Nathan's right, facing his profile, because he has turned and is looking at the bulletin board on his wall. She wills him to look at her.

"Sophie feels drawn there," she says. "It's intuitive, not rational."

"You know… it's ironic," Nathan says. "Although I've practically given up on this film, I kind of thought, after they visited, that we might be able to figure things out for the future, delay shooting, make it work somehow, after… She seemed to be feeling better, getting her shit together."

"So, deciding to have a baby in your own way, and making that your priority instead of your career, is *not* getting your shit together?"

Nathan looks at her then, gives a slight, tight smile, bewilderment in his eyes. He is hurt, she can tell. She has brought "that" into the conversation, whatever "that" is. Her own childbirth history perhaps, or some kind of female-centered ethos that he feels excluded from. She stands up, suddenly restless. Nathan stands too.

"Do you know what I've been working on for the past few days?" he says. "I've been dredging up back-burner projects with procrastinating writers, looking for story editors to help them. I've been wracking my brains to come up with casting ideas for scripts that aren't even through their second draft yet. I've been scrolling through bios of potential replacements for Sophie in this film. I've been trying to bullshit my way through talks to investors, putting the right spin on all of this, making it sound like a minor delay, with a promise of even bigger returns at the end. And I've been occasionally taking a peek at our bank account, which, in case you haven't noticed, is not exactly growing."

"Of course, I've noticed. I'm not a financial illiterate," she says. But her annoyance is tempered by her awareness that she adds nothing to that bank account. Nothing she has earned, anyway. Her money is tied up, and off limits as far as Nathan is concerned.

Lately, instead of focusing on these practicalities, she has been wondering what it might be like to pick up and go somewhere. She has fantasized, sunlit and watered by Sophie's words, about getting away, instead of being the present partner that Nathan needs.

"It's stressful, all of this," she says. "But if we can try to talk about it without blaming Sophie? If you can try to separate all the worries this is causing you from her intentions?" She stops momentarily, then says: "I've noticed that if you give people the space they need, they're more likely to come back to you, in the end."

Nathan runs his hand through greying hair. "That all sounds great in a psychology textbook," he says.

The next day, to her surprise, he tells her to go ahead. Say yes. Do what she thinks is right. Anne is not sure if this is because she has gotten through to him, or because he has given up on getting through to her. She takes him at his word, though, emails Sophie to see if she still wants to use the cottage. When Sophie responds with a tentative yes, Anne feels an unusual surge of energy. Over the next few days, she gets in touch with Mary Ellen and Bob in Nova Scotia. She pays a cleaning company to overhaul the cottage, telling Nathan this is something they need to do anyway, if he wants to put it on the market.

As she makes these plans, memories of Nova Scotia keep coming back to her. Rudy digging in the pebbly sand behind the house, the feel of his toddler legs wrapped around her waist as she piggy backs him out into the shallow water, with his inflatable arm bands and goggles on. He never liked the feel of the silty sand, the seaweed lazily flicking his knees.

Whatever happens, whether they sell the cottage or not, she knows she will someday revisit Nova Scotia. This possibility shines in her mind, as if she's headed somewhere, moving towards something new and more light-filled than dark winter days in this landlocked town.

One day, at the mall for groceries, she passes a children's clothing shop and impulsively picks up a couple of sleepers for Sophie's baby, imagining herself presenting them to her. She also considers passing on Rudy's baby clothes as hand-me-downs. They sit, folded neatly, in a clear plastic storage bin in the attic, of no use to anyone now.

On her way to the mall exit, she sees a backpack on the sale rack of the luggage store. It's perfect for Rudy. On impulse, she buys it. She has stopped insisting that he go with her to buy his clothes or other needs, regardless of what the mental health literature says about life skills. As she gets out her debit card, she remembers taking small items home to Rudy's school-aged or toddler-sized self, when he was small enough to sweep up in her arms or take on her lap to comfort.

In the parking lot, a woman of her own age is walking with a teenage son. The kid is teasing his mother. He pulls the car keys out of her hands and dangles them, just out of reach. "What, don't you trust me?" he laughs. Eventually, he tosses them to her, saying "Mom, Mom," shaking his head and rolling his eyes. The woman, too, is laughing as she gets into the car.

Anne watches, smiling a little. Later, when she picks Rudy up from his day-program, she lightly ruffles his hair with her fingers, before pulling out of her parking space. She chats to him about her day, tells him about buying the baby clothes, and hands him the backpack.

"Hope you like it," she says, but does not wait for a response or try to meet his eye.

The New Year begins without any household celebration, but with the sound of fireworks coming from other parts of town. The noise starts early; perhaps people are testing their stock of explosives beforehand. She and Nathan sit in the living room with their respective laptops. Anne scrolls through healthy recipes and checks out plans for the Poughkeepsie women's march. She reads a chatty email from Mary Ellen in Nova Scotia. Attached are snapshots of Mary Ellen's children.

The sound of fireworks intensifies. Anne wonders how loud they are in Rudy's room, but she does not go to check on him. They are three people at stasis in their comfortable home, surrounded by the partying of others. She's grateful for this calm.

On her way to bed, she knocks on Rudy's door to say good night—a habit she has consciously decided to take up. When he opens the door, she kisses him the way she used to when he was little, but on the cheek instead of his forehead, which she can no longer reach flat-footed.

"Happy New Year," she says, ignoring his immobility and silence.

She is walking down the hall, thinking about who she is when she's with him, and who she wants to be, when she hears him say, "Happy New Year to you too."

| **25** |

ON NEW YEARS' DAY, SOPHIE anticipates that Tim will need to sleep in after his gig, so she makes a salad with avocados, putting the dressing beside it in the fridge, and mixes an omelette to be ready to throw in a heated pan once he emerges. When he finally gets up around noon, he eats the meal with relish. As he digs into a slice of the key lime pie she bought at a local bakery, she considers how to tell him that she has spent the past few days planning a completely different birth scenario from the one they have discussed. Predictably, just as when she told her parents about the baby, she finds herself blurting it all out like some kid, her voice strident and alien to her ears.

"I don't think the birthing centre option is going to work for me. I've been thinking about a home birth actually."

Tim's fork stops midway to his mouth.

"When did you decide this?" he says, carefully.

"I've been thinking about it for a while. And, you know, that conversation with Anne about that woman they know, their neighbour in Nova Scotia? It kind of solidified my feelings."

"The neighbour," he says confusedly. She realizes he probably wasn't even paying attention to an exchange that prompted her to make two phone calls.

"You know," she says, trying to keep from sounding impatient. "The friends of theirs who had a midwife-attended home birth. Anne was saying how quickly she recovered."

"So," says Tim. "Are you thinking of this woman in your hometown that your mom mentioned? I've got to say I'm surprised, Sophie. I thought the birth center was something we were both on board with. I didn't think you were planning to completely follow your mom's example on this."

Sophie's gut clenches. "Oh God. I'm not following my *mom's* example!"

Seeing the surprised confusion deepen in Tim's eyes, she tries to even out her tone. "I don't want to go home to have the baby. I was thinking of going to Nova Scotia."

"*What?*"

"Okay, I know this sounds weird," she prefaces in an even tone, still trying to banish the strident child she keeps channeling. "I've been thinking of Nova

Scotia ever since I got back. I really feel drawn to it, and… I got the number of the midwife from Anne's friend and called her yesterday morning."

"Weird? That sounds 'weird'? You are proposing to run off to *Nova Scotia* to have this baby?"

An echo of their conversation in August. *You have to go to* Nova Scotia *to get your creative juices flowing?*

"No…not run off…at least not on my own. I meant, run off with you… If you can't join me right away because of what's going on here, I'll understand. But I'm feeling like I have to get away. I can't explain it. The city, the politics, stuff is driving me crazy."

"So go stay with your parents for a few days. If you have to do this home birth thing, I suppose we could go with the midwife your mom recommended."

"That wouldn't be getting away," she says. "My family is one of the things I need some distance from."

Tim's eyebrows are raised in an exaggerated question mark.

"If we do this," she says, "we can wait until after the Women's March."

"What the? You think the *Women's March* is what I'm worried about right now?"

"Yes, um no…" Why *had* she brought that up? "I'm just talking about the timing, and also I want to say that I think it's great you've been so involved in the protests. I think it's too important to miss."

Sucky, and people-pleasing, she thinks. Going to a women's march to mollify her "boyfriend," the only word to use in that scenario. She's torn between laughing and crying.

"Sophie, if I understand you, we are not talking about a vacation here, we are talking about you leaving the country and having our kid in someone else's home, attended by a woman you've never met, for reasons you won't explain."

"You're right. I'm not explaining it. I can't, fully. I'm just… feeling like I have to get away," she says again.

She stares at the salt cellar on the table between them. Behind it, Tim's hand is toying with a teaspoon, letting it run through his fingers to fall gently on the tabletop, over and over. Something makes her reach over to stop this movement. She longs for there to be stillness between them, a stillness resembling peace.

"Why?" he says in a weary tone that, despite everything, she registers as slightly comic. Her long-suffering boyfriend. She takes her hand away.

"I just need to think," she says.

"I don't understand you," says Tim. "You need to think so you want to bury your pregnant ass in some Nova Scotia backwoods in the middle of the winter? What the fuck *are* you thinking, Sophie?"

"Their place isn't in the back woods. It's in a small town, quite near the main road. The nearest hospital is only a twenty-minute drive away, and I haven't decided for sure yet."

Has she not decided? Had she not decided when she called Anne after their visit? Had she not decided when she put on her most calm voice, in response to Anne's question: "How does Tim feel about this idea?" When she took down details about the midwife, the nearest neighbours? Had her body not decided when the thought of that beach, that landscape, made her suddenly relax, the wheeling images in her mind suddenly slow to a halt?

She knows he is right in many ways. This is crazy. She knows that Nova Scotia in the winter will not be anything like the peaceful, sunny haven that enveloped her after her encounter with the sea. She knows she is running away, instead of doing what she's supposed to be doing—planning her future, thinking long term, carrying her baby towards something stable and safe. Yet, nothing feels stable or safe. Not New York, not her career, not her family, not even Tim, the person she would most like to be at one with.

"Obviously, you're gonna make this decision regardless of what I think," he says.

"Tim, it isn't that crazy. The midwife, Claudine, sounds amazing, and Anne's friend had her for all three of her children…"

"And there aren't any competent midwives in all of New York? No decent birthing centres? No *sane* options?"

"This is a sane option. I'm not going into this blind. I'm not going to put my health or the baby's safety at risk."

"Flying is always a risk," Tim says.

This coming from someone who will hop on a plane at a moment's notice if it means a paid gig.

"I'm only six months along," she says, trying to keep her voice calm. "People fly places all the time at that point in their pregnancies." Her voice rises in spite of herself: "I bet if this were some tour you wanted me to go on with you, you wouldn't be complaining." She regrets this as soon as it's out. Notices the beat of silence that follows.

"I wouldn't bother asking you because I know what the answer would be. Sophie gets what Sophie wants."

How did they arrive here? To this place she thought they had left behind months ago? And his implication, that she's a spoiled brat with no empathy, infuriates her, hardens her resolve. There is something about the way he's looking at her that reminds her of Bill.

Fuck it, she thinks.

Then fear washes over her. Is he right? *Is* she spoiled? Selfish? She was oblivious to Jack's pain when they were kids. She readily accepted the attention lavished on her acting career by her mother, without noticing Jack being shortchanged. Despite her guilt over inconveniencing Nathan, she hardly thought of Bill and his screenplay when she left the film. She has been so wrapped up in thoughts about this birth that she has hardly planned for afterwards, for how she will care for this baby. And now, she is distressing Tim with her wild ideas. Whatever her intentions, there will always be some way she messes up, every move she makes to deflect harm from herself has a way of ricocheting back to hurt someone else.

She tries, yet again, to focus on her breathing: in two, out two, in three, out four.

"That's not what this is about," she says. "Me getting what I want and not giving a shit about anyone else."

Tim is silent.

"Could you just entertain the possibility that this might be a really wonderful thing? A chance for us both to get away and focus on what's important? Each other? Becoming parents for the first time?"

"You think I don't know what's important? You haven't noticed that I'm out there trying to change things? You don't realize that has to do with this kid that's on the way?"

Although she's touched by this sentiment, she can't help thinking there must be more direct ways of preparing for the baby's future, like finding a regular gig to pad their dwindling bank account. But she's immediately ashamed of this thought, knowing she has recently jettisoned her main source of income.

"This winter I was planning," he says, as if reading her mind, "to see if there is any more work at NYU, even just music theory tutoring, and then getting back to the solo album, start sending out demo tracks, and getting some bookings for the summer." His voice is quieter now, almost as if he is speaking to himself. "I told the band today that I don't want to tour any time before that, because of the baby."

Sophie exhales. They are finally on some kind of common ground, have found their footing, if tenuously, in order to continue this conversation without doing irreparable damage.

"Nova Scotia would be the perfect place for you to work on the solo album, away from distractions. And maybe you could offer online theory help to Chris's students at NYU? I'm sure we can set up a spot in the house to make that work. And, I never told you, but I have been talking to Patty about some voice work. I know Farid has done that when things are slow. Patty suggested I do a demo reel, and I thought, you know, you could help me with that.”

“And what about paying the midwife, and the trip up there?”

“I could withdraw some money from my *Liza* savings. It’s not as if I’ll never work again.”

There is a brief silence.

“Yeah well, financial planning is not my strong suit,” he says. “I’ll just have to keep my ass in gear. Keep working on booking the band. Maybe talk to Samara. See if she knows of any session gigs I can do remotely.”

In the downturn of his gaze, Sophie sees that he too is on unsure footing, that the material practicalities of parenthood are as daunting to him as they are to her.

“This is kind of off topic,” she says, “but I’ve been thinking that if we have the kid in Canada, it could be a dual citizen. Kind of cool.”

He’s looking at her with that speculative gaze again. She can feel the distance between them re-establishing itself. When he speaks, there is a dangerous coldness in his voice.

“Are you saying that instead of making a change here, we should just run away? Become Canadians?”

“What? No! Of course not!”

Her feeling of panic returns, and with it, the nausea which she thought she was finally free of. “Why does everything have to be so black and white with you? Why do you have to put words in my mouth? All I’m saying is that it would be good for a kid to have more than one option in life! For the future, for education and stuff like that.”

“We’re Americans, Sophie! My parents are American, my whole family is American.”

“Did I say we weren’t?”

“And speaking of family,” he continues as if he hasn’t heard, “What are *my* parents going to say about all this? Having the kid in a birth centre is radical enough for them. Just wait till I tell them you’re planning to abscond to another country and have the kid in a hot tub like your mom or some fucking thing.”

Stung, she feels a weird pull of loyalty towards her family, even now when she wants to get away. Hasn’t Tim always said she was too hard on her mother? Something flips over inside her mind, almost like the baby when it’s restless.

“For fuck’s sake! Of course, pleasing both our families is top on my list of priorities right now. Here’s a thought. I’ll tell my mother I am having a home birth in a water tub with a shamanic healer, and I have to go up there because I was told to, by my spirit guide. You tell your parents that we’ve found a top-notch obstetrician who just happens to practice in Canada, and you could add for good measure: 'What Sophie wants, Sophie gets.' That should cover all the bases."

Amazingly, she sees the corners of Tim's mouth twitch.

"You're crazy, you know that?" he says.

"Yeah, I know that. And if I forget, I guess you're there to remind me."

"Damn straight."

She can finally risk meeting his eyes, and when she does, they are the eyes she knows.

| 26 |

Sᴏᴘʜɪᴇ clutches her homemade sign *(This is what feminism looks like)* and thinks: I am out of here. I am where I'm supposed to be. She wraps her other arm around her belly—shielding it from the sharp corners of the placards jutting into the aisle of the subway car. The slogans and signs surrounding her both inspire and intimidate. *Pussy bites back… I can't believe we're still having to protest this shit.* (This last one is held by a formidable looking woman with white upswept hair, who must be at least eighty.)

Sophie has spent the past few weeks planning her move to Nova Scotia. Last week, a bureaucratic hassle over getting her medical records released by her doctor's office kindled a slow fire of outrage within her. It's *my* body, she repeated to herself, *my* baby. But this mantra did nothing to empower her when she told her mother of her plans over the phone. In the silence that followed, Sophie thought she could hear something quietly rupturing—a membrane, a cord. Then the questions came. *When is all this happening? How long do you plan to be there? What do Tim's parents think?* Not, Sophie noticed, *Why?*

At her back, Tim's body shields her from the crush as they are propelled through the opening train doors and upstairs onto the street. They are supposed to meet Samara and Farid at Greenacre Park, along with Paul and Miranda, Tim's NYU friends who have been on parental leave. But a policeman standing by a barricade of yellow tape tells them they have to move on to 2ⁿᵈ Avenue.

"Shit," says Tim starting to text furiously, until Samara appears holding a placard with a purple background and hands drawn on it. The three words— "Love, Sanity, Compassion"—float above the hands as though written in the night sky. Samara's long black hair is tucked behind her ears. Delicate beaded earrings hang from her lobes. Sophie, bundled in her wool sweater-coat, carrying her monochromatic sign, feels dowdy by comparison, then immediately thinks: What am I comparing myself to her for? This is not what feminism looks like.

"I've let everyone know the meeting point's changed," Samara says. "Apparently no one can get the livestream, the carriers are all overloaded. We're rocking the planet, guys!"

And when they get to 2nd Avenue, closed to traffic and streaming with bodies—male, female, old and young—Sophie does feel a rock concert vibe. The baby does a kicking and spinning maneuver within her. Bill, with all his crap about "the left half of American idiocy" should see this.

Paul and Miranda meet up with them. The baby, a wool hatted, indefinable bundle, is strapped to Miranda's belly. At the same time, Sophie sees Farid swimming through the crowd towards them and smiles. Her affection for him is untinged by the guilt and worry that colour thoughts of her real brother.

Farid hugs her, feels the bump through her coat and says, "We've grown a bit since that Halloween party."

"That's the way it works," Sophie says.

"Yeah. But it's like, bizarre, in the flesh. Anyway, I kind of forgot. Have a lot on my mind…"

"Oh?"

"Benny and I are getting married."

"Wow! Congratulations!"

"THIS IS WHAT DEMOCRACY LOOKS LIKE!" the crowd around them chants. Tim brandishes his sign *(Make America Think Again)* over his head like a tomahawk.

"Where's Benny?" she asks Farid.

"Had to work," says Farid. "I think he would have chickened out anyway. He can't handle this kind of thing. It makes him feel claustrophobic. Best sign idea he could come up with was, 'I'm not a sign guy, but Geez…'"

As Sophie starts to laugh, a woman in the crowd with a *Pussy Bites Back* poster yells, "I DON'T WANT YOUR TINY HANDS/ANYWHERE NEAR MY UNDERPANTS!". There are scattered giggles. Taking up the call with a chorus of female voices, Sophie feels like she's back in junior high.

"I am so glad you're here!" she says in Farid's ear, after a few more minutes of edging forward.

"Me too," he answers. "Kind of a survival impulse. Things are getting pretty fucked. Benny and I are scared to hold hands in public, here in New York, for Christ's sake. All the racist and homophobic cockroaches coming out of the woodwork."

"RACIST, SEXIST, ANTI-GAY, DONALD TRUMP, GO AWAY!" yells Samara, who is behind and to the right. Sophie wonders if she has been listening. She wants to say to Farid: "It's going to work out. Look at all these people. Feel the love," or something like that. The kind of thing Samara would say. The kind of thing Samara probably does say, when she and Farid are alone. Sophie wonders how much older than Farid Samara is. She has never asked.

An image of Jack, striding ahead of her on Boxing Day, shoulders hunched against the wind, passes through her mind. He had expressed no interest in coming to the march when she invited him. Now, a slow, distant ache in her heart quietly makes itself known, in the background, beneath the analgesic and contagious euphoria of the crowd.

But the sun shines on, warming her shoulders through her wool coat. Amazing weather for January. Today, she will not speculate on apocalyptic reasons for unseasonable warmth. She links her arm through Farid's, and they catch up to Tim. For a while, she becomes part of an odd, lumbering threesome. Tim on her left side, with his arm around her, and Farid attached to her elbow on the right. Tim and Farid break the threesome to raise their phones over their heads, trying to snap a picture of the crowd behind. Farid is the first one to manage it, and when Sophie looks, she sees people stretching back for blocks and blocks. Tim, checking his own phone, makes a joyful whoop— part wolf howl and part laughter. The ache in Sophie's heart eases. In that moment, she loves Tim unreservedly. She would like to keep marching by his side forever.

After what seems like hours, they have only moved forward a few blocks. Miranda passes around small bites of peanut butter sandwich, for which Sophie is grateful. There is a container of trail mix in her own pocket, but the bread and oily peanut butter feel more satisfying.

Her sign awkwardly stuffed under one arm, she's wiping the peanut butter off her fingers with a tissue when Tim points to a toddler riding his father's shoulders, sporting a cardboard sign taped to his belly that says *I still need naps but I stay woke.*

"HEY HEY! HO HO! GENDER VIOLENCE HAS GOT TO GO!" rolls through the crowd towards them.

At once, Sophie feels a knife-like pain in her crotch. Her doctor has assured her this is normal. Lightning pain—appropriately named—her pelvic ligaments stretching to prepare for the big event. She breathes cautiously, works on relaxing down there. On the other side of Tim, Paul and Miranda's baby is being transferred, in its sling, from its mother's to its father's belly. It wails in protest. After they have shuffled a few more feet, Sophie feels a treacherous pressure in her bladder, and says reluctantly into Tim's ear, "I have to pee."

Before Tim can answer, Paul comes over. The baby hangs immobile on his belly now, out cold. "What say we cheat?" he says.

"Cheat?" says Tim.

"Yeah, take a shortcut. We could head west on Fiftieth to Fifth Avenue, and then north to Trump Tower to join the end of the march. "The baby is just about done in."

Sophie sends a silent prayer of thanks to the baby. After chanting, WATER IS LIFE! SCIENCE IS REAL, the pressure in her bladder becomes more urgent, and a charley horse starts in her right calf. Trying to ignore it as they make their way along the comparatively deserted 50th Street, she tells Farid about quitting the film.

"Even though I think I made the right call, I feel really guilty when it comes to Nathan," she says. "He's been so nice about it. Bill, on the other hand…" She tells him about the phone call, doing a surreptitious dance to relieve the charley horse, standing on one leg and shaking her foot back and forth. "To be honest," she adds, "I think I need a break from acting. Not sure I need this shit—all the off-set drama."

Farid glances over at her skeptically, catching the dance.

"We both need that shit, Sophie. It may not be a replacement for therapy, but when I'm not acting, my personal life gets so fucked over, I have to run for cover. Talk about drama."

She considers this, reviewing the last few months of her life, and tries to put weight back on her right foot.

"We're taking another detour, on Third Street to a Bagel shop," says Tim, after conferring with Paul and Miranda.

"Yeah," says Paul, gesturing to the baby who still hangs immobile on his chest. "Need to find a bathroom. This guy's getting kinda soggy."

A new mood of hilarity takes over. Sophie's swollen bladder reminds her of drunken nights on the town with Farid in L.A., and here in Manhattan on nights off from their *Glass Menagerie* run. When they get to the Bagel shop, she makes her way to the bathroom stall and squats in relieved ecstasy over the toilet without letting her bum touch the seat. The others, once she's joined them, have ordered bagels to go round.

Later, her bladder comfortably empty and her belly sated by a bagel and cream cheese, she decides that life is good. She and Miranda and the baby sit in the only chairs left, while the others hover, munching. Fragments of conversation between Tim and Paul float above their heads: *And what about Chris*, Tim is saying. *Did he ever make it to Europe? Always loved playing with that guy, but Jesus, he could suck oxygen from the room. Remember his bee-bop faze?*

Farid and Samara stand slightly apart, out of earshot, and Sophie gets up to join them.

"Did Tim tell you about our plans to go to Nova Scotia?" she says.

"Just as long as we don't lose you guys up there forever," Samara says, putting her hand on Sophie's arm.

"What the?" says Farid, his mystified expression reminding Sophie uncomfortably of Tim on New Year's Day. "Nova Scotia? When?"

"My flight leaves tomorrow. Tim is finishing up some NYU work for Paul, and then he'll drive up in a couple of weeks."

"And it sounds like you have an awesome place to stay, right on the water," says Samara.

"Right on the water in Nova Scotia in January?" says Farid.

As she tries to verbalize her reasons for leaving, explaining about the cottage and midwife, Samara nods encouragingly, but that might just be due to today's female solidarity vibe. On the other hand, Farid's urban, beautifully groomed face takes on deeper and deeper layers of astonishment, until Sophie starts to laugh.

"Okay, so maybe I'm crazy," she says. "Maybe I'm fucking my life over with drama because I'm not acting."

"You said it, not me," he croaks out. "Is your next project about a woman who gets lost in the Canadian wilderness and gives birth near an iceberg?"

"It's Nova Scotia, not the far north. The weather's actually warmer than here in the winter, usually."

"So you're there until the spring?"

"Yup, planning to come back when the baby's about a month old." A shiver of excitement runs through her as she says this, accompanied by a stirring in her womb, as if its inhabitant knows it's being talked about.

Tim, she notices, is making his way over to the trash bin with everyone's bagel wrappers, and Paul is putting on his coat. Walking back to Miranda's booth to retrieve her own coat, Sophie sees Miranda's baby is awake and bright-eyed, looking around the shop from the vantage point of his mother's lap. A magnetic force draws Sophie to him. She reaches out her arms and says, "Want me to hold him while you put your coat on?"

The baby's weight is hardly more than that of Blackie, her childhood cat, and when she brings him close to her body, she notices his astonishing warmth and softness. Holding him somewhat awkwardly, next to her belly bump, she makes sure he can see his mother the whole time. He doesn't seem to mind, and after a moment, she can't resist stroking the skin of his tiny hands and looking into his eyes, which she finds mesmerizing.

"You'll have your own soon," smiles Miranda, after taking him back. "Just you wait. It can be crazy at times, but I can't imagine him not being here."

As they leave the shop and head towards Trump Tower, more signs come into view. WELCOME REFUGEES, says one held by a plump fiftyish woman.

YOU'LL DIE OF OLD AGE. I'LL DIE OF CLIMATE CHANGE! reads another, held by high-school-aged girl with enviable long wavy red hair.

On the TV screen of Sophie's mind, unbidden catastrophic images appear— desperate-eyed refugees, children's bodies buried in white rubble or washed up on Turkish beaches. Plastic islands rising from the sea, cities of garbage emerging from South American slums, commuters donning masks during smog alerts. Dead songbirds falling from the sky.

She does her best to laugh with everyone else as a large banner is lifted up depicting a giant presidential tweet: *Very small march. Sad.*

By four-thirty, they agree to call it a day. Paul and Miranda head to Brooklyn for pizza, but Farid, Samara, Tim and Sophie go to a restaurant in the Time Warner Center where Farid's boyfriend works. Benny is just finishing his shift, and joins them at their table after serving them appetizers—all they can afford on the menu.

"I'm so envious you got to march," he says. Farid rolls his eyes at Sophie, without anyone else noticing.

"And look at you, Sophie!" he continues. "I had no idea."

Sophie dips her beets (appetizer #2, "Ruby and Golden beet salad") into her creamed goat cheese, and takes little bites to make the food last.

"I only started to show about a month ago," she says.

"You wear it well."

"Thanks." She watches through the window as, four storeys below, people leave the march, many of them weaving their signs between the rails of the barriers around Trump Tower.

"Look at them all!" says Benny. "Pretty shitty optics for the 'Manhattan Whitehouse'. Shitehouse is more like it."

By the time they head out onto the street into the rapidly chilling night air, Sophie is aware that the march is truly over. Blissed out by the warm memory of the restaurant's plush seat under her tired bum and thighs, she's too content to join in with much fervour when her companions groan as police clear away the signs from the barriers in front of Trump Tower.

She and Tim stay a while longer than the others, but eventually, by tacit agreement, they start to move off. Looking back, she sees the police removing the last of the signs and the sidewalk, littered with discarded pamphlets, white in the evening light and fluttering in the wind like the dead songbirds still in her mind.

| 27 |

It's the dying bird dream—back again. After the strangely soothing dream he had a couple of weeks ago in which he was convinced he saw his Great Aunt Lucy, Fred thought he was done with wounded animal nightmares for good. He has not told anyone about the Lucy dream, does not want to face the skepticism and fear in his mother's eyes, or hear Aunt Flo's speculations about spirits and omens, which, in his present state, seem too pat, too obvious somehow.

But he would like to recapture the floating feeling that new but familiar face brought him. Way better than what the dying bird dream leaves in its wake—Jamie ambushing his thoughts at 3 AM. He remembers, with new clarity, packing his things in the early hours of the morning of that last night, Jamie pale and sweaty, saying 'It's okay…It's okay. Don't go.' Seeing his own bottled-up rage reflected on the face of the man who had once been his lover, companion and soul mate. "What is *wrong* with you man?" Jamie had yelled. "What's your problem, anyway?"

In this unlit room with its narrow twin bed, he's not surprised to meet, along with the ghost of his ex, his old friend, worry, shouting into his brain like a chorus of harpies. Not enough money in the bank, not enough hours in the café. Not enough tips at the resort to justify his gas expenses. What is he doing, waiting on tables at his age?

Not enough meaning and connection in his life.

Coming home to an empty apartment. Avoiding any kind of nightlife. Jamie's name still hanging in the air like an invisible speech bubble when he meets old friends. And he is still unable to imagine starting up with anyone new. That song from his mother's old seventies Motown record album, "I'll Never Fall in Love Again," pops into his mind, bringing with it memories of his mother working in the basement office, responding to Fred's complaints about school by saying, "If I could go back then and do what you kids are doing now." That damp basement where she strived so hard to cover up their family's crises and to improve herself, the same basement where she found his father.

Fred knows there are other reasons for his current drop in mental well-being. He has been consuming too much news—global warming, the reality shit-show of US politics. There are protest marches today, all over the world, even one here in Parade Square, which he should probably join. But he was offered a shift at the café, and couldn't afford to say no.

Yet another worry: If he doesn't get back to sleep, he will seem hungover at work, maybe screw up an order, maybe drop something. He can't force it though, still has no effective strategy for these insomniac nights. Books don't work. Screens make it worse. Journalling spirals him into the heart of the worry, leaving him trapped and gasping for air.

Going to the kitchen for a glass of water, he sees his sketchbook on the kitchen table, and takes it back to the bedroom. Holding it close to his chest, he climbs into bed and surveys the room. Curtains on the window that he has had since college. A slight gleam from the mirror reflecting the flash from the smoke detector in the hallway. Turning on the overhead light, he thinks, fuck circadian rhythms anyway. Something is brewing inside him that needs to come out.

He doesn't want to reproduce what is in front of him, map out the room, render its angles and shadows. Instead, he begins to draw the dying bird from his dream, grounded, but with wings uplifted, trying to shake free. As he works, he finds he's less interested in the emotional weight of its sickening spasms and the prickly metamorphosis. He focuses on the feathers, enjoying the way his hand feels making the curve of the animal's chest and beak. Without trying for anatomical correctness, he reaches for a suggestion of movement that struggles at the back of his mind, struggles to make its way through his hand and fingers and onto the page.

| 28 |

ON THE WALKWAY OVER the Hudson Bridge in Poughkeepsie, Anne is flanked by a somewhat anxious-looking elderly woman on her left, with a sign saying, *We shall Overcome*, and a smiling, fortyish Black man on her right with a megaphone and a sign saying *Black Lives Matter*. They have been told by the March organizers to march three abreast, and in a strange way, she feels protected by these people she doesn't even know. For a moment she is a child again, swinging between her parents' outstretched hands, walking on a trail somewhere, near Bard maybe, or along the Hudson, on some long-ago winter day like this.

The man beside her shouts into his megaphone, "*When women's rights are under attack, what do we do?*"

"*Stand up fight back!*" people yell.

She supposes being here today is fighting back. In real life, she has never fought for anything much.

Except for Rudy, says a steady and calm voice inside her head. Except for Rudy.

From the bridge, she can see the midday sun glinting on the river. If she squints her eyes to avoid the buildings on the far bank, focusing only on the purplish hills and the thin winter sun above them, she can imagine this valley as it used to be, over a century ago, in the stories of Washington Irving and Fenimore Cooper. Writers almost no one remembers now.

"*Donald Trump, you can't hide. We can see your sexist side!*" yells her companion with the megaphone. "*Donald Trump, you can't hide. We can see your racist side!*"

Here and there, fists are raised. The three-abreast plan has disintegrated, as people move at their own pace and overtake each other.

"They were predicting three thousand, but I think there are more than that," says the woman on Anne's right.

Anne smiles and keeps moving, adjusting her strides to the woman's. To their right, a young girl holds a sign that reads *I am made in my own image.* Below these words, she has photoshopped her face onto a poster of Rosie the Riveter from World War II. Anne can't count how many times she has seen that image. It's probably new to this girl. Better than Anne's own childhood role models: perfectly made up, energetic mothers in seventies sitcoms; idealized ladies in Dickens and Austen, embroidering and knitting by the fire.

Together we are stronger, reads another sign in her peripheral vision.

She would have liked Nathan to join her today, but she wasn't ready to leave Rudy alone, and bringing him would never work. The crowds and noise. When she told Nathan she planned to come, he looked up from his laptop and said, "Go, Anne. You need to do this."

Some people have already reached the other side of the river and are coming back. Anne shuts down her knee-jerk surge of grief at the sight of teens everywhere, smiling, cheering, taking selfies. She's at the halfway point of the bridge now. Among all the joyful and fist pumping teens, one girl catches her eye. Neatly dressed in a black quilted jacket almost identical to the one Anne is wearing, the girl is hatless, windblown, sign-less, and silent. Her coat is partially opened to reveal a sweatshirt on which Anne can make out the words "Stop the" before the rest of the sentence is hidden behind the zipper. She seems completely alone, a look of concentration on her face. Anne's heart goes out to the kid. She wonders what her story is, where her adults are.

Here, even on her day away from Rudy, she can't stop being a caregiver. Pathetic.

Is it her caregiver impulse really or the empathy she feels for the loneliness in the girl's eyes? Lonely. The word resounds surprisingly in her brain, a counter chant to the slogans being shouted around her. Her own loneliness calls to her, through the gentle, intelligent eyes of the woman by her side who is convinced they will overcome, and the easy camaraderie of the Black man with the megaphone. She has neglected the friendships she once used to value. All her personal expectations have been put on hold, sucked into the hole that is Rudy's illness.

And she and Nathan are like two people signaling to each other through a fog. The intense longing for love that used to wash over her like a tide in her younger years only comes occasionally now—when listens to romantic music or is startled by an erotic image in a piece of art. Usually when Nathan is away. There has to be something more than this, she thinks. There has to be something more than feeling like a spectator to every event she takes part in that doesn't involve her troubled son.

I am an intelligent woman, she thinks. I am not that old, yet.

At the end of the bridge, Anne turns, a few paces behind the elderly woman and the megaphone guy.

She should confide in someone, bear witness to the numbness that has slowly crept up on her over the years. She pictures Nathan, hunched over his computer, lifting his eyes to tell her she should go to the march. She thinks of all the times she has fought with Rudy on his bad days, when he refused to get out the door to his day program or an appointment. *You will get up right now or I will sit here beside you all day and we will do nothing else.* Is he thankful, or does he still hate her for that? She sees her mother at Christmas, fatigue pulling down the skin below her eyes as she struggles to make conversation about the latest happenings in her seniors complex. She feels a strange, barely uncontainable dread in the pit of her stomach.

There is a Dixieland band on the bridge, made up of white-haired trumpets, trombones, saxophones. Their smiling faces, grey beards and glasses have been reminding her of neighbours and relatives throughout the years she has lived in the Hudson River Valley. Suddenly, she notices that their enthusiastic rendition of "Down by the Riverside" has quieted, or perhaps it is just further away.

And another faint sound, a nasal, bland, generic melody, is coming from her pocket—the ringtone of her phone.

She pulls it out, sees Nathan's name, and is immediately on alert. The noise of the march fades into the background. She swipes her phone and puts it to her ear, thinking Rudy, Rudy, Rudy.

But when Nathan's voice comes on, it takes a moment for her to hear and understand.

"Anne," he says. "It's your mother."

Two hours later, Anne watches her mother's sunken face, half hidden by an oxygen mask, the mechanical rise and fall of her chest in rhythm with the life support machine. Her mother's torso and the top half of her scrawny, wrinkled arms are clad in a flower-patterned johnny shirt. She is as still and shrunken as the mummified ice man from Rudy's computer screen, and no more responsive.

A nurse comes in to check tubes and machinery. The nurse's movements are businesslike but also slow, like someone making a pass at housecleaning, when there is nothing else to do. She looks really young to Anne, in her twenties still—fresh, baby-faced complexion, blond hair in a short bob.

"Are you sure she's not cold?" Anne says, then wonders if the nurse can hear her.

She moves closer to the bed and gently pulls the turned-down sheet from under her mother's tiny forearms to cover what she can. The words of the doctor—hemorrhagic stroke, quite significant...we will see—replay in her mind on a continuous loop.

"Feel free to go get some sleep," says the nurse. "We'll call you if there is any change."

"Thank you," says Anne, without moving.

On her phone is a text from Nathan, who has gone home to be with Rudy. He suggests she come home too, and he offers to bring her back in the morning.

There is no way to know, she thinks, if it makes a difference, being here. She has heard stories of comatose people being completely aware of what is going on around them, the voices, the pings of monitors, the touch of a hand.

Her father's death was so different from this, shocking and sudden, even though they all knew the risk was there when he went in for heart surgery.

A part of Anne's mind observes that she is drawing parallels, as if this is a fait accompli. Is it possible, she wonders, that her mother is aware of these thoughts she's having, of being written out of the land of the living, sent elsewhere? Anne's father would have called that nonsense, would have told her not to be morbid. His death was appropriate to his personality—sudden, no grey areas. Rudy had been only one year old then, and a source of constant distraction for Anne. Her status as Rudy's mother was an anchor in her life, a simple set of tasks and a daily rhythm that kept chaos and angst at bay.

Even in the past few years, when motherhood has been an instigator of chaos and angst, that daily rhythm has given her the strength to see it through.

When she came here, directly from the Women's March, Nathan met her in the corridor. There was no Rudy in sight. He's fine, Nathan told her. Discombobulated by it all but nothing else. There was a moment of silence after the words, 'nothing else.'

"It was his choice to stay home," Nathan said. "But I think that's mostly because he doesn't want to get in the way."

Get in the way, Anne thinks now. Poor kid. But this is a passing moment of compassion only, the kind she might feel for any adolescent, not one of the punch-in-the-chest stabs of anguish she usually feels for Rudy.

Another hour, and her mother does not move. Nathan comes into the room, which disorients her for a moment. She thought he was home, and in her mind, home seems like another country, at least a plane ride away instead of twenty-minutes on country roads.

"Let's go get some sleep, Anne. I'll drive you."

"My car is in the parking lot."

He shrugs. "It can stay there overnight. I don't think anyone's checking."

There are only a few hours until morning anyway, so she agrees, sits in the passenger seat of his car, encapsulated by winter darkness on the drive home. Later, she lies, awake or dozing, she's not sure which, by Nathan's side. Nathan breathes deeply, snores, breathes deeply again. In Anne's conscious and unconscious mind, her mother's face and bony arms on the hospital bed swim in and out of focus. Hospital corridors with painted arrows and signs, white and pastel clad nurses, blend with the faces in the crowd of the Women's March. It's a relief to see a soft glow in the sky outside her window, observe the slow shuffle of dawn towards full daylight.

They drop Rudy at his day program at the entrance to the mental health ward, on their way to the ICU. She sees him stop in front of the doors to talk to a blond, beefy young guy smoking a cigarette. Anne has seen the smoking guy's face before. Mark, she thinks, or Mike. She remembers, a month or two ago, asking Rudy who he was, because he had made her laugh. It was Day One of a yoga class that Anne had insisted Rudy try, thinking it might loosen up his stiff walk, improve his sleep. When she came to pick Rudy up, Mike was right in front of her as she stepped out of the elevator, lying on the polished floor like an overturned beetle, waving his feet in the air in the happy baby pose, saying, "Man this feels *good*." The nurses stepped around him with slight smiles on their faces. For one moment, the ward had lost its air of cautious calm, felt like a street corner or a high school cafeteria.

Now, Anne wonders briefly what Rudy is saying to Mike, if he might be sharing what is happening with his grandmother. He has not been protesting about going to the program lately, even though mornings are still not his best time. She wonders if it's possible that Rudy has a friend.

Nathan backs the car up and drives to the emergency entrance. Once they have entered the ICU, all thoughts of Rudy vanish. Her mother is still a life-sized rag doll. All the machines in the world can't pump enough oxygen into her to bring her back to life. Anne supposes she could sit by her bedside and pray, if she believed in anything resembling a benevolent God. Or she could close her eyes and meditate, hoping to send 'healing thoughts,' if she believed there was anyone in there to receive those thoughts. She could have brought flowers to brighten the room, but that would only make a difference to her and the nurses, not to her mother.

She sits in the thoughtfully provided chair near the bed, touches the papery skin on her mother's hand, considers getting a book to read from the gift shop in the hospital lobby or doing an online crossword puzzle, but instead finds a focal point to stare at, the gleam of metal under the bedside table that reflects the window-light of the wintry sun.

Nathan sits with her for a while, but she can feel a restless energy start to build. He needs to solve catastrophic events, not observe them as they slowly unroll. She knows this about him, knows this is what makes him good at what he does. It also made him helpful in the midst of crises with Rudy, even if he was absent for a lot of the aftermath.

"My car's here, remember?" she says. "I'm okay to hang out on my own for a bit."

"What about food? I can get you something from the cafeteria or go for takeout."

"The cafeteria's fine. Whatever you think."

She sees him make an effort to not move too quickly, tiptoeing to the door, his shoulders relaxing. He comes back a few minutes later with a tuna sandwich and an apple. "Best I could do," he says. "You'll call me if anything changes, right?"

"Right," she says, accepting his kiss on her cheek, his hand giving her hand a squeeze, as if he is attempting to pump blood and warmth back into her body, just as the life-support machine pumps air into her mother's.

In the afternoon, standing by the window looking out over the parking lot, she hears the attending physician come in. He pulls a chair up beside her mother's bed and asks Anne to sit down. She does so, first removing the half-eaten sandwich sitting on the seat in its clear plastic container, slightly embarrassed as she stuffs it into her handbag. The doctor pulls a second chair up and sits beside her. He is a middle-aged man with the customary hospital five-o'clock shadow on his chin. Trim and fit-looking, though. Probably jogs on his off time, she thinks.

"I'd like to call in a neurologist to take a look at your mother," he says.

"Okay…" she says.

"He'll perform a series of tests to see how responsive she is."

Anne can think of nothing to say to this.

"Depending on the results," he continues, "we'll repeat the tests in six hours' time."

She has the feeling that he's following a memorized script, one he has said many times before. Why six hours?

"Yesterday we spoke about how the bleed in your mother's brain is too deep to operate. So, her prognosis does not look good. We feel she has slipped into a deeper level of unconsciousness."

Deeper than what? Anne thinks.

"If your mother is unresponsive to all the tests, we wait and repeat them, just in case that unresponsiveness has to do with other factors. But with initial negative responses, I usually warn families to prepare themselves to start thinking about how long to keep their loved one on life support."

Loved one, she thinks.

"I see," she says. This is an expression she almost never uses. An all-encompassing, non-committal affirmative. It's an expression her mother used to use, she realizes, whenever she disapproved slightly of a tactless or over-sharing remark from someone in the room.

Anne supposes she should call Nathan. This development represents change, if not the kind of change he meant. Then again, maybe this is the kind of change he meant.

"When…" she begins.

"The neurologist can be here in half an hour," says the doctor, "and you are welcome to be present for his exam."

She should call and tell Nathan that this is probably it, the 'it' looming large in her mind, swollen with mystery. He will be picking Rudy up in an hour anyway. Maybe best to wait and see what the tests reveal… Her reluctance to call has something to do with the action of holding the phone to her ear, of opening her mouth to answer questions, to make herself understood, the way this doctor, who is no doubt a decent guy, is trying to make himself understood.

In the time that elapses between the doctor leaving the room and the neurologist's arrival, the living, sentient being that used to be her mother begins to haunt Anne. She remembers her mother making trays of asparagus rolls to share with the faculty and graduate students at English Department Functions; mixing the softened and chopped vegetable with mayonnaise in a pale blue bowl and letting it chill in the fridge. Rolling the sliced bread flat with a rolling pin and spreading on the asparagus mixture, then slicing the rolls into elegant little bite-sized morsels, leaving a few for Anne and her babysitter. Her six-year-old self watches her mother remove her apron, check herself in a full-length mirror, and throw a colourful scarf over her shoulders in preparation for the evening ahead.

She remembers her mother working in the garden of the family home, digging deep under the stubborn roots of dandelions with a trowel, tossing the long roots in a wheelbarrow, then coming in to wash the dirt off her hands.

She feels the warmth and weight of her mother sitting beside her on her bed, reading from a book of fairy tales.

She has later memories of her mother joining her and Nathan and Rudy at the cottage in Nova Scotia, gamely swimming in the frigid sea, her seventy-five-year-old body still active enough to manage a passable front crawl through the waves.

Then she remembers her mother, a few months ago, telling her for the first time of a pre-marital honeymoon trip to Nova Scotia, hinting about skinny dipping in the Bras d'Or lake. Anne wonders how many other untold stories lie beneath that sunken face, within the soft rise and fall of the shrunken chest. She wonders if that is, in fact, where those stories lie, or if they are instead swirling like dust motes in the sunlight, dissolving into nothingness.

She chooses to leave the room when the tests take place, both the first and the second time. Cannot watch her mother's body being prodded, ankle tapped for reflex, water poured into the eye. She cannot stand the indignity of it. The woman who bore her—those words come to her as if directly from a novel or screenplay—the woman who bore her, shrunken to nothing on that bed, at the mercy of well-meaning, but ultimately indifferent, strangers. We will all come to this, she thinks, and hopes, without much originality, she supposes, that when her own time comes, she will be past caring.

When she tells Nathan how things stand, he says he should be there with her, and so should Rudy. She does not protest about the Rudy part, as she might have done a few months ago. But she suspects that her reasons for wanting Rudy's presence are different from Nathan's. She believes, uncharitably perhaps, that Nathan is still trapped in the idea of normal. It is normal for a seventeen-year-old boy to take part in momentous, even tragic, family events. It is not normal for them to still be sheltering him. These thoughts ruffle the surface of Anne's mind but leave very few emotions in their wake. What she feels, in contrast, is a growing certitude that, despite whatever psychic pain this will cause Rudy, leaving him home would be worse.

So, she sits, holding her mother's hand, feeling its treacherous warmth, which she is afraid will disappear as soon as the ventilator is shut off. The film roll of childhood memories and images has sped up and is blurrier now, faded in contrast to the starkness of this room, and the arrival of a nurse and doctor, who solicitously approach her, as if she's the patient.

"I'm waiting," she says, surprised to hear a note of panic in her voice, "for my husband and son."

They arrive fifteen minutes later—Nathan, her partner and friend for all these years, and Rudy, the only grandchild her mother has ever had. She feels tears start unexpectedly when the nurse suggests they should all leave while the feeding tube is removed. "Then," says the nurse, making firm eye contact with her, "you are free to stay with your mother as long as you like." Anne is grateful for the firmness, for someone else taking charge.

In the hallway, no one says anything. She will remember observing the subtly faded grey and beige pattern on the tile floor beneath her feet. She will not recall being whisked back into the room, only the silence when she sits again by her mother's side.

"Maybe you want to go sit on Grandma's other side, Rudy," Nathan says. "If there are any last words you want to say…"

Rudy obeys but stays predictably silent.

"Her hand is still warm," says Anne.

Rudy looks over at her, takes his grandmother's hand, gingerly, as if afraid it is broken or maimed, as if he might injure it further through touch. The dead hand from his computer screen flashes through Anne's mind once, twice, and then is gone. She closes her eyes, tries to think of what she would like to say to her mother.

"Thank you," she thinks. "Thanks, Mom." But no spoken words form.

The sterility and chilly practicality of the room evaporate around her within this silence, an almost sacred hush.

| 29 |

In the late afternoon, when the sky begins to approach twilight, Sophie meets her new neighbour Bob at the Halifax airport. Bob is picking her up at the behest of Anne.

"I can get a taxi," Sophie had said when Anne told her of the plan.

"He doesn't mind," said Anne. "He works near there, and his shift ends just around the time your flight gets in. They are lovely people, Bob and Mary Ellen. They can take you to Bridgewater to find a car rental until Tim drives up."

Mary Ellen, Sophie thinks. The woman Nathan said could have a baby, then bake a four-course meal afterwards.

Bob has a beard and wears an unzipped parka and ski hat. He says he has left kindling on her front porch, and that Mary Ellen has put a pot of soup on the kitchen stove.

"I normally keep the key to the place," he says. "But now it's yours."

He produces the key with a slight bow and flourish of the wrist, like a Shakespearean jester. But with the wrong body type, Sophie thinks, watching him heft her suitcases into the trunk of his Corolla as if they are plastic shopping bags.

Back in August, when Sophie had taken the cab ride with Nathan and Bill to the resort, the scenery outside had rushed by in a blur of tree and sky and sameness, a watercolour wash of summer greens and deep blues. On this ride, Bob points out some more off-beat landmarks. A green plastic dragon's head in the lake on the side of the highway. A giant milk carton towering above them at the dairy co-op where he works. A boulder on the side of the road, painted like a giant Rubik's Cube.

"You won't see this stuff in the guidebooks," he says.

The landscape is barer and scrubbier than upstate New York, the trees smaller, the terrain hilly, but no mountains in the distance. There is less snow than she was expecting, only a few drifts clustered around trees, and lots of bare yellow grass.

"Yeah, we didn't get much real winter this year, not like two years ago," says Bob. That was a shit-show, pardon my French. Snowbanks higher than houses. So many school cancellations we should have just homeschooled the kids and be done with it."

By the time they have pulled off the highway and turned onto the Point Road, a deep country darkness has fallen. The car headlights a luminous tunnel ahead. To the right Sophie can see only the shadows of tree branches, and to the left vague outlines of houses, the occasional bright living room window. As the car slows and prepares to turn into Anne and Nathan's driveway, she notices Bob and Mary Ellen's house next door—a small, cozy-looking white bungalow. Anne and Nathan's place is taller, with vertical clapboard, stained to what Sophie thinks is a natural wood colour, although it's hard to tell.

"Mary Ellen lit a fire," Bob says. "You can let the oil furnace take over if you want, but you can't beat wood heat."

Looking out for ice beneath her feet, she follows Bob, who has her larger suitcase, carefully along the driveway and up the steps, holding a duty-free bag in one hand and a carry-on bag in the other. When Bob opens the door and turns on the light, a waft of warm air hits her, along with a mix of aromas she associates with her parents' house—beeswax, pine, woodsmoke, and from the kitchen, chicken soup. Beyond the front hallway, the house is small but uncluttered, with an open floor plan. A kitchen island instead of a table. Taking off her shoes and walking in Sophie notes, beyond the kitchen and to the left, a small room with a TV and to the right, open pine stairs leading to a bedroom loft. On the ground floor next to the stairs is another bedroom which she mentally claims as her own, with white sheets, grey-blue blankets, and rice-paper blinds on the windows.

Bob is still wiping his boots on the doormat.

"When Anne and Nathan bought the place, it was pretty much a run-down shack," he says. "They totally redid it." He points out the dark, solid wood of the exposed beams on the ceiling. "Some job. Kept a few people employed around here, I can tell you. Soup just needs to be heated up," he adds.

The pristine and shiny stainless-steel burners of the propane stove make her nervous, thinking of her burnt turnips at Thanksgiving. Mary Ellen's soup pot is less intimidating, its surface slightly scratched, its base blackened. Aware of Bob standing behind her, she rummages through her duty-free bag and extracts a bottle of wine.

"Thank you so much for picking me up," she says. "And the soup smells awesome. That was really thoughtful. I thought you guys might enjoy this."

Should she have written a card, or would that be overkill? She can't think how to reimburse him for the groceries without offending.

"No problem. Mary Ellen'll enjoy this." He taps the bottle of wine absently on his thigh and brings his right hand up to his ear. "Well," he says.

"I'll stop by tomorrow to thank her for the soup."

He backs closer to the door frame, saying something on an inhale that sounds like: "Yuh," with a glottal stop. The corners of his eyes crinkle when he smiles, changing his face from awkward stranger to friend. "If you need anything, you know where to find us," he says.

"Absolutely," she says, smiling back

After he leaves, Sophie looks out the back-facing kitchen window. Layers of darkness and shapes that must be trees, the suggestion of open space beyond. The sea is not near enough to be audible. Only forty-eight hours ago, she was marching through Manhattan with two hundred thousand people. The baby shifts inside her. She feels a foot, then possibly toes or fingers, lightly brushing the walls of her womb.

At 6:30 AM, crows and seagulls wake her, their calls loud enough to penetrate the airtight windows. There is also a less familiar avian sound, a lower-pitched, raucous, many-voiced honking. Through the kitchen window, she sees a flock of at least thirty geese in the backyard. Their black necks and heads ducking now and then to peck something out of the dead grass.

The bay is open water, not frozen like the lakes and ponds in winter in her hometown. Sophie sees an island within swimming distance of shore, and another one further out. Both are covered with spruce trees, erect and clustered like the hairs of a brush. On the island closest to shore, one tree leans diagonally away from all the others, ready to embark on a slow slide into the water. It has probably been growing like that for years.

After putting on jeans and a coat, she walks outside, moving quietly, but only gets within ten yards of the geese before they lift off, wings beating in unison with a sound like the thwacking of a loose-skinned drum. They settle, honking, on the water near an outcrop of land behind Bob and Mary Ellen's house. She navigates the scattered, grey-green goose shit down to the shore where a seawall of smooth boulders separates the edge of the lawn from a pebbly, seaweed-strewn beach. Perching on one of the granite boulders, she wraps her arms around her belly. Although it's warmer here than in New York, the damp seeps through her clothes. An outcrop of land to the right of the island has a dilapidated, rust-coloured boathouse on it, its lopsided structure lodged between the steel grey, wrinkled water and the white sky.

Turning her head to face the house—her house for now— with its windows staring at the sea, she's aware of something intangible hovering in the air, alive on her steaming breath. The word that comes to her mind is "safe." Safe is where her breath comes most easily, where she can imagine the birth of something within her, something just as significant as this spinning, kicking baby, but nameless and unformed.

After a minute or so, the cold seeps into her bones, and she goes back inside, only to find that the fire in the woodstove, which she stoked before bed, has gone out. Five minutes and many matches later, it's still a smoldering mess of old newspaper and blackened kindling. Keeping her coat on and making toast from the bread Bob and Mary Ellen left her, she watches three YouTube tutorials on her phone about how to lay a fire. She will not turn on the oil furnace. Her father, who taught her to lay a fire years ago, would be astonished at her ineptitude.

Kneeling again by the stove, the task of fire-building gradually and inexorably asserts its authority over her. She begins to feel that nothing is more important than the satisfying crackle of a tentative flame being coaxed into a blaze. She lies on her side on cushions in front of the stove, feeling the baby move slowly, thickly. Her awareness of the cushions and floor beneath begin to fade, her thoughts loosening like her wobbly, hormone-loosened joints. Finally, the baby is quiet, lulled, like her, by the heat.

She is on a film set in her nightgown and bare feet, trying to find Bill, knowing he wants her to make everything right in a script about a girl with blue hair and no lovers, a girl with light feet and a laugh that she's supposed to offer up to Bill like mouth-to-mouth resuscitation. She's late for her call time, but she can't seem to move quickly. There are cracks in the pavement, and randomly scattered goose shit to be avoided. And there is a baby in her belly.

A text from Tim buzzes her awake. *Sleep well? House okay? Yes and yes,* she answers. *Sitting by a wood stove. Saw some Canada Geese this morning.*

Each day she will text him some blissful image like that, something that lets him know that, in coming here, she has done the right thing.

Someone knocks at the door as she's heating soup for lunch. She opens it to a short, plump woman with long brown hair in a loose ponytail, who introduces herself as Mary Ellen. Sophie starts to thank her for the soup and groceries, but Mary Ellen makes a dismissive gesture with her hand.

"My youngest is over there asleep, so I can't stay" she says. "Just wanted to let you know that you're welcome for tea any time. Also, I'm planning to go to Bridgewater to shop tomorrow morning, so if you need to do any errands…"

In contrast to Bob's slow syllables, this woman's delivery could rival a hip-hop artist's. Sophie has just enough time to accept the shopping invitation before the conversation is over. Afterwards, she pours her soup into a mug and sips it while staring through the living-room window at the cattails and yellow grass across the road and, beyond, a faint glimpse of water and mauve coloured hills.

A thick blue sweater that must belong to Nathan hangs in the hallway. When Sophie puts it on under her coat, it envelops her the way Nathan's hugs used to envelop her on set. She and Nathan's sweater move together to the front step. Another bout of riotous honking announces the geese, who appear overhead in a V formation, like a military air show. Surprisingly low to the ground, almost skimming the telephone wires, they fly across the road towards the marshland. Sophie feels small, despite her burgeoning belly, as she starts walking, turning to the right, towards the end of the point.

Other birds—crows and seagulls mostly—populate her walk. One huge gull perches on top of a telephone pole, lifts its beak into the air, throat heaving as if about to vomit up a golf ball, and emits a resonant croak. Another gull lands beside the weathervane on the roof of a dilapidated rust colored barn, does a little shimmy, and shits. The birds call back and forth many times over, like the signals pinging around on a radar screen—Hitchcockian.

Sophie reaches the other side of the bay where a corrugated metal shed perches on a wharf, lobster cages piled up beside it. Ducks, oblivious to the cold, land on the slate-colored sea. Turning back towards home, she meets only one human being, an elderly woman with sunglasses and earmuffs, who nods and smiles, but does not stop to chat.

The next day, shopping with Mary Ellen and her toddler, whose name is Daniel, is both invigorating and exhausting. Daniel keeps hurling things out of his car seat and onto the floor, then yelling because they are out of reach. He shrieks in protest when they stop at the lights coming into town, and again when Mary Ellen lifts him into a shopping cart at the grocery store. Once the cart is moving, he adopts a trance-like quiet, so they practically run through the aisles, hurling food into the cart as they go. By the time they get to the cash Sophie is breathing hard. The baby kicks her in the ribs, sharply. Just a reminder, just a little something to freak her out even more about impending motherhood.

"Sorry about this," says Mary Ellen, fishing in her wallet for her debit card. "My sister claims he's an 'indigo child.' More like a royal pain in the ass, but we love him anyway. Don't we Daniel? Oh shit, he's dropped his bunny, do you think you could possibly?"

In the mall, Sophie manages to sort out her phone account while Mary Ellen and Daniel are at the drug store. When she again meets up with them, Daniel tries to climb out of the drug store cart and leap to the ground, a distance twice the height of his pudgy little body. Sophie reaches out to catch him, but

Mary Ellen is already on it, lifting him from the seat and plonking him in the main basket of the cart, from which he also tries to climb.

"I can take you to the car rental place, but do you mind if we make one more stop?" she says over her shoulder. "I'm dying to get a pair of jeans at Frenchy's, and it would really help if you could watch him a couple of minutes while I try them on."

"Frenchy's?" says Sophie, wondering if she can keep the kid from injuring himself.

"A Nova Scotian tradition. You are in for a treat. I get my whole wardrobe there."

"I could use a warmer jacket."

"Mmm…" says Mary Ellen uncertainly, eyeing Sophie's Citizens of Humanity maternity jeans, her Blundstones and soft mohair coat.

Frenchy's turns out to be like the Good Will stores back home, racks and bins of second-hand clothes smelling of cheap detergent and fire retardant. Mary Ellen works with her usual speed, wheeling a red plastic basket around and rummaging through the bins. Sophie gets a parka for ten bucks which she's not sure she will wear, but she doesn't want to seem like a pampered rich bitch. Which she isn't, given her stagnant bank account, given the work she has turned down, given Tim's meagre part-time pay at NYU. She thinks about the voice-acting demo reel he has agreed to help her with, and vows to start preparing material for it when she gets back to the cottage.

Squatting down with Daniel in the play-center by the changing rooms, she wheels dinky cars around his legs, which he ignores. But he squawks with glee when she finds a spongy ball and chucks it at his chest. This game takes up the rest of the time, Daniel clapping his hands, missing the ball over and over.

Later, pulling out of the car rental parking lot, breathing in the brand-new Nissan Sentra smell, Sophie notices the silence of Daniel's absence. A mix of snow and rain hits the windshield and slides down it like soggy cream of wheat. It's a relief to arrive back at the cottage, although she's already worried about the rental price, which was way more than it would be in the States. Tim would have haggled for a better deal.

Mary Ellen is pulling into her driveway next door, so Sophie rolls down her window and shouts her thanks across the lawn. Mary Ellen waves back with one hand, pulling Daniel from his seat with the other. The last Sophie sees of her is her backside as she picks a sippy cup off the ground. Snatches of monologue accompany Daniel's wailing.

"Yeah, I know it's crap, little guy, but there it is…Here we go, lunch, then nap time."

Sophie likes the sound of the words 'nap time.'

| 30 |

The next day, Sophie buys a pool pass at the resort, on Mary Ellen's advice. Apparently, they are a good deal in the off-season. Her sense of déjà-vu as she approaches the inn's revolving glass doors is tempered by the mounds of slightly blackened snow that line the curbs of the parking lot. Once inside, she's drawn to a wall of windows at the far end of the lobby, which look over the equally wintry beach. Aware that the woman at the front desk is eying her back inquiringly, she turns and asks for the pool pass, then adds, "I stayed here in the summer."

"I *thought* I recognized your face," says the concierge, who has exquisitely polished nails. Her name tag says: "Hi, I'm Sylvia."

"Does a man named Fred still work here?" Sophie asks. "I'd like to say hello to him."

"He's not in until this evening, but I can put a note in his cubby if you like." Sylvia's smile is still professional, but her eyes are suddenly more alert.

"Sure," says Sophie, as casually as possible, taking Sylvia's hotel notepad and pen. "I'd also like to go for a swim right away." As she says this, she writes: *Hi Fred, Sophie Langstraf here. You helped me out, back in August after I had a mishap* (Anne's word again) *on the beach. Would love to get together for tea sometime. Feel free to give me a call…*

The guy will think she's crazy, maybe stalking him in some way. This is a thought she would never have had in New York, she realizes later, as she sits on the surprisingly utilitarian, hard wooden benches facing rows of lockers in the women's changing rooms. In New York, surrounded by her community of friends, any unexpected encounter was a source of casual laughter only. The word "stalking" was reserved for spooky walks home at night and troublesome exes. But it's different here. She feels off her social game.

After quickly changing into her stretchy one-piece bathing suit, she heads for the pool, which she has been assured is heated to a pleasant temperature. When she slides her legs and protruding belly into the water, her body does not agree.

The only other swimmer is an elderly man with a bathing cap, goggles, and grey-looking skin in folds on his belly. Sophie does a few unenthusiastic lengths before taking refuge in the hot tub. From her perch on the hot tub seat, she watches the man do a sort of slow-motion front crawl, and feels her whole life slowing down. Even the sound in here—the boomy, echoing splash of the old guy's arms hitting the water's surface—is like music being played at the wrong speed on her parent's old turntable record player.

In the afternoon, she has her first appointment with Claudine. Claudine is blond and fortyish and sits on the sofa in the cottage's TV room as if she has come for a neighbourly visit. She asks about Sophie's medical history, food and drug allergies, exercise habits, whether the pregnancy was planned. "Yes," Sophie answers, not wanting to give the wrong impression—single motherhood, relationship issues, emotional instability. She's only too aware that she could have ticked each of those boxes at various points over the past six months. Onward and upward, as her father would say.

Claudine washes her hands in Anne and Nathan's pristine bathroom, before gently probing Sophie's belly. She suggests Sophie lie on her yoga mat for this, which Sophie finds both weird and oddly reassuring. The baby does a little flip and Claudine laughs. "Knows I'm not you," she says. "Active little critter." She takes measurements and writes them down, saying that everything looks normal for six-and-a-half-month mark. Once Sophie is again sitting beside Claudine on the couch, she peers at the clipboard on Claudine's knees. There is an elaborate chart, with bi-weekly spaces, in one of which Claudine has just completed a mysterious little diagram, showing a curly little upside-down "g" which must represent the baby, hovering over an upside-down triangle, which must be her pelvis and birth canal.

When the appointment is over, Sophie offers Claudine tea, which Claudine accepts and drinks unhurriedly. Sophie can't help contrasting this woman's easy silences with her Brooklyn doctor's hurried questions and note taking.

"So, I have to ask you," says Claudine, as she's putting on her boots to leave. "Have you seen the white deer?"

"The what?" For one unnerving moment, she wonders if Claudine is a member of some pagan cult, not the practical ex-nurse Mary Ellen described.

"There's this albino deer people have seen on this road. Not pure albino, apparently, it has a little splash of beige on its head. But still, pretty striking. People are starting to get competitive on Facebook about who's seen it and who hasn't."

"Wow," says Sophie. "I'd like that to be in my Facebook thread."

"No kidding," says Claudine, and they both laugh. "That's what people post when they live out in the boonies for too long."

"I think it's great. Beats the news from home. I bet even shots of his backside are easier on the eyes than Trump's face. If I see him, I'll tell him he should cultivate his image. Visibility on social media is half the battle."

"You might not see him for a while, but this road is overrun with deer in the spring. Watch out for your tulips. They love those. Pretty animals, though. Can't imagine wanting to shoot them."

"Absolutely not," says Sophie, horrified. Then she remembers where she comes from, all the hunters in her hometown, going out in camouflage every fall. Even though her mother always shuddered pointedly when they heard shots, they occasionally attended venison suppers at friends' houses. "I'll look out for the celebrity when I go for my walks," she says.

"You do that," says Claudine, briefly patting her belly. "A white deer is supposed to be good luck."

That night she calls Tim to tell him about the appointment.

"It was so relaxing," she says. "So different from doctor's appointments."

"That's great," he says, in a slightly distracted voice.

"How are things there?" she asks.

"Oh you know, the same old shit. You've probably heard about Trump's Muslim ban."

To her shame, she has not. Aside from glancing at the odd headline on her phone, she has not watched any news since she arrived here.

"Does he really think this thing is going to stand up in court?" Tim is saying. "All those people being held in airports? There are demonstrations planned for Kennedy. Just imagine how Samara and Farid must be feeling. Their parents were refugees."

"Of course," she says, feeling even more guilty.

But her heart lifts when they talk about Tim's plans for joining her. He says he will probably stay with his friend Joshua, the singer-songwriter in Maine, on his way up.

"You'll be amazed at the scenery when you come, even if it *is* the middle of winter," she says. "I bet you'll write all kinds of music. And you'll like Mary Ellen and Bob. Bob was impressed when I told him you were a musician. He plays guitar."

"Oh great. Tell me you didn't commit me to jamming with him to three-chord Country & Western."

"Don't make assumptions. I got a glimpse of the CDs in their car. Eclectic and tasty. Radiohead. Buena Vista Social Club. Florence and the Machine."

"No shit!"

"Are you playing a lot these days?" she asks.

"This and that. The band's squeezing a practice in between protests this week. And Samara says she has news to tell us. She won't say what, but she sounds excited, even though she's so bummed out about this Muslim ban thing."

After hanging up from that call, Sophie resolves to start watching the Canadian news in the cottage's comfortable TV room, but she will not dive down too many online rabbit holes. She puts down her phone, but picks it up again when she hears the sound of a text.

Hey Sophie, Fred here, she reads *Nice to hear from you. Be happy to get together for tea before my shift next Wednesday. Does 2 PM work?*

| **31** |

F RED ASSUMED HE WOULD NEVER see Sophie again. Back in August, she checked out early, ahead of the men. He figured her stay here in Nova Scotia, and its trauma, would be something she would rather forget. So last Friday, when Sylvia handed him her note, he had momentarily blanked, thinking surely this must be from another Sophie, someone from high school whom he had forgotten about maybe? He wondered how many ghosts from the past he was supposed to encounter before the message from the universe, or whatever his Aunt Flo would call it, would get through.

Today, when he tells Sylvia he's meeting Sophie in the dining room, he notes Sylvia's raised eyebrow. All the staff must know he's not interested in women, even if he has never officially come out to them. He started here not long after the split with Jamie, and was in no mood to talk about anything personal.

The place is pretty dead this time of year, aside from conventions. The churning grey sea, visible through the lobby's wall of window, contains the odd, forlorn-looking buoy, where the odd, forlorn looking seagull occasionally perches. Even the birds are seasonal temps. On the cement patio above the beach, the drained and abandoned swimming pool is covered in heavy green plastic. The only deck furniture left consists of some heavy wooden chairs that are bolted down. Fred wonders if it's still worth coming out for fifteen hours a week, holding on until the tourist season.

When he enters the dining room, he sees, with a sense of anti-climax, that Sophie is not yet there. There is only a grey-haired woman at a table by the window, with a kit bag by her side and, closer to the middle of the room, a pregnant woman checking her phone. They both look like pool pass locals. Fred goes to the buffet table and selects a chai rooibos from a crystal jar of colourfully wrapped herbal teas. He has started avoiding coffee in the after-noon, to improve his sleep. A faint cinnamon smell wafts up to him when he pours boiling water over the bag. He turns around, stirring, and sees the pregnant woman rise. Her face wobbles in his memory and reconfigures itself. Sophie's face.

This is the second time he has had to reinvent her, since he met her all those months ago. The glamorous guest to whom he served coffee on the balcony morphed into the punch-drunk woman he walked beside on the beach, and now, this third Sophie. Rounder, but with a buoyancy and grace to her step as she walks over and takes his hand. She seems older, closer to his age, as if she has transitioned to a new phase of development. Some new knowledge informs her eyes when she smiles and says: "Hey, how *are* you?"

They move over to the table together and he sits across from her. They are both laughing softly, he is not sure why. Fred thinks he could get to know her. He thinks she could be anyone from anywhere.

"It's so good to see you," she says.

"You too…Sophie," he tries out the name like a new menu item he's reading aloud, suddenly aware that the music playing over the café speakers is crap. Probably the local radio station, because Sylvia has been too lazy to choose a CD. It's at mosquito level volume, almost imperceptible, but annoying all the same. He stirs his tea. Inhales another waft of cinnamon.

"So… What brings you to this part of the world? Are you…working?" He can't remember if he told her he knew she was an actress. Would she find it creepy or flattering that he has looked her up on IMDB? Her burgeoning belly adds another layer of awkwardness to this conversation, another unspoken question.

Sophie's face registers a cross between a smile and a wince. It reminds him of her character in that film. What was the name? Cordelia? Clarissa?

"Unemployed at the moment, I'm afraid," says Sophie. "Or, as they say, 'in between jobs.'" She puts a hand on her belly. "This is going to keep me busy for the next few months."

"I'll say." He's relieved she was the one to bring it up. "When are you due?"

"The middle of April."

"And you're here until…"

"Around the middle of May. Long story."

He waits, sensing this is going to be interesting. Like watching one of her films. He sips his tea, which descends his throat into his belly, warming him through. In the back of his mind stirs a faint unease. He hopes she's not in crisis, running away from an abusive boyfriend or something. She doesn't have that look.

"My partner and I live in New York city. You can't imagine what it's been like the past few months." She stirs her tea in slow circles. "The Trump election, the demonstrations, the craziness. Don't get me wrong, I joined the Women's March in Manhattan, and it was great."

Point taken, he thinks. She is not one of *those* Americans.

"I just felt a need to get away from the city, from the country in fact. And this was the place I thought of. Nathan, you remember Nathan? He and his wife have a cottage here. They gave me the name of a midwife, who is excellent, and things just kind of fell into place. It seemed meant to be."

"Wow," he says, thinking: Some people really live like this. Go to marches in Manhattan. Have babies in Nova Scotia. Some people pick up and leave a city, a country, when the fancy takes them, when it's 'meant to be.'

"Your partner," he says, avoiding a gender-specific pronoun, just in case. "Is your partner up here too?"

"He will be soon. He's just wrapping up a few things."

There is a pause. When she speaks, it's as if she intuits his next unspoken question.

"I've been here for a week or so, and every time I drove by this place, I thought of you. You were so kind, back in the summer, helping me on the beach, taking me to the clinic." She avoids his eyes as she speaks, looking at her teacup and then out the window. Then she turns her head and smiles directly at him.

"It was no big deal, really," he says. "Actually, it was kind of fun. Broke up my day. Added some drama to my week. I'm glad you were okay."

"And I'm glad you happened to be on the beach. I was kind of a mess at the time, if you remember."

He says nothing. Doesn't tell her that he was on the beach because he was looking for her. Doesn't tell her he was sick with anxiety, flashing back to one of Jamie's botched experiments with suicide.

"Maybe when Tim gets up here we could have you over for a meal sometime, on a day when you're not working," Sophie says.

Is this an attempt to recompense him for his trouble? Does she feel a debt of gratitude that she wants to get out of the way? It's not as if he pulled her out of the sea or anything. He didn't save her life.

"Well, that's very kind of you," he says, feeling his waiter's voice creep back into the room. She doesn't seem to notice.

"So, tell me about yourself, Fred," she says. "Do you live around here? Were you born and bred in Nova Scotia, or are you a 'come from away,' as they say?"

He tells her about growing up in Halifax, and his brief stint in Montreal for university. He notices her watching him attentively, as if she's memorizing something about his face, his speech patterns. Maybe this is what actors do— soak up the characteristics of others so they can adopt them for future roles. She still seems undefined to him, dissolving back and forth between the scared and disoriented young woman on the beach and this softer-edged person who is listening to him now.

"I believe you're an actor," he says, throwing caution to the wind. "You were working on some project with your friends when you were here…"

She straightens her spine and pulls back a little, takes a sip from her tea. "Nathan and Bill," she says.

Perhaps he has pried into unwilling territory. But she's the one who wanted to chat. She has probed into his life, and seemed truly interested, not just today, but back then on the drive to the clinic. He remembers her manicured hand fingering the wooden cross in his windshield. Her voice saying: *Are you Catholic?*

"We were working on a film," she says. "I've made two others with them. Bill is a talented writer—really smart. He does amazing things, even though he kind of learned on his feet in the business. He's more of a literary guy, only took a few courses at film school. But you'd never know it. He's a good director, too. His editing process is quite something to watch. …"

She stops and takes another sip of tea. Something about the way she's speaking reminds Fred of how he used to talk about Jamie. *He does amazing things with colour.* Whenever he had to describe Jamie's work, back then, he used to repeat what other people said about him. When he looked at Jamie's pieces, all he felt was baffled pride, unable to distance the work from the man he loved, unable to decide anything about its intrinsic merit.

"I actually saw one of your films," Fred says. "It's on Netflix."

She looks surprised. "Up here? I had no idea. I know Nathan was thrilled about landing that Netflix deal for the first one, and I guess he was right… it's getting out to a much wider public than the art house and film festival circuit."

"Actually, there is a film festival here in Halifax," he says.

"Oh, I didn't mean to imply…" she says, a crease between her eyebrows. Shades, again, of the awkward, winsome girl in the movie.

"No, I know what you mean," he says, feeling a boost to his confidence—that rebalance of power when he puts someone at ease. "We're not exactly a cultural mecca in this part of the world."

She smiles tentatively.

"Actually, I don't know what you are in this part of the world. It's all new to me. I haven't even been to Halifax yet. Maybe you can show me around sometime?"

Maybe you can take me to the clinic. She said those words in the exact same tone of voice.

"It may not be Manhattan," she goes on. "But I bet it's more of a cultural center than my hometown in upstate New York. Deer hunting and the Super Bowl were *our* major events."

Fred imagines himself walking around the city with Sophie. Where would they go? Jeff's café? The new library? The Art Gallery? What the heck is there to do at this time of year? What could possibly seem interesting to her, coming from New York? At least in the summer there are festivals, the waterfront, the boardwalk, and food kiosks.

"Yeah, well," he says slowly. "Halifax tries. There's a symphony, an art gallery, a good alternative music scene…but it's an uphill battle if you actually work in the arts." He takes another cinnamon sip from his teacup. "I used to own a small gallery downtown," he says.

"Really? How cool is that!"

"That's what I thought when my partner suggested it. I loved the idea. We staggered along for two years, but we finished with nothing to show but a truckload of debt."

Staggered along, he thinks. That about sums it up. He has an image of himself staggering along a deserted road somewhere, with the weight of Jamie on his back, making him stumble.

"And is your partner…an artist?" says Sophie, who is fiddling with the rolled white linen napkin on the table beside her teacup. He senses her reticence, notices how she, in her turn, has avoided the use of a gender-specific pronoun. Time to get that little fact out of the way.

"Ex-partner, actually," he says. "He's an artist and currently living in Montreal. I lost touch with him when things got messy." He sees that last night in his mind's eye once more, but also acknowledges that the process of losing touch actually began when he and Jamie were still staggering along, when Fred was enduring the bad times and clinging to the relatively calm ones in-between.

Sophie looks up at him. "And you're still here in this beautiful part of the world," she says.

"I guess you could say that."

They smile at each other again. He is finally used to her new face and body, has integrated them with his memories from the summer.

The word "friend" enters his mind, tentatively, like the cloud wisp of a distant memory, like the light, fingertip touch of hope.

| 32 |

FROM THE COMFORT OF THE SOFA, warmed by the wood stove, Sophie watches the TV news. She sees shots of the familiar Kennedy Airport, its exterior crammed with sign-waving people. Tim is there, somewhere, she knows. Two hollow-eyed Iraqi girls appear on the screen. They tell a reporter that their visa-carrying mother has been detained in the airport.

"We've only seen her once since she arrived and she's crying and terrified," the older one says.

"We just want our mother," the younger one says.

Sophie remembers a night she once spent in the Philadelphia airport, when one of her flights home from California got overbooked. She remembers trying to sleep on seats with fixed armrests digging into her ribs, covered by a foil blanket handed out by the airline. The cold seeped into her bones, and she was hustled to another spot by a security guard at two in the morning. This was her only experience of suffering in an airport, detained, not by a hostile government, but by corporate screw-ups and indifference. When dawn came, the airport TV was endlessly scrolling shots of Prince William and Kate's royal wedding. All the stranded passengers stared, bug-eyed and stringy-haired, as a gold carriage, thousands of miles away, passed throngs of people on a London street.

The story about the Iraqi girls is interrupted by a commercial for snow blowers at Canadian Tire. Sophie adjusts a cushion at her back and wraps her arms around her belly. The two Iraqi girls come back on the screen, talking in surprisingly deadpan voices. As the camera leaves their faces for that of the cautiously sympathetic interviewer, Sophie feels the baby kick, hard. She sucks in her breath.

After the news, she tidies the remains of her evening meal, noticing the totality of the silence, no cars passing, no sound of human voices. Stepping out on the back porch to dump food scraps into the green bin, she is astonished by the winter sky. The Milky Way hangs overhead like a pin-pricked canopy, Orion and Taurus clearly visible, seemingly within touching distance. She tries to recall the last time she saw the stars this clearly—a winter hike back home with her dad, maybe? He, filling her head with facts and figures about galaxies and nebulae, she, convinced at some visceral level, as she is now, that she was looking at a vast, living organism, calm, indifferent, breathing the earth, with its teaming life-ridden surface, in and out, in and out.

Tim calls the next morning, and Sophie mentions the demonstrations at Kennedy, just to let him know she hasn't lost touch. But surprisingly, he moves on from politics to talk about the band. Samara has landed a gig for them which is colossally important, he says, at the Ballroom.

"Oh my God," Sophie says. She doesn't have to fake how impressed she is. They have been to the Ballroom to see some of their own favourite bands, the place always sold-out and hopping. It's a far cry from the pub or festival gigs that barely covered the expenses of the band's last tour.

"Yeah, it's amazing," says Tim. "We've been trying to get in there for ages. Usually they book months in advance. Some other band cancelled at the last minute, and I guess the publicity package Samara last year sent made an impression."

"So, when is it happening?" asks Sophie.

There is a slight pause.

"That's the thing," says Tim. "It's not until March eighteenth."

"Oh," she says.

"I realize the timing is shit, Sophie, but I can't see driving out there and driving back before the gig. We'll need to rehearse, and a couple of session gigs have come up that I shouldn't say no to."

There is an uncertain, pleading note in his voice. She feels her internal calendar rearrange itself like tiles on a scrabble board, re-calibrates her solo time here from two weeks to seven. All of her daydreams about Tim attending appointments with Claudine, of relishing that warm-bath sensation of togetherness she had felt when she realized he was happy about the baby, when he held her hand to his lips in the car on the way home from the airport, when he cried as they saw the ultrasound. All of that, put on hold.

"I'll be with you for the last month when you really need me," he says.

When you really need me. Maybe she has been overdoing her perky little texts about the geese and the scenery? But anything that boosts Tim's career is a good thing. She's the one who gave up income and insisted on coming out here. They have to work as a team to pay the rent. They have to behave like adults. She knows this is what couples do, especially couples who have children dependent on them. She thinks of the demo reel that Tim was going to help her with when he got here. She has been hoping to talk to him about that, hoping he can build her self esteem about this new work possibility, although it seems like a long shot right now. Today, she clicked the voiceover button on her only paid casting website, and ruled out five in-studio jobs, all of which required voice acting experience anyway, and found only one remote job for a headphones commercial that paid $100.

Before she mentions any of this, she must show him her support, the way couples do.

"I understand," she says. "You have to do this."

"Sophie…"

"What a great opportunity," she says.

"We can call, skype, as often as you like," he says.

As often as *I* like, she thinks.

"I just wish I could be there to hear you guys at the Ballroom," she says.

"We'll be sharing a ton of photos on our Facebook page. Samara is excellent at that kind of thing."

"I know it." Sophie pictures once more Samara's colourful sign at the Women's March. The baby stirs within her, softly. She takes a deep breath and says, "I know this show is super important, but I was hoping we could talk about my voice-acting demo reel. I really need your help, so I guess it will need to be delayed until you get here."

"Not necessarily."

"But I haven't got a clue, and I don't have any equipment."

"Let me look some stuff up. What you need will only cost a few hundred bucks. Then you just have to find somewhere kind of soundproof, hang up some blankets, or go in a closet or something. I can talk you through it."

Can he though? Usually when she asks for his help with technology, he takes over. She notes, with a sense of inadequacy and envy, that while he has landed his dream gig, her current attempts to find work involve spending instead of earning. Then she recalls all the crap gigs he's endured while she got to join Nathan and Bill's movie shoots.

"I was hoping to get you to edit it, and maybe even provide music," she says.

"Once you have something, you can send it. I'll work on it from here."

"Okay," she says cautiously. She should be grateful for his ideas, but instead, is dismayed at the thought of doing all this alone, contemplates hours of no one's company but the little guy inside her. Lately, she has been imagining Tim caressing her neck, kissing her cheek from behind, the way he does.

"I'll miss you," she says softly.

"Me too."

After they hang up, she thinks of the energy in Tim's voice as he spoke of the gig, imagining his excited hand gestures. She pictures his solid, warm presence in their apartment and feels herself, far away in this breathtaking rural landscape, fraying at the edges, becoming paler and more ill-defined by the minute. Despite the growing baby inside her, she feels she could walk out onto the back lawn and blow away over the water with the sea gulls and no one would notice. Which is ludicrous. Which is her attention-hungry, stage-addicted inner child talking. Not the person she wants to be.

The next day, she goes to a café on the shore road with her laptop, to check her emails. Pulling into the parking lot, she notices a tabby cat perched just inside the café window. About half a dozen customers are sitting drinking and looking at their phones or laptops.

The place apparently belongs to a sweet, hippy-looking family. Two kids under five, a tired-looking mum in the kitchen and a dad—tall and bearded, with an unwashed-sexy look. Sophie starts an email to Patty, telling her a demo reel is in the works. She tries to sound cheerful and professional, wondering if she will ever stop feeling like a kid pretending to be a grownup whenever she tries to take her career in hand. After clicking send, she watches the hippy dad passing his kids off to an older woman—probably a grandmother, who puts a coat on the youngest one, humming a tune that sounds like a hymn. Jack's face pops into Sophie's mind. His cheekbones, his down-turned head, his eyes looking everywhere but at her, his shoulders hunched against the wind. After ordering a green tea, she opens a blank email and types Jack's name into the address box.

Her fingers freeze over the subject line, then go straight to the body of the email, and write "How are you." She deletes that, writes "I miss you," then deletes that. Staring into the middle distance, she types: "Hey, I have no internet at the cottage so I'm here in this cute hippy café." She describes the cat in the window, the bearded dad, the grandmother humming a tune as she dresses the little boy. "I wonder if they're fundamentalist Christians," she writes, "like the Brennan family back home. Remember? The ones that kept having kids that all looked the same?"

She stops typing, deletes the last two sentences, avoiding the thorny territory of shared childhood memories. "How are you?" she types, but instead of "I miss you," she adds: "You are welcome to share my rural bliss if you feel so inclined, either before or after the bambino is born." She goes back to the subject box, writes "Hippy bliss," and hits send.

Next, she writes to Anne. Mary Ellen has casually mentioned that, at

Anne's request, a cleaning company did over the house a week before Sophie arrived. Sophie thinks of the calm downstairs bedroom and of the geese in the back yard. She feels familiar guilt about Nathan and the film, passing through her in waves, ruffling her edges. She will do something to pay Anne and Nathan back for everything they have done for her. She imagines Anne as she saw her at Christmas time, calmly pouring tea. The way Anne held her teacup carefully aloft as she seated herself.

She writes about the geese, about her shopping trip with Mary Ellen and her upcoming appointment with Claudine. She writes about Nova Scotia as if it were heaven, and while she types, she believes it is heaven. She writes to Anne as if Anne were a big sister, or a mother. As the words appear on the screen before her, she imagines them flying across the border to New York, touching Anne's face like snowflakes in the wind. Feeling the baby lightly explore the walls of her womb, Sophie imagines its fingers, tiny and translucent.

When she finishes writing to Anne, she can finally focus on emailing her parents, but can't think of anything else to say. So, she highlights chunks of the letter to Anne and cuts and pastes them. Her mother will sit in the kitchen, her new reading glasses perched on her nose, and read this email aloud to her father. Sophie imagines the surprise and gratification in her mother's voice at the letter's descriptions of nature, its unexpected verbosity. Sophie wills these words, even though originally intended for Anne, to settle at her mother's side like old friends, recalling the friends the two of them used to be.

| **33** |

Aɴɴᴇ ɢᴇᴛs ᴜᴘ ᴇᴀʀʟʏ, ɪɴᴛᴇɴᴅɪɴɢ to take Rudy to his day program. But after sitting on the sofa for a while, staring at the columns of miniscule print in the *New Yorker*, a heavy lassitude descends on her. She eases down onto her side, her head resting on a throw cushion, the embroidery on its slipcover pressing into her cheek. Her glasses dangle from the fingers of her outstretched arm, daring her to drop them, rather than place them carefully, as she does, on the coffee table.

There is a constant ache in her chest. The physical origin of the word heartache, she thinks. Pressing her cheek deeper into the cushion, she hears Nathan's feet on the stairs, hears him stop, halfway between kitchen and living room, then go back up. His quiet voice speaks through Rudy's closed door. "You up?" Anne cannot hear Rudy's muffled reply.

"I'll take you to the day program," says Nathan. "Your mother's asleep down there, so let's see how quiet we can be."

Good luck, she thinks, hearing Nathan tiptoe back down to the kitchen. She should either get up, or go back to bed, but her body obeys neither of these commands, is instead flooded with an ecstasy of relief at not having to drive Rudy.

She wakes to the sound of Nathan letting himself in the front door and sits up, smoothing her hair. He comes and perches beside her on the arm of the sofa. Takes her hand.

"I can't face going back to the apartment, today," she says.

"You don't have to," he answers. "Everything's packed, except the furniture."

"The books."

"Which will take about ten minutes to throw in boxes and bring here. There's lots of room in the attic. We'll do it next week, before the furniture sale."

She looks out the bay windows at the winter landscape of their back yard. The wind insistently shakes the dead leaves that cling to the uppermost branches of the elm tree. The bird feeder is deserted. She has forgotten to put seeds out, again.

"I'm tired," she says.

"I bet."

"I don't mean just from dealing with Mom's stuff. I'm just… really tired."

Nathan shifts in his seat. Glancing over at him, she sees that he's staring at the corner of the room, the same corner where Rudy has seen his shadow people. He must be tired too. She had insisted on being the one to box her mother's things and label them, but Nathan had emptied the apartment of all the big stuff. He called the Episcopalian minister and helped arrange the memorial service, which is tomorrow. It will be a pitifully small affair. Her mother was not a regular church goer, and her closest friends are either gone, or shut-ins for one health reason or another.

Anne has thanked Nathan many times for all he has done, but this morning she is certain that is not enough. She should reach out and wrap her arms around him. Show him, not just talk about it.

"Thanks for driving Rudy," she says.

"No problem."

She stares out the window, then down at the phone in her lap.

"I got an email from Sophie yesterday."

"Oh?" he says, letting her hand go and standing up.

"It was quite sweet. She went on and on about the scenery. I think we did the right thing, lending the cottage to her."

One right thing, she thinks.

"I suppose," says Nathan.

She has a mental image of Sophie in the kitchen of the cottage. For some reason, she can only picture Sophie there in summertime, maybe because she herself has never been there in the winter. The sun is shining outside the cottage window, and Sophie is barefoot. Barefoot and pregnant. No one says that anymore.

"I'll reply today at some point," she says. "When I got it, I was in the middle of emailing everyone about Mom." She, too, stands up, to look for her laptop.

"Have you had breakfast?" he asks.

"I'll get something later," she says.

The memorial service is as sad and small as she imagined it would be, but she's impressed with how well Rudy copes. He even holds her hand, briefly, after passing her a tissue from Nathan, who stands on Rudy's other side. She has never known Rudy to take the initiative on things like that. He stares straight ahead during the minister's words and does not blink. The coffee and conversation hour afterwards will probably be too much for him, so he and Nathan go for a walk afterwards, while she stands and accepts the frail hugs and condolences from her mother's few remaining friends.

She's surprised to see Alan Blake, one of her father's former students, now a journalist—balding and barely recognizable. He takes her hand and says what a classy lady Mrs. Jamieson was. Goes on to reminisce about those asparagus-roll-fueled English Department functions.

"I remember having a conversation with you when you were a teenager, Anne, all about post-structuralism. I was impressed at the time. Guess I shouldn't have been, given who your parents were."

She has absolutely no recollection of this conversation. Her teenage self pretending to know more than she did, faking poise and intelligence, completely unaware that she was succeeding. In fact, she barely remembers Alan, other than his name. But she smiles as if he is a long-lost friend and thanks him for coming.

After they have dropped Rudy back home, she and Nathan go out again to meet with her mother's attorney. Nathan, more than Anne, is astonished at how much money her parents had stashed away, most of which is willed to them, because Anne was their only child.

On the way home in the car, Nathan says, "I guess I shouldn't be surprised. All that railway money from your mother's father—and being a tenured prof in your dad's day was a good gig."

She supposes he's right. She has never thought about her parents' money much, which speaks to her privilege, she knows.

Once home, she tells Nathan she plans to move money out of her trust fund to pay off Rudy's overdue day-program fees—and sees a shadow of that old defensiveness in his eyes.

"What difference does it make?" she says. "We'll be fine once we settle the estate."

"No difference," he agrees. She can guess what he's thinking. He is wondering how he has come to a place where his wife's inheritance is a necessity, not a gift.

It's only money, she wants to say. None of this—the film hiatus, the unpaid bills, Rudy's illness—none of this is your fault. There are no fuckups here. This is just the way it is. My mother having a grandfather who was a railway magnate. Your grandparents having to escape the Nazis. Sophie quitting the film. My mother's stroke. Rudy's brain becoming scrambled at age sixteen, for no good reason that anyone on earth can see.

She has still not responded to Sophie's email. Should it be a polite note or a detailed personal letter, like the one Sophie sent? She pours water over coffee grounds in the French press, descends the plunger. Now that her mother's apartment has been dealt with, her days are beginning to feel dangerously empty and free-floating.

Nathan comes in with his laptop perched on his right arm, so she reaches into the cupboard and retrieves his favorite mug, the one Rudy gave him years ago for Christmas, a hideous red thing with snowflakes on it. He always says it's just the right size.

"I got an email from Bill," he says.

"Oh?"

"That's two emails in a week from those two."

"Those two?"

"Bill and Sophie."

He associates Sophie with Bill. For Nathan, the film set is Sophie's context, she supposes. A possibility emerges in her mind like the plot of a mystery novel, momentarily distracting her from her sadness.

"Were they ever a couple?" she asks.

"Bill and Sophie? No. They've always had creative chemistry, but as far as I know, they never did anything about it. Better that way. Just imagine how much more of a snit Bill would be in now."

"What does he say in his email?"

"Seems to have lost interest in the film entirely. Says he's working on something new. I think he's been influenced by current events, or, in his words, *the weird turn this fast food, fast talking, fast fuckup nation of ours has taken.*"

There is a slight smile in Nathan's voice, like an indulgent teacher quoting a brainy ten-year-old. Anne takes her own mug out of the cupboard and puts it, with a slight clatter, on the counter next to Nathan's.

"So, what's the new project about?" she asks.

"He didn't say. He wants to send me a treatment. I'll take a look at it. It might appease the backers to know I have something else up my sleeve. It'll definitely be a different genre, though, so I'm not sure about that."

"Did he say it was a different genre?"

Nathan half smiles, pours his coffee with his free hand. Something about him seems bewildered, lost. Anne is suddenly reminded of how he looked when they first got Rudy's diagnosis. He scrolls for a moment.

"What he says is: *I admit I am losing interest in the whole quirky, light romantic comedy genre that I seem to have fallen into like a frog in a soup pot.*"

Anne's mug freezes halfway to her lips. "A frog in a soup pot?" she says. "Jesus. I think he needs an editor."

"Well, he does add in brackets, *no offense to your work on those films, which has been stellar.*"

"Big of him."

Nathan goes back to his office with the coffee. She hopes he will not spend all his time writing Bill. He told her he was planning to get in touch with other writers he's lost contact with, Jason and Olivier.

Anne has never met Jason, can't remember what he and Nathan worked on. But she remembers Olivier, a nice person, and a good writer. That civil rights TV drama, which moved her to tears. Nathan was in a great mood during that shoot. Soon after, he started working with Bill. All that script development, helping Bill get to the core of what the story was about, he said. She worried, at the time, about him investing so much energy, putting all his eggs in that one basket. But when she read Bill's screenplay, she had gotten excited about it, too.

She sits back on the sofa with her laptop and coffee and embarks on her email to Sophie—a soothing and absorbing process. She writes about Nova Scotia, about her mother. She does not once mention Bill or the film.

When Nathan comes out of his office again, she's surprised to see that it's already three o'clock. He says he's going to get Rudy, and she's relieved to be able to go on writing.

Forty minutes later, she is standing at the fridge, trying to decide about supper, when the car pulls in the driveway. Through the kitchen window she sees Nathan get out, followed by Rudy. As usual, Rudy is dressed inappropriately for the weather—sneakers instead of boots, jacket open, no scarf. She has given up insisting he wrap up. Rudy stands irresolutely by the car door with his knapsack dangling in front of him, while Nathan walks towards him, saying something. She turns back to the fridge, hears the front door open and then, surprisingly, Rudy's voice.

"Yoga," he says.

"Yeah?" says Nathan. "An okay time or shit?"

"An okay time, I guess."

"What else?" says Nathan.

This sounds like an interrogation, something Rudy's psychiatrist has warned them against.

"Group," says Rudy.

"What was the topic today?"

"Career counseling"

"Yeah? Okay or shit?"

There is a pause.

"Shit," says Rudy, in a firm voice.

Would he be that honest with her? Anne wonders.

"Got it," says Nathan. "Then?"

"Meds counseling."

"Yeah?"

She can guess how he feels about that one.

"Shit," he says.

They have both come into her field of vision now, around the corner from the front hall into the living room. She thinks of asking them what they want to eat, but something stops her.

"Anything other than yoga that's not on the shit list?" asks Nathan.

"Lunch is okay I guess."

Nathan, who is sitting on the sofa now, snorts with laughter. Rudy, his hand on the stair banister, shows no sign of beating his usual retreat to his bedroom.

"What do they give you?" says Nathan. "Share a sample menu from an okay lunch."

"Little cups of apple juice with foil lids," says Rudy in his deadpan voice, "reconstituted scrambled eggs, cooked frozen vegetables, toast."

"Jesus…and that's an *okay* one? Anne, did you hear that? After all your efforts to give the kid a healthy diet?" He turns towards the kitchen, meets her eye, winks. She can't remember when he last did that.

"The toast is gluten free," says Rudy.

Anne risks a sideways glance at her son. It takes her a moment to recognize that he's laughing—silently, not with the raucous bray he used to have when he was little. But still. He is laughing. To her own amazement, she starts to laugh too.

| **34** |

Sophie is at the Shore Café once more, reading some links Patty sent her on how to record a voice acting demo reel. On Tim's advice, she has downloaded recording software on her laptop. To save on overhead, Tim has sent his own mic and cable by courier, but she still needs to buy a digital audio interface, whatever that is, and a mic stand. Miraculously, a music store in Bridgewater has both. She plans to go there this afternoon, and take time tomorrow making recordings in Anne and Nathan's closet.

Tim has been enthusiastically supportive, maybe because he feels guilty. At moments she shares his enthusiasm, as she contemplates doing two demos—one for commercials, another for audiobooks—remembering how she and her friends spent their downtime in theatre school tossing around celebrity impressions and wacky accents. But she also winces at spending money on a venture that might never pan out, and panics about her lack of experience at non-acting jobs.

Her table is nearest the window, where the resident cat sits, serenely. Sophie orders herbal tea from the sweet, wholesome-looking woman, who is doing both cooking and waiting today.

There is an email from Jack in her inbox. Her heart starts thumping as she opens it, thinking, What if he says yes to her invitation? Will he like it? And how long will he stay?

But Jack tells her he's moving to California. Noah has opened a café in L.A. and has invited him down to wait on tables for a while. *Thanks for the invite,* he says, *but I'll take my hippy bliss with a dose of sunshine. I thought it was cold here at 28 degrees. But I looked at the forecast for next week in Nova Scotia and they're saying <u>five</u> degrees there. Or minus 15 on that weird Celsius scale Canadians adopt to scare everyone. Fuck me.*

Reading this, Sophie feels a huge lump in her throat. Something about the email's gentle teasing puts her to shame. Of course he can't just put his life on hold to come up here and hang out with her. Just like Tim, he needs money. How would he even get to Nova Scotia? In that beat-up, borrowed Yaris?

Anyway, he is a grownup, not some lost puppy she is responsible for. She missed that boat long ago. She should be relieved by his self-sufficiency, by the tone of his writing, his careless bandying around of the word "fuck." She looks again at the screen and reads, *Speaking of hippy bliss, watch out for that sexy unwashed café proprietor. You'll be huddling with him for body warmth, if Tim doesn't turn up soon.*

There is also an email from her mother, whom Sophie will probably call today, reading the email's not-so-subtle hints about missing Sophie's voice. No mention of Jack. She wonders if he has even told their parents about his plans.

He's right about the weather. The temperature has plummeted. A light snowfall has now frozen into crystalline whiteness. The sun sheds no heat, hanging in an impossibly blue sky, making the outline of every ice-coated tree branch shine like a hand-blown glass ornament. Sophie has been keeping the wood stove at the cottage stoked and uses the oil furnace as a back-up at night. In New York, she would be worried about the stores of fat on her hips, afraid they might linger after the baby is born, but here, with no one around to see them, they feel like comfortable woolen underwear. She wonders momentarily what Tim's reaction will be when he catches sight of her bulk, but his arrival seems a long way off, not quite real.

Then she wonders what Bill would think. She remembers him commenting on Barbara, who played Sophie's mother in his last film. How he stared into the middle distance as Barbara came on set, saying sotto-voce to Sophie, "Someone's been going for the free donuts a little too much I see." She felt uncomfortable at the time, like she was in a mean girls movie, but she doesn't remember saying anything.

The cat, still perched on the white painted windowsill, begins washing its fur, bathed in sunlight. As she sips her tea, it jumps down and winds itself around her calf, rubbing its whiskers against the leg of the table, then wanders off.

Anne has also written. Sophie scrolls down the length of the message, surprised at its heft.

Dear Sophie, she reads. *I loved your email. I loved hearing about our cottage in the winter, because I've never been there at that time of year. I enjoyed hearing about Mary Ellen and Claudine and the sea gulls and geese. Especially the geese. We get flocks of them here, in the Spring and Fall. Not so much this time of year, though. I have heard there are more geese on the South Shore of Nova Scotia than there used to be. The story is that a bunch were transported there from Ontario because they were so plentiful in the cities that goose poop became an issue. Ontario's loss, Nova Scotia's gain, in my opinion.*

Anne goes on in a sweet, old-fashioned way about how glad she is that Sophie is enjoying their "little sanctuary up there" and says she has felt guilty in the past about leaving it empty for months. She does not seem to regret her generosity.

Sophie reads the next part more slowly.

I'm afraid we've had a very difficult time down here. My mother had a massive stroke a week ago and sadly, she died within twenty four hours. She was very elderly, ninety in fact, and had seemed frailer lately. Still, it was a shock, probably because her frailty did not extend to her mental capacities. Everyone always commented that she was sharp as a tack. In many ways, she was the same person I grew up with, although saddened by my dad's death a few years ago, and slowed down by a fall which impaired her mobility and took away some of her independence. I knew her time was dwindling but I didn't expect her to go so suddenly, and in such a dramatic way.

Sophie suddenly feels like a teenager. She has been obsessing over make-believe and accents, worrying about her weight, feeling lonely and abandoned because Tim has been delayed and Jack has turned down her invitation. But here is someone who has real difficulties, real reason for sorrow. And by Anne's side, there is Nathan, also troubled by this loss, no doubt, and already inconvenienced by Sophie's abandonment of the film that he put his energy and resources into.

She keeps reading Anne's email.

It's a cliché to say, "You don't know what you've got 'til it's gone,", but looking back, I regret that my time spent with my mom sometimes felt like a duty rather than a gift, and that my attention was often occupied elsewhere...I've started notifying people and sorting out her stuff and her finances. It feels like I'm spending more time and energy on her now that she's dead than I did when she was living.

A school bus pulls to a stop in front of the café window, air brakes hissing. A child gets off. He is all bright colours: red parka, multi-coloured, puppy emblazoned paw-patrol backpack. He bursts through the door, runs into the kitchen and hugs his mother's waist briefly before heading upstairs.

Looking back at her phone, Sophie reads: *I'm really unburdening myself here, Sophie. Sorry. Your email was so beautifully written that it put me in confessional mode. I'm glad you are well, and that Mary Ellen and Bob and Claudine are making you feel cared for. You must be getting big now... what an exciting time. When is Tim joining you?"*

Sophie notes the x's and o's Anne puts next to her name at the end of the email. She's touched, both by the letter's honesty and by the formality of its language: *I'm glad you are well... her time was dwindling ...*

The baby inside her moves sleepily. Sophie briefly indulges in a flight of fancy about the near future. The baby in Tim's arms, the baby on her belly in a sling with Tim by her side, the baby reaching out, smiling, burbling its first words, even scrambling around like Mary Ellen's toddler in a shopping cart.

But then she has a new and less rosy vision of the future. She imagines the baby's birth as the first in a series of inadvertent but devastating abandonments. Anne and Nathan's son, who is rumored to be mentally fragile in some way. What must that be like, when also grieving the loss of a parent? She pictures Anne's mother in her nursing home, occasionally visited by her dutiful daughter but ultimately dying alone in an increasingly alienating world. She wonders how anyone can stand it.

Later that afternoon, after stowing the mic stand and audio interface in the bedroom closet, Sophie calls her parents. She decides not to mention Tim's delay.

Her mother's voice, when she answers, is slightly breathless.

"I found a seat sale," she says. "To Halifax."

"*What?*" When have they discussed this? Is her mother planning to hover in the background of all her midwife appointments, or worse, cheer her on at that final agonizing moment when she has to push the baby out, all sweaty and screaming?

"For after the baby is born," her mother says. "In April. It's a few weeks past the due date you told me."

Sophie exhales. "Wonderful," she says. "Just you? Or Dad too?"

"Both of us. We wouldn't miss this for the world. And we want to check out this Nova Scotian home that you've adopted."

"For the time being," says Sophie.

"It sounds pretty small there, and we don't want to impose on you and Tim," says her mother, "so we found a little Airbnb to stay in for a week."

"Wow...are you sure, Mom? I mean that sounds kind of expensive." Sophie has a flashback to her mother's impulsive flights to L.A. and wonders, not for the first time, how she afforded them on her dad's janitor's salary. Things are better now, but still.

"Don't you worry about that. We'll manage just fine." Her mother's tone is warm, but also final and decisive.

"How's Jack?" Sophie asks cautiously.

There is a pause. "Your brother is a restless soul," her mother says. "I take it he's told you about his California plans?"

"Yes."

She waits for something from her mother, she is not sure what. She would like to build a bridge between them based on their mutual love for Jack. She would like to confess to the lump in her throat, the ache in her heart about his distance, even if she can't share what she knows, or thinks she knows, about Jack's reasons.

"Say hello to your father," her mother says in an overly bright voice. "He's sitting right here."

"Of course."

In the brief silence that ensues, Sophie recognizes her mother's decision not to discuss Jack as probably a good idea, but also feels defeated by a thousand unspoken words.

When her father comes on, Sophie tells him how expert she is at laying a fire in the wood stove, and how much he would like the scenery up here. She mentions the geese, and Anne's theory about them being shipped from Toronto because of the goose shit problem. Only she says: "goose poop", like Anne did. She doesn't mention Jack, or Tim, or the baby. She avoids talking about human beings at all.

The next day, she sits on a straight-backed chair in Anne's closet. Clothes on hangers, including Nathan's sweater, surround her laptop and mic stand, to eliminate reverb. Her laptop perches on a child-sized folding table she found tucked away behind Anne and Nathan's TV. She reads sample scripts from a free website Patty sent her, in various suggested vocal styles. "Casual conversational"—which reminds her of her character in *Liza*. "Bright"—which reminds her of Dorothy in Oz. "Warm"—which reminds her of her mother's yoga DVDs. She has no idea how she will keep the finished product under three minutes. She plans to enlist Tim's editing help to make her reel fit the average casting agent's attention span.

Although she feels slightly claustrophobic amongst the jeans and sweaters, she admits that this is kind of fun. Like playing house under the sofa cushions in the living room when she was little. When she finishes with the commercial demo reel, she embarks on one for audiobooks. Her sample scripts include the passage from *Jane Eyre* that she recited for Anne, only this time she's not pretending to be eighteen. She no longer filters Jane's passion through her younger self. Instead, she floats with the cadence of the dialogue, inhabiting a Yorkshire accent the way she inhabited Nathan's old sweater—with bittersweet nostalgia. She spends considerably longer on the audiobook reel, even though she knows the commercial one is what is most likely to bring her paid work in the short term. As she speaks, and all outside preoccupations fade, she is less aware of her heavily laden body, as if her voice, spoken into the darkness lit only by the glow of her laptop, is all that exists.

| 35 |

THE FOLLOWING DAY, SHE CALLS Mary Ellen and invites her for tea. Mary Ellen says it would be easier if Sophie came to her, with Daniel and all. "We might even be able to talk in peace while he's napping."

"Okay, but let me bring the tea, and some cookies."

"Bring on the cookies," says Mary Ellen. "Just be prepared for a messy house. Apologies ahead of time."

"No worries."

"How are things going over there anyway?" says Mary Ellen.

"Not bad. But it looks like I might be on my own for a bit longer than I planned. My partner has an unexpected work commitment back home."

"Bummer," says Mary Ellen lightly.

"Yeah. You wouldn't happen to have a line on a cheap vehicle, by any chance? I was only planning to rent this one for a week."

"I can ask Bob. He has a friend at work who owns a used car lot."

"Thanks. That would be great."

Daniel's voice in the background interrupts the call and Sophie rings off to make the promised cookies. She rifles through Anne's cookbooks and chooses a ginger snap recipe. Her mother used cookbooks too, when she and Jack were kids, but Sophie mostly finds her recipes online. There is no flour or sugar in the kitchen, so a trip to town in the expensive rental car is necessary.

The cookies are still warm when she shows up at Mary Ellen's door, but she and Mary Ellen only manage to eat one each before Daniel decides to lick his fingers and run them along all the rest, staring in fascination at the cookie he has in his other hand, and eventually smushing it onto the coffee table. He goes down for a nap within a few minutes.

Mary Ellen comes back after putting him in his crib and sits beside Sophie.

"Bob and I talked about your car situation," she says, reaching for one of the spit-contaminated cookies. "You could probably get some rust-bucket for a thousand or so, which would be cheaper than renting for the next two months, but it would be totally unreliable. We seriously would not mind if you wanted to share our Toyota on the days I have it. All you'd need to do is fill up the tank once in a while."

Sophie thinks of being indebted yet again to this woman whom she hardly knows, imagines having to phone Mary Ellen every time she wants to go to the pool or the café.

"I couldn't do that," she says. "You need your wheels."

"Here's the thing," says Mary Ellen, as if she has read Sophie's thoughts. "I could give you our spare key, so you wouldn't need to call me up every time you need it. We could just talk once a week to figure out when each of us needs to drive. Some planning involved but not that much. I really only ever use it to go to Bridgewater for shopping and to take Ella to her gymnastics class. And even on the weekends when Bob is here…It's pathetic, I know. But we're homebodies in the winter."

"Well…" Sophie considers again her dwindling bank account. "Thanks for the offer. I'll think about it."

She hasn't heard from Tim in a couple of days, which leads to a fair amount of hormone and loneliness-fueled speculation. She imagines him having a blast in rehearsals with the band, sees Samara's face, her eyes shut as she sings into the mic, then gets pissed off at herself for these thoughts. They are like exploring an abscessed tooth with her tongue. For the first time, she can almost understand Tim's anger in the summer about her "going off with those guys" for the film consult.

At the time, his anger or possessiveness, or jealousy, or whatever it was, had briefly made her want to chuck everything. It was only for a moment, but still, the line between staying or leaving the relationship felt so thin. How easy it might have been to say "fuck this," to justify abandonment with all the ready-made phrases about personal growth, moving on, self-realization. How easy it could have been to float away from Tim, just as she has now floated away from the film project. At this thought, she finds herself probing the other ache in her heart, to do with her brother's flight to California.

She's about to call Tim when the phone rings.

"Hey Sweetie," she says in her cheeriest voice.

"How's it going?" he says predictably. She has teased him in the past about that phrase being his phone mantra.

She embarks on some funny local detail, keeping it light, keeping it entertaining. She tells him about the hippy café, and prepares to mention her tea with Fred, and Mary Ellen's offer of a car loan, when she notices that Tim has been silent for a while.

"Can we talk?" says Tim. "It's about the gig at the Ballroom."

Her heart momentarily leaps with anticipatory joy. Maybe they have moved the dates up? Maybe he won't be delayed quite so long? She won't allow herself to hope that the gig has been canceled. She's not that unmoored from his need for this break. She is not that shitty a partner, or wife, or whatever she's supposed to call herself.

"Samara found out a few more details about the band we're replacing," Tim says.

"Yes?" She tries to keep her voice neutral.

"They're from Iran. They were planning a North American tour. They can't come because of the Muslim ban."

In the brief silence that ensues, Sophie hears a chorus of sea gulls rising from the shore.

"We're getting the gig because of Trump shafting some innocent artists," says Tim.

The gulls are just outside the window now, one perched on the telephone pole that stands on the border of Bob and Mary Ellen's property. It's hard to tell from the ruckus they are making, whether they are outraged and angry, or loudly greeting each other. Sophie tries to focus on Tim, on the surprising note of uncertainty in his voice. She tries to imagine what kind of moral dilemma the canceled Iranian band poses for him.

"Shit," she says, to buy time.

She would be happy for them to cancel in the name of political scruples, if it weren't so important for his career, if it weren't for the baby and her dwindling bank account. And…what good would cancelling do for the musicians in Iran, anyway?

She searches her mind for the snippets of news she has heard on the car radio over the past few days.

"That judge blocked the order," she says.

"Doesn't matter," Tim says. "No one in their right mind is going to try coming here from one of those countries. It's had the effect they wanted. And Trump and his cronies will appeal the decision."

There is another silence. The seagulls have piped down, but now she can hear distant honking. The geese are back. Maybe that's what the gulls are pissed off about.

"Samara's devastated," says Tim. "It hits home for her."

"Of course."

Knowing that Samara's dilemma is way more personal than that of her white male band mates, Sophie wonders if they will just follow Samara's lead. She realizes, however, that she does not want this to be Samara's call. She does not want the band to cancel because Samara is devastated, and is ashamed of this thought.

"I don't know what to say," she says. "I know you all will decide what's right to do."

Lame, she thinks. But something about this whole conversation feels lame. Her thoughts are as disconnected and mind-numbing as the images on the news—the sign-waving protesters, the hollow-eyed refugees being turned away at the border, Trump leering about women and their pussies, gangs of women and men she never knew existed cheering him on. The whole surreal and bathetic jumble of images on her Facebook and Twitter feeds. And here she sits, letting her thoughts stray from the point at hand, from the person at the other end of the phone. Whom she is supposed to support. Whom she is supposed to love.

She carefully asks him what he thinks is the right thing to do.

"Fuck knows," he says, which endears him to her more than any political statement.

"I love you," she says.

"Love you too."

The next day at the café, Sophie rereads Anne's email, to which she has not yet replied. She notices again its warm and beautiful phrasing, imagines Anne typing it, perching her glasses on her nose like her mother does.

She wants to create a beautifully scripted and well-thought-out response. She wants to sound both mature and supportive, like a friend, instead of like a needy kid. She starts to compose the letter in her mind when her phone rings. Tim again.

She holds the phone up to her left ear and covers her right, to block out the chatter from another table where an elderly couple and another elderly woman are having an animated conversation about Trump.

"So, what's the story with the gig?" she asks.

"We're gonna do the show," Tim says. "But we'll mention Trump's ban and the circumstances to the audience. Samara will do a Persian song in homage to the other band, and to all Iranian nationals who are barred from entering the country. We started learning the song today."

Part of Sophie thinks all this sounds a little too easy, but who is she to judge? She tells Tim it's great news.

"I guess. It still feels shitty though."

"I get that," she says, thinking, it would do no good to have him come out here ahead of schedule, jaded and frustrated by a missed opportunity. She's imagined him contentedly playing guitar in the cottage living room and recording a CD up in the loft. She imagines him touring with the band, but not too soon—in six months or so, when the baby is older. And she imagines him joyfully coming home to Brooklyn and their sweet little family, sweeping the baby up in his arms—the three of them making a sunlit tableau like the closing frame of every sentimental movie or show she has ever seen or acted in. But it won't be acting, it will be real life.

After she hangs up, she decides to accept Mary Ellen's offer of the car. To show Mary Ellen she's both organized and responsible, she sets herself a schedule of regular trips to the resort, putting them into her phone calendar. Even if all she does is float like a whale in the heated pool and go to the café afterwards, she will have a shape to her days. She will keep an eye out for voice acting jobs. Once Tim has finished editing and adding music to her demo reel, which he promised to do by next week, she will send it to Patty. Maybe she will get in touch with Fred again. And at night back at the cottage, she will stare at the stars instead of at the TV news.

Then she looks back at her laptop where Anne's email still lies open and begins to write, watching her typed letters emerge on the screen.

So sorry for your loss, Anne. And I loved your email too. It was sad, but not depressing. You are an amazing, strong woman and I am so grateful to you for letting us stay in this beautiful spot. Being here has helped me step back from my life and look at it in a new way. I wouldn't have done that if I hadn't gotten away from New York.

She looks out the window, where her reflection floats weirdly against the telephone wires and ice-coated tree silhouettes across the road. Turning back to her laptop, she starts to tell Anne what she didn't tell her mother. That Tim has been unexpectedly delayed, that she's on her own until the middle of March. That the cottage has lots of room.

I know you have enormous responsibilities down there, she writes, *but maybe getting away wouldn't be a bad idea for you too? Obviously, this is your house, and obviously, there is room for you to stay, if my belly and I aren't too much of a crowd. Think about it.*

| **36** |

With Sophie's email still open on her laptop, Anne is surprised by the way her mind has leapt to practicalities. Puzzle pieces falling into place.

"I want to go," she says, more to herself than to Nathan. "I want to wrap up a few things here and then go." She hears her voice the way he might hear it, saying, "This is what I want. I want this."

"Okay," Nathan says, cautiously. "For how long?"

"Maybe a couple of weeks? I'm not sure."

There is silence.

"Can you manage?" she says, not looking at him, staring at her screen without seeing the words. "Rudy's pretty stable these days."

"It'll be a transition for him, being without you."

"Me too."

She wonders whose transition will be bigger, Rudy's, hers, or Nathan's.

"I can call every other day or so," she says. She imagines the dead silence on the other end of the phone and Rudy's monosyllabic answers. "Or skype."

"I know you need a change, Anne," Nathan says. "I know how tired you are. But…" there is another pause while neither of them looks at each other, "are you sure this is what you want? Drive all that way? Hang out with a moody, pregnant woman in our cottage in the middle of the winter?"

"What do you mean, moody? I don't find her moody. She seems a pretty straightforward person to me. Are we talking prenatal hormones here?" she asks, thinking of her own prenatal moodiness eighteen years ago, her insecurities, and later, her postpartum blues. All those times when Nathan came home from a film shoot to a messy house and a woman who doted on her son but was bewildered by the constant quick-witted improvisation it took to be a parent. She looks back to how much she relied on him in those days. The tears on the shoulder. The rants about some domestic disaster that ruined her day or week.

She would take back those moments in their marriage if she could. After years of caring for the teenage Rudy, she can't fathom why her former self struggled so to manage the day-to-day care of a healthy toddler. She would like to time travel back to replace that young, frazzled, fragile woman, or at least talk some sense into her.

She doubts Sophie is anything like Anne was, back then. In her mind, the gaunt but chic Sophie at the café in Manhattan, talking about morning sickness and the Nova Scotia seaside, blends with the seemingly well-rounded, self-assured Sophie sitting on the sofa at Christmas, discussing childbirth and politics.

"I like her," she says.

"Well of course. I like her too," says Nathan, sounding annoyed. "She's an amazingly talented actress."

He stands up and runs his hand through his greying hair.

"Can you manage?" she asks again. This time she looks him in the eye. A shared gaze, a brief silence, swollen with awareness of their son's presence upstairs and of the next conversation that will have to take place.

She waits until it's nearly suppertime before going up to talk to Rudy. There is a pause before he answers her knock, during which he's probably shutting down his computer. She offers up a silent prayer that he's not looking at a misogynist porn site or someone's crazy right-wing manifesto. She thinks again of the iceman pictures she found there, the accompanying article telling how the ice man had been shot in the back of the neck, how they did an autopsy on him and tried to take pictures of his brain but couldn't get a clear image because the scope kept hitting ice. She remembers seeing what she assumed were Rudy's words written below the cut and pasted article: *"Ice on the brain is not a good thing."*

When Rudy opens the door, she asks, politely, if she can come in. She sits in the computer chair across from the bed, on the edge of which he perches, his feet flat on the floor and his legs bent at an awkward angle.

"I'm thinking of going away for a bit," she says.

"Yeah?" His eyes look past her face, over her left shoulder. Not in an intense way, more as if he's placing his gaze somewhere neutral and safe.

"You remember our friend Sophie? The actress in Dad's last two films who came for a visit that day at Christmas?"

"Mmm?" The gaze doesn't shift.

"She's staying at our cottage in Nova Scotia for a while and has invited me to join her."

"Oh?" The gaze shifts upwards, closer to the ceiling.

"Sophie's on her own out there. Her partner Tim can't join her for over a month. She's expecting a baby, and I think she'd like company, for some of that time, anyway."

Why does she have to couch it in those terms, as if she is rescuing someone in need—always the caregiver, the manager, the helper?

As she expected, she's greeted with silence. "I was just wondering," she says. "If you're okay with that."

Maybe this isn't the right thing to do. It smacks too much of asking permission, or forgiveness. Either way, a move that could potentially shut down whatever honest communication they have with each other. When he was little and she had to leave him in preschool, she remembers the teacher telling her it's best to make a clean break, something she was never able to do. She remembers his worried, tear-filled eyes that left her sick at heart. How they finally reached a compromise: She promised to peek at him through one of the flower decals on the window before getting into the car, making him laugh through his tears.

After a moment, she adds: "Dad will be able to take you to the day program and everything. He's home for the winter because he doesn't have any projects on right now. And if you need anything…"

She realizes that he is looking at her, and unlike his former toddler self, his eyes are not tear-filled. Startled. Interested maybe. Eye-to-eye. Which is so rare she can't remember when it last happened. She looks away first.

"You're going and Dad's staying?" Rudy says.

"Well, yes."

"Are you and Dad okay?"

"What?" She's so surprised she can't quite find her footing, and although she knows the way he's looking directly at her, the way anyone else might, is a huge step forward, it unnerves her as well. There is a shadow on his jaw, which only started appearing a year ago, and there is also a solid look to his cheekbones that didn't used to be there. Even though he's still a skinny, lanky kid, there is a hint of solidity to his body as well.

"Just wondering," he says. "I know there have been arguments."

Her heart sinks, remembering her outburst in front of the tree back in December. She frantically searches back to other arguments she may have had with Nathan over the past few months, when Rudy was up here in his bedroom, plugged into his computer, she thought. Oblivious, she thought. And what were those arguments about? The cottage, money, Sophie, their future. But mostly Rudy and his care.

"Wait. No…" she says, feeling her neck tense, her head making quick little negating movements. "Rudy, you've got the wrong idea. That's not what this is about."

"No?"

"No. It's just…your dad and I argue, sure. All married couples do. I just…I need a change of scene I guess." Which sounds even worse, she thinks. Because Rudy himself is "the scene." The scene is Rudy and Nathan.

"I'm sorry if our arguing has upset you," she says.

"I'm not *upset*," he says, an edge to his voice. "I just noticed. And you saying you need to get away. It's a logical conclusion to make. Even I'm capable of logic sometimes."

"I never said you weren't," she says quickly. But he is right. In this conversation, she has been taken aback, not just by the clarity of his sentences. But by their logic.

"Okay," she says. "Maybe you're right. Maybe the arguments with your dad are part of my need to get away. But having time away from each other is normal part of married life too. Even though we've been apart because of your dad's film shoots, I haven't had much chance to be on my own for the past few years…"

"Because of me," he says.

"Not only!" she says, again, too quickly. "Grandma too. And now that she's gone…" her voice breaks a little. It surprises her to be ambushed by tears now, when they are talking about something else, something that has nothing to do with this latest grief, this weighted blanket sitting on her chest, overlaying the ever-present weight of Rudy's illness.

"It's okay, Mom," he says.

When was the last time he called her that? When was the last time he called her anything at all? She has grown accustomed to him answering her questions in monosyllables. And she still dreads the possibility of him spouting some hallucinogenic nonsense while staring past her into that troubled, parallel world of his, a world which has rubbed up against their world and ripped their everyday lives to shreds.

"You need to get away. It's all good," he says. "I'm doing better now."

She has been staring at her knees, but now she looks up.

"Are you?" she says.

"Yeah, better…maybe not normal. But everyone keeps telling me normal is overrated."

"You better believe it is." She runs the flat of her fingers across her eyes. "When you say 'better,' what I want to know is…is it easier? Is anything getting easier?"

There is a pause, during which she is unable to look at him. She becomes aware that she's holding her breath, and consciously opens her chest to send air into her lungs.

"I guess you could say some things are," he says finally.

"Like?"

"Triggers like stress and anxiety. I'm getting better at managing those."

The auto-pilot parroting of medical terminology is depressing. He is reverting back to passive patient-hood in front of her eyes. "But…Rudy," she says, almost on a whisper. "Are they still there? The, you know, voices, the people…" She will not say the word 'demons.'

"Less," he says, shortly, with difficulty, as if he is speaking through cotton wool.

"Yeah?"

"Yeah."

"Even," she says, voicing the fear that has been haunting her for the past four months, "even with the medication being reduced?"

His answer comes quickly on an exhale, as if he, too, has been holding his breath.

"So far so good."

She sneaks a look at him. There is none of the shiftiness she has seen in the past when he has lied about hallucinations or pretended not to be having them. But there is no rejoicing either.

"So, less, but not gone completely?"

"Mom," he says, once more presenting her with that unfamiliar, direct gaze. He reminds her, suddenly, of Nathan.

"It's okay for you to go," he says. "I'm okay to be here with Dad. That's what we're talking about, right?"

"Right," she says.

The ensuing silence envelops them both, and this time it is a silence she is not inclined to break.

| **37** |

Aɴɴᴇ ɪs ᴅᴜᴇ ᴛᴏ ᴀʀʀɪᴠᴇ ɪɴ ᴛʜᴇ ʟᴀᴛᴇ afternoon, and Sophie is thankful for the lengthening daylight hours as she laboriously but aggressively cleans, avoiding too much squatting or bending. The place seemed okay last night, but now she's acutely aware of every spoon left in the sink, every fluff of lint on the carpets. When Anne still hasn't arrived by five, she starts chopping vegetables, adding them to the chicken soup with which she hopes to reproduce the homey welcome that Mary Ellen provided on the day of her own arrival.

At 5:30, Anne pulls in the driveway, and is already unloading her suitcases from the trunk by the time Sophie makes it outside to meet her. They hug briefly, shyly.

"Are you tired from the drive?" Sophie asks.

"Not too bad," Anne says. "I spent the night in Maine at a hotel Nathan and I stayed in once. It's gone downhill a bit since then, but the bed was comfortable." She rolls her largest suitcase to the door, carefully avoiding an ice patch. "No, no, I'll get that," she says, as Sophie makes a move to bring in the smaller one. "I was really lucky to avoid snow squalls."

On entering, as if on cue, Anne says the kitchen smells great, and notices how clean and tidy the house is.

"Wow, I forgot how small it is. Hope having me here isn't going to drive you nuts."

"Are you kidding?" says Sophie. Which sounds like she's desperate for company.

In fact, after her initial invite, she has been having second thoughts about a roommate experiment in the last few months of her pregnancy. What kind of host can she be when she has to pee every hour and nap most afternoons? Then again, she's not exactly the host in this situation.

As they eat, Anne asks if she got the vegetables at the farmer's market, which apparently happens every Thursday morning. Sophie feels like a newbie, not knowing this.

"I couldn't ask for a better meal after a day of traveling," Anne says. She insists on doing the dishes, and Sophie notices that the cupboards are organized slightly differently after everything gets put away.

They dig out an old DVD to watch after supper. Kaufman's *The Unbearable Lightness of Being*.

"I loved this when it first came out," says Anne.

Daniel Day Lewis, all sex and sleaze, seduces Juliette Binoche in an opening scene. They watch in silence, until Anne says, "I forgot how much sex there was."

"My parents rented this when I was seventeen. I watched it with them," says Sophie.

"Awkward."

"Tell me about it."

Sophie remembers liking the sweeping romanticism of the film but also cringing at the scene where Tereza romps naked around Sabina's photography studio, all white skin and gamine charm. Even at seventeen, she recognized something bogus there. A straight guy's fantasy about women loving women. Would she have pointed that out, if she had been playing the part? Unlikely. She wonders how many takes Binoche had to do.

Thankfully, she and Anne don't make it to that scene. Forty minutes in, Anne suggests they stop and watch the rest the next day. As if she has been hearing Sophie's thoughts, she adds:

"I don't know how actors do it. Juliette Binoche is incredible. If you asked me to play a role like that, when I was that age, I'd be mortified."

"There are challenging moments, I guess."

"Any acting aspirations I had died when I was about ten," says Anne, stretching her legs towards the wood stove. "Too much of an introvert."

"Introverts make great actors. It's the best way to hide. You get to be someone new with every role."

"I suppose," says Anne. "But everyone watching me? I couldn't stand that."

"It just takes practice," says Sophie. "And good directors."

The topic of Bill looms suddenly in her mind. She would still like to classify him as a good director—thorough, perceptive, attuned. She used to think those qualities were character traits, not just professional skills, but they had been nonexistent in Nova Scotia. He accused her of being on automatic pilot, but looking back, his heart seemed even less into it than hers. Bill had wanted her there, Nathan said, but why? Her mind shies away from the memory of that kiss at the airport. She thought they were friends. She thought they were colleagues. She thought he wanted to hear what she had to say, maybe know who she was when not playing one of his invented dream girls. At these thoughts, yet another ache arises in her heart—not what she needs right now. Fuck him, she thinks. Fuck the shame she still feels about leaving, the shame she has always felt about unfinished projects—Bill's film joining a legion of childhood drawings, journals and crafts, sitting mutely at the back of her closet.

"Well all I can say," says Anne, bringing Sophie back to the present, "is I have the utmost respect for you folks."

You folks, Sophie thinks. Actors.

"There are so many crap jobs out there," she replies. "I feel pretty lucky to make a living this way. I've never even had to wait on tables."

This is true. She is lucky to do what she does.

"I waited on tables for six months when I was a student," says Anne. "Hated it. They had me working in the kitchen until I turned twenty-one because of their liquor license. Everyone told me how great it was to serve—tips and all that. They made a big deal of my birthday and my promotion to waitress. But it turned out I liked bussing tables and washing dishes better. You don't have to talk to anyone or keep anyone's order straight." She laughs quietly. "Guess I never had a bright future in the restaurant industry."

Sophie tries to picture Anne waiting on tables and being bad at it, or being bad at anything. She tries to picture her as a teenager.

"I know a waiter," she says. "Works at the resort here actually. He helped me out when I had that run-in with the sea in August. I decided to look him up when I got here. He's a nice guy—smart, and a good waiter too. Doesn't seem to mind doing what he's doing."

"I imagine he might mind the low paycheck, although I think it's better up here than in the States," says Anne.

She's looking at Sophie curiously.

"His former partner is an artist," says Sophie. "Kind of a messed-up guy, I'm gathering, reading between the lines. They used to run an art gallery together."

Anne's face and body relax slightly. Sophie imagines saying aloud, *No, I have not come up here to have an affair with someone during my sixth month of pregnancy. I may be a flake, but not that much of a flake.*

"So, in the few weeks since you've arrived, you've already made a friend?" says Anne. "Impressive. Does he live nearby?"

"In Halifax. He's offered to show me around the city. Take me to a few art galleries. You probably already know Halifax well, but if you'd like to come…"

"Might be fun," Anne says.

"That's settled then," says Sophie. "I'll see when Fred's free and we'll make a date."

When she calls Fred in the morning, he says, "It's great to hear your voice, Sophie."

They arrange to meet the day after next at a café in the city after his lunch shift is over.

"You and your friend will like Jeff, the owner," he says. "He's a painter." Fred texts her directions to the café. He even checks the forecast as they speak. "Yeah, we should definitely wait until Thursday. There's weather on the way tomorrow."

Weather on the way. Sophie likes this turn of phrase. Snow, she assumes, or maybe more ice pellets? The careful way Fred checks all the details reminds her of her father, always looking into practicalities none of the rest of the family ever considers.

When she hangs up, she relays their conversation to Anne, who says, "There's a new library in Halifax that's supposed to be a big deal. I've seen pictures. They even talked about it on CNN—the architecture. It's supposed to look like a stack of books." She pulls up two photos on her phone. Sophie sees a glass exterior, the angles of three stories, each facing in different directions, like a precarious Lego construction. She sees an open sunlit interior with escalators that remind her of the Time Warner Center, except without the giant ads and store fronts. Sophisticated, urban. Definitely a contrast to this country road and its sea-and-sky landscape. She hands the phone back to Anne, who scrolls some more, to the site of the Provincial Art Gallery.

"This looks interesting," she says, handing the phone back.

It's an ad for an exhibit by a painter from Newfoundland called Maggie Piper. Sophie has never heard of her, but she is supposedly well-known. There are photos of still-life studies of food, luminescent and pleasing to the eye. The subject matter is somewhat repetitive, as if the artist spent all her time in the kitchen. Sophie checks the woman's dates. She would be in her eighties now.

One exception to all that domesticity is a painting of an animal carcass (deer? moose?), strung up in a garage. It looks like a torture victim hanging by its heels—human-flesh-coloured stripped ribs, splayed legs.

"Yikes," says Sophie, handing the phone back to Anne and feeling an involuntary contraction of her pelvis. She puts her hand on her belly where the baby sits a bit too heavily this morning.

"Yeah I know," says Anne. "That one's kind of raw... Whoops, no pun intended. I meant, you know, raw as in disturbing... as in..."

"I know what you meant," says Sophie, meeting Anne's eyes. They both laugh, Anne a little longer than her. Something shifts. Once more, Sophie feels a connection with Anne that has nothing to do with Nathan, or Bill, or the film, or even with her gratitude over this cottage. It is what made her confide in Anne across a table in Manhattan, made her recount her baby dreams over the phone, prompted her to invite Anne to be with her now, at this confusing and endlessly changing time in her life.

"I'm glad you're here," she says, impulsively.

Anne's eyes register surprise, briefly. Then she smiles a slow, warm smile that makes Sophie understand why Nathan must have fallen for her.

"I'm glad too," Anne says. "You have no idea how much…Actually, the timing of this is perfect. Nathan and I haven't been up here, or anywhere, for quite a few years. My son has been struggling with mental health issues, and there's been my mother to care for…but things are different now."

Touched, Sophie notes the pacing of this confessional speech, a little too rapid fire to be unrehearsed. It's the only time Anne has ever seemed nervous. And for the first time in Anne's presence, Sophie feels like they are on an equal footing.

| **38** |

Anne sleeps late and wakes to silence, broken only by the soft grit of snow hitting the window. There is the sound of Sophie trying to move quietly in the kitchen. The thwack of the toaster. Cereal poured into a bowl.

Morning languor makes Anne's body feel as if it does not quite belong to her. Her body knows she doesn't need to make Rudy's breakfast, or watch him take his morning meds, or drive him to his day program. It knows she doesn't need to go out to visit her mother, or keep that awful silent vigil at her mother's bedside, or deal with the sad leftovers in her mother's apartment. Having let go of all that, her body has slowed down so much that it doesn't know how to stop slowing. Lying there, listening to the toaster pop, Anne imagines herself entranced and comatose, like a bewitched princess in a fairy tale. She imagines herself in a white and sunlit chamber instead of this neutral beige-and-grey loft bedroom. She imagines herself young again, younger than Sophie, her long blond hair flowing over the pillow.

Snow builds steadily against the windowpane. Layer upon layer of silence. She and Sophie won't be going anywhere today. She realizes they don't have snow shovels in the house. Why hadn't she thought of picking some up when they were in town? It's the kind of practicality she would always remember at home. She will have to borrow one from Mary Ellen and Bob. Looking at the size of the flakes coming down, she decides it's pointless to start shovelling anyway.

As she did yesterday, she dresses with care. The mauve sweater Nathan gave her for her birthday last year. Earrings to match. Beige trousers. A circular scarf that contains the hues of both the trousers and sweater, but darker, bolder. She spends a long time sitting on the side of the bed, brushing her hair. She has to be gentle with her hair these days. Now that grey is mixing with the blond, it has become fragile. She remembers when she could haul the brush through and it would emerge from the ordeal shiny and smooth, like something from a shampoo commercial. She remembers Nathan pulling that hair—sometimes playfully, sometimes with passion when they were in bed together.

When she goes downstairs, she sees that Sophie is in the leggings and sweatshirt she wore to bed. Her legs are slim and shapely despite the bulging belly above them. Her face is still puffy with sleep, like the face of a young child. She wears fuzzy, pink and white striped socks. They look thick and extraordinarily comfy, and Anne knows she would never wear them in a million years.

"Claudine is supposed to come today at four," says Sophie. "She might not want to drive in this snow, though."

"Who knows?" says Anne. "It might stop by noon."

"My phone's dead so I can't check the weather."

"There's always the radio," Anne says, amused.

"Right," says Sophie, looking over at Anne and Nathan's ancient stereo system as if it might explode.

Anne verifies on her phone that the snow is due to end early afternoon. A fair accumulation though.

"It depends on how soon they're able to plow the road," says Anne. "I would say there's a fifty-fifty chance she'll make it. How are you feeling? Everything okay?"

"Oh yeah," says Sophie. "Way better than in my first trimester. Claudine is great."

"I bet she is. Anyone that comes with Mary Ellen's recommendation is okay by me." She finds the coffee where she usually keeps it but has to search for the bread. Sophie has stored it in the cupboard above the toaster, with some granola bars and crackers.

"I had an appointment with a doctor at the walk-in clinic the other day," Sophie says, sitting at the counter with her hands wrapped around a mug of tea. "Claudine recommended some blood tests and stuff."

Anne goes to sit beside her while she waits for her toast.

"The doctor seemed a nice enough guy," says Sophie, "but when he found out I was doing a home birth, he just lost interest. Filled out the forms and sent me on my way."

"It's a weird system," says Anne. "They all have their own turf. I've taken my son to see a naturopath a couple of times, and I downplay it whenever I talk to his psychiatrist or MD. If you do anything outside their area of expertise, they either discount it, or make patronising 'hmm' noises, like you've confessed to a secret fetish or something."

Sophie laughs. "I know what you mean," she says. "I know home birth is right for me. Claudine's amazing, and totally professional. Still, I wish things didn't have to be so complicated. My mother was always at war with doctors. She questioned everything, from antibiotics to vaccines. She was always explaining why I shouldn't eat certain junk food, or use certain hair products. I used to wish our family could be like everyone else."

"Sounds like she was doing her best," says Anne, tentatively.

"Oh, I know she was." Sophie stands up to rinse her mug.

Anne thinks about the recent restrictions she has put on Rudy's diet, and all the advice she has given him since he's been sick, about taking his meds and reducing his meds, about sleep, computer use, going to the day program. She wishes she could find another way to be with her son, but what are her choices? Someone has to take responsibility. Someone has to help him find a path out of that dark psychotic hole. And even though he's now slowly crawling his way forward, there is no guarantee he won't continue to periodically slide back for the rest of his life.

"Bob's coming over," says Sophie, looking out the window.

Anne goes quickly to the door and opens it, thankful that she dressed before coming downstairs. Bob looks the same as he did the last time she saw him, red-cheeked, bearded, maybe a bit more heavyset.

"It's so good to see you," she says hugging him and getting wet from the snowflakes on his parka. "I've been meaning to come over and see Mary Ellen and all your little guys. How's the new one?" She wracks her brain for a name from Mary Ellen's emails, but comes up blank.

"Keeping us busy," Bob says. "Just wanted to let you know that I'll be over to clear up this mess after I've done our driveway."

"You know you don't have to do that," she says. "I was going to borrow a shovel from you later, though."

"Only take a few minutes."

"Well at least bring an extra shovel so I can help."

"Older kids have a snow day," says Bob, as if he hasn't heard her. "They'll be out soon enough making snow forts. Mary Ellen's telling them they have to make at least two, before she'll let them watch cartoons." He grins. "She says come over once they're in their snowsuits and out of her hair."

"We might do that."

It's another half hour before they see Mary Ellen's kids emerge on their snow-covered lawn. Between the older two is a toddler in a one-piece snowsuit—a fat oval in bright red polyester who can barely stand, like one of those egg-shaped toys from Anne's childhood—*Weebles-Wobble-but-they-don't-fall-down*. Except he does fall down, repeatedly. On the third go-round he lets out a wail. The older girl picks him up like a sack of potatoes and goes to the front steps, where Mary Ellen emerges in a sweatshirt and rubber boots to retrieve him.

Sophie and Anne wait ten minutes before going over. By the time they are at Mary Ellen's door, the child has stopped wailing and Bob has started shovelling.

"Remember what I said about that extra shovel," says Anne over her shoulder to him as she hugs Mary Ellen.

"Don't worry about it," says Mary Ellen. "He loves it. Happy as a pig in shit. He's got this big frigging scoop thing that makes him feel like the abominable snowman." She gestures to the child clinging to her leg. "This guy, on the other hand, thinks a walk in the snow is only marginally better than being waterboarded. I thought it was worth sending him out with the other two, but no go."

Daniel stares at them while they take their coats off and, for lack of free coat hooks, drape them over the washer and dryer. His eyes are enormous and deep brown, like Mary Ellen's.

"He's the size your oldest one was when I was last here, and the middle one was just a baby," says Anne.

"It's been a while, for sure."

They enter the living room, where Daniel picks up a tot-sized mallet and becomes absorbed pounding pegs through holes in a pounding bench. The pegs have happy faces on them which disappear down the holes and then pop up again. Did Rudy ever have a toy like that? Anne remembers big plastic Duplo blocks, and a yellow tonka truck. She remembers Rudy's hands stacking the blocks, but she can't remember his face, or the sounds he made.

They sit on the sofa while Mary Ellen makes tea.

"Won't be long before you have one of these guys to entertain you," says Anne, gesturing to Daniel.

"Don't I know it," says Sophie.

"Don't sound so terrified," Anne laughs. "It'll be great."

"It's just starting to hit me that I'm kind of unprepared. I mean…not for the birth, but for afterwards. I'm so clueless. I don't have anything."

Mary Ellen comes in with the tea. "Like what kind of anything?" she says.

"Well like a crib or a stroller, or toys or stuff."

"You've still got two months to go," Anne starts to say, but Mary Ellen cuts in.

"You don't need any of that. Your boobs and diapers…That's all you need for the first month. Well okay, sleepers and receiving blankets and onesies."

"Onesies?" says Sophie.

"Not the adult kind," says Mary Ellen. "You know the little shirts that you pull down and snap, so they stay in place. They're easy to undo when you change diapers."

Anne remembers those little shirts well. But what the heck is an adult onesie?

"My point is," says Mary Ellen, "you can get most of that at Frenchy's, or the drug store. No big shopping trip required." She starts to look purposeful. "A sling's not a bad idea," she says. "I happen to have one of those. A bouncer too, maybe. I can dig that out of the attic."

Sophie puts her tea down on the coffee table and then scoops it back up again as Daniel comes over.

"The crib thing is your call," says Mary Ellen, "but I can honestly say, after three kids, that the easiest is just to have the baby in bed with you for the first few months, if your man's okay with that."

Anne searches her mind for her memories of Rudy's infancy. Yes, she nursed him through the night. Yes, he sometimes came to bed with her. But he didn't spend the whole night sleeping there. Would Nathan have been okay with that? She has no idea, she realizes.

"That's what my mom says," says Sophie.

The mom again. Anne thinks. Is she imagining the weight, the hesitation in Sophie's voice?

"Your mom's right," says Mary Ellen. "Saves a ton of hassle for nursing. And you get more sleep. Also, I always thought the crib was way too big for them when they were newborns. They look so lonely in there. If you need somewhere other than your bed, look for something smaller. An empty drawer would do."

Anne gasps. "An empty drawer?"

"Taken out of the dresser and lined with blankets, obviously," says Mary Ellen.

The three of them start to laugh.

"That did sound a little weird," says Sophie.

"I have never tucked any of them away with my socks and underwear, even if I may have been tempted," says Mary Ellen.

There is the sound of machinery outside. Daniel charges to the window and stands with his hands on the sill, bouncing his knees up and down as if he is dancing. The snowplow comes into view, churning snow and depositing it in a heavy pile at the end of the driveway where Bob has been shovelling.

"Well holy crap," says Mary Ellen. "That's the earliest the plow's ever made it. Maybe Francis at the end of the road complained to public works. He's always saying he's going to."

"Okay, now you have to show me where the extra shovel is," says Anne. "I'm not leaving Bob to deal with all of that and our driveway as well."

"Well if you're really determined," says Mary Ellen.

"I am."

"Then take my gloves. Those little wool things will be soaked in minutes."

Anne goes to the front hall, locates the gloves and shovel, and pulls on her snow boots. She realizes she does not want to stay and talk with Mary Ellen and Sophie. Sophie's belly, the presence of Daniel, and the warmth of the wood stove, which she would normally love, all feel oppressive to her.

As she starts to work silently beside Bob, lifting the snow and tossing it until her arms and shoulders ache, she wonders if she will ever be able to hear joyful mommy talk without painful stabs of jealousy and regret, if she will ever be able to remember Rudy's early childhood without putting it under a microscope in search of clues to his current condition, or manage to let go of her need to find a reason, to assign blame. Over the years she has blamed, in varying degrees, the doctors, Nathan, and most of all, despite everything she has read or been told, herself.

While Sophie is in her appointment with Claudine, Anne walks down the road to the water on the other side of the bay, which is unfrozen, but still as glass. The low sun gives the snow a faint pink hue, and the water, in which the trees are reflected, is a deep orange. This beauty is where she would like to live, if she could let go of the past, forget about her aging body and her worries for Rudy. How often, she wonders, does she manage to feel present in that way? Snow shovelling today, she thinks—using her arms and hands to do a task with a clear beginning and end. Helping Rudy, she thinks, when she can in fact help, and is not condemned to merely witness his awkwardness, pain, or delirium. Having sex with Nathan, she thinks, with an ache of sadness at how long it has been —nearly two years, a situation for which she acknowledges her share of the responsibility. Driving up here, she realizes—feeling free and rootless in her small vehicle, moving past trees, through unknown towns, leaving her home, and Rudy and Nathan, behind.

Turning back the way she came, she sees a fallen branch, its forked twig fingers beckoning from a snowbank, and immediately thinks of the frozen hand on Rudy's computer screen, and Rudy's sentence, "Ice on the brain is not a good thing." These words, and others, start to play in her brain to the rhythm of her footfalls, and keep her company all the way to the newly shovelled cottage driveway. Claudine's car is gone, and when Anne lets herself in, she sees that Sophie's bedroom door is closed. Anne remembers those last two months of her pregnancy, when she used to nap like an octogenarian or toddler every afternoon.

As quietly as she can, she removes her coat and boots and tip toes upstairs to her loft bedroom. Rummaging in her handbag, she finds a pen and the journal she bought at the Morgan Library four months ago, and whose pages are still blank. The mantra that has been following her repeats itself in her brain and starts to spill onto the page.

Ice on the brain is not a good thing, you say, she writes. *Think of it as protection,/think of it as dormancy/awaiting spring./The skeletal clutch/ of the ice man's hand/is not your hand./Your brain isn't millennia old,/your body is not pierced by arrows,/but by demons of sight and sound/*

beyond what your senses see and hear.

She feels Rudy's presence in the room as she writes, almost expects to see his boy-man face looking at her when she raises her eyes from the page.

If I could, I would give you peace,/ she writes, *but can offer only a piece of myself —/the piece you took with you/when you left my body all those years ago./ It has stayed with you,/even when you thought you had lost yourself/even when I thought I had lost you.*

She looks up then, and barely aware of the tears sliding down her face, she speaks aloud to the empty room. "I haven't lost you, have I?" she asks. Words she knows she will never say aloud to Rudy, at least not anytime soon. Despite this, her heart feels lighter, calmer, almost free.

| 39 |

AT JEFF'S CAFÉ, THE CONVERSATION has become lively. Sophie's pregnancy has inspired talk of baby naming, and now they are all comparing stories of people with ridiculous names.

"A high school classmate of mine," says Jeff, stroking his beard. "Richard Head. And he was, I'm sorry to say, the proverbial dickhead."

"My mother's gynecologist," says Fred. "Dr. Sperm."

"You're making that up," says Anne.

"It's a name," he says pulling out his phone and starting to scroll. "Look. Here, see? There are four Sperm families in Indiana."

"What the? How did he find that out so fast?" says Jeff, addressing Sophie and Anne. Ever since Sophie introduced Anne to the table, Fred has been noticing Anne's understated elegance, her relaxed conversational style and warmth. He hopes he will give off a similar vibe when he is her age, in ten years or so. As he thinks this, he recalls his doppelganger experience—the older Fred with the kind eyes.

"Mr. Phone-Hands here," Jeff continues, "is on his device whenever he has a moment. I, of course, outrank him in technological savvy…" He flourishes a flip phone that looks like it was bought in the nineties. This schtick with the flip-phone is not new. The phone, the shaggy white hair, the striped suspenders showing above the apron, are all accessories to a persona Jeff has been cultivating for years, Fred imagines, but who is he to judge? The guy's heart is in the right place.

Anne adds to the weird name-dropping: "After I had my son, I was referred to a lactation consultant whose name was Sally Udder."

"*No,*" says Sophie.

"Yes," says Anne.

A customer walks in, the only one they have seen so far, and Jeff takes him a menu. When he returns, there is a slight lull in the conversation. Fred notices Anne's eyes surveying the room, taking in the art on the walls—still mostly Jeff's paintings. But Fred's pencil sketch of the wounded bird is also there, framed and mounted directly across from them. It seems a bit out of place, he thinks now, although he was secretly thrilled when Jeff wanted to display it.

Noticing the direction of Anne's gaze, Jeff says, "As well as phone-hands, our friend Fred is rapidly developing art-hands. That one's his."

Right away everyone stands to look more closely at the drawing—except Fred, who says "Oh God" and covers his face with his hands. Not wanting to be histrionic, he lets his hands fall back in his lap. But Sophie has caught the gesture out of the corner of her eye and, laughing, comes over and rubs his shoulders.

"Fred hides his light under a bushel," says Jeff. "I gave him a couple of drawing tips a few months ago and he took the ball and ran with it. Remarkable. He went from remedial sketches of fruit bowls and furniture to this, out of his own head, apparently."

"It's so beautiful," says Anne, who has been standing, transfixed, in front of the drawing. "Can I buy it?"

She turns to look at Fred, who stares back at her, mouth slightly open, hands now resting on the tabletop.

"Um," he says.

"Whoo-hoo!" says Jeff. "Your first sale, man! Remember it happened here, at my humble establishment."

"Think about it," says Anne gently. "You don't have to name a price right now, take some time and let me know when you come up with something you think is fair."

"You'll also want to get an image of it up on your future website," says Jeff. "Or Instagram thingy or whatever..." He walks over to take the lone customer's order. Sophie reaches over to rub Fred's shoulders again, making him suddenly aware of their bony tightness. "Congratulations," she says. "I didn't know you were an artist."

"Here's my email and phone number," says Anne. "And I meant what I said. Choose a price you think is fair. It's a beautiful drawing. If you do get a website up, please send me the link. I'd be happy to share it with friends."

She gathers her coat and scarf and starts to rummage in her purse.

"I'll get lunch," says Sophie.

Fred watches them wrangle over the bill until Sophie wins. "We should probably get going if we want to check out the gallery," he says.

"Did we tell you we went to the new library before coming here?" says Anne. "I was impressed. I'd like to go back on a sunny day to see how bright it gets inside with all those windows."

"A sunny day. I guess we'll get one of those sooner or later," says Fred, winding the thick, maroon-coloured scarf his mother gave him for Christmas around his neck.

He notices Jeff talking avidly to Sophie at the cash, as Anne also bundles up, her practical, quilted black jacket at slight odds with a beautiful green scarf. Moving closer to Sophie and Jeff, he catches the tail end of their conversation.

"Thing is," Jeff is saying "I'm involved in a community theatre. I do set design and the occasional bit role. We're amateurs, but we take it seriously. For the love of the craft, so to speak. We're in rehearsal for a show in April… Tennessee Williams' *The Glass Menagerie*."

"No kidding!" says Sophie. "I was in the *Glass Menagerie* about eight years ago, off-Broadway.

Fred cringes inwardly at the juxtaposition of Sophie's New York theatre creds with Jeff's Halifax community group, and regrets mentioning that Sophie is an actress. Jeff's next words do nothing to reassure him.

"There's a rehearsal this weekend," says Jeff. "Not sure if you're interested in coming back to the city, but if you were to pop in and give feedback, everyone would be thrilled."

"Sure," she says, a bit too quickly. God love her, Fred thinks. Trying so hard not to be a snob.

"Don't know how much help I'll be," she adds, more cautiously. "It's been a while since I've done any theatre, and I'm pretty rusty. But I could watch for a bit."

Meanwhile, Jeff is beaming, no other word for it, like a puppy who has been given a bone.

For this time of year, the city is surprisingly crowded. No parking to be found on the streets anywhere near the gallery, so they drop Sophie at the entrance, and Fred directs Anne to a parkade on Purdy's Wharf. He insists on using his card to pay, freezing his fingers as he inserts it into the machine. As they walk along Upper Water Street, the wind from the harbour blasting them, he pulls his scarf tighter around his neck.

They are a few paces from the corner of Hollis Street when Fred sees him, walking towards them on the opposite side of Upper Water. Unmistakable. Little has changed, surprisingly, except that he has shaved his beard but kept his mustache.

Jamie.

Anne says something about the gallery exhibit and how the artist comes from Newfoundland. Except she says '*New*funlund,' the way Americans do. Instinctively, Fred pulls his scarf up around his face, speeds his pace, and takes a sharper turn onto Hollis than strictly necessary. With the wind, there is no way to hear if there are any footsteps behind them. In fact, he can barely hear

Anne's words, but that might be due to a roaring in his ears that has nothing to do with the weather. He feels submerged, trapped, and fighting for air.

"Hey," says Anne. "Can we slow down a bit?"

Guilt shoots through him. And when he apologizes for rushing, strategically glancing over her shoulder to check for Jamie, the guilt is compounded by a feeling of deep shame, he has no idea why. He hopes the breathlessness in his voice can be put down to the cold. For the rest of the walk he tries to focus on Anne's words while he replays what he just saw. Was Jamie thinner? Did he look like he was actively using? Impossible to say. It was odd to see that abstracted look, the one Jamie always had when walking, from a distance, as if witnessing the face of a stranger.

Fuck, Fred thinks. Why can't I leave this alone?

When they finally enter the gallery and see Sophie waiting by the ticket booth, smiling, he finds he can breathe again. Jamie would never come here. Too establishment, too pricey. The warm central heating and the bright expanse of the foyer make Fred feel as if he has reached dry land. Just like when he found Sophie on the beach all those months ago, he would like to hug her. But this time, she is the one rescuing him.

The guide to the exhibit is a middle-aged woman, probably not much older than Anne, but her carefully enunciated Grace Kelly speech, coupled with a Hilary Clinton pantsuit, make her seem like a different generation entirely. The show is impressive for its sheer volume of work, completed, apparently, in-between household chores and raising kids, while Maggie Piper's more famous husband focused on his career. Fred knows that he has little to complain of, in comparison. At least he's not stuck in some godforsaken Newfoundland outport, painting household objects in his spare time. But it isn't all jam jars. There are some striking portraits. Standing in front of a painting of a crouching nude woman with a shadowed, distrustful face, the guide explains, with weird glibness, that the model also posed for the artist's husband and was having an affair with him. Fred hears a sigh of obvious impatience from Anne.

After the guide has left, they hover around a beautiful still life of jars on a windowsill. Glancing back at the nude, Anne whispers: "Imagine spending your whole life trying to create something in your own right, only to have people interpret it based on the state of your marriage."

"Yes," says Sophie cautiously. "It's a little weird. I didn't expect an HBO pilot as art-interpretation."

"Definitely cringe-worthy," says Fred. "Thought I was going to have to excuse myself. TMI in a big way."

There is muffled laughter.

"Do you want to go for tea?" says Sophie, shifting positions and rubbing her back.

"Sure," says Anne, adding, "It's just the imbalance that makes me angry. I bet they don't go on about the husband's marriage when they talk about *his* work."

"Who knows?" says Sophie. "In my world everyone's life is public property. But the movie business is its own kind of skewed. Excuse me for a sec."

While they wait for Sophie to come back from the bathroom, Fred wonders what to make of Anne's gender-based anger. On one level, he is surprised by her vehemence. On the other, he can relate. At one time, he seriously thought Jamie was a genius, that if he supported him and did everything he could to keep him painting, he could somehow bask in that creative glow. And where did that get him? Hiding his face and running away from the guy on the street.

He thinks about his recent foray into art and wonders, if he had he pursued it in his twenties, would he have dived down a well of self-indulgent careerism, or worse, like Jamie? Would being famous have become the goal? Today, although flattered by Anne's interest, all he really wants is for this new skill to warm his daily life, hold angst at bay.

"Hey," says Anne, touching his arm. "You look thoughtful. Everything okay?"

Surprised by this attention, as he was by Sophie rubbing his shoulders earlier, Fred is astonished to feel a lump in his throat. He looks at her face, which is motherly, in a way his mother has never managed to be.

"Yeah," he says. "I saw my ex on the street earlier. Bit of a shock. That's why I sped up. Sorry again."

"Ah…" she says, as if this is the most natural thing in the world. "No worries."

In the café, Sophie tells them about Jeff wanting her to help his theatre group.

Fred laughs. "That's Jeff all over. He loves to schmooze. He'll introduce you as his old friend, the movie star."

"I'm hardly that," says Sophie, panic rising in her eyes.

"Believe me, to those people you are."

"Well, I'm happy to go," she says uncertainly. "But it doesn't seem practical. Coming back to the city and everything."

Anne picks up on this. "I wouldn't mind spending more time at that library. Where is the rehearsal? Maybe we can come for the afternoon, get a meal. What are you up to on Saturday, Fred?"

"Working at the resort."

"Shoot," says Anne. "It'd be nice to see you again."

Once more, Fred feels touched by her kindness. Still, he's not too sorry to be working that night. He would like to absorb what has happened today, renewing his friendship with Sophie, finding a possible new friend in Anne, seeing Jamie. Despite the gas money, he's glad the resort gives him an excuse to get out of town.

He tells them about a Sushi place just around the corner from the church basement where the rehearsal is to happen.

"We can eat there," Anne says to Sophie. "I'll go to the library while you're at the rehearsal, then come along to…"

"Rescue her?" says Fred.

Both women laugh, and Fred joins in. The tight, hollow feeling he has had since seeing Jamie is softened by their smiling faces. Their presence here with him is a talisman against the familiar darkness from which he once thought he would never be free.

| 40 |

Through email, Anne and Fred have settled the price for his bird drawing. The price seemed low to her, but she wasn't about to haggle up. When Jeff comes into the Sushi place where she and Sophie have just eaten dinner, he hands her the drawing in a neatly wrapped parcel. With his other hand, he shakes out an umbrella, an odd thing to carry around at this time of year, but she supposes it's protection from the melting snow, the icicles hanging from buildings.

"I wanted this white stuff to last a little longer," he says, sitting down beside Sophie, across from Anne. "The light was amazing this morning. I took some pictures at Point Pleasant when the snow was still fresh. The chickadees were making a ruckus. Other than that, not a soul or their dog out. Heaven. Absolute heaven."

Jeff tends to punctuate his remarks with these kinds of assessments, Anne has noticed —

Heaven, absolute heaven, or *amazing, beyond astonishing!* Or *shit, unqualified, bottom of the latrine sewage.* Apparently, he is not inclined to recognize middle ground.

"Our winters have changed," he says, and then asks Anne: "Where did you say your cottage was?"

When she answers, Jeff surprises her by telling her he grew up outside of Chester Basin, not far from the point. "You wouldn't believe it," he adds, "but we used to skate on the bay in January and February. It froze over all the way to Tancook Island."

"And people in our so-called government say climate change is a hoax," says Sophie.

"Don't get me started," Jeff says, and then starts. He enters into a long and complicated conspiracy theory which encompasses climate deniers, big oil, the Russian government, and Trump's rise to his current unthinkable position as head of state. Who knows? Anne thinks. These days she is prepared to believe anything.

A waiter comes over and Jeff orders sencha green tea, checking to see that it's loose leaf, not bagged, and that it comes from the Shizuoka province. Anne avoids Sophie's eye and stares down at her own teacup, biting her lip to keep from smiling.

When the waiter is gone, Jeff gestures to her package. "Fred's a great guy," he says in a hearty, bro-like kind of way. "Talented artist too. I keep telling him he should do something with those drawings of his." He nods to Anne in an almost seigniorial way. "Will you be joining our thespian evening?"

Thespian evening? Anne isn't sure, looking at Jeff's cherubic, whiskered face, if this is a joke, or genuine verbal pomposity. His eyes are oddly intense. My God, she suddenly thinks. Could he be flirting?

"I might come by later," she says hurriedly, making a mental note to time it so that Sophie is ready to leave when she arrives. "Have a few errands to do." She stands and Jeff stands too, with a little flourish and another nod of his head. Anne finally makes eye contact with Sophie, who is now sitting still, her nail picking and hair fiddling abandoned, a look of amusement on her face.

"Have fun!" Anne says brightly, heading for the door. "Text me when you need to be picked up."

Once outside, she feels the cold air enter her lungs like a tonic. Her car is in a two-hour parking spot and the library is only a couple of blocks away, so she decides to walk there. The sidewalks are surprisingly slushy, snow-covered in spots, forcing her to occasionally walk on the side of the road. She's surprised how few people seem to be out on the night streets. Cars go by, most of them slowing politely to avoid spattering her.

She sees the library: lit from within, its oddly stacked stories jut into the sky, flanked on either side by the silhouettes of two bare maple trees. When she enters, a gust of warmth greets her, and the sound of hushed voices. She looks forward to climbing the expansive, inviting staircase to revisit the clean white lines of the bookshelves on the second and third stories, their rows of window-facing tables where earnest young people sit with laptops. When Anne was their age, she didn't have anywhere that nice to study. Her university library's darkened windows faced other buildings on campus. She remembers the card systems and microfiche. She also remembers becoming lost in thought while taking handwritten notes on some poet or novelist, no laptop in sight, coming up for air after minutes, sometimes hours, to look around at other faces, similarly rapt, similarly lost.

She heads towards adult fiction and, for a time, wanders from shelf to shelf, taking books out at random, enjoying the crackle of their cellophaned jackets. Without searching for any particular author or subject matter, she allows herself to follow impulses based on titles, colours that catch her eye. Words on book spines dance together, intertwine themselves at random in her thoughts. *Ancient. Anger. Life. Random. Penguin. Mystery. Grace.*

At the end of one row of shelves she comes across a poster for a talk by a local mystery author, happening in ten minutes. Might be interesting. She hasn't been to an author-reading in years, since before Rudy was born. Cultural events have been mostly limited to film festival Q&A's, which she attends mainly to support Nathan. She never manages to completely relax at these talks, her mind often distracted by Nathan's preoccupations with the film, or by her own preoccupations with home and Rudy.

She climbs the stairs to the third floor. The room for the talk is more classroom than auditorium, with hard plastic seats and a whiteboard with a podium up front. Only half a dozen other people. She takes a quick survey: three other middle-aged women, one slightly professorial looking man, a young guy about Rudy's age, and, at the back of the room, an older man in a tuque and bomber jacket. A young librarian is setting up copies of the author's books on the whiteboard ledge. They all have spooky images like x-rayed skulls, or shadowy faces on which titles appear in bold, red letters: MAYHEM, MADNESS, MURDER, reads one. SWEET NOTHINGS IN MY HEAD reads another. Anne's heart sinks. Maybe she can make a discreet exit and go back to her blissful perusal of classics on the second floor, but just then, a fortyish guy with a well-maintained five-o'clock shadow on his chin walks in. He is wearing jeans and Blundstones and a blue blazer, and is trailed by about eight people, including two teenage boys.

After chatting briefly to the librarian, the author takes the podium and announces that he does not plan to follow the usual format and read from his work. Is this a new thing? Anne wonders. People not reading from their novels at readings? Instead, the guy gives an overview of his writing career, and short summaries of each of the books on the whiteboard ledge. The plots seem mildly interesting—espionage thrillers and mysteries involving hospital or psych clinic settings. Anne's wariness increases when the writer embarks on a lengthy description of the protagonist of all these novels, a detective who, like him, is a forensic psychologist.

"I think what drew me to the field of psychology, with a special interest in psychopaths, was my natural distrust of people."

Well, at least he's honest about that, Anne thinks.

"It's a distrust most people share."

Debatable.

"Here's a case in point," the author says. "If someone holds a door for you at a store or a restaurant, how many of you would just walk on through?" He moves away from the podium to demonstrate. "Wouldn't you instead take the door from him because you're afraid he might grab you or something?"

No, Anne thinks automatically, although she supposes he might have a point. It would depend where. Brooklyn? Manhattan? Her hometown? Surely not here? Several people in the audience are nodding their heads. They smile encouragingly at the guy. It appears, from various off-the-cuff remarks and greetings made to the audience, that most of them are either colleagues or family members. She assumes that the remainder are avid perusers of narratives about psychopathic or delusional murderers. Sitting on her plastic chair, stony-faced, Anne is acutely conscious of her immobility, as if the rest of her body has turned to stone as well. She can't figure out a way to leave quietly and discreetly, as the only door is up front, directly beside the author.

In front of her, this well-groomed, athletic-looking man starts to describe some of the cases he has seen and used as fodder for his novels: a murderer who claimed he was zapped by a secret military weapon which caused his aggression on the night he stabbed his girlfriend. A six-foot-four drug dealer with a history of multiple assaults on police officers: "I was inexperienced and had placed him between me and the door… 'How quickly can you make it to the door before I get my hands around your neck?' the guy said at one point. So, I just thought a bit and said: 'Are you flirting with me?'" Appreciative chuckles from the audience. More humour: "This guy at a party I gave was in pretty bad shape because his girlfriend had left him…alternately sinking onto the floor and sobbing, and punching the wall, and all I could think was—Jesus, I hope I don't lose the damage deposit on this place. That's when I knew being your average therapeutic psychologist probably wasn't my life's work."

Good thing.

Aware of a flush rising to her cheeks, she has a sudden memory of her thirteen-year-old self in middle school being forced to listen to a biology teacher talking about *One Flew over the Cuckoo's Nest*, which had just aired on TV the night before. He claimed expertise in mental illness, because he had a distant cousin who had been hospitalized for "manic depression." She remembers her outrage at his condemnation of the movie's skewed portrayal of the medical establishment. True, Nurse Ratchett was way over the top, she recognizes now. But at the time she had loved that film. What outraged her most, she remembers, was the teacher's patronising smile when he said he didn't want the class to be "disturbed or frightened" by the movie.

And what, she wonders, did that little bespectacled man have in common with this writer? She has more reason now to be offended by a writer bent on exploiting people he's been hired to study and heal, people not so different from Rudy. Now the author starts to talk about the subplot of his latest book, which has to do with speaking in tongues. Anne tries to pay attention, wanting to give him the benefit of the doubt. It's a topic she is actually interested in. She remembers reading about trance-like states in a first-year psychology text, and being enthralled as a child by the story of the Tower of Babel, read to her by her mother from a large, beautifully illustrated children's Bible. Bible stories, D'Aulaire's Greek Myths, D'Aulaire's Norse Myths: all essential for true literacy, her father used to say.

Suddenly, behind Anne's back, a new voice starts speaking. It is soft, with an unidentifiable accent—Acadian maybe? Without turning, Anne suspects it's the man in the tuque and bomber jacket. She sits quietly with her head bowed, listening. She can hardly hear the words, but she starts to gather that he is rambling incoherently... She looks up to see the writer's face, suddenly still, as if he has deliberately blanked it, smoothed out all lines of tension and animation.

"These tongues..." the voice behind her says. "I've seen some movies... There's a pattern to do with fire and death. I've always heard about mission control being in another language...Those tongues..." And then, in his strange accent, he utters Anne's favourite phrase of the night: "To me it made no nonsense."

Noticing how quiet the rest of the room has become, Anne wonders how the writer will extricate himself. Eventually the bomber-jacketed guy gives him an out, saying in relatively clear English: "Where does it come from, this speaking in tongues?" Grasping at this question like a life buoy, the author starts to expound on the history of evangelical Christianity and religious fervor, refers to a church in Nova Scotia, the only place he knows of in the province where this still takes place, although there are congregations in the Southern United States, the Bible belt..." *You'd better believe it,* Anne thinks.

All the while, she is noticing something about this moment, that she does not feel the need to rescue the possibly drug-addled, possibly schizophrenic man asking the question. She feels no anxiety about him disrupting this social occasion. In fact, she's grateful. What's more, the adolescent sense of rage that was brewing earlier has vanished. Somehow, this rambling man, coupled with what she recognizes as fear in the writer's eyes, has freed her. There is a slight flush on the author's cheeks as he wraps up his answer and asks for more questions from the floor. Soon the reading ends and people stand to leave. Anne slips out while the author stands surrounded by friends, and does not look back to see if the rambling man is behind her.

| 41 |

"So what are we going to do the rest of our lives?" says a tiny woman with short, almost white hair. "Stay home and watch the parades go by? Amuse ourselves with the glass menagerie, darling?" She's wearing glasses on a chain around her neck, and she puts them on her nose occasionally to peer at her script. The other actors are off book, although there have already been some stumbles and outright fuckups.

This woman is too old for the part of Amanda, thinks Sophie. Tom and Laura, the adult children in the play, would be in their early twenties. That would make Amanda the same age as her own mother—or Anne. These calculations give Sophie an odd sensation, like a coin dropping into a slot in her head.

Of course, this is community theatre, so they have to go with what they have, and makeup and costuming can solve a lot. But, with heart sinking, Sophie watches the woman struggle with a bogus Southern accent transposed onto a genteel Canadian one. She sees tight shoulders where there should be expansive histrionic grace.

Sophie remembers being thrilled to get the role of Laura in this play, after *Liza* was cancelled. She saw it as a creative leap, from bubble-gum teen tv to Tennessee Williams. The director was a woman who reminded Sophie slightly of Pam, her cherished drama teacher, another plus. But in the end, she found limping around as the paralytically shy Laura, playing to half-empty houses night after night, depressed her. She felt ambivalent about the actress who played the crazy ex-Southern bell of a mother in that production too.

"I've seen such pitiful cases in the South —" the tiny woman in this darkened church hall continues, her shoulders reaching up to her ears, hands grasping the script, "barely tolerated spinsters living upon the grudging patronage of sister's husband or brother's wife!—stuck away in some little mousetrap of a room—encouraged by one in-law to visit another—little bird-like women without any nest—eating the crust of humility all their life! Is that the future that we've mapped out for ourselves?"

Here the director, an overweight seventyish man with his own spectacle chain around his neck, intervenes. His voice is overly patient, and he rubs his forehead like John Houseman in *The Paper Chase,* that dreary old show from the eighties which Sophie's mother used to watch reruns of, for some reason.

The director starts talking about verbal emphasis—*pitiful, mousetrap, nest, humility.* He's right as far as that goes, Sophie thinks, but he should drop all that right now. The woman playing Amanda is already too tied up in words, she needs to get her body into the character. The woman struggles on. Thankfully, the younger actress has the bulk of the lines in the next part of the scene. She isn't half bad. She's got the physicality down, from the slight limp to a nervous gesture of picking at her finger nails every once in a while. But the scene ends on the older woman.

"Vivacity and—charm! That's all you have to do... One thing your father had plenty of—was charm!"

Everyone gathers for director's notes. Her heart sinking again, Sophie realizes this guy's default strategy is sarcasm. He waves his glasses around in faux jocularity and then starts to hone in. Instead of saying: "Remember to cheat to the audience," he says, "This is a piece of theatre, folks, not a private dinner party." Instead of "Stay planted," he says, "Our bodies are not gyrating on a strobe-lit dance floor, they are giving and receiving information." Instead of reminding them to stay in character when receiving someone else's lines, he says "Try to look at least a *bit* interested, people." Sophie is ignored, even though, according to Jeff, this man knew she was coming and was looking forward to her feedback.

Watching the actors, she sees serious reverence in their eyes. They consider this throwback to another century an expert. She wonders what his day job is. The younger woman smiles slightly at a compliment thrown her way, but there is discomfort in her eyes when he goes on to say curtly to the older woman: "Denise, off script is mandatory for the next rehearsal, and please ditch the glasses, at least until the scene where she's doing her "Homemaker's Companion" pitch." He again waves his own glasses around, perches them on his nose to demonstrate, then goes on to say: "One assumes she's a vain woman who is horrified by the passage in time as it relates to her own attractions. So do your best to look the part." Sophie sees with mounting compassion and anger the older woman's shoulders rising higher and higher, her head nodding perfunctorily, anxiety in her eyes.

"Of course," says the director while making a sweeping gesture that encompasses Sophie, "I should let our guest join our conversation." He pats a chair beside him. "Come join us Sophie," he says, as if they are best friends.

Shit, she thinks. Well, I got myself into this. Sitting next to the director, her anger makes her opt for sun-dazzling positivity. She is all smiles. She introduces herself, downplays her career, says she played Laura a few years back and found it an amazing and challenging experience.

"You all did *great*," she says, aiming extra sunbeams in the direction of the older woman. She's aware of Jeff at the back of the room, who has paused in his painting of a set piece. Trying to think of something intelligent to say, she starts to talk about how difficult it is to capture the mixture of obedience, terror and suppressed anger that Laura must feel, how important it is to make Amanda seem real and understandable—a product of depression-era hardship and the limited options women had back then. Practically quoting her New York director verbatim.

The players move on to the "Homemaker's Companion" scene. The intro by Tom is flat, colourless. In spite of herself, Sophie remembers Farid, imbuing all his monologues with so much subtext: guilt, anger, compassion, his voice melodious, his eyes warm.

The director does not intervene. It's as if, in his eyes, Tom's narration is just stage direction. But he leans forward and perches on the edge of his seat to watch Denise, the Amanda actor, continue to struggle, using her glasses as a prop, now, and pretending her script is her magazine subscription list. She mimes the telephone receiver, since they don't have that prop set up yet, and alternates between sitting and standing. When she stands and starts to pace, the director says, "No, no, stay *there*. The telephone cord. I'm sure we all remember those? There were no cell phones in the nineteen thirties."

Sophie would like to stand and pace, too. In fact, she would like to pace over to the director's chair and overturn it. This is only the third rehearsal. The production is months away. Why is he insisting on everyone being off book so early? Then again, they probably only meet weekly. It can't be easy, this amateur theatre thing.

She stands. "You're doing fine," she calls out before she can stop herself. "Just relax."

I've just interrupted, she thinks, overridden the director. She avoids looking at him or at Jeff, who has come up to turn a chair backwards and sit in it, resting his arms and chin on the back, three paces away from her. The woman has stopped, and is looking at Sophie, slightly confused. Sophie knows she can't abandon her now. "Maybe you could hear what the woman on the other end of the line is saying in your head. Picture what she looks like, if your character knows her personally." Without thinking she says: "Here, I'll be her. Don't look at me though, pretend I'm miles away." She smiles, hopes to God she hasn't just muddied the waters further, and says, "Go back to the question about the sinus condition…"

She finds herself slipping easily into her Southern drawl from the New

York production, interposes "Well now, not too good, Amanda," before Denise can rush on with her next line, and then exclaims in over-the-top horror, "I think my casserole is burning!" which elicits laughter from Jeff and titters from the actors. Again, she doesn't look at the director, but says, still facing the stage, "Now do it over again, imagining all that." She watches, relieved, as the woman stands still to deliver her lines and doesn't do too bad a job, pausing at the right places to listen, forgetting about her glasses. Thank God, she thinks, when the other actors and the director chuckle appreciatively at her outraged exclamation: "Heavens!—I think she's hung up!"

She sits down briefly, feels the baby kick, then a need to pee. An excuse to leave the room. And when she is sitting in the surprisingly clean and modern ladies' room at the back of the church, she finds herself breathing as if she has just run a marathon. She does not want to go back in there. The next scene is audible through the door—an explosive argument between Tom and Amanda, the kind of thing that requires pacing and precision, something these guys are in no way able to achieve at this point. She decides to go outside for some fresh air for a bit.

Back inside, she listens a bit more, makes a few discreet comments on blocking, and then tells them Anne is on her way to pick her up, which is true, since she has just texted her.

"I'll say bye now," she says. "Don't want to distract you in the middle of the next scene. No stay there," she adds hurriedly to Jeff, who is making moves to walk to the door with her. Then turning to the actors taking their places on stage, she calls: "You guys are great! Can't wait to hear how the run goes."

Sophie hopes her exit looks nonchalant rather than hasty. Anne arrives ten minutes later.

Thank God," she says as Anne pulls away from the curb.

"That bad?" says Anne.

"Not the actors so much," she says "They were fine. It was the director."

"Oh?"

"Let's just say he was not what they needed."

They drive through town in companionable silence and take the ramp to the highway. Staring into the darkness, Sophie tries to recover her equilibrium. It was only an hour of her time after all. And she's all for supporting community theatre…but the thought that it's community theatre irks her even more. Those people *volunteered* to be bitched at by that guy. It's different if you're at least getting paid. Well maybe not that different, she thinks, remembering Hugh Wilkinson's unkindness, and worse, according to Farid, to kids who were as young as sixteen on the set of *Liza*.

Bill hadn't been like Wilkinson, or this community theatre guy. He had listened to actors' ideas, experimented with dialogue to make people more comfortable. There was the odd exception, of course, when he really didn't click with someone. Like Barbara Shelby who provoked that fat-shaming episode that made her feel like a mean girl. Bill was definitely way more sarcastic with Barbara than he should have been. Sophie thinks back to the younger actress's eyes tonight when that guy had praised her and put down Denise. It felt like that on set with Barbara. But had she, Bill's director's pet, done anything? Said anything? Only to Barbara, after the fact. Never in the moment. Never to Bill. Instead she had basked, albeit shamefacedly, in the fact that Bill had never spoken that way to her.

"He was a shithead, actually, the director," she says.

"Oh no, really?" says Anne absently. She turns on the windshield wipers as a few snowflakes settle on the glass.

"Some people think the definition of genius is being an asshole. You know," Sophie adds, glancing over at Anne's profile. "Nathan never falls into that trap. He's always kind. Always a gentleman."

"Well," says Anne, sounding somewhat unsure of herself. "I'm glad to hear that."

"Everyone loves him," says Sophie quietly. "You're lucky."

"And what about Bill?" says Anne after a moment. "Does everyone love Bill?"

"I used to think so," says Sophie. "People talk about how 'empowering' he is to work with. You know, in interviews at film festivals and stuff, when everyone's saying nice things about each other."

"And is he? Empowering, I mean?"

"Up to a point," says Sophie, and falls silent again, thinking again about Barbara. All the stuff Bill said to Barbara about authenticity and the limits of technique, pronouncing "technique" like it was a swear word, looking Barbara in the eye with a slight sneer as he said it. It comes to her, as if on a tidal wave, that Bill didn't know what he was talking about. Barbara was a beautiful actress. But at the time, Sophie had been unsure, wondered if he was right, even though she deplored his rudeness. She had been spineless.

Another flood of memories comes upon Sophie—memories of theatre school, of her family, of always being the person treated with cotton gloves, because she was talented, because she was pretty, because she never opened her fucking mouth to disagree with anyone who might give her a good role. She thinks about her blindness to potentially criminal abuse happening on the set of *Liza*. She thinks about her blindness to what happened to Jack.

There is only dark sky outside the car window, and the darker silhouettes of trees, the fluorescent-painted road lines zipping by.

They pass a sign that says: "Bridgewater-95 km."

Sophie's phone rings, and when she looks at the screen, she sees it's Jeff.

"*Sophie,*" he says in a momentous voice after she answers. "Didn't get the chance to say it, because you left so quickly, but you were *brilliant. Absolutely brilliant.*"

She winces. All she had done was parrot her former director's notes, then try a simple exercise that they might well have used back in theatre school. "Not really," she says. "They all seemed to be doing fine with the play, anyway."

"Denise, in particular, was grateful for your suggestions," Jeff sweeps on. "Harrison too."

Harrison?

"I would imagine it is excruciatingly difficult to direct one's spouse. I wouldn't know of course, never having entered the state of matrimonial bliss, myself."

"Of course," Sophie says faintly.

"I have been told to say you are welcome back anytime and there will be free tickets at the box office for you."

"Thanks! Have a good night, Jeff. And thanks for inviting me. It was a pleasure to meet everyone." Almost true, she thinks.

When she rings off, she says, "I don't believe it."

"What?"

"The nasty director I was telling you about? Turns out the actor he was being the nastiest to is his *wife.*"

"Ah…" says Anne, turning up the speed of the windshield wipers. "A depressing little detail. It might have been helpful to know that ahead of time."

"Jesus. I nearly told him to fuck off on her behalf!"

"Well, at least you avoided that little social faux pas."

"Holy shit. Married people should never, *ever,* work together."

"You're probably right. Good thing I'm not an actress and you're not a musician," says Anne, laughing slightly. It's companionable laughter, unforced and untroubled.

Hesitantly, Sophie joins in, but beneath her laughter, her compassion for Denise doubles, triples. "I guess we're both lucky," she says.

The snowflakes fall, the windshield wipers swish, and the fluorescent lines zip by.

After a moment, Anne says quietly, "Yes, I think we are. Thanks for reminding me of that, Sophie."

| 42 |

Aɴɴᴇ ʟɪsᴛᴇɴs ᴛᴏ Nᴀᴛʜᴀɴ's ᴠᴏɪᴄᴇ on the phone as she drinks tea, propped up in bed with pillows piled against the headboard. It takes a while for her to compute what he's saying.

"A dog?" she says. "You want to buy Rudy a dog?"

"Not buy," says Nathan. "Adopt. There are all kinds of strays in shelters who need homes."

"But why a dog?"

"I just think it would be good for him to be responsible for something, or someone."

"I'd settle for him being reliably responsible for himself," says Anne.

"He's not doing badly," says Nathan. "He's eating okay. Taking his meds. Getting exercise. He'll get even more exercise if he has a dog to walk."

Anne tries to picture Rudy's forlorn frame with a dog on a lead. Fails. Then hates herself for failing. Why shouldn't Rudy be capable of looking after a pet? Why should she assume this idea has no merit?

"Does he want to get a dog?"

"Hard to say," says Nathan. "But when I mentioned the possibility, he didn't shut it down."

"But what gave you the idea?" she says.

"We went for a hike at Poet's Walk Park a few days ago and met someone with a beautiful dog. It got me thinking."

The name Poet's Walk Park evokes childhood walks with her parents, her father telling her the story of Rip Van Winkle as they went. It also brings back the memory of Nathan and a ten-year-old Rudy sitting on either side of her on a handmade tree-limb bench, eating the cheese sandwiches Rudy used to like. She remembers reading to him there—*A Wrinkle in Time*? Narnia?—an October wind ruffling the pages. She was always the one to initiate that kind of outing, in the spring or fall. At this time of year, it would be too cold and snowy for Nathan and Rudy to sit on that bench.

"It's great you went to the park," she says. "Makes for a change of scene."

"Yeah well, bit of a chore to get him to go," says Nathan. "Not only did I have to climb the stairs and hammer on the door to break through the kid's online world, when we got in the car, I realized he was wearing sneakers. Claimed he didn't know where his winter boots were."

"Tell me about it," says Anne.

"Anyway, I told him I'd warm up the car while he looked for them. He found them eventually, but Jesus. In four months the kid will be eighteen."

Hearing Nathan relay an experience she has lived daily for years is strangely unsettling. She wonders if the remark about Rudy being nearly eighteen is a judgment on her parenting. Does Nathan think she has coddled Rudy, done too much for him? She's not sure if she would have waited patiently in the car while Rudy unearthed the boots, or gone in to find them herself.

"Actually," says Nathan, "the dog owner at the park was someone Rudy knows. Kim, the yoga teacher at the day program?"

Yoga. Another one of her ideas. The teacher. Blond shoulder-length hair. Pretty face. Sweet disposition. Not unlike some of the young actresses Nathan has championed over the years. Not unlike Sophie.

"I thought Rudy was really taken with the dog. But you know what, Anne?" Nathan continues. "I think I misread the signs there. Turns out he was actually more taken with Kim."

She puts her teacup on the night table and sits up a little straighter. "Are you sure about that?" Are you sure you're not projecting? she thinks, but does not say.

"Rudy pretty much told me."

"*What?*"

"When I said afterwards that I noticed he was interested in his friend's dog, his exact words were, "Actually, it's not the *dog* I was interested in.""

Anne can hear a new note in Nathan's voice, not just amusement, but exultation. He has been bewildered and disempowered by Rudy's psychosis, and probably feels now that *this* is something he can get a handle on. *This* is something he understands. She herself is torn between joy and compassion, imagining Rudy blurting out this oblique confession. He must know he hasn't any hope in that quarter. Kim is at least twenty-eight—plus morally and legally bound to keep her distance. And Rudy can barely look anyone in the eye.

"But Nathan," she says, "if it wasn't the dog he was interested in, why do you still want to get one?"

"Like I said, I just think it would be good for him. And when I suggested it, he didn't object to the idea."

Well he wouldn't, thinks Anne. He is master at saying nothing at all, unless he is in mid-psychotic break. Then she thinks back to the time she heard Rudy banter with Nathan about the food at the hospital. She remembers her conversation with him before she left, when he said, "It's all good. I'm doing better now."

Which must be true, if he's confessing crushes to Nathan. There is a pain just below her left ribs, like a slight echo of the pain that prompted her to say 'I haven't lost you, have I?' after writing that poem, if that's what it was. But this is what she wanted. Nathan taking time with Rudy, getting closer to him, while she took a break.

"Well, I suppose…" she says slowly. "Talk to him some more. If you think it's the right thing to do…"

"The dog won't be your responsibility, I promise," says Nathan. "I'll be on it if Rudy lets the ball drop."

Nathan grew up with dogs. She has seen photos of one named Bailey in an album his mother showed her in Montreal. If Rudy hadn't gotten sick, maybe he would have suggested this sooner.

"What do you think?" he asks. He sounds like he's pleading now. Does he really feel the need to do that? Is that how she comes off, as some kind of domestic tyrant? When did that happen in their marriage?

"It's fine. Do what you think is best," she says.

There is a brief silence, during which she wishes she could say more, something about the shift she felt inside herself when she wrote those words about Rudy, something about how sad she feels that they cannot be close and spontaneous, the way they used to be.

"Any other news?" she asks.

"Not much," he says. "Bill sent me the new treatment."

"Oh? Interesting?"

"Not to me. He wasn't kidding when he said it would be different from his other work."

"How so?"

"It's called *When the Time Comes*," says Nathan.

"Sounds ominous."

"It's ominous all right. I can't decide if it's an attempt at satire, or a satire of a satire, stuck in some endless post-modern feedback loop. If that's Bill's reaction to the 'soup pot' of romantic comedy, I think I'd rather be the frog."

"The frog?"

"You know, boiling alive?"

"Oh, right." She had forgotten that ridiculous metaphor.

"What's it about?" she asks.

"Let's see," says Nathan. "Orating politician babies. People hard wired to their virtual-reality gaming universes. Face transplants that also transplant celebrity neurophysiology into the brain…"

"No way!" She starts to laugh.

"Well it does make a person laugh, but probably not for the reasons Bill intended. I've reread the thing about five times, sure I must be missing something, but I'm lost. I'm pretty certain the film-going public would be, too, but who knows? These days, there's an audience for everything."

"So what are you going to do?"

"Look up who is behind the latest crop of dystopian and satirical stuff and suggest some names to him. It would have to be TV, I think… Much as I'd like to have a new project to work on, I can't see doing this. I'll tell him the genre doesn't fit our partnership."

She can imagine him searching for the best wording in order to avoid Bill's prickly side, if Bill has any side that isn't prickly. From what she's gathered, Bill's prickliness has encompassed his whole being lately, like a blowfish on alert.

"Anyway, how are things up there?" says Nathan. "How's Sophie?" In his voice, she hears an unspoken, additional question. She is fast approaching the two-week mark of this odd little holiday, her tentative end date. And then what? A return to family life with a dog thrown into the mix. Nathan slowly climbing out of his career hole, maybe even working with Sophie again, once her baby is born. Normalcy coming back to their lives, if Rudy can stay on track.

She tells Nathan about the bird drawing she bought from Fred, and then about the art exhibit they went to, and how much she loves the new library. He listens, putting in the odd question here and there, with the cordiality of a good talk show host or diplomat. She hears his warm, confident voice, something she has always loved about him, but she hears it like the soundtrack of a classic movie. She hears him in fifties' black and white.

"It must be time for you to pick up Rudy," she says, glancing at her bedside clock.

"It's an hour earlier here than there, remember."

"Oh…Right."

"Anne," Nathan says. "I want you to know that whatever you need, it's fine. Stay up there for as long as necessary, or come back as soon as you want…"

Does she know what she wants? She feels a tightness in her throat, thinks of Sophie's assessment of Nathan, when they were driving back from Halifax last week. *He's always kind. Always…a gentleman.* She remembers her surprise at hearing that antiquated word from a young woman's lips. She clears her throat.

"Thanks," she says.

Her voice sounds dead to her ears. The voice of someone tone deaf, hearing a famous piece of music but shut off from its beauty. *Everyone loves him*, Sophie said. *You're lucky.*

"Thank you," she says again. "It sounds like Rudy is doing okay, right?"

"Absolutely."

"Then, maybe I could stay for another week or so. But don't hesitate to call if it feels like things are going south.

"You bet. We'll talk in a couple of days."

He's a good father. She can't deny that. They are not where they were a few years ago. Even if a kid sinking into psychosis was beyond him back then, a recovering kid, showing glimmers of normality, is not beyond him now. He doesn't need her to rush in and take charge.

She goes downstairs to find Sophie restless, pacing, staring out the window at the road, which has recently been scraped clean by the plow. In the space of ten days, snow has fallen, melted to slush, frozen to ice, melted again. Now another light dusting has come down. Even though it's late afternoon, the sun is visible, a testament to the lengthening days.

"It looks beautiful out there," Anne says.

"Want to go for a walk before it gets dark?"

"Sure, let me just get these dishes out of the way…No, don't worry about it. I'll have them done by the time you get your snow boots laced up."

"You have a point," says Sophie, waddling—there is no other word for it—to the front hall. She has definitely gotten bigger since Anne arrived. Once again, Anne questions the length of her visit. She knows she can't stay forever, but the thought of heading back to New York fills her with heaviness. A sad little heap of her mother's photo albums, clothes, and keepsakes will be waiting for her when she gets back.

She and Sophie walk all the way past the mailboxes and down to the lobster house by the water's edge.

"Want to keep going?" she asks, slightly surprised by Sophie's unflagging pace.

"Yeah, let's go right to the end of the road. I've only done that once since I got here."

They continue on. The air is sharp as it enters Anne's lungs but there is no wind. The bay, on their right, is still as glass, the treeline of the coast road reflected in it like a careful student watercolour, the islands in the distance also doubled. Each time they pass another wharf and abandoned summer home, Anne thinks Sophie might be ready to turn around, but they keep going. They head past the last of the houses, a bungalow set high up on a hill, its front lawn bordered on one side by a swath of trees.

"Oh look!" Anne says, spotting movement at the woods' edge. "Deer."

There are six or seven of them, stalking into the open, nosing around for any green shoots they can find hidden in the snow-powdered, mostly dead grass. "They must be hungry this time of year," she says, then stops, surprised by a flash of white among the tan-coloured coats.

"What on earth is that? A goat?"

Sophie grabs her elbow. "Oh my God!"

Anne looks at her in surprise.

"I think it's a white deer!"

Anne shades her eyes to see more clearly. In the uncertain, late afternoon light, the odd-looking animal seems almost supernatural, a living shadow, or an underexposed double of its peers. It moves in and out of the herd, looking for a spot to graze with skittish energy. Suddenly it lifts its front hooves and takes a run at another deer of its own size, pushing it out of the way. Anne and Sophie both laugh.

"It must be a young one. Knows what it wants, anyway," Anne says.

"This is amazing!" Sophie says. "I didn't think I'd get the chance to see it, not before spring, anyway. Claudine says everyone's talking about it on Facebook. She says seeing it is good luck."

"I can believe that."

"I wish we could get closer."

Anne says nothing, but leads the way. They move past the ditch that separates them from the grassy slope and start to slowly walk up the house's driveway, but the herd of deer, still at least eighty yards away, immediately freeze-frame, heads up, ears twitching. Anne and Sophie do the same. When the herd goes back to grazing, Anne and Sophie edge forward a bit more, but the deer closest to the woods suddenly leaps into the trees like there's a wildfire behind it, and all the others follow. The flash of the white is swallowed up in the commotion. Then there is stillness, as though they were never there at all.

They walk home in joyous camaraderie. Sophie talks about the deer that come into her parents' backyard. Anne tells Sophie about the barn owl that once nested near her and Nathan's campsite at Bear Mountain Park, the strange hissing noise it made if anyone came near. That camping trip was their honeymoon, the only holiday Nathan could afford back then. She had loved the park, snuggling in with Nathan at night to keep warm, crawling out of their tent every morning to take in the sunrise while he slept on.

Anne notices that the deer sighting has given Sophie a new lightness, a buoyancy to her step that propels her along, right until she has crossed the threshold of the cottage and is in the front hall, bending to take off her boots. Then she suddenly sits down heavily on the storage bench near the coat rack. Anne has a moment of anxiety, wondering if the flimsy thing, bought at a local antique shop years ago, will hold.

"Easy!" she laughs. "Need some help with those?" Then she notices that Sophie is not smiling, but instead grimacing, her hand on her belly.

"Jesus," Sophie says. "Everything's gone tight as a drum. It hurts. I haven't felt that before. Oh shit…"

"Okay…" Anne hears herself take on the deliberately calm tone she uses with Rudy. "Let me get your boots off."

As she unlaces the boots, she looks up to see panic rising in Sophie's eyes. A hint of tears as well. She remembers how vulnerable she felt when she was pregnant, how her sense of self shunted back to emotional, as well as physical, toddlerhood.

"It's a false alarm, Sophie," she says gently. "They're called Braxton Hicks contractions. I got a pile of them with Rudy."

A more specific memory. She and Nathan taking a tour of the maternity ward, the nurse hooking her up to a baby monitor "just for fun" and then insisting she stay there for the next two hours for observation because of slight contractions Anne couldn't even feel. But Sophie can obviously feel these ones.

"I've read about them," says Sophie. "But I haven't felt anything like this before. What if? I'm barely into my seventh month. Tim's gig isn't for another two weeks."

"Whoa. Hold your horses," says Anne. Where did that come from? Her mother's phrase —her lips piping those words like a ventriloquist's dummy. "Try not to overthink it," she says. "We probably just overdid it with that long walk. And remember the white deer? Good luck, right? Not bad."

Sophie's face is downturned. She's breathing slowly as if meditating.

"Here," says Anne. "Let's get your coat off and we'll go into the living room, okay?"

Sophie lets Anne remove her coat and hang it up and then walks slowly across the kitchen floor. Anne wonders if she should take her arm.

"Here's what we're going to do," she says. "You're going to sit on the sofa with your feet on this little footstool here." She nudges the worn and stained artifact up to Sophie's shins. "We'll watch a dumb movie on TV. I'm going to get you a hot water bottle." Her mother again. Hot water bottles being the main panacea of their family home. "And if you're still concerned," she finishes, "you can call Claudine and see what she says." Anne keeps her voice light, but at the same time walks over to the kitchen plug where Sophie's phone has been charging, unplugs it and takes it over to Sophie.

After calling Claudine, who says she will come within the hour, Sophie chooses one of Rudy's old Harry Potter DVDs from the movie shelf, confirming Anne's belief about pregnancy sending people back to emotional childhood. Each to her own escape, she thinks. She read a pile of Agatha Christie novels when Rudy was at his worst. During the movie, Sophie closes her eyes and resumes her yogic breathing a couple of times, but doesn't say anything, and Anne opts not to ask. She lets the perky child actors and Scottish scenery wash over her, without hearing a word of dialogue.

Forty minutes in, Claudine shows up. She waves away Sophie's apologies, saying that she was returning from the city when she got Sophie's call. "Your house is totally on my way," she says, pulling an old-fashioned stethoscope from her bag—a reassuring bit of Norman Rockwell technology.

"Braxton Hicks, our little friend," says Claudine, after getting Sophie to listen to the baby's steady heartbeat. "Everything looks totally normal for where you are in your term, Sophie. These are just little practice moves your body's decided to scare you with."

The woman exudes calm like lavender oil from a diffuser.

"If you're okay with it," Claudine says, "I'm going to leave a tincture here. It's something a naturopath I know recommends. Totally harmless to the baby, although you should put it in boiling water and let it cool before taking it, so the alcohol evaporates off." She goes to the kitchen sink, washes her hands with the dish soap, locates the kettle and fills it from the tap. "It's called skullcap, but don't let the scary name fool you."

"I've heard of it," says Sophie quickly, her voice sounding less tremulous, much more like the Sophie Anne knows. "My mother used to take it for... something. I'm not sure what."

Maybe mothers get to redeem themselves in times of crisis, Anne thinks.

Even the mere ritual of pouring the boiling water over a few drops of the strange-smelling brown liquid is soothing. As Claudine shows Sophie how much to use, Anne can see the last vestiges of anxiety drain from Sophie's face. She wishes she had had someone like Claudine around when she went through this with Rudy, instead of a worried twenty-five-year-old nurse staring at a fetal monitor.

Claudine suggests Sophie make an early night of it. She stays until Sophie is safely in bed with her door closed. Anne's respect for the midwife deepens.

"I can't thank you enough for taking all this time," she whispers, when they are alone in the kitchen. "Would you like a cup of tea or something to eat before you go?"

"No worries," says Claudine, reaching for her coat. "I had an amazing meal in the city with some friends from nursing school. I'm full of tea and cheesecake."

"So, the skullcap is the thing…" Anne says tentatively.

"Ideally, just before she goes to bed, to keep her from waking up at night with these little contractions and getting worried. She can take it in the day occasionally if she feels anything major. I figure when they happen a lot, it's the body's way of saying 'take a break, put your feet up.' Just like you got her to do." She nods in approval in Anne's direction. Anne feels like a school kid who's just gotten a gold star. "Doctors sometimes recommend bed rest if they're really serious," Claudine adds, "but I don't think that's necessary here. It'll just make her more anxious."

"I know what you mean," says Anne. "Sophie isn't exactly the bed rest type. Have you ever seen her act?"

"No," says Claudine, pulling on her gloves. "I'd like to though. She's done some TV shows and movies, right?" The way she says 'TV shows and movies' makes it sound like an exotic hobby—archery or bonsai tree shaping.

"I'll write down a couple of titles for you," says Anne. "She really is lovely in them, so much energy and intelligence." She wonders if Sophie has explained their friendship to this woman. For all she knows, Claudine might think she's Sophie's older cousin or aunt.

"So…." says Claudine. "Sophie's partner's arriving in three weeks?"

"Just over," says Anne, retrieving the calendar she has taped to the fridge to check the date of Tim's gig.

"And you'll be here at least until then?"

Anne looks up. Claudine's face is relaxed, but there is a certain purposefulness to her expression, as if she is resolving one last piece of business.

"Yes," says Anne.

"Good," says Claudine, who takes the scrap of paper with the jotted-down movie titles and smiles. "It's great that you guys saw that deer. It'll be a story for her to tell the kid when it's old enough."

"The kid…yes. Yes, it will be."

After Claudine leaves, Anne roams the house for a while, tidying things that don't really need to be tidied, thinking of Nathan, thinking of Rudy. Glancing up to look out the window into the black winter night, she examines how she feels about saying yes to staying until Tim's arrival. How, in the back of her mind, she imagines more solitary walks in this wintry beauty, more relaxed conversations that have nothing to do with Rudy, or joint marital decisions about his care, finances and the future. The relief she feels about uttering that one-syllable word is almost as great as her relief that Sophie is okay.

| 43 |

Tim has returned Sophie's commercial voice-acting reel, fully edited, with guitar, keyboard and even a banjo in the background. She's blown away by how pro it sounds. Anne laughs out loud at the banjo track behind a promo for granola bars.

"If he's this good on the commercial reel, I can't wait to hear what he does for your audiobook one," she says.

"He's planning to send that one this week. He thinks it just needs some very subtle transition music. He doesn't want to overpower the words."

"Sensible of him. So what's the next step?"

"I'll send it to Patty. Also keep an eye out for markets."

"Good plan. Especially since you can do all of that with your feet up and a cushion behind your back."

"Hmm, says Sophie, "too much more of this taking it easy and any muscles I may have managed to maintain in the past few months will turn to flab."

Although March has arrived, the ice has settled back in on the Point Road. Sophie would love to repeat the wondrous experience of the white deer sighting, but the road conditions have made that impossible. The one time she tried going for a walk, Anne wanted to hold hands like kids on a playground. It was kind of sweet and companionable, until Anne also skidded, nearly toppling Sophie, and was so unnerved that she insisted they turn back then and there.

"You could always do a prenatal fitness video," says Anne now.

"No, I really think I want to get out. Not on the road though," she says in reply to Anne's look. "I'll go down to the shore behind us. The snow in the backyard isn't slippery, and it's just sand down there."

"Well okay," says Anne, with a slight frown. "But take your phone so you can call me, just in case."

So, after laboriously donning her snow boots, Sophie marches through the snow down to the shoreline and paces back and forth on the sand, like a sentry on duty. There is a tightening in her belly once, but she breathes through it. She assumes these little twinges are as comparable to giving birth as a bumpy bus ride is to an earthquake.

This small wintry stretch of waterfront bears no resemblance to the beach behind the resort. She can barely recall that other, slim-bodied Sophie, pacing the endless expanse like a refugee, uprooted and unnerved. She picks up some scallop shells, washed clean by the winter tide, and puts them in her pocket so she can arrange them around a tulip bed on the house's south side. The tulip bed is nothing but frozen dark earth now, but Anne says the red and yellow blooms are lovely in the spring. Sophie doesn't mind the numbing cold on her fingertips when she takes off her gloves to place the shells. She knows she will soon feel the sting of blood rush back into them when she goes inside and stands by the wood stove.

When she enters the house, Anne is drinking tea in the kitchen.

"It's still freezing out there," Sophie says, unwrapping her scarf and hanging her coat above the storage bench. "But something is shifting, you know? A whiff of spring, maybe."

"Don't you believe it," says Anne. "Mary Ellen says snow in April is almost an annual tradition. Who knows, your little one might be born in a blizzard."

"Well as long as Claudine can make it. And as long as Tim doesn't get trapped in weather on his way up."

Tim will be here in sixteen days. Sophie's anticipation of this event expresses itself in a small series of bubbling sensations in her belly, not unlike the early flutterings when the baby was still the size of her hand. She doesn't feel the yearning ache she used to feel when Tim was away, and she was home alone in their apartment in Brooklyn. Again, it must be the little acrobat inside her, keeping that at bay.

"How's he doing?" says Anne.

"Great. The band is practicing like crazy for the Ballroom show. They've got a gig at a local pub this weekend. A dress-rehearsal." She manages, grunting a little, to get her boots off, then heads to the fridge to hunt for some yogurt.

"Wanted to talk to you about that," says Anne. "Not the gig, but Tim's arrival. Are you okay if I stay until he gets here? I'll take off the next morning. Just remind me of the date again." She puts down her mug and picks up her pen, searching in her purse for something to write on.

The joyful flutterings Sophie has been feeling suddenly cease.

"Anne," she says. "This is your house not mine."

"Oh, I don't see it that way." Anne has her motherly face on, the one she had when Sophie was panicking over the Braxton Hicks contractions. "This is your space for the time being, Sophie," she says. "Yours and Tim's and the baby's. I've enjoyed sharing it with you for the past few weeks though."

"Well, in that case, there's no rush for you to leave, even when Tim gets here. Unless," Sophie falters, "you need to get back to Nathan and Rudy? I hope you're not staying longer than you want to, just to keep me company?" For a moment, her newfound joy in female companionship fades. She misses the straightforward camaraderie of the guys on set or Tim's musical buddies. Men can be dense, but they don't dance around each others' feelings the way women do.

Anne picks up her tea mug again. "Nathan and Rudy are doing pretty well without me actually. Did I tell you they're getting a dog? There's a litter of puppies at the local shelter. Once they're old enough to be weaned, one of them is ours."

"Really? What breed?"

"A lab-shepherd, apparently, which sounds like a noisy and active mix."

The look of dread on Anne's face is so out of sync with her usual calm demeanor that Sophie starts to laugh. Anne smiles, runs her hand through her hair. "I told Nathan to go ahead, do it if Rudy seemed keen, because it could be a good father and son bonding thing. But honestly, I'm not much of a dog person. Part of my reason for wanting to stay another two weeks is so that the thing will at least be house trained by the time I get home."

"Well, since you're going back to puppy chaos, I guess I can admit that I was hoping you would stay, even after Tim gets here." This thought, only half-formed in Sophie's mind before she utters it, begs another question which she feels too shy to ask.

"Sweet of you." Anne has lost her motherly look but there is a softening in her face. "I can't intrude on you and Tim though," she says. "I imagine you will need some alone time before all this happens. It's a pretty big deal in your lives."

"No kidding," says Sophie. "I thought it would be a walk in the park. You know, just another day at the office."

Anne exhales. "Have you talked to Tim about me hanging around like a third wheel?"

Sophie looks down at the table. "Well, not exactly," she says uncomfortably. "But I told him how great you've been, how relieved I was to have you here when we called up Claudine about those contractions. He's really glad you're with me."

"I'm glad I'm with you, too," says Anne softly.

Sophie meets Anne's eyes, so blue, so calm. It seems like the most effortless thing in the world to pose her next question.

"You can say no to this if you like. But, aside from Claudine, I would love it if you were there for the birth. You've helped me so much, lending me this place, being here for me. I feel like you're part of it all, sort of. I'd like to think of you as a godmother to this kid. I'd be honored, actually."

Anne's eyes have widened. She lets out a sound that is half-way between a laugh and a gasp. A sound that Sophie would never have associated with her.

"Well! That would certainly be an experience to write home about! My God! *You'd* be honored! Sophie…I don't know what to say."

"Just think about it," says Sophie, noticing that and that Anne's eyes are slightly teary, and that her own flutterings of joy have started up again. There is the sound of honking outside. The geese are back, ready to waddle all over the back lawn, shitting their hearts out, letting Sophie and Anne know that they consider this place to be their home, too.

In the afternoon, they go to the Shore Café with their laptops to catch up on their emails. There is a buzz of conversation around them. Three high school students—two girls and a boy—throw words and occasional articles of clothing at each other. Sophie, stirring almond milk into her tea, hears one of them, a slightly heavyset girl with shoulder length brown hair, say, "Ever been to the States or Mexico?"

"Nope," says the other girl.

"Florida once," says the boy.

Glancing up, Sophie sees a map of North America open on the brown-haired girl's laptop. Must be geography homework.

"What I want to know," says the second girl, is if Chihuahua is full of Chihuahuas."

"Yeah," says the boy. "Think about it. Little Chihuahuas everywhere, running around like chickens." He's tall and stoop shouldered, not unlike a fifteen-year-old version of Jack.

Sophie scrolls through her emails, sees one from a name she doesn't immediately recognize. "Jeff McLeod." She looks at the subject heading and opens it. "I just got an email from Jeff, inviting me to another *Glass Menagerie* play practice, 'if I so desire'." Sophie pauses and grins a little. "Maybe he's just hoping I'll bring *you* along," she says.

"Mmm," says Anne, looking at Sophie over the top of her reading glasses.

"Poor Jeff," says Sophie. "He's a nice guy, really. He kind of reminds me of Jonathan, who played my dad in Bill's last film. You know who I mean?"

"British accent? Mustache?" says Anne.

"Yeah. He was a sweetie," says Sophie. "He had this obsessional hobby—exotic birdwatching. Whenever there was downtime he would show people pictures of parakeets and budgies in their natural locales. Spout all these factoids about them. Nobody knew if he had a partner, was gay or straight. But he was certainly passionate about those budgies…"

"Not sure I see the connection," says Anne.

"Me neither, but that's who Jeff reminds me of. It's his enthusiasm." She pauses. "Bill thought Jonathan was really limited as an actor. He had a schtick he relied on too much, but it worked for that role."

"Yes, I remember him now," says Anne.

The kids at the table next door are packing up to go, making a big deal of it, arguing over texting someone named Kira about a party they are heading to. The boy steals the pretty girl's phone and holds it just out of reach.

"Do you have any brothers or sisters?" Sophie asks Anne.

"Nope. An only child. They say it breeds selfishness. Maybe that's my problem," says Anne.

"Oh definitely," says Sophie. "Selfishness is your thing. We can all see that a mile away."

Anne laughs. "Seriously," she says. "I do wonder what I missed, and what Rudy's missing, by having no siblings. I guess the dog is a good idea. You mentioned a brother?"

"Yes. Just one," Sophie says. The familiar ache she has been feeling since Christmas returns.

"Older or younger?"

"Three years younger," Sophie says. "His name is Jack."

"Three years is a nice age gap," says Anne. "I had a friend who had a sister three years younger than her and they were really close. I think the distance between them was enough for her not to feel jealous when they were little, but also close enough that they had things in common."

"Yeah," says Sophie. "I don't remember ever feeling jealous of Jack. The only memory I have of him when he was a baby was my mom putting him down on the middle of her bed for a minute while she went out of the room for something, probably a diaper. I was watching him squirm around there naked and suddenly he shat on the bedspread. I was astonished at the audacity. Maybe a little envious, actually."

They both laugh. "So did you do things together?" says Anne. "Were you close?"

"Really close when we were little, but things changed when we got into our teens."

"Well, that's normal, I guess."

"I suppose," says Sophie. "I was into theater at that point, and he was into…other things." She feels herself flush. Waves of guilt wash over her, waves of grief. "Actually, I was so into theater and my own stuff that I completely missed what was going on with him at that point. Another thing I feel crappy about."

She can't say more without breaking a confidence. Still, it feels good to share that much.

Anne pushes aside her laptop and holds her teacup with both hands, leaning back in her light pine chair. The late afternoon sun falls directly on the table between them, making it hard for Sophie to see her eyes.

"Well, you were a teenager," Anne says. "Teenagers are normally self-centered and into their own stuff. It's a stage of development."

Blurred memories from her teenage years. Climbing the stairs to her bedroom. Jack's angry voice. "How come she gets out of doing the dishes?" Her mother saying, "She needs to run lines for her show tomorrow." Was that before or after Jack's second year of summer camp? Before or after it happened? Jack's adolescence, irremediably torn in two.

"I just found out over Christmas that he had a really horrific experience at camp when he was thirteen," she says. "The kind of thing that can stay with you for life, you know? And he never told anyone about it. We were all completely clueless to the fact. He still hasn't told my parents. I don't think he ever will." Her grief hovers in the background, poised to swamp her if she lets it.

"But he told you?" Anne shifts her position. Sophie can see her eyes now.

"Yes," Sophie says. "I suppose that means something."

"You better believe it," says Anne. "Sounds like you're still pretty close."

Sophie is unable to take another drink from her tea. Unable to do anything but stare at the tabletop. "It's just so sad," she says. "I wish I could have helped him. He was so alone."

When she looks up, Anne's eyes are warm. "I totally get that," she says. "It's really hard to watch someone suffer. I feel that way about my son. He struggles so much. Some things are a huge battle for him." She takes a deep breath. "But one thing I've learned over the past few years is that sometimes you can't help people in the way you want to. Sometimes all you can do is be there for them and watch and wait."

| 44 |

ANNE CALLS NATHAN AT TEN in the morning, while Sophie is still in bed. She's not sure how Nathan will react to her plan to stay until the baby's arrival. Stay as long as you need, he had said. And unexpectedly, she needs this. Being present for this birth is the one thought that makes her heart quicken these days. Nevertheless, the quickening coincides with a sharp pain and a fluttering of anxiety when she thinks of Rudy. Another month away from him.

They have never spent this long apart. Will he misinterpret this desire of hers, in the same way he misinterpreted her leaving in the first place? Will he feel abandoned, or will he care?

As she predicted, phone conversations with Rudy have been deadly, the pauses on the other end so long she finds herself listening to the clock ticking. Sophie suggested she try Facetiming last week, and helped her set up the app on her phone, which made Anne feel about a hundred years old. Rudy, unsurprisingly, was less fazed by the technology than she was, but still no more verbose than before.

The sound kept cutting in and out and the video froze for a full minute at one point, while she stared at a caricature of Rudy's face, eyes large, mouth half open, the thinness of his cheeks accentuated by the light from his computer screen. Realizing he must see a frozen caricature of her as well, she wondered what she looked like. When they were finally able to talk again, she was so rattled that she said, "I'm going to send you an email. I'll keep in touch that way. Maybe you can send me one back?"

Today, the phone rings for a surprisingly long time before Nathan answers.

"Hi…?" he says.

It's the voice he uses with colleagues when in mid-project. A cautious Hi, a circumspect Hi, a Hi that states itself ready to listen, but comes from within a circle of personal privacy. A Hi that indicates he is courteously aware of her circle of privacy as well, that lets her know he has no plans to enter uninvited.

"I didn't wake you, did I?" she says.

"No, I was up."

"I have some exciting news. Exciting to me at least."

"Oh?" She immediately regrets her choice of words. Maybe he thinks she's going to tell him she is on her way home.

"Sophie has asked me to be here for the birth of her baby."

The silence at the other end of the line does nothing to allay her misgivings.

"I've really gotten to know her over the past few weeks, Nathan. I feel honoured that she would ask."

"Mmm…" he says.

"I know this would mean a longer stay. The baby isn't due for another month. How is it going with Rudy? Do you think you can cope?"

Cope. The wrong word. Turning Rudy into a burden instead of Nathan's son. She thinks of how many lengthy filmset absences she has endured from him over the years and feels annoyed at her current guilt. Then she thinks about how, years ago, this separation from her spouse would have been hard regardless of Rudy. Years ago, she would have been saying to Nathan: I love you. I miss you so much. And he would have been responding in kind, the warmth in his voice a balm to all her anxiety and loneliness. When did that stop?

The reality is, she does not miss him very much. She knows if he were gone from her life entirely, the way her mother is gone, she would be heartbroken. But right now, as she sits in this loft bedroom, as she lowers her voice so as not to disturb the pregnant woman downstairs, she does not miss Nathan. The Anne she is now does not miss the Nathan he is now, anyway.

"Rudy's fine," Nathan says. "Another week and we can go get the puppy."

"Is he excited?" she asks.

"That might be too strong a word. The kid's pretty hard to read."

Try, Anne thinks. You're there, in the house with him. You can see his eyes. Hear his voice. Read his body. Nathan is always fascinated with actors' body language. He has described brilliant performances, usually by young and pretty actresses like Sophie, performances that involve subtle moves and encapsulate hidden emotion. Why not apply that kind of professional discernment to his own son?

"I've decided to email with him, instead of talk on the phone," she says. "I sent him something a few days ago. He hasn't answered yet."

"I'll remind him."

"No. I don't want to…well maybe you could, in a casual kind of way. No pressure."

"Well that's me," says Nathan. "The no-pressure guy."

She is both saddened and impatient with the edge in his voice, wonders if he will actually say what he feels if she takes the bait.

"So…are *you* okay with me hanging out here for another month?"

"I told you, Anne. You should stay as long as you like. Do what you need to do."

"I know that's what you said. I'm asking you what you feel."

She lets the silence between them last, hoping it might be fruitful.

When he finally answers his voice is clipped. "I'm okay with it. Right now I'm pretty focused on getting my floundering career off the ground again."

Okay, she thinks. Fair enough. We'll do it that way.

"Any leads?" she asks.

"Actually yes. From Olivier," he says, the edge in his voice replaced by enthusiasm. "You know," he continues. "I really doubted that contacting him would yield anything. All the networking I was doing felt like shooting in the dark."

"Something was bound to turn up sooner or later," she says.

"Yeah, but… I've been feeling pretty alienated from the whole business these days. Thinking I might have done better if I had learned a useful trade."

"Nathan…"

"Don't get me wrong, I love film, the medium. I love what it encompasses—art, technology, music, words. It has everything you need. Like a tasty ripe tomato."

She is slightly surprised by the poetics of his language, then wonders why she should be.

"When I was just starting out," he says, "I had this sense that I could tap into a whole world of creative people. Bring them all together, make magic. Kind of like a modern-day campfire. Only the magic could touch thousands, maybe millions of people that I'd never know personally." He stops momentarily. She hears a cough, or maybe a laugh, she's not sure which. "I guess I can't stop being a naive film buff, even if everyone else in the industry is only about the bottom line."

"Everyone else isn't," she says quickly. "Lots feel like you, I bet." She wills the stirring within her of sympathy and respect to come to life and inform her speech. "Creative motives just get lost sometimes, when money's at stake," she adds.

"Well, money's at stake, for me too. It's still my career. I'm not in this to make a scrapbook in my old age."

She winces. Opts to say nothing. Thinks about the meaning of the word 'career.' Wonders what kind of scrapbook she might make in her old age.

"Anyway," he says. "This thing Olivier is writing. He said he was planning to contact me even before I got in touch. It's based on this amazing book. A memoir by a young schizophrenic woman."

At the word 'schizophrenic', Anne has a hard time focusing on Nathan's words. For so long she has avoided books or movies with reference to anything that might remind her too closely of her son's psychosis, or infuriate her for being off the mark. She thinks about that arrogant prick writer of thrillers at the library. But those were exploitive novels, not memoirs. Still, a claustrophobic feeling starts to creep up on her as Nathan warms to the subject of the potential biopic. He even talks about directing, something he hasn't contemplated since before Rudy was born.

"This woman is so articulate, Anne," he says. "She describes her condition so well, with intelligence and insight. And there's a real sense of pacing and drama to the story. I nearly read the whole thing in one sitting."

She tries to rejoice in the excitement she hears in his voice. "That's great," she says, and then adds, because she feels it's incumbent on her to do so. "Maybe I should read it."

"I want Rudy to read it," says Nathan.

Her claustrophobia doubles down into real anxiety, a hand clutching her gut.

"Are you sure that's wise?" she says. "I mean, if he reads in-depth descriptions of psychosis, it might trigger something."

There is a short silence, during which she feels like an adult who has just pricked a kid's birthday balloon.

"Anne, there are a million things that might trigger something," Nathan says. "Music, books, videos, stress, life."

He's right about that, she thinks. She almost suggests that Nathan talk to Rudy's psychiatrist but stops herself.

"Reading this book could bring some positive change for him," he says. "Anyway, it's his decision. He can figure out if he's interested and able to handle it."

Again, this she can't argue with. She remembers how skeptical Nathan was when she wanted to reduce Rudy's meds and bring him into their monthly parent meetings with Dr. Green. Now, their roles are reversed. He is the one giving Rudy agency, respecting his judgment, acting on faith and hope. And she is the one responding with fear, miles away from Rudy's side.

The next day, Anne gets a reply from Rudy. When she starts reading, the quality of Rudy's writing takes her by surprise. There are a few odd turns of phrase, but overall there is clarity and flow. Rudy used to be a good student, before all this. At least he hasn't forgotten how to string together coherent sentences.

Hi, he says. *Thanks for your email. It sounds interesting up there. Things are normal here.* Normal, she thinks. *The day program is okay. Yoga is okay too.* Cautious answers to the cautious questions she had asked in her email. She had been curious about Rudy's possible crush.

The only times I don't like yoga, Rudy continues, *is when Lilly, that anorexic girl, melts down and has to be led out of class by the nurse that always waits in the doorway. It usually only happens in Savasana, the corpse pose. Lilly had another meltdown in the cafeteria yesterday. I had to shut my eyes and put my hands over my ears. Mike says I should try to ride it out without doing that. He says if I want to put a label on myself saying 'nut job,' that's the way to do it.*

Anne, remembering the jovial Mike dropping into the Happy Baby pose in front of the hospital elevators, is torn between amusement and outrage. But, as she reads on, it is obvious that Rudy is not offended. He appears to have found a friend.

Mike talks a lot about meditation techniques. Kim says stuff like that in yoga too, but I'm not very good at it. I do think the poses help my nervous system. She bites her lip at this careful, clinical language. *Mike's also offered to show me how to work out with weights.*

Work out with weights? Rudy? Anne is pretty sure that Mike's mental health issues have to do with addiction. Weight training must be a strategy to beat cravings. She tries to recall the other day program kids she has met, to see if she can place a face to the name of the poor, presumably skeletal, Lilly. She fails.

Mike says to tell you he's sorry to hear about Grandma. He told me he thinks you're a sweetheart. A jolt of surprise, similar to the one she felt when Sophie called Nathan a gentleman. *He was also really impressed when I told him dad was a movie producer. He thinks having a dad who produces films that are on Netflix is a seriously cool fact about my family that I should share with people more. Way more interesting than having a plumber who beat the crap out of you for a dad.*

Reading this, Anne suspects that the main attraction of this friendship for Rudy is that the oversharing Mike does all the talking. Still, so far she can see, there is no harm in the guy's social advice, which seems to be sticking more than anything she, or Nathan, or Dr. Green, can offer.

The puppy at the animal shelter will be ready to come home soon. It is the same mix of breeds as Kim's dog. Mike and I met Kim's dog when she brought it to the hospital because her roommate was out of town, and it needed to go for a walk. Its name is Lucky. I patted it and Kim said he liked me, but it was hard to tell. All he did was pant, then gulp, then look at my shoes. Kim also said I was doing really well in yoga, but it's hard to tell that too, because most of the poses feel like I'm trying to tie myself up with invisible chicken wire. But it feels great when she says 'release.'

Whenever a pose is really hard in yoga, Mike turns on his side to look at me and mouths the word 'Fuck" really slowly, like, "Fuuuuk."

Anne, laughing, is starting to feel a release. She laughs at her former anxiety about the implications of Rudy's crush, her worry over whether it was good for him to be around the arm-cutting, drug-addicted teens in the program, who mostly only achieved psychosis with the aid of some rogue recreational substance turned sour. She laughs at all the times Rudy's hallucinations have set up a weird dialogue in her brain, when she has taken his psychotic state personally, defaulted to her late, literary father's Freudian interpretation of the psyche under strain, been consumed by mother-guilt.

Mostly, she laughs because, however she reads between the lines, this email contains the writing of an intelligent, self-aware kid. She sees in it someone she recognizes, but also finds refreshingly, enchantingly new.

| **45** |

THE ICE ON THE POINT ROAD has melted, maybe temporarily, maybe for good. The road is finally clear, and the weather unseasonably beautiful. It feels like spring. At nightfall, Sophie takes a bag of trash to the curb and is entranced by the sight of the full moon hanging low in the sky, reflected in the water. The dilapidated boathouse on the rocky outcrop down the road is little more than a shadow now. She tells Anne to come and look, and they go for a second walk down the ice-free road, both hungry to experience once again this newly opened, less hostile external world.

The stars are clearly visible as they walk, so different from New York. The darkness makes everything soft—a mix of grey and sepia, restful to the eye. It reminds Sophie of the black-and-white illustrations in an antique copy of *Peter Pan* belonging to her mother. Thick, hand-cut yellowing paper with elegant print and line drawings, colour plates of duo-chrome paintings reproduced on thin glossy paper. Peter and Wendy flying over a grey and beige landscape, Wendy's bare feet hanging down from a white night dress. Peter with his arms wrapped around her. How erotic was that? Even at age seven, she sensed some hidden power there. As she does now, with the full moon ahead, her body propelled forward by a will outside of it, a force that is not her own.

"That's beautiful," says Anne quietly, her eyes also on the moon.

"Tim would love the sight of that," says Sophie. She imagines Tim striding into the moonlight, exclaiming, carrying his enthusiasm forward and offering it to whoever crossed his path, like a gift.

"Only one more week and he'll be here," says Anne. "He must be pretty excited about this big gig of his."

"And nervous," says Sophie. "I could tell, the last time I talked with him. But he also seemed extremely focused, like he knew for sure that all the work was worth it."

"That's great."

"I know," says Sophie. They walk on a few more paces before she adds, "It's weird. In some ways this time apart seems like forever. In other ways it's flown by. It's been so great having you here."

"I plan to give you guys some alone time," says Anne.

"You don't need to…"

"Yes I need to. I'm spending next Tuesday in the city, all day. I've made lots of plans. So you can be on your own when he arrives."

They are almost to the bend in the road now, the Big Dipper hanging over the bay on their left. Sophie can just make out the outline of the mailboxes on the corner.

"I'm also thinking of asking Nathan and Rudy to come up," says Anne, "after the baby is born. I thought we might spend a few days at the resort before we go back home."

"That's great," says Sophie. She has a hard time taking in any words other than 'after the baby is born,' but she notices uncertainty in Anne's voice, as if she is just formulating this plan now. "From what you've told me, it'll be the first vacation you've had in years."

"Mmm," says Anne. "Well, we'll see what Nathan thinks. He has some work stuff starting up again, but it's all online."

"I'd love to see him. I hope he…"

"He's thrilled for you Sophie," says Anne. "The film thing is secondary to all this. You know that."

Sophie wonders when Anne started picking up her thoughts so accurately. Anne lets the silence between them last for a few more strides. The moon on their left follows them as they walk.

"Maybe," says Anne, "if I'm going to be godmother to this kid, whatever that means these days, could Nathan be godfather?"

"Of course!" says Sophie, feeling yet another urge to cry. The moon and thoughts of Tim, and now Nathan. She thinks of his old, frayed sweater, still hanging in the hall. She notices how comfortable it has become to walk like this, arm-in-arm, with Anne. I've never had this, she thinks, not with friends, not with my mother. The closest she can come is her friendship with Farid. But this is different. She has never had a sister. Maybe this is what it's like.

"I have something to tell you," she says, "but I'd feel kind of uncomfortable if you relayed it to Nathan."

"Sworn to secrecy," says Anne.

"It wasn't just being pregnant that made me want to leave the film. I mean, I thought that was it, at the time, because I felt so sick and everything. But even before I knew about it, I felt like I was drifting away from it, you know? The third film felt all wrong somehow, and I couldn't explain it to myself, let alone anyone else. I still can't quite sort it out."

"Was that because of Bill, some of the stuff you told me?" Anne asks. There is a sharpness to her voice, an alertness that makes Sophie uncomfortable.

"I'm not sure. Maybe," she says. "I was starting to feel stuck in the roles he wanted me to play, which were all kind of one role, to be honest."

"I know what you mean," said Anne. "I watched both films and read the third script. She was cute and clever, but there wasn't much to her."

"No kidding, and I can't imagine playing her again, afterwards…" She touches her belly, where the baby lies heavy, a surrogate for the weight, the gravitas, she would have liked to add to Bill's characters. "You know," she says, "the 'empowering' thing that some actors said they felt with him? I started to realize that he was only empowering me to be that girl, the way he had written her. Even when we weren't on set anymore, I felt like he had this rigid idea about who I was, not just as an actress, but as a person."

"Ah," says Anne softly. "I guess we all get stuck in roles sometimes, whether we are acting or not."

Something in her tone suggests that Anne is speaking from personal experience. And the connection Sophie feels with Anne at this moment, genuinely empowers her to say more.

"One thing I know is that for the past few months, I've gotten to know myself better than when I was acting all the time. It's been hard, though. I'm not used to having this much time on my hands. And it makes me squirrelly not knowing if there's something else in the can."

"Well this voice-acting idea sounds like a good stopgap. And there will be other film roles if you want them," says Anne. She takes a breath as if about to say something else, then exhales. "You're a wonderful actress, Sophie."

"Thanks," she says. "You know, I used to live for compliments like that."

"But not anymore?"

"Not anymore. It doesn't seem to matter that much, how good I am. Who cares? In the grand scheme of things, it's what I choose to do with it."

"I totally agree."

"Anyway," Sophie sighs. "It's really hard right now for me to imagine anything beyond just getting this baby into the world."

"Don't try. It will all come together."

"It will all be different."

"Maybe that's not such a bad thing," says Anne.

Tim arrives, late Tuesday afternoon, his face lighting up as he gets out of his car.

"My God, Sophie! Look at you," he says. He wraps his arms around her, and they stand that way for a full minute, Sophie's cheek resting on his shoulder. She can feel his body quivering, the way it does when he's excited or happy, like a stringed instrument, responding to a change in the weather, or the touch of a hand. She breathes in his smell, nestles into the rough wool of his winter jacket, feels like she could stay here forever. The baby kicks, between them, just under her ribs, and Tim feels it too. He steps back and places his hands on her belly.

"Hello there, little guy," he says.

"Or girl."

"Rug rat."

He starts to bring in his stuff—two guitars, a gig bag and one backpack that looks way too small to hold all his clothes.

"I see you stuck to your priorities when packing," Sophie says, leading the way to the living room, where Tim stands thoughtfully, probably looking for a spot for his gear. "What's up there?" he says, nodding at the stairs to the loft.

"That's Anne's bedroom. She's gone to the city for the day, to give us some space. She's catching a movie, so she probably won't be back until ten or so."

"By which time I will be dead to the world," says Tim. "It's weird how just sitting in the car that long can take it out of you. Thank God I had somewhere to sleep in Maine."

Sophie asks about Joshua, the singer-songwriter who sent his album at Christmas, and Tim starts relaying a long and complex conversation and musical jam he had while he stayed with the guy. She's lost as soon as he starts talking about voice-leading and modes. She surveys the room for a likely spot for his instruments and gear. The heat from the wood stove will affect the guitars, and they can't be anywhere they will be tripped over. The only patch of wall free for them to lean against is in the corner near the back window, where she has placed the rolled-up yoga mat and cushions she has been using to try some prenatal yoga Claudine showed her, to help with breathing. She decides to bring those into the bedroom.

Tim has stopped talking and there is a short lull before he voices the question she has avoided articulating, even to herself.

"So you think this is going to work, Soph? The three of us in this little place for the next month? I know you and Anne have gotten real close. Don't get me wrong, I'm totally grateful that she's been such a big support to you…"

"She's lovely. Really calm, really tactful. I know you've only met her a couple of times, but you'll like her, Tim."

"Well, you obviously do, if you want her there for the big event."

"When I asked her, I knew it was the right thing. I just knew it. Sometimes you've got to follow your heart."

"Really?" says Tim with a sideways glance at her. "You? Follow your heart? I thought you were the analytical, think-it-through type."

"Actually I am, sometimes," she says, feeling a prickle of defensiveness, which she decides to laugh away. Unlike his first reaction to the idea of giving birth in Nova Scotia, Tim has been in an easy-going mood about this latest idea. These days, he's happy, exultant even. Before leaving to come up here, he had sent her photos from the show at the Ballroom—sold out and hopping, the band looking as if they were having the time of their lives. He told her on the phone that he had never played better. Maybe the way he responds to her plans has more to do with his wellbeing, than because she has fucked up the communication piece.

"Anne thinks she might ask Nathan and Rudy to come up once the baby is born," says Sophie, adding quickly, "they'll probably stay at the resort down the road."

Moving her yoga mat out of the way, she indicates the resultant space. "You could put your guitars here."

Tim leans them up against the wall.

"So no hard feelings on Nathan's part, about the film?"

"Apparently not. Anne says he's been hinting about other projects."

She thinks briefly of the possibility of working with Nathan again, if he will give her a second chance, and feels a slight stirring of that old familiar longing. But with the longing comes a heavy languor, a fuzziness in her head which she puts down to hormones. Her awareness of the baby turning slowly in her belly seems to be increasingly demanding stillness everywhere else in her life.

Later, safe in the knowledge that Anne won't be home until bedtime, she and Tim explore each other's bodies, first in the TV room, then in the bedroom. Sophie is amazed and thrilled at how happily she responds, baby or no baby, her excitement turning everything—legs, vulva, breasts, even belly—into rolling waves of pleasure. He doesn't seem to care how big she is, laughing in the shower afterwards and calling her his earth mama. She has never been so grateful to him.

He falls asleep, as predicted, before Anne gets home, but Sophie stays wakeful. She wanders the house in the nightgown Tim gave her for Christmas, stokes the wood stove, tidies the kitchen, mentally plans a drive along the coast with Tim in the morning if the weather stays good. When Anne returns, she and Sophie chat in whispers about Anne's day in Halifax. Anne asks how it feels to have Tim there, and she says she is blissed out, which doesn't adequately describe how alive she feels, shimmering with happiness, her body lovingly encompassing their child and Tim's warm presence. She can't remember what it feels like to be lonely. She doubts she will ever be lonely again.

| **46** |

ANNE TRIES TO MOVE AS QUIETLY as possible around the kitchen. She manages silence while making coffee, but after pouring herself a cup, she inadvertently knocks the stainless steel scoop off the counter. It lands on the floor with a clatter. She swears under her breath.

There is no sound from Tim and Sophie's bedroom. So she continues her breakfast routine, tiptoeing into the TV room to nab a *New Yorker* magazine. It has a review of the film she went to see last night in Halifax. A sort of reboot of "Network" for the digital age, with a young woman protagonist instead of Peter Finch, the corrupt establishment represented by a Google-like internet giant instead of a TV station. The plot was thin, and the young woman's whistle-blowing speech tepid at best, trite at worst. Anne couldn't help thinking Sophie would have been ten times better in the lead.

Sometimes, she regrets being married to a film producer. She knows too much now to just be entertained by a movie the way she used to be, when she was younger. She also doubts if movies on social or political themes will ever interest her again. Flipping through her *New Yorker*, scanning each column devoted to the moral outrages committed by the current occupants of the White House, she is numbed out, slightly nauseated. With this stuff as a basis for comparison, there is no work of moralistic fiction powerful enough to shock or arouse indignation these days. She understands what might have prompted Bill's satirical screenplay.

Tim gets up before Sophie. When Anne offers him coffee, he gives her the sweet smile she noticed when she met him at Christmas. She pushes her magazine aside and they sit at the breakfast table across from one another. Tim says he drove through some weather on the way, a heavy snowfall in New Brunswick.

"We only had flurries here," says Anne, looking out to the road, which has stayed clear, despite some threatening clouds overhead.

"Luckily, by the time I got to Moncton, it let up. Strange town that," says Tim. "My friend in Maine said it was just one big shopping mall, but it actually does have a downtown. I found an awesome vegetarian restaurant. The servers talked to each other in this weird mix of French and English."

"Are you vegetarian?" Anne does a rapid calculation of what she might have in the cupboard to feed him. She and Sophie have been buying separate groceries, using different shelves in the fridge, but have been coming together once a week for a shared meal. Anne had been planning to buy meat or fish for a shared supper tonight.

"No, I like my meat," Tim says, to her relief. "Just thought the vegetarian place might be healthier than the diner across the road."

When Sophie comes out of the bedroom, she's still wearing her night-gown, and stands beside Tim, leaning her elbow on his chair back. Tim puts his arms around her belly.

"I'm heading to the farmers' market this morning," says Anne.

"Oh, maybe we should go," Sophie says to Tim. "Anne says there are lots of vendors, good food."

"I thought you wanted to show me the scenery," he says.

"If you give me a list, I can shop for all of us," Anne says quickly. "I really don't mind."

She's relieved to see gratitude in Sophie's eyes. Her excitement over attending the upcoming birth almost sweeps away her discomfort at being a third wheel here, but not quite. Sophie perches on Tim's lap to take a sip of his coffee. Anne looks back down at her magazine, then reaches for a pen and paper to make a shopping list. Something special to go with the fish—fresh herbs? A bakery pie for dessert. She will tell them it's her treat, in celebration of Tim's arrival. Bit by bit, the three of them will figure out this co-housing thing, just as she and Sophie did back in February. And it's only for a month. Maybe less, if Sophie's size is anything to go by.

Sophie stands up to get herself a cup of tea. As she leaves Tim's lap, Anne notices his fingers trailing along her arm, prolonging their contact for as long as possible. She returns to her shopping list, thinking that she should call Nathan sometime today.

She buys a jar of pesto and a bag of shitake mushrooms to go with the fish, as well as a beautiful clafoutis for dessert from the French baker's table. Who in New York would believe these kinds of luxuries were available at a rural farmers' market in Lunenburg? There is not much fresh produce this time of year, so she settles for packaged, hydroponic lettuce from the grocery store. Pulling out of the grocery store parking lot, she's thinking about how she has been trying to get Rudy to eat more salad by making tempting, mayon-naise-based dressings, and wonders how he is eating with Nathan, who tends to make a lot of burgers. She could check on that when she calls later today, but then again, maybe not. She left quinoa, rice, and gluten-free pasta in the house before she left, and stocked mason jars full of nuts, seeds, and raisins for snacking.

In Rudy's last email, after talking again about Mike and Kim and the puppy, he had said that Nathan's mother had phoned the previous night. *She wants us to move to Canada, but Dad says that isn't happening any time soon.* Anne remembers a visit to Montreal when Rudy was five, how he silently trailed his older cousins around the neighbourhood and how he looked as bewildered as she felt, trying to fathom the family excitement over hockey playoffs on TV.

Montreal is probably the Canada Nathan is thinking of when he shuns the idea of moving up here. But for her, Canada is these narrow, hilly streets with century-old houses that she negotiates to leave town, these cow pastures on the Northwest Rd., the dense and scrubby spruce trees that line the highway.

As much as she misses Rudy, she feels again a claustrophobic dread about going back to their family home. With the dread comes a growing certainty that, just as when she decided to push for a reduction in Rudy's meds, a voice within her is insisting on change. And it's up to her to figure out what form that change will take. Nathan will not take the lead here. But all the sure-footed assertiveness that Anne has learned as she has cared for Rudy, her capacity to respond in a crisis, to organize order out of chaos, to move life forward in the midst of suffering, all of that deserts her when she contemplates her and Nathan's future. She wants to move forward without breaking things irredeemably. She thinks of the marriages she has seen explode into shit-shows of bitterness and estrangement, the children caught in the middle like ragged toys fought over by snarling dogs. No one needs that.

Unlike her, Nathan has always known how to focus on one thing at a time and shut his eyes to the rest. But she cannot shut her eyes and pretend. In this moment, driving home with her fancy ingredients for a planned meal with two madly-in-love twenty-eight-year-olds expecting their first child, all she can identify between herself and her spouse is a passionless, convenient partnership; a partnership that brings them each equal doses of familiarity, frustration, and sadness. No one's fault, she knows, or maybe the fault lies with both of them.

Maybe if there were something else in her life to occupy her, something she felt as attached to as Nathan feels about filmmaking, she could settle into whatever it is that she and Nathan have. She thinks briefly of her awkward but heartfelt poem, how it made her cry, unlocking the tight vigilance that has so soften taken over whenever she thinks of her son. The memory of the pen in her hands, the quiet snowfall on the window as she wrote, warms her briefly, lessens her fear of the future. But, she wonders, if she does manage to rediscover writing at this stage in her life, how she will find the courage to do anything other than tuck her words away in a drawer somewhere, the way she did all those years ago in college?

It's close to four o'clock when Sophie and Tim come in the door on a gust of wind, their cheeks rosy and hair tousled, like children on a Christmas card, Anne thinks.

"Cold out there?" she asks.

"If it weren't for the wind…" says Tim. "Sophie tried to get me to walk on a beach…"

"At the resort," says Sophie. "We made it about a hundred yards. It was even colder coming back, with the wind against us. We spent the rest of the time driving around the Apoptogen Peninsula."

"Did you see Fred at the resort?"

"The mysterious Fred," says Tim. "I'd like to meet him."

"He wasn't working today," says Sophie. "He's there tomorrow but he'll probably be pretty busy. There's a convention or something. The place was dead today."

"We'll invite him over for supper sometime," says Anne. "I'd like him to see his bird up there."

She nods to the drawing, which hangs above the doorway between the kitchen and TV room. The dove-like bird has landed, temporarily, as if it intends to fly away again, as soon as it has recovered its strength. Anne finds the image even more beautiful, here in the cottage. Behind the penciled plumage, the rose-tinted matte paper warms the pale grey of the walls. She wonders what made her choose grey for this kitchen, all those years ago.

"I'd also like you to meet Mary Ellen and Bob," says Sophie to Tim. "Bob has this CD collection, remember I told you, and he plays guitar. You guys would really get along."

Anne takes out the fish and puts it in a glass casserole, basting it with olive oil, herbs, and pesto. She's touched by Sophie's eagerness to share everything and everyone with Tim. She can remember feeling that way with Nathan. She finishes preparing the fish and puts it in the oven.

When she serves the supper, Sophie and Tim rave about the pesto-lathered fish, the fluffiness of the rice and the deliciousness of the clafoutis for dessert. She lets them do the washing up and goes up to the loft to call Nathan, unworried about them hearing her conversation, because they are still chattering and laughing like little high school kids, flicking each other with tea towels occasionally. Tomorrow, Sophie has an appointment with Claudine, the first one that Tim will be present for. Anne decides she will go to the Shore Café while that's happening.

Settling herself on the bed, she brings up Nathan's number on her phone. When he answers, she says, "Hey, how are things going?"

"Fine?" he says cautiously.

She moves on quickly, thinking he may interpret her question as a check-in on his parenting skills. "Just wanted to let you know Tim arrived safely yesterday and all is well with Sophie," she says. "I also wanted to talk to you about an idea I had."

"Oh?"

She closes her eyes briefly. This fluttering in her belly must mean something, she realizes.

"Do you think you'd like to bring Rudy up, after the baby is born?" she says. Maybe take a few days at the resort before we go home?"

In the silence that ensues, the fluttering increases, then turns to something else.

"I miss you," she says.

"I miss you too." His voice is warm, the kind of warm that used to make her go weak at the knees when she was younger. And while she may not be in that youthful, lustful space anymore, at least she no longer hears his warmth as if from a distance, or doubts it is really meant for her.

"The thing is," he adds, "we'll have the dog by then."

The dog…how could she have forgotten?

But then he says, surprisingly quickly, "We could probably work something out…aren't there chalets at the resort? Maybe they allow pets."

He has not shut down this idea, she thinks gratefully. He is applying his movie-producer problem-solving skills to it, in fact. But she wonders: A man, a woman, a teenager and a dog in a beach chalet in April in Nova Scotia. What if it rains the whole time?

"I'll find out," she says.

They talk a few minutes more, about Rudy, inevitably, and she tells Nathan how much she enjoyed Rudy's email. When she hangs up, she has odd feeling of relief. It's as if she has just dodged something, like that icicle she saw hanging from the eaves of a low building in Halifax the other day, which had landed with a smash on the sidewalk, just paces away.

| 47 |

Aᴛ ᴛʜᴇɪʀ ꜰɪʀsᴛ ᴊᴏɪɴᴛ ᴀᴘᴘᴏɪɴᴛᴍᴇɴᴛ with Claudine, there are some sweet moments for Sophie, when Tim gets to listen to the baby's heartbeat, feel around her belly, support her back as she explores birth positions. Trying to practice breathing together is a bust, though. Sophie winds up coaching Tim, instead of the other way round.

"Okay so you're a pro at this stuff," he says. "All that yoga you've been doing lately. You don't need my help."

"Yeah, but I'm not actually in physical agony at the moment."

"Tim, you're doing great," says Claudine. "We can take five minutes to practice during the next few appointments."

"Everything looks good," she says, feeling Sophie's belly and guiding Tim's hand to do the same. "Feel down here? The baby's head. Perfect position. It's turned beautifully. And over here, up to the right? The baby's little bum." She laughs. "It's getting pretty snug in there." Pulling out her notes, she completes another weird diagram of the baby's position on her chart, which only has four squares left, Sophie notices. Tim looks on. His uncharacteristic stillness unnerves her.

"You sleeping okay?" Claudine asks as she writes.

"The side position is helpful, especially with the pillow between my legs" says Sophie.

"It worked for me, both times."

"How old are your kids?" Tim asks.

"Twelve and fourteen. Boy, did that go by fast." Claudine packs away her chart, preparing to leave. As she walks through the kitchen, she notices Fred's drawing. "Well that is lovely," she says.

Explaining the origins of the drawing, Sophie feels an almost proprietorial sense of pride. Finding out that there is more to Fred than meets the eye makes her feel vindicated for wanting to be friends with him, for coming all this way, in such strange circumstances, and finding him again. It's as if she has known all along that, hidden under the kindness and the waiter's persona, there was something special.

But then she thinks: Why does he have to be an artist to be special? Ordinary human goodness is special, a helping hand under the elbow, a voice that soothes a person's reeling senses under the hot sun. All of that is special. Uneasily, she wonders if she has picked up the habit of trying to collect talented people like exotic shells—a trait she has noticed in Bill, in Nathan, in her own mother.

Although she has downplayed it with Claudine, Sophie's sleep is sporadic at best these days. When she lies on her back, the weight of the baby affects her breathing. She gets up to pee at least twice a night and, hard as it is to sneak out without waking Tim, it's even harder, when she comes back, to get comfortable without tossing and turning. Tim is philosophical about the tiny portion of the queen-sized bed he has to himself. When she lies facing him, he says her belly is like a beach ball. He even dreamed once that he was back in California, floating in the pool on an air mattress, next to his little brother, who wouldn't leave him alone. Tim's parents have said they will wait until they are back in Brooklyn to visit, which Sophie is grateful for, but also wonders at. Whatever mixed feelings she has about her own mother's upcoming visit, she can't imagine having the patience to wait until the baby is a month old.

As for her own dreams, they are eclectic, fragmentary, and disturbing. Tonight she dreams she is not pregnant and has never been. The baby has disappeared completely from her consciousness. She is on set with Bill. She's trying to block a scene and is forgetting which way to walk. She's trying out dialogue and stumbles over lines. Bill suddenly explodes, letting out a spew of verbal abuse way worse than anything he has ever said to her, or to anyone, in real life. His face is nearly unrecognizable, his mouth hardly keeping up with the words as they spill out. *You stupid fucking bitch stupid cunt who do you think you are?* When she tells him feebly not to speak to her like that, he yells *I know who you are. I know the bullshit you pass off as real.*

She wakes sweating, with these last words ringing in her head and her heart pounding, torn between fury and a secret, unreasonable guilt that has nothing to do with the film, or even with Bill, precisely. It is something to do with the words *bullshit* and *real*.

Turning away from Tim, she lets her eyes explore the room, sees a chink of light coming through the window. It's almost dawn. In her mind, she sees a crack develop, like the crack of water between two chunks of ice in the marsh across the road. On one side of the crack, she sees Bill and his anger, she sees her brother's downturned face talking in a deadpan voice about his childhood. Her mind's eye pans out further, to capture vitriolic politicians, hateful slogans, harrowed refugees. On the other side of the crack, she sees the sweetness of her lovemaking with Tim. She sees Mary Ellen, with her soup. She sees Fred, sitting across the table from her with his interested eyes behind round glasses. She sees Anne smiling at her, laughing with her in the car, listening quietly to her talk about Jack, with tears in her eyes.

Giving up on going back to bed, she dozes off on the sofa in the TV room, propped up by pillows and covered with the crocheted blanket Anne has placed along its back. But even then, her restless dream life won't leave her alone. She dreams that her baby, a boy, is already a toddler but has just died. Her grief is so unbearable that she has a dream within the dream, conjures him alive again. He talks to her like a benign, revelatory angel, reaching his arms out to be picked up. When she does, he wraps his limbs around her, and suddenly no longer feels like a toddler, more like a clingy but emaciated full grown adult. She staggers under his weight as she walks down the street, talking softly, torn between horror and compassion, still grieving her lost child.

"Tired and stressed," she admits, in answer to Claudine's inquiries at their next appointment.

Claudine suggests herbal tea, a heating pad on her back, journaling.

"Journaling?" says Sophie. "I never thought of that." Tim's mother gave her a journal on her last birthday. She had tucked it in her suitcase before coming here, planning to document her pregnancy and this trip. A plan that has fallen by the wayside, like daily yoga and swimming three times a week. So far, she has only used it for shopping lists.

The next morning, waking in the darkness, she makes tea, then unearths the journal from the bottom of a drawer, and sits with its leather-bound pages on her lap. She almost never writes anything by hand these days. Reminded of middle school, she's tempted to doodle, the way she used to in the margins of schoolbooks. But instead she starts writing letters. A letter to Jack, in which she tells him how sorry she is for her oblivious teen years. A letter to her mother, in which she tries to explain why she had to get away. A letter to Bill, in which she says, 'Look. It's me. I'm still here." Except that she's not sure who 'me' is, if it's the Sophie she feels she has always been, or the one he thought he saw when he wrote those roles for her.

She knows these are letters she will probably never send. As she gets into the flow of writing, her thoughts begin to spiral towards the event that led her back to Nova Scotia and changed her, irrevocably, she feels. She wants Tim to see where exactly her encounter with the sea happened.

So, later that day, she asks him to drive her to the resort. Bundled in their winter coats, they descend the cliffside steps to the beach, bypassing the inn, because she wants this moment to be theirs, and theirs alone.

As they walk, she feels every pore in her body being tugged by the tide. She is drawn to the ocean's edge, in a way that invigorates rather than terrifies. Its magnetic pull at once cleanses her of fatigue and empties her mind of restlessness and anxiety. If it were warm enough, she would take off her boots and walk barefoot.

When she needs to rest, she and Tim find a sheltered spot in the dunes. Tim sits behind her, his arms barely reaching around her belly. Those arms are like a life preserver keeping her afloat, snug and awkward, but a godsend all the same. She leans into him, confident that he can handle her weight. The pressure of the baby on her lungs eases somewhat, freeing her breath.

"So what exactly happened out there, Sophie?" Tim asks.

She decides to give up on rational explanation, and lets memory move through her, become words. How can she evoke, now, that kaleidoscope of helpless body parts, the jumbled soundtrack, her struggling mind revolting against the indignity and implausibility of it all. The choking darkness, the words *'riptide'* and *'undertow'* appearing in neon to her mind's eye. Seeing herself as if in an underwater camera shot from below, the invisible force swiveling her body around, that final wave spitting her closer to shore.

Her words are halting and self-conscious. She knows that, no matter what she says, this event will always be her own experience. She cannot manufacture witnesses, turn it into a performance or a work of art. And like that solitary moment in the undertow, the experience of the baby breaking free of her body will also be something that happens to her alone.

In the midst of this new awareness, she feels Tim's heartbeat, directly behind her left shoulder. He has at times seemed so close, and at others so far away from her. She remembers the moment, early on in her pregnancy, when she saw him as a stranger, even though he was the father of her child. The memory no longer elicits a choking, black panic within her. Tim is also alone. It seems so simple to say that they are two beings, not one, and it is enough that their paths have joined in the creation of another unique, solitary life.

She sees Jack's face now. With him, she shares a signature mix of DNA from each of their parents. Her unlooked-for visions of Jack's troubled and angry face could continue to make her cry and lament the pain he endured, alone, during their shared but sequestered childhoods. Or, she can decide how best, in this present space, to turn up for him now.

"I want to try harder to keep my brother in our lives, after the baby is born," she says aloud.

"Hmm," says Tim sleepily. "Sure, we can make that happen. Bearing in mind he's on the other side of the continent."

"I love him," she says.

The friends she has made in the past few months, their small and large acts of kindness—Fred, here on this beach, Anne, Mary Ellen, Claudine—all of them have given her permission to love, without angst or guilt. This is the love she wants to offer Jack, and Tim, and the baby.

Tim's arms tighten around her, his cheek resting in her hair. After a while, a colder than normal wind picks up, impatiently searching through their clothes.

"Let's go home," he says.

She stands, with the help of his steadying hand.

In the week that follows, Sophie wanders around the cottage, imagining a third person there, a tiny one, but with a lot of paraphernalia attached to it. Mary Ellen has given them the car seat she promised, and Anne gives them a bassinet. "Okay, so maybe that beats a dresser drawer," says Mary Ellen. The bassinet can be raised to waist height on its sturdy stainless-steel legs and wheeled to the bedside for night nursing. Sophie is fascinated by the fabric it's lined with—white, with little drawings of grey fleecy sheep all over it—so soft, she can't resist smoothing it with her hand.

With only two weeks to go until her due date, she and Tim go shopping in Bridgewater for a change table, diapers, diaper cream and powder. Sophie carefully makes her selections based on Claudine and Mary Ellen's recommendations. Tim dutifully follows her into the store, arranging with the staff to pick up the change table at the main entrance. Sophie hoists the small purchases into the shopping cart.

"We can get baby clothes at Frenchy's," she says. "It's this great second-hand place. Everything's really cheap there."

"Let's hold off on that," he says. "I can always come back into town later this week. We should get you home."

She's about to argue, but something tells her not to, and when they get back to the cottage she discovers that Mary Ellen and Anne have put together a sort of baby shower. The kitchen is festooned with paper chains and hand-made cards from Mary Ellen's girls. Anne has baked a chocolate cake, and she and Mary Ellen present Sophie with a box crammed full of every article of pure cotton infant-wear they could find at Frenchy's, washed and ironed, as well as some beautiful sleepers that Anne bought in New York. Bob and the kids come over, and the house is soon noisier than it has been since Sophie's arrival. The girls chase Daniel, while their parents whip valuables out of harm's way with the skill and precision of card sharks.

Tim and Bob hit it off, but not for the reasons Sophie anticipated. They spend at least fifteen minutes discussing the hockey playoffs, and whether the Canadiens or Rangers will make the finals.

"Obviously, the Habs will crush it," says Bob, his eyes alight with a passion she has never seen in them before.

"Yeah but we've got Lundquist!" says Tim.

Ludquist? Thinks Sophie. What the fuck? Did he research this stuff? Back home, he and the guys in the band are into basketball, not hockey.

"*Lundquist?*" Bob says. "Two years ago, our guy Carey Price had the all-time greatest season of any goaltender. Ever. Period."

He invites Tim over to watch on the twelfth.

"The twelfth…" says Anne. "That date rings a bell for some reason."

"It's the opening night of Jeff's play," says Sophie.

"That's it. I take it you got that email too."

"Did I ever," says Sophie, "with a very flowery note attached. Bet yours was even flowerier."

"I doubt 'flowerier' is a real word."

Tim looks from one woman to the other.

"Who's Jeff?" he says.

"Long story," says Sophie.

"I'd like to go to the play," says Anne. "But you should stay put. It's way too close to your due date. I might ask Fred to come."

"I feel bad not going," says Sophie. "For one thing, I'd like to see Fred again."

"Okay, it's time I met the mysterious Fred," says Tim.

"We'll get him out here soon," says Anne. "He can see his drawing on the wall, and meet you, of course," she adds, nodding in Tim's direction.

The conversation turns to hockey once more. Quietly, Mary Ellen says to Sophie, "I might come over here for shelter sometimes when the playoffs are on. Sorry to conform to gender stereotypes, but hockey leaves me cold."

"Of course, come on over," says Sophie.

Anne has a thoughtful look on her face. "Maybe Fred can join me at the play on the thirteenth. She looks at the calendar. "And then come for supper, the next day?"

"That'll be the second game of the playoffs," says Tim.

"Does this guy like hockey?" says Bob.

| **48** |

At the door to the church hall where *The Glass Menagerie* is about to be performed, Fred, standing next to Anne, freezes. He sees an eerily familiar face, minus the familiar beard. Jamie. Standing near the makeshift sound and light table, talking to Jeff.

Why didn't this possibility occur to him? Why didn't he ask Jeff who was going to be here tonight? Why had he felt so safe, with the kind and elegant Anne by his side? As if the new life he created, with its new friendships, could somehow eradicate the old one—that shit-show that continuously follows him around, threatening to swallow him whole.

Still, who'd have thought? The Jamie he knew had zero interest in community theatre. Maybe the guy has burned so many bridges that Jeff is his only helpful contact around here, and he needs to ingratiate himself. Even as Fred's insides curdle with shame at the nastiness of this thought, his intuition suggests it's true. Jeff is the indiscriminate Santa who sees the good in everyone; an easy mark.

He gradually becomes aware of Anne's hand on his arm.

"Everything okay?" she asks.

"My ex," he manages to croak out.

"Oh crap." She holds his arm more firmly and he drags his eyes away from Jamie to look at her face. All he sees there is warmth, no judgement. It occurs to him that she is the perfect companion on this outing. He considered inviting his mother, but is now relieved he didn't.

"What do you want to do?" Anne asks, and he briefly considers bailing, abandoning her for the evening and catching a bus home. But how would he explain his cowardice to her, to Sophie?

"It's okay," he says. "Just give me a second."

And in that second, Jeff spots them and surges forward with the same expansive bonhomie he had shown when Fred met him at the movie theatre, all those months ago.

"So glad you came," Jeff says. He turns to Anne, and starts embarking on a new round of pompous verbosity. Fred can't quite decipher the words, because he has just caught Jamie's eye.

There is a combination of that raw naked look that used to break Fred's heart when they were together, and something else—fear. As if Fred's own fear of this moment has suddenly left his body and landed in Jamie's instead. When he looks at his former love, Fred sees a sad, frightened man. A man who is too thin, but without other obvious signs of using. A man who is diminished. The diminishment is in the set of his shoulders, in the way he half-smiles, as if mocking himself, in the way he raises his hand uncertainly in greeting.

Barely aware of his own legs propelling him forward, Fred walks forward, leaving Anne and Jeff behind.

"Hey," he says.

"Hey," says Jamie. "Didn't expect to see you here."

"Ditto," says Fred. "Have you been in town long?"

"About a month."

"Well," says Fred, feeling at sea in the absurdity of this situation, these feeble words, the bizarre context of this meeting. "Enjoy the play."

He's turning towards Anne when he hears Jamie say, "Apologies," in a tight, awkward voice that Fred has never heard before. He looks back. Jamie's gaze is downcast, focused on something in the vicinity of Fred's left foot.

"For the texts," Jamie adds.

Fred lets the silence last a few seconds before saying, "No worries." As if none of it mattered, as if he really has no worries now. And, judging by his current state of comfortable numbness, he realizes this may be true.

Then Anne is by his side, and they are finding their seat, and Fred focuses on the stage, even though nothing is yet happening, so that he can avoid speculating about where Jamie is sitting, behind, to the right, to the left. And miraculously, when the curtain opens, he no longer imagines Jamie's gaze boring through the back of his head, but allows the sights and sounds of the play to envelop him like a cooling, gentle mist.

However amateur this production might be, Fred has to hand it to Jeff; his staging is cool. A set of shabby, once-elegant furniture perfectly depicts the genteel poverty of the Wingfield family. Behind the actors are three screens on which sepia-toned images are projected. Fred finds these restful to the eye, even though they represent a racially segregated American South, which, for obvious reasons, he can't romanticize. But maybe that's the point, he thinks, watching as gritty layers of family dysfunction are methodically exposed through the play's elegant, nineteen-forties dialogue.

Before coming here, he read up on Tennessee Williams—his financial struggles, the mental illness in his family, his queerness. All relatable stuff. Glancing over at Anne, who sits beside him taking in the play with equanimity, he is again thankful he didn't try to bring his mother. He can only imagine her impatience with the helpless Laura, the self-pitying alcoholic Tom, and, most of all, the histrionic, snobbish Amanda. It would all be as incomprehensible to her as their southern whiteness. Probably a good thing. Lately, he can acknowledge that his mother's commitment to common sense may have saved them both over the years.

"They're doing a great job!" Anne exclaims warmly to Jeff at the intermission. Fred listens without adding much to the conversation, aware of Jamie leaving the building, probably to go for a smoke in the parking lot.

When Anne goes back to her seat, Jeff says, in a kind of grandiose sotto voce, "Hey man. Sorry about any awkwardness. Didn't know he was going to be here."

"Bound to happen," says Fred casually. "I saw him on the street the other day." After a pause, he decides, since he is stuck in this conversation, to get a sense of where the land lies, and what the likelihood is of Jamie being at the intersection of his and Jeff's mutual friend groups.

"How's he doing?" he asks.

"Better," Jeff says. "He found a place. I heard he's cleaned himself up a bit."

A bit, Fred thinks. There is no cleaning yourself up 'a bit' from the stuff Jamie was on. But he says, "Good to hear. I wish him well," realizing that he means it. Despite everything. Still, just to be clear, he adds, "I'd prefer not to have much contact with him, so like, if he ever comes to the café or asks about me…"

"Got it," says Jeff.

After returning to his seat beside Anne. Fred does not turn around to see if Jamie has come back. He's tired of looking over his shoulder.

Anne drives him to the door of his apartment building, even though he tells her he can walk. On the way, she asks him to come for dinner at the cottage the following day. He's touched, but also nervous about this invitation. From the sounds of it, it will be a very straight evening—two hetero couples, even the offer of a hockey game after the meal. All good, he can get into hockey as well as the next guy, but he wonders if Sophie will seem as approachable with a husband by her side. And he wonders what kind of straight the couple next door will be—the no-questions-asked kind of straight, or the embarrassingly friendly kind of straight, which each require different adaptations on his part. He has ruled out the toxic kind of straight, if they are friends of Anne and

Sophie's. Despite the nerves, he says yes. At least dinners on the South Shore won't run the risk of repeat encounters with Jamie. Letting himself into his apartment, he's thankful Anne did not ask any questions, and he's thankful that this one meeting with Jamie seems to have left him intact.

He's also thankful that his landlord has finally fixed his front door, because Krystle, upstairs, has let the skeletal Cory, who stole his bike, back into her life again. Fred and Joan cross paths occasionally and exchange whispered conversations about where Krystle's head is at. But on the whole, the cold weather and his work schedule mean that he doesn't see much of the other tenants. He still likes his bachelor apartment, but is starting to wonder if life might present something better for him, someday. Despite his finances, maybe there are options, if he can just get creative, see his life the way he sees colours and shapes emerging from under his fingers in his sketchbook.

His latest project is a drawing based on the photo his mother gave him of his great aunts and grandmother, except that he focuses solely on his Aunt Luce. At first, he's frustrated by her sunglasses in the picture, because he wants to see her eyes. But tonight, as he works by lamplight, he becomes certain that the mystery behind the sunglasses is a central part of this image, of who she is in his psyche. He tries to suggest, as the photograph does, the shape of those eyes behind the dark lenses, and the way the light hits the plastic frames. Having completed the outline yesterday, he begins shading her face, working to show where the sun reflects in glowing patches of light on her forehead, her cheekbones, her full and glossy lower lip.

Her closed mouth offers a slight smile in the shape of an unfurling poppy or a stylized heart. Although he's working in black-and-white with a hint of brown to emulate the sepia tones of the photo, he can imagine her deep red lipstick. He works well into the morning hours, and in his mind, superimposed on the young face in the photo, there is another face, with his mother's thinness and Flo's eyes, the face of the middle-aged Aunt Luce from his dream.

When he finally drifts off to sleep, he has only one dream, which he will later remember—a momentary vision of his younger self, standing in the bathroom of his and Jamie's shared apartment. He meets the haunted eyes of the younger Fred in the mirror. The panic-ridden, despairing younger Fred, trapped—unable to save his lover from all the literal and metaphorical toxins poisoning his mind and body, and yet, unable to leave.

When he awakens, he feels none of that panic and despair. All he feels is grief, for them both.

Later that day, he calls his mother to tell her about the drawing.

"I'd like to see it," she says.

There is an unfamiliar tone of intention in her voice. As if Fred has offered to lead her somewhere she has always wanted to go, but never asked.

"It's almost ready," he says.

"I want your help with something."

"Okay?"

"You know Flo and I went to visit the Heritage Centre in Birchtown last summer?"

He feels a stirring of guilt, remembering how he had used work as an excuse to back out of that trip. Despite all the celebratory press about the centre, he felt weighed down by the struggles and hardship it represented. Community elders and scholars working for years to keep the Black Loyalist Heritage Society alive, only to watch all their research go up in flames because of some asshole arsonist. Then, through their collective effort, the new centre arising like a phoenix. It is impressive and humbling, but he wonders how they can stand to continue working conscientiously, applying for grants from tone-deaf governments. He wonders how they keep from howling in rage and setting fires of their own.

"That visit made me think," says his mother. "I want to learn more about us, about where we come from."

He is thankful that she includes him in the pronoun 'us.' This is exactly what he has wanted for her, all those times he felt annoyed and mystified by her fascination with European history. What was it that annoyed him about that, anyway? Something to do with his own guilt over the mostly white life he has led, the ways he has tried to outrun her legacy of hardship, his family memories, himself.

"I can help," he says, without waiting to hear her ask the question. "It's probably time I put that history degree to use."

"No kidding," she says.

| 49 |

Sophie listens to Anne and Fred rehash the previous night's performance of *The Glass Menagerie* over chicken and delicious roast vegetables that Tim has prepared. She thinks back to the night she worked with the cast, feels deeply protective of them, actually nervous to hear Anne and Fred's opinion.

"It wasn't bad," says Anne. "I kind of liked seeing it in that church basement. There was an intimacy to it. Did you know it's playing right now on Broadway? Really mixed reviews. Some people saying it tramples roughshod over the subtleties of the text. As imperfect as this version was, it didn't do that."

"Jeff's staging was cool," says Fred.

"And you said Denise, the woman who played Amanda, was okay?" asks Sophie.

"Yeah, not bad," says Anne gently. "I mean I wasn't expecting Joanne Woodward. But there were moments. She got a laugh early on in the play when she was having this phone conversation about a magazine subscription."

Sophie is surprised at how relieved she feels. Triumphant, even. Even though she knows staying home was the right thing for her body and the baby, she wishes she had gone, if only to cheer on Denise. Maybe she can give a congratulatory note to Jeff to share with the cast.

After supper, the evening turns into what Mary Ellen calls a "girls' night," because Bob, Tim and Fred go next door to watch the second game of the playoffs. Tim takes his guitar, in case he and Bob want to jam at half time. Mary Ellen brings over a bottle of homemade blueberry wine for herself and Anne, and fizzy grape juice for Sophie. When the men are safely out of earshot, Mary Ellen says: "Don't know how much rocking out they'll be able to do with the kids in bed down the hall, but that's for them to figure out. I'm taking a break from motherhood." She hands Sophie the juice. "I used to find, when I was pregnant, that if I pretended it was wine, I got some of the same effects… Okay. Not. But do your best."

Sophie has to pee every ten minutes and feels like she's dragging a bowling ball from the TV room to the bathroom when she goes. Her back is killing her. She tries standing. She tries sitting in the lazy boy, propped up with cushions stuffed in the small of her back by Anne. The tired old beached-whale analogy comes to mind. But that image doesn't fit with the expectant energy under the surface of her massive bump, which Anne and Mary Ellen take turns massaging like a lamp out of the Arabian Nights.

After a while they decide to put music on the stereo. As loud as they want. Because they can, says Mary Ellen. "Trust me," she says to Sophie. "It will be a long time before you'll be able to do this again." She has brought over some of her CD collection, selects the Red Hot Chili Peppers, then the Buena Vista Social Club. By the time she and Anne have consumed another glass of wine each, Mary Ellen decides to move the sofa against the wall and dance. Anne helps with the sofa, and then, somewhat hesitantly, joins her, carefully putting her glass on the end table near Sophie. Mary Ellen's moves are raucous and angular, she keeps going down to the ground in a twist. Anne is shyer at first, but after a while Sophie sees her smile and close her eyes, arms lifted, fingers trailing through the air as though touching silk. Sophie watches these two women, sees her immediate future in Mary Ellen's plump, one-year-post-partum body, and her more distant future in Anne's thinner, slightly stiffer middle-aged one. She thinks: It's not so bad. They are here. They are dancing. Maybe I can do this.

She takes her fourth trip to the bathroom, and on her way back, Mary Ellen grabs her hands, stopping her from sitting down. By now, Bob's CDs have given way to a random Spotify playlist of Mary Ellen's "happy tunes." A heavily synthesized drumbeat starts up—the kind of thing Tim would hate. A joyful sounding woman's voice sings over it. Sophie allows herself to be swept along, despite the mammalian metaphors that crowd her mind—whales, dancing bears. Over the drumbeat, the singer lingers on the word "free." Sophie lifts her arms the way she saw Anne do earlier. She looks up at her fingers, sees them waving overhead like tendrils of seaweed on the surface of sunlit waves.

There is light up there, reminding her of the light piercing the waves that dragged her under less than a year ago. Another lifetime, another place, another girl. She takes a deep breath and starts to spin, revolving slowly around the point of light above her that she is brushing with her fingers. Fre-ee-ee-ee belts out the singer on Mary Ellen's track list. And Sophie is free, spinning towards the light, closer and closer.

Suddenly, she feels a dampness on her thighs. Oh my God, I've pissed myself, she thinks. The humiliation of it roars in her ears, drowning out the drumbeat, the ecstatic vocals. She stops dancing and looks closer at the water that is dripping between her legs.

"Stop…guys, can we…stop for a second?" she says. Her voice is faint, submerged by the music. Mary Ellen and Anne keep dancing.

"I THINK MY WATER'S BROKEN!" This has the desired effect.

"Oh my God!" says Mary Ellen, turning off the music.

"Okay, Claudine," says Anne, in a calm, but slightly slurred voice, pulling out her phone. "I've got her number here, saved." Her hand is shaking.

Mary Ellen grabs a tea towel, soaks it under the tap and starts to wipe up the puddle on the floor under Sophie's feet.

"I don't think…" says Sophie faintly, but then a tightening in her belly, way stronger than any of the warning contractions she has felt before, causes her to lean her hands on the counter, panting. When it passes, she says, "Okay, this is going to be painful, I can tell."

"No kidding," says Mary Ellen, who has suddenly teleported to her side and has a hand on her back.

"Claudine's on her way. I just phoned her. It won't be long," says Anne, who has also mysteriously appeared on Sophie's other side. "Sweetheart, let's get you dried off and into a nightie or something."

"Tim," says Sophie.

"I'll get him," says Mary Ellen. "Boy, this is the best excuse I've had yet to interrupt a fucking hockey game. Can't wait. I should take a picture of their faces."

Sophie will remember a series of tableaux representing the hours that follow, interspersed with darkness and vice-like pain. Pacing the kitchen floor with Anne and Tim on either side of her. Claudine running a bath and Tim sloshing warm water over her belly. Still moments when Claudine, amazingly, seems to be asleep sitting up, but then opens wide-awake eyes when Sophie starts to make noise. Anne and Tim by her side always, except for one moment when she hears Anne say, "Tim, are you alright?" and the next minute sees Tim sitting on the floor with his head between his knees, flanked by both women. Sophie rouses herself enough to say, "You'll never live this down, passing out when your kid's about to be born." She sees Tim laughing, maybe crying, but then she is too busy to notice.

She will remember seeing Anne, with a load of receiving blankets in her arms, putting them, weirdly, in the oven. "The pan of water goes on the rack below, and put the oven to about 150 degrees," says Claudine's voice. "They'll be the perfect temperature for the baby."

In the end, just as dawn is creeping through the window, Sophie finds she's unable to leave one patch of kitchen floor, near the wall facing the stove, where she crouches, tries to squat, tries to sit on an odd little birthing stool provided by Claudine. She is supported on either side by Tim and Anne. This is not where she imagined this happening, but then nothing is as she imagined, like the horizon shifting when the world has been turned upside down by the waves, the world rushing into a spinning vortex at her belly. She hears Claudine's cries of *"push"* coming to her from the end of a long black tunnel, and then the tunnel is inside and around her. She hears her own screams and knows this time she will die, wishes for it to happen. There is an O of light ahead of her… the room returns to her consciousness. She opens her eyes and sees the glow of lamplight, feels Tim's hands behind her back, and, incongruously, sees a tiny, grey-and-purple head protruding from her own body, its eyes shut, its mouth closed obstinately against the intake of air.

"I have a cord around the neck," she hears Claudine say, her voice still calm. "Anne, come here while I get my hand in there. Sophie, you *have* to push once more now." Sophie hears an edge to this last command and then she is back inside the tunnel… the darkness and pain are one and the same thing, the roaring noise in her ears is her own voice coming from deep inside of her, so deep that it is as alien to her as a wild animal.

She hears the words "Cord's free. I've got the arm unhooked," and then, unbelievably, it's over. There is just her body crouched on the floor with Tim, Anne and Claudine surrounding her like supplicants around an icon, and in Claudine's arms is a tiny form, which is not crying, but, when placed on Sophie's chest, opens its mouth and turns its head like a mechanical doll. Sophie is astonished to see a tiny penis between its legs and hears Anne's voice, shaken with tears, saying:

"Look, Sophie, a boy, a beautiful boy."

She feels Tim's chest heave behind her shoulders. The tiny penis between the slippery little doll's legs suddenly emits a stream of clear liquid onto Sophie's belly, and everyone laughs.

"His first action," says Tim. "Peeing on his mother. We'll remind him of that when he's fifteen."

Sophie is aware of Anne sponging her belly and thighs with soap and warm water, as though she herself is an infant, while Claudine wraps the baby in the oven-heated blankets.

"If you nurse right away, it may help you to deliver the placenta," says Claudine. Then the baby is back in her arms, its head nuzzling towards her right breast, as though it knows better than Sophie what to do.

"Let's see if we can get you sitting up properly and give Tim's arms a rest," says Claudine.

For the first time, she realizes that she has been leaning against Tim. Everyone props pillows around, below, and behind her. Once again, she feels like some kind of huge stationary goddess, around the altar of which everyone is kneeling. Even more surreal is the sensation of the baby's mouth on her nipple, though he only sucks half-heartedly.

"He's been through a lot," says Anne, wonderingly.

A few minutes later, Sophie feels a pain which is like a tiny echo of the pain she has just gone through and then something slips from between her thighs again. It is mottled red and white and viscous, like a jelly fish or deep-sea creature. Claudine holds it up. It's covered with interlacing veins shaped like the silhouettes of ancient trees.

"Your placenta," Claudine says. "We'll wait till the cord stops pulsing before we clamp it."

"*My* placenta?" says Sophie, and for some reason, everyone laughs again. But the sound, to her ears, is like canned laughter from a distant TV, because the baby has just opened its eyes. In this light, they are dark cavernous pools, darker than the night sky beginning to change to grey outside the confines of this tiny warm room. She stares into these dark pools, fascinated, and cannot look away.

| 50 |

THERE IS A REASON, ANNE THINKS, that women who are pushing fifty do not have babies. One sleepless night and she feels as if she can barely see what is in front of her. Her legs, moving up the steps to her loft bedroom, feel shackled with iron weights. Sophie, Tim, and the baby are all safely tucked into bed but, unable to let go of a certain vigilance, she sleeps for two hours only before her body's habitual rhythms impose morning on her, and when she picks up her phone by the bedside table, she sees a text from Mary Ellen: *Any news????* All is quiet in the downstairs bedroom, so when she calls, she half whispers into the phone that everything is okay, it's a boy, and Sophie and Tim are still sleeping. She's touched to learn that Fred slept on the sofa in Mary Ellen's living room.

When she climbs down to the kitchen for a cup of coffee, her legs only slightly less leaden, she is met by Tim, unshaven, somewhat wild eyed. He hugs her as if she were his long-lost sister, or mother.

"I can't believe how small he is!" he says. "His little fingers and toes!"

"How did everyone sleep?"

"He's just woken up now. She's feeding him. I'm going to get her some of this tea Claudine left."

The tea is on the counter, an herbal blend that is supposed to be good for everything from toning the uterus to increasing milk supply.

"How's the nursing going?" Anne asks.

"So far so good," says Tim. "Sophie's leaking all over the place though."

"That happened to me too," says Anne.

Tim looks embarrassed, and Anne feels more than ever like his mother. Watching him fill the kettle, she wonders if it would have been helpful for her to have had some of those herbs after Rudy's birth. Breastfeeding was a nightmare in the beginning. She definitely had enough milk, but Rudy's frantic, spasmodic hunger movements unnerved her. He never seemed to latch properly. Thank heaven for that nurse, the one with the red hair, whom she still remembers with gratitude, who sat with her while she tried different nursing positions, held her hand when she wept on the third day with exhaustion and post-partum blues. Anne's mother, hearing of her difficulties over the phone, was ready to show up at her door with a crate of formula and a bottle.

"I didn't breastfeed you," she said, "and you turned out fine."

In the end, Anne managed to nurse Rudy for nearly two years.

After Tim has gone back to Sophie, Anne makes a cup of tea for herself, and takes it up to her bed. Memories of Rudy's first days follow her. During the nursing trials right after the birth, wandering the halls to the hospital nursery, in search of a rocking chair to sit in, she saw a pair of tiny, incubated twins, IVs attached to their arms and white patches over their eyes to protect them from the light. They were enclosed in a glass case like museum exhibits. At the time, she wondered how their mother could stand it.

How lucky, she thinks now, to have given birth to a healthy child. How lucky Sophie is to have given birth to a healthy child in this comfortable cottage, with no monitors and flashing lights, no masked physicians, surrounded only by the people who love her.

The word 'love' unlocks something in Anne. 'Love' is the right word to describe her feelings towards Sophie. However close she and Sophie remain in the future, whatever becomes of Sophie's working relationship with Nathan, Anne's circle of people she loves, so recently narrowed by her mother's death, has widened to allow for this young woman. Perhaps it was watching Sophie change and grow as the baby within her grew. Perhaps it was spending two months together in this cottage that was once a haven for Anne's own family. Perhaps it was Sophie's fragile impulsiveness, and her ability to express, in her own garbled way, things that Anne has felt in the past, but has hardly known she was feeling.

She calls Mary Ellen again, to thank her for hosting Fred, and to invite them both for breakfast.

"Okay, but let me handle the cooking part," says Mary Ellen. "You must be exhausted. I've gotta say, even though I've been through it three times myself, I'm not sure I'd have the guts to sit on the sidelines and watch."

"It was pretty dramatic," says Anne. "You should have heard the sounds she made at the end."

"Bob said after my first that I sounded like a combination between a lion and an elephant."

"Not a bad comparison," says Anne.

Did she roar that way when she was pushing Rudy out? It's all a bit foggy, because of the Demerol, but she seems to remember the nurse saying, "No sound now, just bear down."

Within minutes, Mary Ellen and Fred have arrived. Mary Ellen rushes into the bedroom to kiss Sophie and fuss over the baby, Fred peeps shyly around the bedroom door. Anne is grateful to sit and drink her coffee while Mary Ellen takes over the kitchen, making French toast. When it's ready, even Sophie comes out to serve herself, but retreats back into the bedroom to eat. Everyone else hangs around the kitchen, laughing and recapping the night. As soon as Anne's had one piece of toast, she also retreats, up to her loft again, so she can call Nathan.

He answers on the first ring. She realizes it has been about fourteen hours since she first texted him that Sophie was in labour.

"It's a boy," she says, feeling like a TV character from her childhood, one of those white-coated, white skinned avuncular male doctors. *It's a boy, Mrs. Smith!*

"Sophie was in labour for ten hours. But everything went really well. The midwife was amazing. Tim was amazing. Sophie was amazing."

"Oh my God, what a relief," he says.

"I'm almost as exhausted as Sophie."

"I bet."

"It was a wonderful experience. To see that baby come out. To be there when it took its first breath. I'll never forget it, Nathan."

She hears his breath on the other end of the phone, a sigh, or just an exhale maybe.

"That's the way I felt, watching Rudy's birth," he says, his voice wistful. "You were amazing, Anne."

"So were you."

She thinks again: How lucky we were. How much we loved each other.

There is a yipping sound in the background. Nathan says, "No buddy, not the computer charger," and then he hollers casually, "Rudy? Are you up?"

"Is that the…"

"Dog. Yup, he's keeping us busy. Vaccination appointments, house training, crate training, walks. We just started those. I do the morning one, Rudy does the evening one. Last week was all about getting him used to the harness."

His voice has the soothing but purposeful intonations she has heard him use with financial backers on the phone. He's still trying to sell this to her.

"Sounds like you've got it down," she says.

"We had our first obedience class last week and there's another one on Tuesday."

"Does the subject of all this attention have a name?"

"Bailey."

"Like your dog when you were a kid."

"How did you know that?" says Nathan.

"Your mom showed me pictures of Bailey when we visited Montreal. A golden lab, right?"

"Good memory."

She can hear Rudy' in the background, saying, 'Bailey, here boy, come on."

"So," she says a little nervously. "When are you coming up? I checked at the resort. If we book a chalet, we're allowed to have the dog with us. But how will it be, traveling with him?"

"We'll just have to take it slow. We'll stay at Keith and Linda's for one night."

"That will be peaceful," she says. "You've always said you sleep well there."

"Mmm, don't know how peaceful it will be with Bailey around, but they seem fine with us bringing him."

"I checked out the chalets last week."

"And?"

"Small but nice."

Tiny A-frames, in fact. Anne hopes the sunny forecast for the upcoming week holds true. Being stuck inside one of those structures with the smell of wet dog everywhere might derail this vacation idea, and the potential she hopes it holds.

"We'll have our meals in the resort dining room," she says, thinking, *I don't have to cook. The dog can run free on the beach. Maybe we can take a trip to Halifax with Rudy. Go to the gallery. Or a museum.* These ideas bring a little flutter to her heart, even in the midst of her tiredness.

"How's Rudy?" she says.

"You can talk to him if you like," says Nathan. "Rudy? Come talk to your mother. Here Bailey, let's find your toy."

"Wait, Nathan…" she says.

"Yeah?"

"I really love it here."

"That's great. I'm looking forward to seeing it again, too."

If she says more, will her honesty form a bridge between them, or will it turn out, instead, to be the slow beginning of a scorching, annihilating fire?

"I don't want to sell the cottage," she manages, and waits in silence for his reply.

"Hmm," he says eventually. "Maybe we can find some time to talk about that, when I'm up there."

"For sure, it's just… I've really thought a lot in the past few weeks, about what I want, what I need."

Why is she saying 'I', she thinks, when she should be saying 'we'? "I'd like us to spend more time up here," she adds, "at least in the summer. I think it could be really good."

As she speaks, she realizes that she wants to take all the good they have been to each other and let it outweigh the sadness and distance of the past two years.

"I want things to be better between us," she says.

She half expects him to react with the same defensiveness she met when she talked about Rudy's birth, and he had said, "Things could *always* be better Anne." But when he speaks, he doesn't sound defensive. "I know," he says quietly. "Me too."

When Rudy comes on the phone, he tells her about the dog, how he took it to the day program, introduced it to Kim and Mike. There are still pauses between his sentences. She can hear the slight effort he has to make to keep up the conversation, and for once she doesn't try to prolong their talk by asking questions.

"I'll be seeing you in a few days," she says. "I can't wait."

"You'll get to meet Bailey," he says.

He could be any kid with a dog. She feels the tug of that old invisible umbilical cord between them. Hanging up the phone, she knows that, whatever happens, it will always be there, that cord. She will never stop feeling that tug. She will remain forever aware of the weight of her actions and how their effects ripple outward to touch everyone she cares about. Rudy most of all.

And yet, these past few months, during this season of death, separation, and birth, she has allowed herself to imagine that something new is waiting to sweep her along, if she can only take that first step, let the current show her the way.

| 51 |

It's Easter Sunday, the sun is shining, and a pot of hyacinths rests on the passenger seat of Fred's car. The events of the past few days seem like they happened to someone else. He has napped on a stranger's sofa, woken to a toddler touching his face, heard the toddler's mother speaking on the phone and whooping in celebration, then stumbled across the lawn to the cottage next door, where, feeling completely abashed and out of his depth, he saw another transmogrified Sophie, her face soft and blurry, lying on her side, with a doll-like form wrapped in blankets beside her. A tiny arm and fingers emerged from the blankets, grasping Sophie's finger. He could not bring himself to enter the room and break the spell. Neither could he bring himself to look away.

And then there was Tim, another virtual stranger, responding to his tentative congratulations by hugging him like a brother. And Mary Ellen's voice from the kitchen, saying: "I'm making French toast for anyone who wants it."

When Fred went home to Halifax, he shared the news with Jeff over the phone, then begged off work, pleading exhaustion. But in truth, his brain was buzzing. He had never felt more alive.

Easter makes Fred think of his childhood, of singing in choir at church, lilies, tulips and hyacinths crowding the altar, everyone singing "Hallelujah." Whatever ambivalence he feels about religion, those are memories he cherishes. He remembers wanting to share them with the theophobic Jamie—the myth of renewal, the second chance, rolling away the stone. At his warm and fuzzy United Church Sunday school, the myth tended to stop there. Only brief mention was made of the resurrected Christ walking among his disciples, or of the disciples' day-to-day work, spreading the news, facing torture and oppression, carrying on with unconditional hope and unconditional love.

He pulls into Sophie's driveway, just at the hour when the church bells of his childhood would be ringing. Anne lets him into a house that is quieter, but also messier than when he was last here. There is a laundry basket full of unfolded sheets, baby blankets and towels in the kitchen, the remains of dishes in the sink, and in the living room, Sophie sitting on the sofa in the sunshine, nursing her baby.

"Hey," she says, smiling, when he comes and sits in an armchair across from her. Their eyes meet. Despite his embarrassment at the intimacy of this moment, the slurping noises made by the tiny brownish head at Sophie's breast, he's reminded of the other times they have smiled at each other, the times when he has thought: 'She is my friend.'

"Does he have a name yet?" he asks.

"No. Pathetic isn't it?" she says. "We had some ideas before he was born but we can't settle on one. Mary Ellen says it took them a week to come up with Daniel's name, but I hope we decide sooner than that. We can't keep calling him 'baby' forever. My parents are coming in a few days. I'd like to be able to introduce him to them properly."

"Is this the first grandkid?"

"Yup, my mom's ecstatic." She brushes a speck of something off the baby's cheek and smiles down at its face, which is still hidden from Fred. "I can't wait to see my parents," she says. "I think, actually, he looks like my brother Jack. I've seen baby pictures…"

"Is he coming up with the parents?"

"No." A look of trouble momentarily crosses her face, but is quickly replaced by calm. "He's in the middle of a move and career change. I plan to skype with him though." She takes a moment to switch the little brown head from one breast to the other, while Fred looks at the floor. "Before, I was kind of dreading my parents' visit. Family dynamics and all that. I love them but they drive me crazy sometimes. But now…" She looks up suddenly, and her smile draws Fred into her circle like a spotlight. "I feel high with love, literally. Like I can't remember any reason not to love them. And not just them, everyone. Nathan's coming to visit in a couple of days, and I can't wait for that, either. If everyone I've ever hung out with or worked with suddenly showed up on my doorstep, I'd welcome them with open arms."

"Wow," says Fred. "I want some of what you're on."

She laughs. "Claudine, my midwife, says it's oxytocin, commonly known as the 'love hormone.' Apparently it's released every time I breastfeed."

"Hmm, guess I'm going to need the synthetic version."

Sophie laughs. "I'm sure I'll crash sooner or later," she says. "Can't stay on these heights forever. But so far so good. No sign of any baby blues."

She shifts a cushion at her back, tries reaching for a glass of water on the coffee table. Fred, eying this maneuver, gets up and hands it to her. "Thanks," she says, taking a swig.

"Well," he begins, unsure what to say next. "I can't tell you how happy I am for you."

She smiles again. That crooked smile he first noticed when he was standing at the hospital pharmacy with her, the day he found her on the beach.

"I guess you'll be going back to New York, soon," he says.

"In a month or so," she says.

"I'll miss you when you go, Sophie."

"I'll miss you too," she says.

Are those actually tears in her eyes?

"You know, Fred, if ever you feel like coming to New York, checking out some galleries or shows, you have a place to stay."

"That's the oxytocin talking," he says.

"I mean it. It's way too expensive otherwise. You should take us up on the offer, soon. I have a feeling we won't be staying in the city forever."

"No?"

"Doesn't feel like the place to raise a kid. The pace of life up here feels so sane, you know? Of course, it helps that this country isn't being led by our wacko in the White House."

"We're not immune to the wackiness," he says.

"Nowhere is, I suppose." Sophie sighs. She takes another sip from the glass that Fred has made sure to edge closer to her on the coffee table.

"I love New York," she says. "The plays, the concerts, the night life. I don't know, though. Something tells me its days as a cultural mecca are numbered."

"You might be right," says Fred.

Privately, he thinks: Its days are numbered because for every happy free-lance musician or actor like Tim and you, there are at least a hundred waiters, construction workers, cashiers. People trying to keep their heads above water, working two or three jobs, cramming in a bit of creative satisfaction, or just entertainment, on the side. But he feels no envy, bears Sophie and Tim no ill will. Looking at the baby, which has apparently fallen asleep at Sophie's breast, he figures they have their work cut out for them.

"He snores, can you believe it?" says Sophie, gently detaching the baby from her breast, not bothering to hide her nipple behind the receiving blanket. She puts him, still out cold, in a car seat on the floor at her feet. Fred gets his first proper look. Shell-like skin, impossibly long eyelashes, tiny fists that curl and uncurl.

"He seems to like sleeping in this thing as much as in his bassinet," says Sophie. "It's handy to be able to carry him from room to room."

"Sounds like you're figuring it all out," he says.

"I guess so, for now. Wait till he gets to be Daniel's age."

"Ah yes, the toddler next door," says Fred. "I had the pleasure of meeting him very early the other morning."

"Oh dear. Did you really sleep there all night?"

"You bet. It was high drama. You've brought a fair amount of that into my life, Sophie."

"I guess I have…"

There is a slow, peaceful pause, broken only by the baby's odd snuffling noises. Fred thinks about all that has happened since he first met her. Jamie's stalking, his new job, socializing with her and Anne. But what comes to him most are his bird picture, and his drawing of Aunt Luce.

"I was due for some drama," he says. "I'm really glad you came into my life, Sophie."

He risks looking at her, sees her eyes full on him, now that the baby is no longer drawing her gaze.

"Ditto," she says. "You're a good person, Fred."

There is a surprising vigor to her voice. It cuts through her new, blissed out maternal persona, takes him back to the earlier Sophie he has gotten to know and like. "I could tell you were a good person the first time we really talked. You were so kind, so courteous. Why do you think I looked you up when I came here?"

"It was nothing," he says, feeling like the cliché of a humble hero, but needing to say it anyway. "I didn't…" save your life, he thinks, the way he supposes he saved Jamie's physical life, once. "It was nothing special," he tries again.

"Don't you believe it," she says, leaning forward slightly and taking his hand. "It was special to me. I was a real mess when you found me on the beach. And it wasn't just because of what I'd been through out there. Or maybe it was. I don't know. I nearly drowned."

She sighs, closes her eyes briefly, lets go of his hand and leans back. "Even before I came up here for the film consult, and the whole time I was staying in that suite with Nathan and Bill…I'd been feeling all wrong. Like I had been playing a part my whole life. Acting is something I love, but it had taken over. Everything was about, I don't know, looking this way, talking that way, doing this thing or that thing, all to make it right for other people."

Fred wonders if he sensed any of this when he was so mysteriously attracted to her last summer. He has an uncomfortable moment, thinking of his helpful waiter's persona, the blank solitude behind all his offers of tea and coffee to customers. Making it right for other people. Was it that persona who had helped her on the beach, or was it him, for real? Does it matter?

"I was confused, terrified," she says.

In her downturned eyes, her averted profile, there is the ghost of the awkward young woman with bedraggled hair and sand-encrusted skin.

"You were so calm," she says. "You just did what I needed. You didn't expect anything or ask anything from me. You were a real friend."

He can hear the clock ticking in the silence that follows, manages to say, "Thanks, Sophie. You're a real friend, too."

$\cdots\cdots$

FRED IS ABOUT TO BACK OUT OF SOPHIE'S driveway when, in his rearview mirror, he sees something dark lying in the middle of the road. It looks like a glove or some other article of clothing. Smaller than the bundle of Sophie's clothes that he found on the beach that day back in August, but when he turns off his ignition and gets out to take a look, he feels a familiar burst of fear in his gut.

He walks slowly to the center of the deserted road, and looks at the bird. A blue jay. Its belly is touching the pavement, and its tail feathers are spread out behind it. It's alive, but doesn't fly off at his approach. It just sits unmoving, eyes open and blinking. Fred can see no sign of injury. It looks to be merely resting. He walks around to the other side of the bird, squats down beside it. He cannot see a broken wing or missing feathers. He wonders if it has been mauled by a cat or has flown into a car window and been stunned. Standing up, he looks to the right and left. No sign of a car, but he can hear traffic from the main road.

"Shoo!" he says, feeling like an idiot. He waves his arms in the bird's direction, as if directing traffic. The bird still does not move.

Feeling slightly sick, he goes back to his car and reaches into the passenger seat for his leather gloves. His squeamishness about touching the bird is compounded by his memory of the nightmares that eventually prompted him to make the drawing that Anne bought. He has to move the thing off the road.

He puts on the gloves, then returns to the bird, worried he might find, when he lifts it, the messy evidence of a mortal wound. How far will his sense of responsibility extend in that scenario? He squats. The bird still faces forward, eyes open, its breath and heartbeat visible in its throat.

"Okay, little guy, here goes," he says.

He moves behind the bird, marvelling at the brilliant blue of its tail feathers, places each hand palm up on the pavement on either side of the bird's body, and starts to inch them, slowly, towards the creature, holding his breath.

His fingertips touch feather, then move closer to slide gently under the blue jay's breast. At that moment there is an anguished fluttering, a sickening repetition of the flailing wings in his dream, and the blue jay escapes his hands and flies about four feet away from him to the side of the road.

Slightly emboldened, he moves towards the bird again. At that moment there is another fluttering, more purposeful, and the bird lifts, tilts, and launches itself high into the sky and out of sight.

Relief explodes in his chest.

"Thank God," he says aloud. He finds that he's panting.

He knows it's only a bird, not a human being. And he's not naive. He knows the unlikelihood of a sick or wounded animal surviving and thriving in the wild. He knows that the world is a dangerous place, and that the suffering of birds, like all suffering, is beyond his power to prevent. And yet—the jay flew out of his hands. His clumsy gloved fingers managed to set the bird in motion.

A weight that seems to have been smothering him for years lifts. Astonished, he feels how gently and quickly it vanishes, like the blue jay, into the clear April sky.

Thank you to Arts Nova Scotia, whose financial assistance enabled the completion of the first draft of this book.

Many thanks also to the Writers Federation of Nova Scotia and the Alistair MacLeod Mentorship Program.

Huge gratitude to my two mentors: Valerie Compton, who encouraged me to reimagine my earliest draft, and Sharon English, who inspired me to go deep and examine the motifs running through the multiple narratives in this story.

Thank you to Lee Thompson at Galleon Books for taking a chance on a first novel and guiding me through the editing and publication process.

Thank you to the following people who generously offered me their knowledge and expertise: Camelia Frieberg, for insight into a film producer's role; Anna Heron, for fact-checking aspects of Sophie's acting career; and Flowe Hout, for being my eyewitness at the 2016 Manhattan Women's March.

Finally, and most importantly, huge gratitude to the following friends and family who read early drafts and/or supported me at every stage of this process: Charlotte Britten, Peter Heron, Tricia Snell, Cathey Heron, Frank and Will Heron, Dave Clingan, Lib Sircom, Gill Sircom, Sue Murtagh, Katie Cameron, Peter Leblanc, Liam Britten and Colleen Bonomo. Love you all.

Beverley Shaw's short fiction and poetry have appeared in *Queen's Quarterly*, *The Fiddlehead*, *The New Quarterly*, *Grain*, *Event*, *The Antigonish Review*, *Existere*, and the anthology *Best Canadian Stories 2017*. She lives and writes on the South Shore of Nova Scotia, where she also works as a teacher and musician.